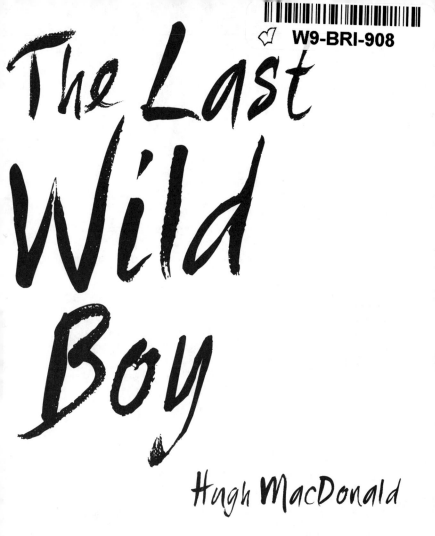

The Last Wild Boy

Hugh MacDonald

The Acorn Press
Charlottetown
2013

The Last Wild Boy © 2013 by Hugh MacDonald

AC🐚RNPRESS

P.O. Box 22024
Charlottetown, Prince Edward Island
C1A 9J2
acornpresscanada.com

Printed in Canada
Edited by Caitlin Drake Smith
Designed by Matt Reid
Cover illustration by Shaun Patterson

MacDonald, Hugh, 1945-, author
     The last wild boy / Hugh MacDonald.

Issued in print and electronic formats.
ISBN 978-1-927502-12-9 (bound).--ISBN 978-1-927502-13-6 (ebook)

     I. Title.

PS8575.D6306L38 2013   jC813'.54   C2013-904718-2
                                                 C2013-904719-0

Canada

Canada Council
for the Arts

Conseil des Arts
du Canada

The publisher acknowledges the support of the Government of Canada through the Canada Book Fund of the Department of Canadian Heritage, the Canada Council for the Arts Block Grant Program.

The Last Wild Boy

I dedicate this book to my wife Sandra and my children: Adam, Matthew, Melody, Andrew, Allister and David.

Part 1

Chapter 1

Mabon was hard at work in the dead zone, clearing the scorched remains of a large bald eagle and dozens of smaller birds and bats that had flown obliviously into the lethal force field surrounding Aahimsa's walls. It was still dark out, and the dampness of the cool morning air seemed to seep right through his skin and settle in his bones.

He'd done the same job, day in and day out, for seven long years. His initial horror at his posting here had softened to monotony and numbness — and loneliness, terrible loneliness. What was the difference if the bodies that fell from the sky were cleaned up, he wondered. Insiders never walked the dead zone anyway. No one would ever come to this place if they weren't forced to. It was home only to him, and death.

He was strolling along, eyes down, sweeping and scooping, picking and cleaning, whistling a tune he had composed from the songs of living birds and the feel of the sunshine, when he heard a faint whimper, then a scream, then a loud rustling sound overhead. He looked up just in time to see a bundle wrapped in pale fabric before it hit him with a powerful, glancing blow, knocking him down and slamming his neck and head against the side of his steel wheelbarrow. As he fell he heard a sickening thud on the ground just beside him.

Mabon reached up instinctively to touch the throbbing spot on his neck, and his large hand came away bloody. He felt his neck again and realized that the lump that held his control device was missing. He waited a moment for the explosion, resigned to death, but it didn't come. He wondered how long he had before they would come to investigate.

After the pounding of his heart slowed enough for him to move, he turned over toward the bundle of fabric and found himself looking straight into the eyes of a young insider. He stared at her in a mix of shock and wonder. She had not so much as whimpered since she had landed, but he could see that she was still breathing. Sixty feet straight down through the air onto rock-hard dirt. It must have hurt like hell.

She was definitely badly wounded. Blood oozed from her ears and the corners of her mouth and pooled in the dirt under her cheek.

Suddenly she blinked, and then her eyes focused blearily on Mabon. "Hide me," she moaned in a soft voice.

"I can't," Mabon said. He knew the penalty for touching an insider, knew it was forbidden under any circumstance. "You're hurt," he said, pulling away. "You should stay still."

"Get me…away from…here," she rasped. "Please."

"But you need help," said Mabon.

"Can't…let them…find me," she said.

"If I lay a finger on you, they'll terminate me," said Mabon. "You must know that."

"Please," she said again. Her voice was soft and sweet as music, but filled with desperation. Her eyelids fluttered and then closed.

Mabon looked down at her small face and her limp body. He'd never seen an insider so close up before. Even broken and bleeding, she was beautiful. In the moments when the moonlight cut through the swift-moving patches of cloud, he could see her long, dark eyelashes and her thin, perfect nose. She was so fragile, like the bird carcasses he carried away from the foot of the wall. As he looked down at her shattered body, he felt something deep down in his gut, a feeling he'd never experienced before. And he knew he had to help her, no matter the cost.

He stood up slowly, then bent and scooped her into his strong arms. There, he had done it. He had touched an insider and he was still alive. It was lucky the control device had come off, he thought, feeling the bloody spot on his neck again. He would be safe for the moment. But he knew it wouldn't be long before they'd come looking for him.

He looked around to see if anyone was watching, but there were only shadows. He took one small step on his powerful legs and then another. He felt the insider's groans of pain more than heard them.

He remembered holding a new puppy in his hand and feeling its heartbeat in his palm, remembered the scent of its soft fur. He could smell the insider's scent even here in the dead zone. It was sweet, like fresh lilacs, but there was a musty undertone to it as well, something he couldn't quite place.

In her close presence he felt dizzy and reckless. He was fascinated by her, almost hypnotized. He did not understand what it was about her that moved him. It was simply a feeling, a sort of tingle that seemed to deny the ache at the nape of his neck, an unfamiliar sense of nobility. He, Mabon the cleaner, was defending the life of this lovely, broken creature from something she feared worse than death. Perhaps it was worth the repercussions.

He ducked his head as he passed through the entryway to his hut, careful not to let the insider's head or feet bump against the thick walls. He felt his way through the darkness, past the faintly glowing embers in his fire pit to the back corner of the hut, and placed her on the mound of grass he used as a bed. She stirred and opened her eyes, but didn't speak.

As Mabon lit a small tallow candle, he caught his pitiful reflection in the small cracked mirror next to his wash stand. His square jaw was smudged with dirt and blood. He ran his long fingers through what was wavy, red-brown hair when it was clean, rubbed the dust from his blue eyes, and splashed some water on his tanned face.

A battered teapot sat on top of the dying coals in the centre of the room. Mabon poured aromatic tea into a dented tin cup and held it out to the insider. "It's good," he said. "Picked it myself. It'll help you feel better."

"Thanks," the young woman said. Her right arm hung limply at her side. She tried to take the cup with her left. The effort made her wince. The cup tilted sideways and some of the tea spilled.

"I'll get you some help," Mabon said, steadying the cup and holding it up to her lips.

"No," she said, sinking deeper into the bed. "No one...can...know..." Her eyes shut again and her muscles relaxed.

Mabon sat in silence for a long time, watching her breathing grow shallower until she wasn't moving at all. He was about to cover her with a blanket when her eyes suddenly opened. Mabon jumped backwards in surprise.

Her eyes searched around the room wildly. "My baby!" she said.

"Your baby?" Mabon said, confused, "What baby? There's no baby here."

"Help him," she pleaded. "Please." She coughed violently and spit blood. Her breath smelled of death.

Mabon lifted the lid of a wooden trunk next to his bed. He grabbed a clean handkerchief. "Here," he said, putting the fabric into her small, perfect hand, which was stained with bright red blood and sputum.

She began to cough again. Mabon wiped her forehead with a dampened cloth. Her cough quieted, but the thin line of blood grew wider and flowed thickly from her lips. Her eyes were cloudy in the light of the dancing flame. It wouldn't be long now.

Mabon had seen death before, during his early training as a forest ranger in the wild and his office training with Dr. Ueland in the manufacturing homeland. Lots of accidents happened. An outsider's life wasn't worth a bird carcass back then. That was before Blanchefleur's time as mayor. He never knew any other mayor's name, but he knew that when the new mayor took power, life had improved in the homelands.

The insider closed her eyes and sunk deeper into the bed once again. Mabon watched her for a long time, noticing the pool of blood under her pretty face getting wider and wider and her breathing getting weaker and weaker. When the rising and falling of her chest finally stopped, tears tumbled from his weary eyes.

Mabon couldn't recall ever crying. It was not appropriate for a forest ranger in training, and even after his fall from honour as a ranger, even on all of those desolate evenings alone in his hut, he had refused to give in to his loneliness and grief.

When the tears finally stopped, Mabon wiped his face and stood up over the insider. Her body was stiff and motionless. The flush from her cheeks had already started to drain away, the life in her face seeping away with it. He wrapped her in the rough brown blanket and lifted her carefully into his strong arms.

Streaks of morning light were starting to invade the darkness outside Mabon's hut. The cleaner carried the insider's body away from the city wall, which loomed high in the faintly glowing sky behind him. He wanted to hide her beyond the ruined ground surrounding the modern city, away from the dead zone that separated the walled-in community from the wilds of the forest.

As he passed into the densely wooded area, smelling the lush riverbank just ahead, he wondered how the unfortunate insider had escaped the worst effects of the force field surrounding the wall. The blast that should have killed her instantly, like the birds and bats whose singed bodies it was his job to recover. He concluded that her fall must have coincided with the brief daily shutdown while systems were checked. But why had she fallen? Was it an accident, was someone chasing her, or had she meant to jump? And what was this about a baby?

Mabon chose a spot under a small red maple on the riverbank and scraped a shallow grave into the dirt with the short-handled shovel he usually used to gather dead birds. He placed the insider's body into the hole gently, then covered her limp remains with bits of stone and what twigs and leaves he could gather from the fringes of the wild. The soil beneath the trees here was free of grass — dark, moist and loose. Carefully, he lifted shovels full of the rich loam and poured it over the shallow grave. When he was satisfied that he had done all he could to hide the body, he shuffled sadly back to the desolation of his hut.

Mabon stirred up the embers of his fire and added a few fresh sticks, then relit the scrap of tallow candle. Its dancing yellow flame fell across the pile of bloody handkerchiefs. These would have to be destroyed. They were evidence of his crime against the insiders. Yet, in spite of his fears, Mabon felt no guilt.

He recalled how little the insider had weighed when he first encountered her, and what a terrible burden she had become as he had lowered her into her grave. One more fragile bird that had fallen from the wall to lie broken at his feet.

Mabon let out a deep, rumbling laugh. He couldn't remember when he'd laughed last. Sometime back in the Manuhome, perhaps. But that was long ago. This morning's laughter was different, though. Filled with remorse. It awaked feelings long buried, long forgotten. If Dr. Ueland heard me now, he thought, he'd have me hauled away. Gradually his laughter gave birth to warm, salty tears that seeped from his tired, young eyes like blood from a wound. The tears, though unfamiliar, felt satisfying. "I will never understand," Mabon whispered as he clutched the bloodied rags and held them to his face. "I will never understand."

It was only then that the soreness on the back of his neck returned. He rubbed it with his strong hand and felt the congealed blood in the place where the control device lump had sat under the skin on his neck. He could not recall a single moment when he hadn't been under the complete power of his controllers. Not even his thoughts had been private. His entire life had been fraught with the knowledge that they could terminate him at any moment. And now, for the first time ever, he was not under their power. He was free at last.

Regardless, he knew he was marked for termination. They wouldn't let him live now, though he'd been free of his control device for only a few hours, especially not when they found out that he'd broken the law of the insiders. And it would be his former colleagues, the forest rangers, who would be coming to do to him what the controllers weren't able to now.

They would be here soon. He knew what he had to do.

Chapter 2

"I hate picking berries," Alice complained. She groaned and flung her graceful frame onto the manicured lawn.

"You wanted blackberry pie." Nora barely managed a smile. "And you promised to help."

Nora brushed her hands off on her jeans and continued plucking fistfuls of the juicy deep-purple berries from the bushes along the pathway by the pond. A few minutes later, she glanced back at Alice, who was still lounging in the soft grass. Even with the sour look on her face, she was still beautiful.

Alice's beauty began at her perfect toes, elegant as small fingers, each nail a rosy petal surrounded by powdered alabaster skin. Her feet were slim and sleek, like a pair of well-crafted shoes. From ankles to waist she was built like a runner; every muscle drew eyes in her direction when she passed by. She carried only enough fat on her torso to give a healthy lift to her unblemished skin. But it was Alice's flawless face, with its shining blue eyes, upturned nose, and full lips, and her blonde head of hair, which bleached almost ivory every summer, that Nora believed granted

Alice much of her capacity to dominate her world.

It was the confidence that came from this power that had attracted Nora to Alice in the first place. Nora still couldn't believe that Alice, who could have had her pick of all the insider girls in Aahimsa, had returned her affection. As the mayor's daughter, she would have been expected to choose a partner closer to her social standing, not some orphan who had been employed in her home as the housekeeping assistant. Nora still didn't understand why she hadn't.

Nora was shorter than Alice by several inches. She wore her hair cropped, and by now the summer sun had bleached it from auburn to a coppery red. Her green eyes sparkled with specks of gold when she laughed, which was seldom, but even more so when she was angry, which was often, although she seldom let it show in any other way. Her body was generous, she thought, a bit too much of everything, but fortunately, only a bit too much.

"Are you done yet?" Alice called, her voice overly sweet. "I'm bored."

"It's fine with me if you want to turn back," Nora said with a shrug. They had walked almost to the edge of the western section of the wall that surrounded Aahimsa. The sun was hot today and there was little breeze near the wall. Nora would be happy to get back to the summer house and cool down.

"You're mad at me," Alice said, grinning, "aren't you?" She smiled and cocked her head.

Nora said nothing. She just continued picking the berries and tossing them into her basket, though perhaps with a bit more vehemence than before.

"And, no, I don't want to go back," continued Alice. "I want the pie." She fluttered her long eyelashes playfully. "I simply adore your sweet blackberry pie," she said in her most impish voice.

Nora set her feet and clenched her teeth. "Then help me pick."

Alice turned her head suddenly toward the grove of evergreens beside the great pond that separated them from the summer house and the city centre. She could see the tall communications tower looming in the distance, its powerful electronic eyes and ears constantly scanning all parts of the city and far into dark and distant wilds. "Shh!… Did you hear that?"

"What?"

"Listen!… Shh!"

This time Nora did hear something — someone's old cat on the loose, perhaps. Yet it didn't sound quite like a cat. It didn't sound much like anything she'd ever heard inside the walls of Aahimsa.

"Let's go see what it is!" said Alice. She sprung to her feet and brushed away the wisps of grass and dirt that clung to the light cotton dress that she had borrowed from her mother's closet in the summer house.

"You go," said Nora with a sigh. "I'll finish picking."

"Leave the stupid berries. Come on!"

Nora shrugged, rolled her eyes, then set down the basket and followed. She scrambled across the well-maintained lawn into a grove thick with willow and evergreen, having a hard time keeping up with Alice. It seemed odd to see Alice in a hurry to get anywhere.

Nora finally caught up, and found Alice staring down at the long grasses in the shade of a weeping willow, a look of wild excitement in her blue eyes.

"Holy mother!" said Alice. "A baby."

Nora moved closer and looked down into the red face of a baby. The child was wrapped in a coarse gray blanket, the sort used at the civic hospital for the poor. Nora recalled from childhood how these rough blankets felt against the skin, and how much she'd missed her mother when she'd lain beneath one alone in the charity hospital as a child. She stared at the baby and waited to see what Alice would say.

"What do we do?" Alice finally asked.

"Call the caretakers, I guess," Nora said. This was the first baby Nora had ever seen, but she knew about the Palace of the Caretakers, where babies were raised before they were returned to their mothers. Her mother had been a caretaker for a few years, and had told her all about it before she'd died.

"Let's take her home and play with her," Alice said. "No one will know. My mother's staying downtown for the next few days, and she'll be in council meetings all day anyways. And no one else would come out here." Her eyes flashed with defiant excitement.

"What about the pie?"

"Forget it! We'll eat the berries with cream instead. Come on!"

"But the security patrols," said Nora. "What if we run into one?"

Alice shrugged. "I can handle them. They wouldn't hassle us, anyways. They're all too scared of what my mother would do. None of them would dare give Mayor Blanchefleur's daughter a hard time." She gestured to the baby. "Come on, just pick her up and let's go."

Nora picked up the silent baby. She felt something firm under the baby's blanket as she did so, and she lifted the edge of the blanket to see what it was. A tube labelled "Infant Nutrifier" was tucked in beside the baby. Nora wrapped the blanket back up and followed Alice toward the pond.

Alice stepped gingerly from the shelter of the trees onto the pathway beside the pond. She glanced in the direction of the wall and caught movement in her peripheral vision. She turned her head to see two police officers striding along the shore of the pond in her direction. Alice quickly looked behind her into the trees and was relieved to see no sign of Nora or the child.

"Hello," she called out to the officers, who were approaching rapidly. The first officer, the younger of the two, she didn't recognize, but the second officer she knew as Nancy. Nancy was a regular around Blanchefleur's residence and the mayor's offices at City Hall.

"Hi, Alice," said Nancy. "Where's your friend?"

"Back at the house," Alice lied.

"You shouldn't be out here by yourself," said Nancy.

Alice watched nervously as the younger officer poked her head into the nearby trees and surveyed the area.

"It's safe here," insisted Alice. Her heart was hammering through her chest, and she felt her hands begin to shake. She hoped Nancy hadn't noticed.

"Your mother wants your companion with you at all times," said Nancy. "You know how she worries about you."

"I know," Alice said sweetly. "I'll head right back. I just wanted a little time alone." She flashed Nancy her most dazzling smile. "You won't tell my mother, will you?"

"Not if you get back right away and promise not to get into any more trouble," Nancy said, giving Alice a wink.

"I'm going. Thanks, Nancy."

The officers waited until they saw Alice turn toward the house and disappear from view before they continued their rounds.

Alice took a deep breath, then circled around through the trees, back to where she had left Nora and the baby. There was no sign of them. Panic gripped her. She turned and raced back toward the house.

When she arrived there, she found Nora waiting, alone, outside the front door.

"Where's the baby?" Alice asked. "I was so scared."

Nora took a moment to suppress her anger before she answered. "She's safe. I hid her back in the grove."

"Go get her," Alice said. "And let's get inside."

Chapter 3

The summer house was twice the size of a normal family housing unit in Aahimsa. Like the children of all the upper level city officials, Alice had certain privileges. Using the summer home when her mother wasn't around — as long as the watchful eyes of the mayor's security detail were close by — was just one of those privileges.

As Alice and Nora stepped up to the door of the house, the sensor above the polished marble entrance emitted a fierce green glow and began to pulsate.

"It's all right!" Alice snapped as she ran her hands through her sun-blonde hair. "It's only a baby, you stupid robot." The light dimmed as the computer finally recognized Alice's voice and the heavy door slid open long enough for the young women to step inside.

The child started crying again. Its tiny hands opened and closed and its little arms waved about as its dark brown eyes surveyed the new surroundings.

"Here, let me have her," said Alice, pushing her hair back behind her shoulders. She turned her almond-shaped eyes excitedly to the baby and then to Nora, who hesitated. "Don't worry, silly. I'll be careful."

"Like you were careful back by the wall?" Nora's eyes flashed gold. "What if the security detail had caught us?"

Alice shrugged and searched the spotless terrazzo floor of the summer house for nothing in particular.

"Fine, then," Nora said, carefully handing the baby to Alice.

Alice cradled the baby in her arms and made soft cooing noises, but it wouldn't stop crying. "Shush, now," she said, frustrated, "or we'll have the police on our doorstep."

"Let me try," said Nora reaching for the baby.

"She's all yours," Alice said, handing the child over. "I'm dying of thirst anyway." She flounced into the kitchen.

Nora held the baby close and rocked it back and forth, but it didn't stop crying. "You must be hungry," Nora said, feeling the bump in the blanket where the nutrifier tube was tucked. "How long has it been since you've eaten?"

Nora carried the baby over to the couch, pulled the nutrifier tube from the folds of the blanket, and removed the cap, exposing a rubber nipple underneath. She held the nipple up to the baby's mouth, and it sucked greedily.

As the child fed, Nora looked down into its soft brown eyes, which focused back on her. It looked almost as if the baby was smiling up at her. Nora's heart beat in an irregular way and felt as if it flipped over in her chest. She tried to look away, but as she did, the child made a gurgling sound. Nora looked at the baby again and it smiled even more brightly. She turned and glanced back toward the kitchen door to make sure Alice wasn't coming, and then quickly kissed the baby's forehead. It smelled like a fresh orange peel, mixed with something slightly musty.

She kissed the baby again and it closed its eyes. Nora did the same, with the scent of oranges on her mind.

"Well it looks like she's finally quieted down," Alice said, coming back into the living room with a half-empty glass of water and a handful of blackberries. She popped the blackberries in her mouth and chewed carefully, trying not to let the dark juice dribble down her chin onto her dress. "I guess that means I can play with her now. Here, hand her over."

Nora lifted the baby gently up to Alice, who rested it against her shoulder. "There," she said to the child. "Now you're not so bad." She started humming quietly, but she was interrupted by a loud, liquid rumbling noise from inside the baby's diaper. Alice's expression went from smiling to shock to disgust in a matter of seconds. "Ugh!" she said, thrusting the baby back at Nora, then looking down at her chest. "Look at my dress! The little rat pooped all over it!"

"I'll change her," said Nora, chuckling. She held the baby carefully away from her as she walked toward the kitchen. "Get out of that dress," she called back over her shoulder. "I'll toss it in the washer."

"Yeah, that would not be nice to explain to my mother," Alice said with a laugh. "Can you imagine what she'd say if she saw her dress like this?" Alice unzipped the dress and stepped out of it, careful not to get any of the baby's mess on her. She left the dress in a pile on the floor and stepped into the bedroom to get something clean to wear. "You know how to change babies?" she called from behind the door.

"My mom showed me," Nora said as she lay the baby down on a towel on the kitchen counter. "It isn't hard. I used to practise with my dolls."

"Poor people are lucky," Alice said, bouncing back into the room in a pink floral sundress. "They get to learn so much about life."

Nora didn't answer. She just scrunched up her nose and worked at opening the baby's diaper without getting any mess on her.

"It'll be nice to play with the baby, won't it?" said Alice, flopping down at the kitchen table. "It'll be like we have our own little family."

"I guess so," Nora said, her mind still on Alice's remark about poor people. "But I'm nervous. If your mother catches us with her…"

"She won't," said Alice. "Besides, she always gets over things quickly. She can't stay mad at me for long. And as long as you're my partner, you won't have to worry either."

Nora finally managed to get the baby's diaper undone. "There!" she said. "Could you watch her while I get the cleaning stuff?" she called to Alice.

"I suppose." Alice wandered over and hovered just close enough to prevent the child from falling off the counter.

"This should do it," said Nora, coming back carrying a basin of hot water, a cloth and soap. There were strips of cloth from a faded old pillowcase draped across her shoulder.

"Finally," Alice said, holding her nose. "I can't stand this for another moment. The stench is unbearable." She headed to the living room and flopped down on the couch.

Nora plugged her nose with one hand and started to remove the baby's diaper with the other. As she did, she uncovered a fold of paper wrapped in plastic that had been tucked inside. She turned to call Alice, whose head was buried in a fashion magazine, but then she stopped herself. Somehow she knew that whatever was in that package was something she shouldn't let Alice see. She made sure that Alice wasn't looking, then hastily wiped the packet on a dry portion of the diaper and stuffed it into the pocket of her jeans.

When she looked back down, she gasped.

"What is it?" Alice said, her eyes not lifting from the magazine page she was reading.

"Alice!" Nora whispered frantically. "You've got to see this…"

"No way! I already know what poo looks like, thank you very much."

"It's not that! Come here!"

With a look of disgust, Alice peeled herself up from the sofa and stomped over. "Holy mother!" she exclaimed as she caught sight of the naked baby. "It's an outsider!"

Chapter 4

Alice and Nora stared down at the appendage that sat between the baby's skinny, pale, feces-coated legs. Neither had ever even seen a picture of a naked outsider before this. They had heard others speak of outsider parts, of course, but this tiny version of something so feared by all of Aahimsa just seemed ridiculous.

Nora snorted, and then laughed out loud. After all she'd heard about the horrors delivered to the world by male dominance over the centuries, the sight of this child, with his pathetic little outsider parts, struck her as hilarious.

"It isn't funny," Alice said, her face going even paler than usual. "This changes everything. My mother would have a fit if she knew that we were hiding an outsider, even if it is just a baby. We'd better call security." She headed toward the communicator panel.

"Wait!" said Nora, her own reaction surprising her. "First we should check the news. There may be something going on."

Alice didn't say anything. She just walked over to the viewer and turned it on. A dark-haired commentator appeared on the screen. The words "BREAKING NEWS: BODY OF AN INSIDER

FOUND IN DEAD ZONE" flashed across the screen in front of her.

The news anchor's clear voice filled the room: "At 7:35 this morning, while carrying out a routine investigation of an interruption in communications with an outsider worker, a member of the ranger force discovered the body of a young insider, which was found in a shallow grave in the wilds just beyond the dead zone. The initial assessment of the victim indicated that she had suffered extensive injuries, leading police to speculate that she may have been brutally beaten."

Suddenly Blanchefleur appeared on the screen, standing behind a podium at what was obviously a pre-recorded press conference. She had an attractive but serious face and the same blonde hair as her daughter, though hers was shorter and quaffed in a tidy bob. She wore a fashionably cut business suit, and her ever-present white lily was pinned to her lapel. She wasn't particularly tall, but there was an air about her that commanded attention and respect. "This incident is being thoroughly and carefully investigated," she read from a prepared statement. "We must not draw any conclusions until we are certain of what happened here. Until the coroner concludes her examination, this will be labelled a suspicious death. So far, there is no indication that this is anything but an isolated incident, or that there is any danger to the residents of Aahimsa. Nor is there any conclusive proof that the injuries the insider sustained were inflicted by an outsider.

"In the meantime, we can expect this incident to spark even greater pressure from the Central Council to eliminate the outsider workforce. I remain adamant in my opposition to permanently severing our link to the genetic past. The new systems of production and reproduction have not proven themselves yet. It will take a few more decades before sufficient generations of cloned insiders reach maturity and these experiments are deemed safe and sustainable.

"Until then, I am convinced that Aahimsa remains a worthwhile area of exception within the federation. Cloning and automation will not eliminate the labouring class. Our outsider workforce produces the best quality and most profitable products in the world. No matter how well the planners do, if we terminate the remaining outsiders, most of their labour and its social consequences will become the daily task of insiders. It will mean the creation of another low-paid working class within the walls. This would only lead to unnecessary conflict inside our city. You have all seen the reports. Aahimsa is the safest, happiest, wealthiest city in the federation. It also has the smallest police unit, and the least crime. If you compare the quality of life within Aahimsa to any other city on Earth, you will see how much better most of our lives continue to be."

As soon as the mayor finished her speech, the reporters in the audience jumped up and started shouting questions at her. Blanchefleur lifted a hand in the air and the room went silent. "Unfortunately, I only have time to take one question this afternoon," she said with a practised smile. She nodded to a stern-faced reporter in the first row.

"We have received information from a reliable source that claims the insider was struck down by an outsider," the reporter said. "Is this true?"

"There are those among us who are impatient for change," Blanchefleur replied. "It is in their interest to jump to such conclusions. They are only too happy to conjure up the violent and Earth-destroying spectre of the world of our ancestors, to place blame on the outsiders in order to strengthen their political position. Until we receive the results of the coroner's investigation, I cannot deny the fact that it is possible an outsider is responsible for this death. However, I am convinced that there is another, simpler explanation for all of this.

"Your source appears bent on creating hysteria in order to strengthen the hand of the Central Council," Blanchefleur continued. "The council isn't concerned with the welfare of the citizens of Aahimsa. But I am. And I can promise you that we are taking every precaution to ensure the safety of every insider in Aahimsa. It is sad to lose a sister, whatever the cause. But let's not make any rash decisions based on incomplete information and confusion. Let us work together to maintain Aahimsa's position as the finest city in the federation." She turned and nodded to an official standing off to the side, then turned back to the audience. "Thank you for coming. The Goddess be with us all."

When Blanchefleur's face faded from the news channel screen, Alice started flicking through the channels on the viewer. "Well, there's definitely something going on," she said, "but it doesn't seem to have anything to do with the baby."

"What if it does?" Nora said. "What if the two stories are somehow connected?"

"That's ridiculous," Alice said, rolling her eyes. "You saw the news report. No one ever said anything about a baby. And definitely not an outsider baby. If anyone else knew about this, it would be all over the news."

"I guess," said Nora, tying a knot in the strip of cloth she'd wrapped around the baby as she'd finished diapering him. "It's weird about the insider girl, though. I wonder what happened to her."

"I bet you I can find out," Alice said. She tapped a code into the viewer and the screen suddenly lit up with an image of the council chamber, which was filled with insiders settling down for a meeting.

Nora gave Alice a questioning look.

"My mother uses this to monitor the council meetings from

here while she's on holiday," Alice said with a shrug. "It's supposed to be secure, but I saw her type in her password once."

A bell chimed in the chambers and the councillors went quiet. Blanchefleur rose and addressed the gathering, using what Alice recognized as her official voice. "Thank you for coming, everyone," she began. "I know it's been a long and busy day for you all as we've dealt with the news of the dead insider. I'm hoping that this meeting will help us shed some light on the situation. There's been much discussion today based largely on hearsay, including some rather indiscrete conversations with the press." She paused and turned accusingly at Gloria, a councillor in opposition who regularly lobbied for the opinions of the Central Council of the World Federation, and who glared brazenly back at her.

"Perhaps we can begin by having the coroner, Dr. Doris, inform of us of the facts from her examination findings." Blanchefleur turned and nodded at a serious-looking woman with black hair cut evenly to shoulder length. "Please go ahead, Doris."

Dr. Doris pulled a thick document from her case. She wasn't a person who could be hurried. She lifted her silver-framed reading glasses to her face, adjusted them carefully on her pert nose, and began to read, her light-brown eyes focused on her report: "The body that was discovered today belonged to a thirty-one-year-old insider named Minn. Prior to her death, she suffered from mild malnutrition. Other than her physical injuries, there was nothing obvious that could have contributed to her death. Upon examination, I found that she had compound fractures in the femurs of both legs, and a broken pelvis, clavicle, and wrist. It is almost certain that she died from suffocation and heart failure due to massive injuries to her lungs and spleen."

"And the cause of these injuries?" snapped Gloria. "She was violently attacked, wasn't she? And afterwards one or more of *them* attempted to hide her body out there."

"It is my informed opinion that no such thing occurred," Dr. Doris explained. "The victim's injuries were not consistent with such an attack. It is almost certain that she died because she jumped, fell, or was pushed from somewhere very high. Only a fall from a great height could have resulted in the type of injuries she sustained. Her body was also covered in minor plasma burns, which leads me to hypothesize that she fell from the top of the wall surrounding Aahimsa. However, while her skin does show significant burn tissue, it's obvious from the integrity of her remains that she somehow missed the full force of the wall's energy field."

"If her death was the result of the fall," Gloria persisted, "why don't you explain to the rest of us why that outsider fled from his post? Why would he run away if he wasn't responsible in some manner for her death?" She paused, arms crossed, waiting.

The doctor did not react. She simply continued calmly, "I know nothing about the outsider or his motivations. I can only draw opinions from my observations of the physical evidence. I am a coroner, not a member of the city police."

Blanchefleur rose from her seat and turned to Gloria with an audible sigh. "Gloria, we would all appreciate it if you would allow the good doctor to finish her report before you begin your interrogation. You appear well-prepared, if ill-informed, about certain aspects of this incident. We can talk about the outsider's disappearance after the coroner finishes her report. Doris?"

Blanchefleur looked toward Dr. Doris, who hesitated. The mayor gestured with an open right hand for her to continue. The doctor still hesitated.

"Go ahead, Doris," insisted Blanchefleur, her lips pursed. "Continue."

Dr. Doris took a deep breath before she spoke. "There's one more thing. The victim had recently delivered a child."

A scattering of whispered conversations erupted throughout the large room.

Blanchefleur cleared her throat loudly and the council quieted. "Thank you, Doris." She nodded at the doctor, who packed up her papers and exited through a side door.

"From what I understand," Blanchefleur continued once Dr. Doris had left, "after security identified the victim, they ran a check on pregnancy authorizations. No one by the name of Minn was on the list. However, the name appeared on another list. This insider had gone missing from her job at the Temple Donors more than seven months ago."

There was silence as Blanchefleur adjusted herself in her seat. "Of course, the case remains under investigation. There are a few loose ends. The outsider cleaner has, indeed, fled. But there are several extenuating circumstances. Traces of human blood were found in the dirt below the wall and on the inside of the cleaner's cabin. We think he came upon Minn and felt compassion for her. We believe his sympathy overpowered his good sense and he carried her into the shelter of his home."

"How horrible it must have been for her," Gloria cut in. There was a murmur of agreement from some of the councillors. "The thought of that creature carrying an insider into his filthy hut makes me sick to my stomach. He could have done anything to her that entered his disgusting mind."

"The cleaner in question, a former ranger-in-training, was working in the dead zone as punishment for the use of bad judgement caused by misplaced kindness and an inclination towards softness of heart," Blanchefleur said. "I can't imagine anything he might have done to her or to what purpose. There have been no indications that he was anything but kind to her. Dr. Doris's autopsy indicates that he may have served her tea. Her burial site was primitive and basic, but she had been laid out respectfully.

There is no question that he broke the law of contact. Like all outsiders, he knew the rules, and the consequences for breaking them, so there can be no question as to why he would have fled the scene following her death. When he's found, he'll pay his debt to this law, however unjust that law may be under these circumstances."

"So you sympathize with the outsider," said Gloria.

"Draw whatever conclusions you must," continued Blanchefleur. "We will nonetheless use the incident as a warning to insiders about the hazards that lurk beyond the wall and of the dangers posed by all outsiders, though not just because of their violent history. It is more the danger that nature inflicted on us that we must worry about, the danger of temptation."

Blanchefleur took a sip of water from a glass in front of her, then continued. "As the doctor said, Minn was employed at the Palace of the Temple Donors. Apparently she was one of the technicians who collected the temple fluids, and was thus in regular contact with the outsider donors. At one point she applied for compassionate leave to visit her mother, who she claimed was seriously ill. She was granted two weeks, and more if required. When the holiday was over, she never returned to work.

"At first there was a slip-up in reporting that she was missing. Most missing persons cases clear themselves up in due course. The authorities figured this one was no different." Blanchefleur paused and let her eyes sweep the room. With a sigh, she continued, "I spoke to the palace manager. She remembered Minn as a kind but troubled young woman. Apparently she had developed an unhealthy attachment to one of the donors. The manager was relieved when Minn stayed away from work."

"Are you saying that Minn had an inappropriate relationship with an *outsider*?" Gloria asked incredulously.

"Minn had been repeatedly warned to maintain the proper

decorum and dignity when dealing with her donors," Blanche-fleur explained. "She was informed that her tendencies were being noticed and that she was at risk. I cannot confirm that she had illicit relations with an outsider, but the signs seem to indicate that this is the case. I repeat: the real danger, the danger of temptation, still exists within certain of us."

"That's ridiculous!" snapped a red-faced Gloria. "We have a dead body on our doorstep and you expect us to sit here listening to nonsense about the weaknesses of the victim?"

"As I said," Blanchefleur's voice cut through the air like ice-hardened steel, "it is likely that Minn got herself pregnant in the Palace of the Temple Donors. If she jumped from the wall, it is probable that she did so after giving birth to a child outside of the gender determination. No child has been found. She may have jumped with the baby in her arms, which would mean that somehow the child is now somewhere in the wild, or she may have left it behind in Aahimsa. Either way, we have no way of knowing whether the baby is alive."

"And what would possess her to leave her baby?" Gloria spat sarcastically. "After what she'd done to keep it?"

"Minn could have asked permission to keep the child," Blanche-fleur said reluctantly. "She would have been punished for insubordination, but her wishes would have been granted. It has happened before. Unless..."

"Unless what?"

"Unless the newborn child was an outsider."

The chamber fell silent as a tomb. The councillors looked from one to the other in shock.

"One outsider baby is not a danger in itself," Blanchefleur continued soberly. "However, if it exists, this unauthorized child could furnish the spark needed to ignite some very real danger to the future of this world."

"And that's why all outsiders should be terminated!" Gloria shouted. Her face was bright red and her dark eyes flashed. "This is *your* fault, Blanchefleur! It's you who poses the greatest danger to all of us. You still won't acknowledge the danger inherent in your refusal to accede to the demands of the World Federation."

"That's enough, Gloria," Blanchefleur interjected, shooting daggers from her icy blue eyes. "This event occurred because the primal instinct to pair with the outsiders still clearly exists within us. We have been assured by our scientists that Mother Nature will eventually extinguish this deep-seated urge, the vestige of an earlier age. With lack of use, the theory goes, it will, like the appendix, shrink and eventually disappear. And once it does, the advantages of controlling the outsider workforce will far outweigh the risks we've taken to secure it. It's taken several generations, but we've almost completely overcome our primal instincts, and we've come much too far to give in on our stance toward outsider labour now. However, I can't caution enough that these urges, and the oppression that results from them, could return in a very short time if we let down our guard." She scanned the room, meeting every councillor in the eyes before continuing. "Babies have more power over us than we could ever imagine. That child must be found and destroyed. It is the only way that we can sleep in safety."

She picked up the stack of paper in front of her and cracked the edges on the desk to bring them in line. "This meeting is adjourned."

Alice clicked a button on the control panel and the screen faded to black. She turned around to face Nora, who was cradling the sleeping outsider baby in her arms. The blood had drained from her face, and there was a look of sheer panic in her eyes.

Chapter 5

"They'll kill him, won't they?" Nora said, her hazel eyes squinting like a cat's. The answer was obvious.

"Of course," Alice said, noticing the tears welling up in Nora's eyes. She held her arms out, took the sleeping baby, and looked down at his peaceful face. "It's hard to believe he'd grow as ugly and dangerous as the rest of them."

"The rest of who?"

"Whom," said Alice. "Outsiders, of course."

"What are we going to do with him?" Nora asked, blinking back a tear.

"*Do* with him?" Alice asked. "We're not going to *do* anything with him. My mother and everyone else in the council know all about him. They'll be searching for him all over Aahimsa, and on the outside. They won't stop looking until they find him, one way or the other. The security group will want to find evidence as soon as possible because the pressure will be intense. We'll have to get rid of him."

Alice handed the baby back to Nora, who took him in her arms and wrapped the blanket around him a little tighter.

"Look, Nora," Alice said, putting a hand on her arm, "I know how you feel. I'm caught up in this whole thing, too. But think of the future. Soon we can have our own babies. Babies no one can take away. I'll be eighteen in a few days, and you only have a few months before you're of age. You know that this baby shouldn't be alive anyway. He wasn't authorized. He doesn't officially exist. Security will deliver him to the terminators and he'll be dealt with humanely."

Nora drew the baby closely against her. "How long can we keep him?"

"The sooner we get him out of here, the better. If they find him here my mother will be furious. We won't say anything. We'll take him somewhere close, but off the property. We'll call in an anonymous report."

"All right," said Nora, fighting to hide her turmoil. The baby squirmed against her breast in response. She rocked him gently in a way that was already second nature to her, and she sang to him inside her head as she breathed in the citrus of his hair and skin. "But let me do it. I need some time alone to say goodbye to him before I give him up."

"Fine," said Alice. "But be careful. If the one of the search parties catches you out there with him—"

"They won't," Nora cut in. She looked down at the baby again and wiped a smudge of dirt from his face. "You want to hold him before I leave?"

"No, thanks," Alice said. "From now on, he's all yours. I've held him as much as I want to. I know when it's time to say good-bye. You should, too. Some things you just have to do." She rose up and swept from the room.

Nora bundled the baby up in his blanket and then placed him in the wicker basket she'd used to pick the berries. She placed another small blanket over the basket so no one would be able to see inside if she were stopped. She lifted the basket carefully and went to the window to peer outside. When she was satisfied that no one was out there, she grabbed a flashlight and slipped out the door into the warm evening air.

The sun was starting to set, and the sky was a brilliant pink. Nora would normally have stopped to admire it, but tonight there was no time. She scurried into the trees near the house, careful not to shake the basket too much as she ran, and followed a path down to pond. It was darker under the canopy of trees, and she had to take care not to trip over their roots as she walked. When she reached the water she stopped and put the basket down among the reeds, then looked around furtively. When she was convinced there was no one else around, she sat down on a rock, pulled the packet she had found inside the baby's diaper out of her pocket, and opened it. Inside she found a note scribbled in a shaky hand. She lifted it up and tried catch enough light from the dying sun to read it.

Dear Friend,

I pray you are a kind person. I don't know who you are, or what you'll do with my lovely child. But, whatever you decide, try not to be cruel.

I want you to know who deserted this boy and why. My name is Minn and I am his mother. I conceived this child the way our ancestors did. I was in love with the outsider who put the life in my belly. I could not save him from being terminated once he was no longer deemed of use to the

Palace of the Temple Donors, but I swore to myself that I would do everything I could to save his unborn baby.

When I was a child, my grandmother used to tell me about how life was lived in the olden times, stories she had heard at her grandmother's knee. Stories that were forbidden to tell, but that had survived and been passed down nonetheless.

It was very long ago that I first contemplated love as it was in the days of our ancestors. It was when my grandmother told me a story from one of the forbidden books. A story from long before insiders and outsiders. A story about a first woman and a first man. The woman was Eve, and the man was Adam.

My grandmother said that perhaps someday there would be another first man. Well, I want you to meet Adam.

If you find this note, then I am likely dead. I have jumped from the wall to see if I can find a way to smuggle Adam out of Aahimsa, some secret door or passage that can only be found from the outside. I know the fall from the wall will almost certainly kill me, but I have no other option. I've tried everything I can to find a way out of Aahimsa, but all of the exits are monitored by security details and the wall extends too deep into the ground to dig under. I couldn't bear to bring Adam with me over the wall for fear that I would have to watch him die. I pray that if I do not make my way back to him, someone will find him alive and take pity on him.

If you have found Adam, I beg you to take care of him, and to try to do what I couldn't. Take him, hide him, raise him as your own, keep him safe. He is our last chance to return the world to the way it was meant to be, to the ways of our ancestors.

There is a hiding place nearby that you can stay in if you need to, the basement of an old church that has been buried underground since the uprising. My grandmother took me there once as a child. It is where I have lived these past few months, and where Adam was born. There are supplies there, and infant nutrifier for Adam. I've enclosed a map to the entrance with this letter.

I know you will probably give my baby to the authorities to be terminated. But I pray to the Goddess that you are merciful. If there is any way you can find it in your heart to take pity on him, you must *get him out of Aahimsa.*

Please, please,
Minn

Nora sighed as she unfolded a stained bit of paper that had been fastened to Minn's note by a small paper clip. A crude map was drawn on it in blue ink. She immediately recognized the landmarks from an area very near the mayor's summer house. A rush of adrenaline pushed her racing heart rate higher.

She lifted the blanket from over the basket and looked down at the child inside. He opened his eyes and gazed straight up into hers, as if he were staring right into her soul. Nora admired him for a long time before he stirred lightly and made a quiet mewling sound. "Adam," she said aloud. He was so small and fragile. How could anyone fear him?

Nora didn't know what to do. She knew she couldn't keep Adam, no matter what his mother's letter said. But she also couldn't bear the idea of leaving him all alone under the darkening sky for the authorities to find. And what would happen to him when they did was simply unthinkable. She sat there for a long time, looking down at Adam and trying to figure out what she could do next.

"You must be getting hungry again," she said finally. As if on cue, Adam started to whimper. Nora picked up the baby and rocked him in her arms. "I suppose I can't leave you here without feeding you first," Nora said. "You could die of starvation before someone found you."

Nora knew what she had to do.

Chapter 6

Nora placed Adam back in his basket, then unfolded the map once again. This time, she studied it more closely. When she was satisfied she knew the direction she needed to head in, she picked up Adam's basket and hurried along as quietly as possible through the fading dusk. She felt bright and warm, and the prospect of matching the map to the geography cheered her mightily.

Nora knew the surrounding landscape well. She had walked through most of it with Alice. But even though she was very familiar with the large, wooded area that had once served as a public park, in the twilight it looked like a different place. She was relieved when she recognized the dense grove surrounded by relics of long-abandoned public buildings where she and Alice had found Adam only a few hours ago.

The air in the grove was charged with the perfume of wild flowers and sweet grass and the damp of the evening dew. "Can you smell how fresh it is?" Nora whispered to Adam as she once again followed the narrow path that led toward the weeping willow where Minn had hidden him. Nora checked the map again, then walked past the willow and followed the path toward an area near the wall. She carried Adam's basket through another opening in the trees and they were suddenly on a narrower path that led into a lush, green field.

She and Alice had walked here once, and she remembered that in one corner of the field they had noticed a huge slab of worn concrete, which jutted up from the ground like an irregular obelisk. Here and there, rusted rods of steel protruded from the concrete like unkempt whiskers.

Nora had intended to ask Alice about that erratic hunk of rock the first time she'd seen it, but the excitement of being there with her new and powerful companion had pushed the question from her mind. But now, as she and Adam approached it in the fading pink light, she was positive she was looking at the landmark indicated on Minn's map.

"Come on, Adam," Nora said, stopping to adjust the blanket over his basket. "Let's go see if we can find you something to eat." She switched on the flashlight and picked the basket back up. As she approached the huge rock, Nora saw signs of recent traffic. The grass was worn and bent, creating a narrow path that seemed to dip and disappear up ahead.

She followed the path as it twisted and turned around the concrete behemoth. When she noticed a narrow slit in the soft earth at its base that could possibly lead below ground, she set the basket down and moved as much of the dirt away as she could to uncover a small opening. With a bit more work, the hole had been widened just enough for her to fit through, though it would be a very tight squeeze. "Your mother filled this in well," Nora said to Adam as she brushed her dirty hands off on her jeans. "She must have wanted to keep it hidden in case she ever needed to come back."

Nora looked around the meadow furtively in case Alice or someone else had followed her. When she was satisfied that she and Adam were quite alone, she wiggled as quickly as possible through the narrow opening.

It took a moment for her eyes to adjust to the darkness as she shone her flashlight around the dingy room. The air was dank and musty, but the space looked safe enough, so she squeezed back up through the hole and returned, pushing Adam's basket through ahead of her. Now she'd be able to have a proper look around.

The room was sparsely furnished. A small cot was set up along the wall beside the entrance, there was a shelf with some supplies on it on one wall, and a table and two chairs stood in the middle of the small room. On top of the table sat a glass lamp half-filled with rank-smelling fuel. Nora had used lamps like this a few times before, during the rare interruptions of electric power to Aahimsa from the distant wind farms of the manufacturing homelands. Beside the lamp sat a small metal box. Nora lifted Adam up out of the basket and placed him down gently on the narrow cot, then walked back to the table and picked up the small tin box. She struggled for a few moments with its tight-fitting lid before she got it open. Inside she found several dozen waterproof wooden matches.

She wondered if the matches would still light in this damp, stagnant room. She put her flashlight down on the table, then struck a match along the side of the metal box. The blue head exploded with fire. Nora touched it to the darkened edge of the lamp wick and watched as a smoky yellow flame began to dance across it. She adjusted the wick and replaced the glass globe. The flame brightened. It gave off a pleasant, warm light and lit up the room enough for her to see the room's unpainted walls. She guessed by the discoloured cinder blocks that she was in the sub-basement of a church from the previous civilization.

Nora walked back over to the bed and checked on Adam, who seemed contented with his place on the cot and had fallen asleep. On a small table beside the cot she discovered several pairs of shoes and a neat pile of clothing. She picked up one of the shoes and held it against her foot. It looked like it might fit her. She unfolded a dress from the top of the pile of clothes and held it up to her chest. It, too, looked to be about her size, though maybe a bit snug. On a shelf above the table she found a stack of tubes with labels that read "Infant Nutrifier."

Above the cot, a yellowing calendar displayed the page for December 2055. In its faded picture, a bearded outsider in a flowing crimson and beige robe stood high on a hill addressing a large assembly of similarly dressed outsiders.

Beside the cot, an open door led somewhere deeper in the basement. Nora found a second glass lamp in a corner, wiped its globe clean, lit it, and stepped through the open doorway and into a long corridor. She could see more open doors up ahead to her left and right.

Before exploring further she stepped back to check on Adam. She knew she should rouse him so she could feed him, but he was sleeping so peacefully that she couldn't bear to wake him.

Nora didn't really want to venture farther into the dark corridor, but she knew she wouldn't have another chance to look around and, although she couldn't admit it to herself yet, a dangerous plan was forming in her mind, a plan that would require her to get to know this place. For the moment, she told herself it was only a brief adventure. She was free of Alice for a little while and could roam wherever her heart desired. In a short time she'd have to be back at the summer house, and that would be the end of exploring.

As Nora made her way through the shadowy hallway, she

passed half a dozen open doors. At the end of the corridor, another door opened into a second hallway, which came to a sudden dead end to the right, but continued on into the distance to the left. She followed it for a few feet, until she came up against a pile of broken concrete and dirt that sat beside a crude hole in the floor. Perhaps this was Minn's attempted tunnel to the outside. Nora set the lamp down and climbed into the hole. It was deeper than she had expected. It was much too dark down in the hole to see clearly, but with her hands she could feel solid concrete along the side of the shaft. The wall. Nora imagined how frustrated and disappointed the Minn must have been when she'd found out how deep it went.

Nora lifted herself up out of the hole, picked up the lamp, and cocked her ears, listening for sounds from the child. Satisfied that Adam was content, she headed back toward the first hallway, passed through the door, and entered the first room on her right. A dusty table sat against the wall. Tiny chairs circled it in anticipation of five small bottoms that would never arrive. A shelf along one wall held several tins of wax crayons and a sheaf of yellow wooden pencils of various lengths. It must be some sort of schoolroom within the church, Nora thought. There was a stack of red hardcover books, all identical, beside the pencils. Nora picked one up and read the words emblazoned in gold letters on the front: "Holy Bible." She opened the cover and read the inscription: "High Park Presbyterian Church." Must be some old religious text, she thought to herself. She slipped the book back on the shelf and left the room.

She entered another small room, which was empty aside from a coat rack hung with metal hangers, one of which held a miniature blue blazer. She removed it from the hanger and inspected it. It looked strange to her. At first she didn't know why, but then she noticed that the buttons were on the wrong side. She had never seen a coat with buttons like that. She looked at the label inside. "Frisky Fellows: clothes for active boys." So this had been the jacket of an outsider child. That meant this church must have been wrecked sometime before the uprising, when outsiders still lived among the insiders. The building had probably been covered over and forgotten, or perhaps used as an underground classroom after the transformation.

Perhaps the jacket had belonged to a young outsider who had been born too late. Nora wondered what had happened to him. Was he killed following the transformation? Did he live to see the world improve, go from violence and hatred to a place of peace and contentment? Had he become a slave to the insiders after they had successfully wrested the earth from the muscled arms of his forefathers?

Suddenly a shrill cry pierced the air. Adam had woken up. Nora ran down the hallway to the main room and shut the door to the corridor tightly behind her.

Adam settled in against her body when she picked him up, his tiny pink tongue bobbing in and out of his mouth.

"You must be hungry again," Nora said, shifting him to one arm and grabbing a tube of nutrifier with the other. She removed the cap and held the nipple up to Adam's mouth. He sucked at it greedily. Nora rocked him back and forth and sang to him as he fed. Holding him close felt good, and she was disappointed when he dropped off to sleep again.

She set him back on the cot and watched him breathe under the orange glow of the oil lamp. She didn't know how long she'd sat like that, but she suddenly started awake, realizing that she'd been gone from the summer house for hours and she ought to get going. Alice would be starting to panic by now. But she didn't want to wake Adam up, and she knew she probably wouldn't get another chance to explore the basement.

The cot squeaked and moved under Adam as she rose. He stirred, but stayed asleep. Nora picked up the lamp and hurried back up the length of the hall and into the room opposite the one she'd been in earlier. Its ceiling had partially collapsed onto a huge metal tank of some kind, perhaps a boiler for some sort of a heating system. She looked around. Against one wall ran a wooden workbench. From a panel above it hung a variety of carpenter's tools. Under the bench sat a rusted lawn mower. Nothing much of interest here.

A storage room next door held dusty stacks of tables and chairs, pitted with rust where the paint had cracked and peeled away. The next room proved more interesting. Its walls were lined with books. This is a room she could spend some time in — but for now she wanted to explore as much of the underground hide-away as possible.

The next room was stocked with gardening tools and equip-ment: hoes, shovels, and forks, trowels and clippers. Rows of tin boxes with faded pictures of flowers, fruits and vegetables were lined up along shelves on the walls. She pried open the cover of one and found that it was still full of seeds. She wondered if they would grow after all this time. She squeezed a few of the seeds between her fingertips. They seemed firm. She closed the tin tightly and placed it back on the shelf carefully.

Nora decided to return to the long, narrow service corridor where Minn's hole was. As she entered the hallway, she felt a sudden chill breeze, which seemed to originate from somewhere farther down the corridor. She took a few steps past Minn's hole, then stumbled as her foot landed on something hard. She held the lamp down in front of her and shone its light on the floor to see what it was. The moment her eyes focused enough to discern what had tripped her, she let out an involuntary cry and almost dropped the lamp.

The unmistakable form of a human skeleton was propped against the wall in front of her. Nora had never seen a dead body, let alone a skeleton, and the sight of it terrified her. But something about it was strangely intriguing, as well, and she couldn't help but take another peek down at the sad pile of bones beneath her feet. A discoloured paper notepad lay on the floor next to the skeleton. Nora steeled herself, then bent down picked up the pad, trying her best not to look at the skeleton. She fanned the dust off the pad, then tucked it into the waistband of her jeans.

The fresh breeze felt a bit stronger here. Nora wondered where it was coming from. She squeezed her eyes shut and took a moment, then inhaled deeply and leapt over the skeleton. She ran the rest of the way down the corridor, until she reached a pile of concrete boulders, metal pipes, steel girders, and debris that reached from the floor up to the ceiling. A cave-in.

Nora spent a few moments looking over the damage, trying to see if there was a way over the pile. It didn't look like it, but she decided to climb up and see if she could shift some of the debris out of the way. I wonder if Minn tried this, too, she thought to herself. Probably. She would have done anything to find a way out of here.

Nora tried putting the lamp down on the ground so she'd have both hands to climb, but its glow didn't reach far enough for her to climb very high before she would be in complete darkness. She'd have to bring it with her. She picked the lantern up with her left hand and steadied herself against the pile with her right, then shifted her left leg up onto a boulder and shimmied up on top of it. Her knee scraped against the concrete and she winced as she felt the burn from where the rough boulder had scraped off the skin. She'd have to be more careful. With considerable effort, she managed to climb almost to the top of the pile without hurting herself again. She was just about to try shifting some of the boulders out of the way when a sudden gust of strong wind blew out her lamp, leaving her in complete darkness.

Nora panicked. She grasped at the boulder in front of her, trying to secure herself against it. But as she did so, her left foot slipped from its toehold and she slid down, dropping the burnt-out lamp as she groped wildly at the rubble in front of her for a hold. She heard the lamp smash on the ground beneath her just as her hand grabbed on to a metal support wire sticking out from a boulder. She gripped it with all of her might and managed to steady herself. She let out a sigh as she found a boulder just beneath her outstretched legs that was large enough to stand on.

Nora dropped down onto the boulder and caught her breath. She wanted to scream, but she was afraid that she would wake Adam, even from this distance. She thought of him lying alone in the room up ahead and gritted her teeth. "I'm okay," she said to herself quietly. "I'm okay."

Nora's jeans had ripped as she'd fallen, and she could feel blood dripping down her leg. She touched her wound with her finger, but she couldn't tell how deep the cut was. She patted at it with the sleeve of her shirt to dry it off as best as possible, then carefully reached down with her foot, searching for something she could step down onto.

A few feet down and a little ways to her left, she could just touch the edge of a steel girder. Nora crouched down and swung her legs over the side of the boulder, then slowly lowered herself down until her feet were balanced on the girder. With her hands still gripping the edge of the boulder above her for support, Nora stretched her right leg out below her, and was surprised to feel solid ground only a few inches beneath the girder. She felt around the floor, careful to make sure that there was no glass from the shattered lamp where she was about to step, then let go of the boulder and shifted her weight down onto the floor. Relief washed through her as she brought her left foot down onto solid ground to meet the right.

Bit by bit, Nora shuffled her way away from the debris pile, kicking glass shards out of her way as she went. When she got far enough away from the pile that she'd be safe from stepping on glass, she picked up her pace slightly, using the wall beside her as a guide as she headed back toward the main room and Adam. As she started nearing the spot where the skeleton was sitting, she slowed down again and stayed as far to the opposite side of the corridor as she could. Even so, she still managed to accidentally kick something that she guessed was its outstretched foot. She swallowed a scream and kept going, shuffling her feet carefully now in anticipation of the large hole that Minn had dug.

A few moments later, Nora reached the pile of dirt that ringed the sides of Minn's hole. She hugged as closely to the wall as she could and navigated around it carefully. When she had passed it, she reached her arms out to feel for the doorway that led to the next corridor. It took longer than she expected to find it, and the cramps in her stomach taunted her that somehow she had taken a wrong turn. But reason assured her that no other branches to the service corridor existed.

Her hands finally found the doorway, and she passed through it thankfully. There was a faint light escaping from under the door up ahead at the end of the hallway, and she raced toward it and flung the door open.

Chapter 7

It took a minute for her eyes to adjust to the dim light in the room, but as soon as they did she looked down at Adam. He was still sleeping peacefully, blissfully unaware of the ordeal Nora had just been through.

Nora lay down on the bed beside him, glad to feel the warmth of his body beside hers, drinking in the security of finally being back in the safety of the lamp-lit room. She lay there for a long while, smelling Adam's citrus scent. She realized then that the slight mustiness she'd smelled on him before was the same odour as the stale air in the room.

When her breathing had evened out and her heartbeat had slowed to its normal pace, Nora sat up and examined the wounds on her leg. Her knee was scraped up a little, but it was already starting to scab over. She poked through the rip in her jeans to see how deep the cut on her leg was. There was dried blood all down her leg, but luckily, the cut didn't seem very serious. Just a surface wound, really. She cleaned her leg off as best she could with saliva and a strip of cloth, then tied the cloth around her leg to stop it from bleeding more.

When she was finished, she pulled the skeleton's yellowed note pad from her waistband. The paper had turned acid brown and brittle along its borders and edges, so much so that it crumbled even under Nora's careful fingers. The first page was disappointing — the writing was so faint that it was impossible to read. She turned to the next page and found that she could make out many of the words.

...all over now, it seems. I was one of the few to survive the last battles and I came here and fou   everyone dead. Then the army of the women arrived with their prisoners. I tried at fir   to insist that some of us were different...   oo late, though. The laws make it impossible to continue. Military all gone...refused to go to the homelands...so many dead and dying. I hoped to ride out the craziness. The rangers found me on the outside, murderous traitors that they are...hurt bad...scaped back inside here through   nnel ... cave-in blocked the way back out... I miss you, Cheryl, and our children. I miss the old world with all its flaws.

Nora turned the page, but there was nothing more. The rest of the book was empty. She closed it and placed it carefully on the table next to the bed, then looked down again at the sleeping Adam. His breathing was starting to sound rough and irregular, like his lungs were congested. His nose was running. She picked him up and kissed his forehead. The air in here must be bad, she thought to herself. I'd better get him out of here. But still she didn't move.

Nora knew she should have left Adam hours ago, placed him

in some safe spot and said her goodbyes like she'd promised Alice. *Alice.* She'd be absolutely beside herself with worry by now. Maybe she'd even be out searching for her.

But even though Nora knew all of these things, knew that she couldn't stay here in this place with Adam, she still couldn't bring herself to leave. Or to leave him.

As she gazed down into Adam's peaceful face, willing herself to do what she knew she had to — put him down, head back to the summer house, and call in an anonymous tip revealing his whereabouts — she thought she saw something move near the small opening that she'd entered through. It's probably just some dirt falling down from where I packed it in the hole, she thought to herself.

But then she heard the sound of muffled voices. Insider voices.

"Sacred Mother!" she whispered. She jumped to her feet and backed away from the opening, holding Adam close.

"Looks like there could be something down here," said one of the voices, getting closer.

"It's probably just some animal burrow," said another. "A fox den or something."

"I suppose we should still check it out, though. Orders were to leave no stone unturned."

"I'm not digging down there if there's a chance there's something alive in there."

"Fine. We'll just gas it out for now. Come back to check on it later if we have time before the shift ends."

As Nora's frightened eyes focused on the opening, she saw a heavy leather military boot jut down through the packed dirt. It quickly disappeared back up through the hole it had made. Nora heard some rustling from above ground, and a thin metal nozzle was thrust inside the opening. A cloud of gas burst out from it, spreading fast.

Nora didn't hesitate. She grabbed a woollen blanket off the cot and turned and blew out the lamp, first noting the location of the door. Then she raced into the hallway and closed the door tightly behind her. She dropped the blanket to the ground and shoved it into the narrow gap under the door, trying to keep the gas from spreading. She'd heard of this gas before; the guards used it to prevent animals and vermin from entering Aahimsa. It was extremely toxic to humans, as well, especially in a small space like this.

Nora's heart was on the point of bursting. She held Adam's face close against her chest, trying to keep him from breathing the toxic air, as she made her way away from the door. She hoped he couldn't sense her terror. When she reached the end of the hallway, out of danger from the gas fumes, she sat down and cradled Adam in her lap. While she sat she could think of nothing other than getting out of that basement and getting Adam away from danger.

She knew now what she'd been suspecting all along, though she hadn't been able to admit it to herself. She couldn't leave Adam, couldn't let them terminate him — *murder* him. No matter what the cost. But she couldn't hide him in Aahimsa, either. And the basement was no longer safe. There was nowhere left to go.

As she sat in the pitch-dark hallway, listening to Adam's raspy breathing and trying to figure out what to do, a cool breeze caressed her face. She remembered the breeze coming from the tunnel beyond the cave-in. The note in the skeleton's pad had mentioned that he'd escaped from the outside through a tunnel on the other side of the cave-in.

Nora had made it that far earlier, but could she do it with Adam? And would it matter? It was likely that both Minn and the skeleton man had tried getting over the pile of debris before, and neither of them had made it. But she didn't have any other choice. She would have to try. But not until she could get back inside the room to get the lamp and some supplies.

Nora sat there for a very long time, not knowing what time it was, wondering if the guards would come back. Sometime later she awoke in blind darkness. Adam was lying in a clump between her outstretched legs. It was so damp and cold. She wanted to look at him but couldn't. Then she remembered the small, electric torch she had taken from the summer house and left on the table in the other room.

"I wonder if it's safe to go back inside," she said to Adam, just to hear the sound of her voice. "I'm going to set you down and have a look. Wish me luck." Adam gurgled.

Nora walked to the end of the hallway and carefully removed the blanket. She waited a few more minutes, then by slow degrees she opened the door. The room seemed still and safe. She couldn't smell anything, but she supposed the poison might not have a detectable odour. She stepped inside.

The damp, stale air of the basement had got to her and now she was rasping and sniffing, much like Adam. She lit the lamp on the table and then brought a tube of nutrifier to Adam, who she carried back into the room. He drank about half the tube, but would have no more. Nora burped him, then set him on the cot while she changed his diaper.

When she was done, she gathered a few essentials: some woollen blankets, the tubes of nutrifier for Adam, a few bottles of water, some canned food and an opener, a small pot, a container filled with kerosene, the box of wooden matches, the few items of clothing left there by Minn, and some squares of cloth for diapers. Nora put as much as she could into two canvas bags she found under the cot. She picked up the bags, slung them across her shoulders, and then placed Adam back in his basket.

"We'd better hurry up and get out of here," she told him. "The guards could be back any minute."

Nora took a deep breath of the stagnant air and immediately succumbed to a fit of coughing. After her lungs settled down, she switched on the flashlight. She surveyed the long corridor, up past the rooms, and then turned it off. She didn't want to use up the batteries when she knew she might need the light more later.

She remembered there were three doors to her left before arriving at the end of this corridor. She shifted Adam's basket to her right arm so her left was free to feel along the wall and count the doors as she came to them.

The only sound in the cold, dark corridor was the distant, faint hum of moving air. Nora counted steps aloud as she walked, "one, two, three, four," then the first door, "one." Adam's breathing was really loud and Nora could tell he needed his nose cleaned, but she couldn't do it now. She had to keep going. She passed door two without counting. The concrete block walls were rough and the peeling paint and aging concrete felt abrasive and dry to her cold hands. "Three," she said as she came to the last door.

She groped around and found the end door, then carried Adam through, careful not to bump the basket against the jamb. Already the air was cooler and cleaner. When she was through she turned the flashlight back on. She didn't want to risk tripping and falling into Minn's hole while she was carrying Adam.

More quickly than she expected, she and Adam passed the hole and arrived at the bones. The journey had seemed so much longer the last time, when she'd been stumbling through the pitch dark. She continued down the corridor to the cave-in, set Adam's basket down far away from any danger of falling debris or glass, and planned her climb up the unstable pile of concrete, plaster, and steel. When she'd found what she thought was the safest path to the top of it, she put the flashlight in her mouth and started climbing up the debris, careful not to scrape her knees this time. When she reached the top, she cautiously made her way from one wall to the other, looking for ways over the rubble or holes she could squeeze through. There were none. The concrete boulders and steel girders blocked off the whole corridor, from floor to ceiling.

Nora tried pushing some of the smaller boulders out of the way, but aside from a few bits of plaster that cascaded down the pile here and there, nothing would budge. "No wonder your mother gave up and tried going over the wall," Nora called down to Adam. "This is hopeless." She made her way back down the pile and sat down beside Adam.

"Now I understand how your mom must have felt," Nora said, picking the baby up and sitting him between her crossed legs. "We're trapped here, just like she was, and just like the skeleton man was. It's not safe for you up in Aahimsa, just like it wasn't for him. And if I don't find us a way out of this basement, you'll probably die down here, just like he did." A picture of a tiny baby skeleton lying on the bare corridor floor flashed into Nora's mind, and she had to stifle her scream. Tears gushed out of her eyes and she started sobbing uncontrollably.

When her sobs finally subsided into weak shudders, Nora wiped her eyes and looked down at Adam. He was still sitting between her legs facing her, and he had managed to grasp onto the shiny silver button on the front of her jeans.

Nora laughed despite herself. "I'm sitting here, bawling my eyes out because I can't save you, and all you're worried about is a shiny button?"

Adam smiled and grasped the button even tighter.

"Wait a second..." Nora said, a huge smile brightening across her face. "I think you might just be on to something, Adam!" She carefully unclasped Adam's fingers from around her button, then stood up. "Wait here!" she said as she placed him back down in the basket. "I'll be right back!"

Nora raced down the corridor, past the skeleton and around Minn's hole, her flashlight leading the way ahead of her. When she reached the doorway into the other hallway, she turned into it and then kept running until she reached the room with the coat rack in it. She grabbed the little boy's blazer from the rack, then continued on to the room with the gardening tools. She bounded over to the barrel where the shovels, hoes, and rakes were stored and selected the largest shovel. Its edges were heavily blunted, as if they'd been repeatedly bashed against a hard surface, and Nora briefly wondered if this had been the same one Minn had used to dig her hole. Probably.

Nora ran back through the corridors to where Adam was lying in his basket and checked to make sure he was okay. He gurgled happily when she shone the light on him. She picked the basket up and set it down a little farther away from the pile, just in case, then headed over to the cave-in with the shovel and blazer in tow. She draped the blazer around her neck, then carefully started climbing up the pile, the flashlight in her mouth and the shovel still in her hand. It was tougher to climb with the shovel, and it took her a long time to make it to the top of the pile.

When she finally reached the ceiling, she planted her feet onto two pieces of concrete and grabbed onto a metal girder with her left hand for balance, then manoeuvred the shovel under a boulder with her right hand. She put all the weight she could onto the shovel, trying to lever the boulder up, but it wouldn't move even an inch. She tried again, but the boulder still wouldn't budge.

Nora shimmied over to another small boulder closer to the other wall and tried the same thing. This time the concrete moved, but just barely. Nora smiled. She tried again, and managed to lift the boulder about an inch above the one below it. She let the rock fall back into place, careful to leave the blade of the shovel wedged underneath.

"You okay down there, Adam?" Nora called as she held onto the shovel handle tightly with her right hand and slid the blazer from around her neck with her left. She wasn't really expecting an answer, of course, but she figured hearing her voice might keep Adam calm. Instead, he started to cry.

Nora's heart quickened as soon as she heard Adam's wails, and she had to fight the deep-seated maternal instinct within her that made her want to jump from the pile and run to him to make sure he was okay. "Hush, now," she called to him in the most soothing voice she could. "It's okay, Adam — I'm right here."

Adam's cries grew louder, and Nora could feel the blood rushing through her veins. She wanted so badly to climb down to him, but she knew she had to finish what she started. She looked down at her feet to make sure that they were both perched in stable spots on the girder below her, then leaned forward with her left hand and positioned the blazer in front of the boulder, making sure the metal buttons were facing down. When she had the blazer in place, she shifted all of her weight onto her right arm and pushed down on the shovel handle as hard as she could. The boulder lifted up off the one beneath it, and Nora quickly shoved the blazer underneath it with her left hand. As she did so, she lost her balance and fell sideways, just managing to get her hand out from under the boulder before it crashed back down on to the one below it.

Adam's wails had intensified and now he cried out at the top of his lungs in loneliness and desperation. Nora felt every mournful sound in her gut and she wanted to weep or to scream in desperation. But there was no one to help them. It was all up to her. "Hold on just a little longer, sweet one!" Nora called. "I'll be there soon!" She steadied herself against the shovel handle, then, when she was sure she'd managed to regain her footing, pulled the shovel out from under the boulder and dropped it. It clattered down the pile noisily, then skidded across the floor a few feet before it came to a stop.

Nora turned her attention back to the boulder, trying to tune out Adam's cries so she could focus. She squared her feet on the girder below her, then tugged on the blazer with all her might. She could feel the metal buttons scraping against the concrete below them as she inched the boulder closer and closer to her. It was working! She stopped and caught her breath, then tugged on the blazer again. This time the buttons slid a little more easily, and she managed to drag the boulder almost all the way to the edge of the pile. She shuffled her feet down the girder a little further and inched away from the path of the boulder, then reached over and gave the blazer one final pull. The boulder slid forward and then fell down over the edge of the pile. It crashed down to the floor with a mighty bang, and a cloud of white dust exploded up from it.

"I did it!" Nora exclaimed. "Adam! I did it!" She poked her head through the hole where the boulder had been and shone the flashlight through it, down the tunnel. She couldn't see much, but she could feel the cool air against her face as she leaned into it.

Adam let out a mighty wail, which cut right through Nora's reverie. "It's okay!" Nora called down to him as she started to make her way down the pile. "You're going to be all right, Adam!"

When Nora reached the bottom of the pile, she ran over to Adam, picked him up, and held him tight. "You're going to be okay," she whispered to him as she kissed his head. "I'm going to get you out of here."

When Adam had calmed down and his cries had subsided to whimpers, Nora lay him back down in his basket and picked up the canvas bags filled with the supplies. Since she knew the guards could come back at any time, she decided to make two trips up the pile, one with the bags and the second with Adam. This way she could move as quickly as possible, and it wouldn't be as dangerous as if she were try it with both the heavy bags and the baby.

She put one bag over either shoulder and took the flashlight in her left hand, leaving her right hand free to move obstacles and pull her upwards, or to catch her if she fell. She knew that if she were seriously hurt, all of this would be for nothing. She took a deep breath and started up.

It was slow going and much harder than she expected. The bags made her heavier and more unstable. The debris underfoot kept shifting, causing bits of concrete and gravel and dirt to rattle downwards. Every time this happened, she lost her balance and almost fell. Several times her legs or her arms scraped against the jagged bits of broken reinforcement steel that stuck out here and there like the antennae of grotesque concrete insects.

After fifteen or twenty minutes, she'd finally managed to make it through the hole at the top of the pile and down the other side. She left the bags at the base of the tunnel and carefully returned for Adam. It was much easier climbing without being burdened by the bags, and it only took a few minutes for her to make her way back to Adam. She picked his basket up and began climbing the pile as cautiously as she could. Once again she felt the frequent razor-like cuts and bruise-inducing impacts against rock and metal. But this time she found comfort and purpose in Adam's warm presence.

She breathed a sigh of relief as they reached the very top of the mound. Manoeuvring through the hole with Adam proved to be a bit of a challenge, but Nora managed it with minimal injury. When she reached the other side, she rotated her legs down carefully, then felt her way to the bottom of the pile. She set Adam down and kissed him.

Nora looked down the tunnel ahead of her. There was an almost imperceptible light coming from farther down, enough for her to make out the shapes of her baby and the bags. She picked Adam up and, after rummaging through the bags, found the remains of his tube of nutrifier, which he swallowed down with happy gusto. As she sat with him feeding on her lap, she examined her legs and arms. She was sore from battling the pile of debris, but aside from a few scrapes and bruises and the cut on her leg from her last time climbing down the pile, she seemed fine.

There was no more time to waste. She didn't know how long it had been since the guards had pumped the gas into the room, but she was sure several hours at least had gone by. Maybe more. Their shift would have to be ending soon.

Nora loaded the bags onto her shoulders, put Adam back in his basket, and headed down the corridor. A short ways down, it made an abrupt turn to the right and led into a breezy tunnel. The light was brighter here, and Nora was able to turn the flashlight off and find her way through the shadows to the end. The tunnel led into a huge concrete pipe, some kind of ancient storm sewer, Nora guessed. She looked both ways. To her left was nothing but darkness and the slow drip, drip, drip of falling water. To the right, she saw in the far distance a pinpoint of brilliant, clear light.

Nora stepped into the sewer. There was water leaking into the pipe from up towards the city. Probably irrigation water seeping down from the lawns, parklands, and fields above, Nora guessed. There was a pasty residue on the bottom of the sewer, and she didn't want to imagine what she was stepping in. The subdued, but still somewhat pungent, odour that arose from the residue didn't make things better. As Nora progressed, she had to step carefully around occasional mounds of unpleasant, unknown substances.

Nora made her way slowly through the pipe, and as the light

coming from the end of the tunnel intensified, she found she had to squint to fight it from burning her sore, tired eyes. She was eventually able to make out a heavy metal grille covered in moss and slime at the end of the sewer. She hoped that didn't mean that after all her hard work they were now stuck in a concrete prison. When she reached the grille, she felt both excitement and fear. Looking through it, she could see green grass and a quick-moving stream running past. The sky was overcast, but it wasn't raining. She breathed in the warm summer air, and held Adam up to the grate so he could fill his lungs as well. They were so close, but it could all be for nothing if she wasn't able to get the gate open. And even if she did, she had no idea what awaited her outside in the wild.

Nora located a dry area of the pipe where the wall curved up away from the floor and set down Adam's basket and the bags. Adam turned his head toward the light and seemed perfectly happy in spite of the fact that his diaper was most certainly full. Nora resolved to wait until they were outside to clean him up.

Nora examined the gate. Luckily, there didn't seem to be any locks on it, and the door was fastened shut with wire. Nora unwound the wire and the grille swung open on well-greased hinges. "Well, that was easy," she said cheerfully as she picked Adam back up. "Maybe our luck has started to change."

She took Adam to a dry place under a tree and returned for the bags, which she set on the nearest bit of dry ground outside the sewer. She swung the grille closed, then climbed up onto the pipe and rewired it shut. Finally, she picked up her things and returned to where Adam's basket was lying under the tree.

Nora changed Adam's messy diaper quickly, then rinsed the old one out in the stream. When she was finished, she used another of his clean diaper cloths to wash the dried blood and dirt from her legs and arms. She spread the two wet cloths out on a nearby rock to dry, then picked Adam up and curled up with him under the protection of some low branches. She needed some time to rest before continuing. She held her baby tightly in her arms, rested her head against the bag of clothes, and fell fast asleep.

Chapter 8

Alice had never seen the room look like this before. In the air floated a wisp of fog that smelled of decay and glowed and danced as if the summer house were on fire. She glanced around the room, thinking for a moment that she must be somewhere else. Everything about it, though, appeared to be in its proper place: the heavy curtains, the pictures on the walls, the cushions scattered over the sofa.

Nora sat in a chair in the corner, holding the doomed child. Alice's cherished companion smiled invitingly at her. The picture filled Alice with conflicting emotions, not the least of which was jealousy. She had always been aware of her possessiveness, but to be jealous of a mere baby, and a condemned outsider child at that...

Nora's shirt was unbuttoned and opened wide. The back of the baby's head moved softly and hungrily as it nursed from her breast. Alice could hear the slurping sounds of feeding and see the contentment in Nora's face. Alice moved up closer to her friend just as the child turned its head toward her. A scream of rage and fear leapt up from the deepest recesses of her feminine soul and soared around the empty spaces in the room.

What should have been the baby's soft round face was suddenly the face of a large rodent, beady eyes staring viciously at her, pointed teeth threatening her from its gaping, frothing mouth. Suddenly, Nora disappeared completely, and as the fog cleared Alice woke up and found herself in bed. She sat up, heart pounding, and rubbed her eyes.

Thank the Goddess! It had been a nightmare!

Alice looked down to see that she was lying on top of the covers, still wearing the dress from the day before. A magazine was splayed out on the bed beside her. I must have fallen asleep as I was waiting for Nora to get back, she thought to herself. She looked over at the clock on the wall. It was nearly four in the morning.

She got up and walked out into the main room to look for Nora, but there was no sign of her. She searched the rest of the house, calling Nora's name out, but the longer she searched, the more obvious it became that she was home alone.

Within moments Alice was close to panic. Nora had been gone for hours, and there were no signs to indicate that she had come back home during the night. Alice closed her eyes in hopes of quelling her dizziness. She had to think this out properly. Should she call security? No, it was too soon. And what could she possibly tell them?

"What have you done, Nora?" Alice said out loud.

Alice returned to the bedroom and hurriedly changed into jeans and a sweatshirt. Then she ran out into the main living area and began to search for a flashlight. As she yanked out drawer after drawer, she realized just how much she normally relied on

Nora. Nora knew where everything was stored and had always been so willing to wait on her. At first it was just because she was paid to do so, but later on it became clear that she took such good care of Alice because she cared about her.

Finally, just as Alice was about to give up, she found a working flashlight. She grabbed it, threw her sneakers on, and burst out the door. Outside, the moon shone brightly in the night sky and the grounds were alive with shadows. Alice became more and more frightened as she moved from moonlit patch to shadow. She wanted Nora to materialize out of the darkness and return to her before it was too late. That was their only hope. It was madness for her to try to avoid the authorities. There was nowhere to hide inside of Aahimsa unless you were rich and powerful enough to buy safety. Nora was neither of these. Without Alice and her mother to protect her, there was nothing ahead of her but servitude, or worse.

By now Alice was completely aware of just how dangerous a game she and Nora had been playing when they'd picked the baby up and taken it home. Yesterday everything had been under control. They'd been safe in the summer house. They could have dropped the baby off somewhere and it would eventually have been discovered. Now everything had changed.

Alice spent hours combing the grounds of Aahimsa, searching for Nora. But as the sun started to rise, she still hadn't been able to find even a sign of her. Her search eventually brought her to a grassy meadow below the wall that surrounded Aahimsa. A long set of steps led up to the top of the wall. She remembered the last time she had climbed up those steps to the top: feeling the frightening power radiating off the electronic moat, seeing the trees spanning out for what seemed like forever into the wild, following the river as it snaked along through the countryside, and taking in the magnificent view of the vast sea, dotted with ships carrying manufactured goods from Aahimsa to the other remaining cities of the world.

Before she was even aware of a plan she found herself slowly making her way up the steep and winding stairway, holding tightly to the rusted iron rail as she went. As she neared the top she read the signs that warned of the dangerous energy moat. She was nervous as she drew nearer to the powerful wall defenses. Even standing as far back as she could from the invisible barrier that guarded the entire dome of Aahimsa sky from unwanted intruders, she could feel her hair responding to the forces and standing excitedly on end.

She stepped out of the terrifying current and into the tiny insulated guardhouse to her right. Immediately she felt relief from the pulsing energy that had been coursing through her. She walked over to the window. From here she could see a long way up and down the wall. The area immediately below and outside the wall was bleak and desolate. The silver-white glow of the full moon emphasized its starkness. The only break in the monotony came from a miserable hut that sat on the edge of the dead zone.

Alice stared off into the distance, watching how the moonlight danced on the vast sea and glinted here and there on the narrow face of the Humble River, emphasizing the pathetic emptiness of the dead zone and its little hut. She squinted and stared into the outside, searching for any sign of Nora, even though she knew in her heart there was no chance her friend could have made it out of Aahimsa. A silent tear rolled down her cheek as she turned and headed back to the house.

Chapter 9

"Nora didn't return with you?" asked Blanchefleur as Alice walked into the kitchen of the main house later that morning.

Alice considered telling her mother everything then and there, but for the moment she lied. "She was tired."

"Odd thing for Nora to be tired," said Blanchefleur. "She wasn't sick, was she?"

"Oh, no. She just didn't sleep well last night. That's all."

Blanchefleur gave Alice a searching look, then took a bite of her toast.

"If you don't mind, Mom, I'm going to go back to the summer house once we've had our breakfast. I want to pick some berries for a pie."

"Of course I don't mind," said Blanchefleur, wiping a crumb from the side of her lip. "Oh, how I envy you, my darling. It's good that you're indulging your whims while you're young. In the future, you'll look back wistfully on these times. When you come into your inheritance, and should you, as I expect, elect to try on the shoes of the mayor, you'll discover that they pinch.

You'd not believe the day I had yesterday."

"The dead woman and the outsider child," blurted Alice.

Blanchefleur turned sharply toward her. "What would you know of this *outsider* child?" she snapped.

"Nora and I watched the news and part of the council meeting on the viewer at the summer place," Alice answered as matter-of-factly as she could. "I know I shouldn't have been snooping on council business, but I missed you and felt like looking in." She hadn't anticipated this reaction, and she worried how well her mother would read her face.

"I don't recall discussing an outsider child, even in council."

"But you said that the dead woman's baby could be a male. You did, Mom. I watched you say it on the viewer."

The mayor didn't answer. She chewed quietly on her last corner of toast, then pushed the plate away and took a sip of her coffee.

"What happened to that woman?" Alice ventured. "Is there anything that wasn't brought up in the council chamber? Was that outsider really just trying to help her? I thought outsiders were all dangerous?"

Blanchefleur cleared her throat before she spoke. "I'm not aware how much of the deliberations that you overheard, but overall the evidence seems to point to a simple hypothesis. It appears that the woman, Minn, became pregnant through elicit relations with a young temple donor, and in an act of remorse for her actions or carelessness on her part, she jumped or fell from the wall around the city."

"Are you sure she was pregnant and that she had a baby?"

"Positive...absolutely positive. All of the signs were in her body," said Blanchefleur. "And the baby?" Alice asked. There. She'd done it. She'd asked the question she'd wanted to ask. She hoped she hadn't given too much away. She put on her best poker face and waited for Blanchefleur to answer.

"The child was never found. It may have survived the fall somehow, or it may be somewhere inside the city, left behind by its distraught mother. Minn disappeared from work months ago and must have gone underground somewhere in the city. Maybe the baby is still there. Either way, the danger to the city is very real, and will remain so until we've found the child."

"Oh, Mother!" Alice said, trying to sound nonchalant. "It *is* only an infant, for heaven's sake. How much trouble could it possibly cause?"

Blanchefleur's voice turned cold as granite. "Babies grow up. An infant male will become an adult male. Just one outsider could potentially return the world to turmoil and suffering. At the very least, this incident could give the federation the reason they need to involve themselves in our city politics. We can't let that happen. You, of all people, must learn this fact. If you don't, you may live to regret it."

Mother and daughter stared intensely at one another.

"There is something important I have to tell you," Alice finally said. She watched as one of the housemaids walked into the kitchen and starting clearing the breakfast dishes. "In private."

Blanchefleur turned and led her daughter to her office, then closed the door behind them. The two women sat down on a small sofa under the office window.

"Well?" said Blanchefleur. "What do you have to tell me that's so important?"

Nora braced herself for her mother's reaction and the cross-examination to come. "Nora's gone."

"What do you mean, 'Nora's gone'?" Blanchefleur asked, concern washing over her face. "Nora's gone where?"

"When I went to sleep last night she was there in the summer house and when I got up this morning she was gone." Alice knew she couldn't tell her mother the whole truth, but she had to at least account for Nora's disappearance. There was no way that her mother wouldn't notice that.

"Did you look for her on the grounds?" Blanchefleur asked.

"I looked everywhere," Alice said, breaking down into tears. "I went all around the grounds. I even called the transporter office, but they hadn't registered any pick ups anywhere near the house last night."

"There has to be more to this than you're telling me," Blanchefleur said, putting her arm around her daughter. "Sometimes you don't treat Nora as respectfully as you should. Did you have a disagreement?"

"Not really a disagreement," Alice sniffed, "just a stupid little tiff. I was rude to her yesterday, treating her like a servant."

"I've spoken to you about that before, Alice," Blanchefleur said sternly. "Nora isn't a servant anymore. You have chosen to take her on as your companion, and we have welcomed her into our home as part of our family. You will have to learn to treat her with more respect when we find her."

"*If* we find her," Alice sobbed almost hysterically. "I don't know what to do."

"We'll find her," Blanchefleur said, stroking her daughter's long blonde hair. "Don't worry. I'll put out a search order at once." She looked straight into Alice's eyes. "Is there any more to this than you're telling me?"

"No, Mom," Alice lied.

"Forgive me for asking," said Blanchefleur. "But we're in the middle of a major crisis, and now all of a sudden we have another minor one — or let's hope it's minor. I just had to make sure."

Alice lay her head down into her mother's lap. She stayed there, crying, for a long time. She couldn't recall the exact moment she fell asleep, but it came while feeling regret that she hadn't told her mother the whole truth.

Chapter 10

Nora was awakened by the sound of loud, unfamiliar, alarming feminine voices in the distance. *The police.* Her legs were hurting badly from the fall she had taken from the debris pile, but she forced herself to stand up and prepare to head out.

It was a warm day. Judging from the overhead sun, it was nearly noon. The sound of the voices was getting closer, and there wasn't a minute to waste. Nora scurried about, smoothing out every footprint and mark she could find, then gathered up her bags and picked up Adam's basket gently, careful not to wake him. She limped quietly down the grassy bank and into the stream, moving her painful legs slowly in the soothing, cool water so as to make as little sound as possible.

She stumbled along the gravelled riverbed until she discovered a narrow path that led in the opposite direction of the voices. She followed it in grim silence, her heart drumming in her chest, her aches and pains forgotten in her desperation. She had no idea where she was going, or what dangers awaited her in the wild.

Adam was awake now, wheezing softly in his basket. Nora stifled a cough as she watched the expression on his pale, chubby face as he glanced curiously around with his dark brown eyes, as if mesmerized by his surroundings.

The path opened up to a clearing on top of a hill. Nora adjusted her load as she paused and scanned the horizon, peering into the blind distance. After a few moments of searching — for what, she had no idea — she came to a decision and began to move. After a few moments, she turned to glance back toward the city wall, now barely visible. It hit her, right then and there, just what she'd done when she'd taken Adam from Aahimsa. She had, by an act of her own will, given up her position of privilege and luxury for a life of uncertainty, or possibly even death. She could never go back to the safety behind those walls. The enormity of it all came crashing down on her. But there was no time to mourn.

Her heart heavy, Nora hurried along, trying to leave as much distance between her and the threatening voices — and whoever else might be roaming these woods.

What seemed a long time later, she left the path and climbed a steep bank into an area of shadowy trees and rustling grasses. Nora stopped for a moment. For just an instant, she thought of Alice, and wished for the protection of the summer home.

Adam gurgled cheerfully, breaking Nora out of her trance. She looked down to see him swaying in a kind of mystic dance in response to some inaudible music. "What are you so happy about, little one?" she asked him, following his gaze up to the fluffy clouds floating in the sunny sky. "This is all just an adventure to you, isn't it?" He made a small contented noise and she felt herself smiling.

Nora ventured on, dragging her heavy burdens, trying to put as much space between herself and the wall as possible. Time seemed to stand still as her weary legs carried her along the path, which stayed monotonously the same. Her throat was killing her, her legs were sore and swollen, and she felt hot and nauseous. She was ready to collapse. Only her fears for Adam's safety kept her moving.

She drew in great gasping breaths and focused on the purity and the sweetness of the air, which improved as they travelled deeper into the wilderness. She wondered which of the many plants and flowers she'd seen was the source of the amazing smell. But there was nobody to ask. Her heart seemed to shrink as she realized how alone she was and how lonely she would always be from now on. She walked on, deep in contemplation, until she realized that she had almost forgotten to listen for the voices. She stopped and cocked her ear in the direction she'd come from. She couldn't hear or even imagine them here. It was like they had never existed.

There wasn't a single sign of Aahimsa this far into the forest. There were tall trees on every side and the great wall had long since disappeared over the horizon. A gurgling river flowed beside her. She could hardly believe that she was here in the wild, travelling as quickly as possible into forbidden acres, carrying a dead woman's child.

Every instinct warned her of the insanity of what she was doing. She felt a huge sense of uncertainty. She had done this to save Adam, the outsider child. But to save him from certain death, she may have killed them both. At very least, she'd killed any chance of a normal future. But on top of all her fear and loss, she also felt an odd excitement. And, for the first time in her life, freedom.

Nora continued walking even as the sun started its descent toward the horizon. It wasn't until Adam started to cry that she finally stopped for a rest. She found a small clearing and set her load down, then carefully lifted Adam out of his basket. He needed something to eat and a diaper change. Nora located what she needed and accomplished both tasks. When she was finished, she did her best to clean the diaper off without using too much of her water. She made a mental note to fill her bottles up the next time she came to a river or pond. After she had finished cleaning the diaper, she hung the wet cloth from her belt and hoped it would dry quickly so she could return it to one of the bags.

By the time she stood up to leave, the sun had nearly disappeared below the tree line. She gathered her things, noting that the light was fading much faster than she liked. She decided to keep moving until darkness put an end to her travels.

She walked for a while longer, getting more and more apprehensive as the light faded and unfamiliar sounds emerged from the shadowy forest around her. Suddenly she felt the sudden compression of the air, heard the friction of wing against the sky. She ducked down instinctively and raced forward through the trees, too afraid to look back and see what had swooped down so close to her head. She wasn't used to this life in the raw, where things were totally outside of her control.

Back in Aahimsa, where all things were measured and controlled, walking at night was a time of contemplation, of silence. On the inside, the moon cast its blue light around the still shadows of the grass. It was safe. There were no wild animals to be wary of. Nothing flitted in the shadows or scurried under the trees. But here in this place, wild things lurked in the dark shadows and decided if passers-by represented danger or food.

Nora shuddered as she felt a tiny creature crawling across her bare skin. A bug of some kind, biting her neck up close to her hair. She shook it off, but it just buzzed around her ear and then attacked her with vengeance. She checked on Adam, and almost screamed in disgust when she noticed several tiny flies crawling across the baby's face and around his big eyes. She quickly brushed the insects from his face and rearranged his clothing and blanket to shelter his skin from the hungry creatures. She had to stop and find a way to protect them before they were eaten alive.

Nora found a sheltered spot in a small, open clearing nearby and set Adam down. She tugged two large, heavy blankets from one of the bags. She spread one over a low branch like a tent and placed the other one on the ground underneath it. Then she picked Adam up out of his basket, lay him down on the blanket, and crawled in beside him. Tired and scared, she and her baby curled up in the warm comfort of their simple shelter and fell asleep.

Chapter 11

"Where do I go?" Mabon asked no one in particular. He was used to talking to himself, a consequence of having no one else to talk to for so many years. He was wandering about aimlessly, not far from the dead zone. He stopped at the stream for a drink, and then, out of curiosity, stepped up on the treed bank to investigate what looked like a path. He focused his pale blue eyes on the ground and found signs of others having been there.

He had heard a commotion earlier from his hiding place farther back in the trees — lots of loud insider voices. He figured the police had been called about the broken woman's body. He had known enough to stay far away from them. The insider police were even more dangerous than the rangers — they were just as ruthless, but had much more power.

Mabon knew he'd best get away from this spot fast. If the police were ahead, he had to see them before they saw him. He stepped back over the bank and into the cold water and began to follow the stream, continuously searching for signs of the police or rangers on either bank. It gave him something to do to take his mind of the loss of his home.

He was not used to his newfound freedom of thought. The monitoring device had connected him to his controllers every moment since his childhood posting with the rangers. It seemed odd to him that he could make his plans and travel anywhere without worrying whether he was breaking some rule, or being afraid that some controller's voice would break in, and a blistering headache — or even the stabbing pain he'd heard was a precursor to instant death — would be triggered. Now he could go anywhere and say anything and even think whatever thoughts pleased him. To his knowledge, he was the first ranger ever freed from the device without dying first.

Mabon continued along the stream, which he knew would deepen up ahead where it poured into a much-wider river. After travelling several miles, he finally managed to convince himself that he wasn't being followed. He relaxed a little then, and allowed himself to enjoy the warmth of the sun and the pleasant sound of birdsong filling the air. He took a bar of harsh laundry soap from his supplies and stripped down. The water was so cold it numbed his fingers, but he was relieved to finally have a chance to clear away the dirt and the grime from his work in the dead zone. When he was satisfied that he had scrubbed off as many of the stains as possible, he shook out his red-brown locks, dried himself off with a portion of towel, and dressed.

As he continued on his way, Mabon checked every possible gap in the brush along both banks, no matter how small, for signs of recent passage. He soon came upon a place where there was a dampness in the ground that might have come from a person or persons leaving the stream for dry land. He stopped and listened for sounds of movement, or voices, or any indication that there was someone nearby. But all he heard was the babbling of the creek and the lonely song of a single bird.

Mabon stepped gingerly toward the bank on his left-hand side and saw the imprints of a pair of small shoes. They disappeared in the thick grasses and ferns beyond the reeds. The grasses were bent enough that he was able to follow the path the person had taken. He moved slowly forward, heart beating with nervousness and excitement.

In the past, such physical responses would have been enough for the controllers to raise an alarm and, even though he knew he was free of the device, he braced himself for a pain that never came. He took a few deep breaths to relax and a moment or two to lean against a large oak and rest his eyes.

He wondered whose tracks he was following. From their size, they certainly didn't belong to one of the rangers. He figured they were probably some insider police officer or guard's. It was strange that the insider police would be this far out into the wild, though — insider officers never ventured much farther than the dead zone, and they didn't even come that far unless they absolutely had to; the insiders always sent the rangers to take care of any business in the wild. Either way, he figured it would be safer for him to follow the insider's trail than the other way around.

Mabon brushed himself off and continued on the trail of the mysterious small feet. He carried on this way until dusk, when the air became filled with hungry insects. He stopped and reached into his bag. Inside he found a jar of paste he had made from herbs that grew near the dead zone. He took a small bit of the paste and spread it across his face, neck, and hands and then continued on, brushing aside the few bugs not put off by the smell of the paste.

Darkness would not have normally stopped him on his journey, but as the sun disappeared over the horizon he found he could no longer detect the signs that marked the insider's trail. He decided to stop until the light returned. He knew that once he lost the trail, all hope of picking it up again would disappear. He gathered his things and rolled up under the low branches of a fir tree. He breathed in the rich smell of the needles and sap above him as he formed a nest in the cool soil below. He would be safe and secure under here, and in the morning he would continue his quest.

Part II

Chapter 12

Mabon was packing his gear when he heard the screams of terror. Alarm immediately spread through him, as though his racing blood contained ground glass. He grabbed his bags and dashed toward the sound, watching out for a broken hardwood branch large enough to serve as a weapon as he ran. He found one close to the path and barely slowed down as he plucked it from the ground. He picked up his pace and as he approached the location of the screams, he could make out another sound: frenzied barking and growling. He sprinted even harder until he arrived at a clearing, where he found a pack of wild dogs snarling and snapping at a young insider cornered against a tree.

Suddenly, a vicious-looking black dog leapt up and attacked the insider, clamping powerful jaws on a corner of the brown blanket she was holding. The dog started tearing at the blanket, trying to pull it free, but the insider just clutched the bundle tighter. The dog yanked the blanket savagely and pulled it down far enough for Mabon to see that there was a baby tucked inside.

The insider yelled at the dog defiantly, but her green eyes were those of a trapped animal resigned to death. Mabon was deeply moved by her beauty and her helplessness and the way she held her ground for the sake of her baby.

Out of nowhere, a small brown dog, barely more than a puppy, leapt at the black dog and knocked him on his side. The black dog let go of the blanket and twisted around to attack the brown one, clamping his strong jaw on its leg. The brown dog howled and tried to tear his leg free, but the black dog just clamped down tighter. The girl yelled again, and the black dog suddenly let go of the brown one and turned its attention back toward the baby. It stood up on its hind legs and grabbed the hanging corner of the blanket, then tugged at it with all its might. The young woman screamed and kicked at the dog as the baby started to slip from her grasp.

Before he knew what he was doing, Mabon found himself charging at the dogs, wielding the branch over his head. "Ar-reeeeeeeew!" he howled, trying to get the dogs' attention off the insider and her baby. His plan worked. The pack turned and moved together toward him. The black dog let go of the blanket and snarled at Mabon, white foam dripping from its mouth. Then it reared back on its haunches and pounced at the young man. Mabon's muscles seemed to ripple and roll in anticipation as he waited for the dog to draw close. As it leapt up at him, fangs reared in anticipation of meeting flesh, Mabon swept the dog aside with one easy swing of his stick. The dog landed still near Mabon's feet, and Mabon, his pale blue eyes fierce and threatening, let forth a second howl.

It was clear to Mabon that something must have snapped in the brain of one massive, well-muscled black and tan dog. It separated itself from the pack and let out a menacing roar. The rest of the pack froze in their places. This dog was obviously the pack's leader. It thrust itself toward Mabon, leaping with the full force of its powerful legs for the young man's throat. Mabon stood his ground and waited. Then, bringing to bear his formidable natural strength on the swinging of the club, he inflicted a mortal blow to the angry dog, whose momentum knocked Mabon to the ground. The rest of the pack roared and lunged forward.

Mabon picked up the leader's limp body and heaved it in the midst of the pack. The dogs changed their focus and leapt on the carcass of their fallen leader, tearing its flesh apart. Mabon stepped back from the pack slowly and made his way around them to the insider and her child.

"Come with me!" he said, gesturing at the insider.

The girl cringed at him with narrowed cat's eyes. She appeared to fear him every bit as much as the dogs.

"We have to go!" Mabon said, trying to sound less commanding this time.

The girl still didn't move. She just clutched her baby tighter and stared at him with a look of horror in her green eyes.

"You have no choice," Mabon tried. "It's not safe here. As soon as the dogs have finished with their meal, they'll turn on us again." He held his hand out and smiled at the girl. "I won't hurt you or your baby. I promise."

The girl looked over at the dogs, who were now fighting over the last of their leader's remains. They would be finished soon, and looking for more. She picked up her bags and basket, then took a tentative step toward Mabon.

Mabon gestured for her to follow, then disappeared into the woods.

Chapter 13

"I'm Mabon," the young man said as he held a branch back for her so she could get by.

Nora stepped past furtively, keeping as much distance from him as she could. She'd never seen an outsider this close up before, and she'd never imagined they were quite as large or as strong as this one was. The outsider's broad shoulders and well-muscled arms showed through his rough-hewn tunic and gave him an air of power. It scared Nora, but also thrilled her in a strange way she couldn't quite understand. Still, she stayed as far behind him on the path as she could. "I'm Nora," she said, her eyes cast down in front of her.

The outsider didn't say anything more. He just kept on picking his way through the dense forest, clearing a path for Nora wherever he could.

"Where are you taking me?" Nora finally asked.

Mabon stopped and turned to look at her. A boyish grin played across his tanned face. "To be honest, I have no idea," he said, his blue eyes twinkling. "Away from those dogs. And away from the city."

"How did you know I was trying to get away from the city?" Nora asked.

Mabon looked down at his feet, then turned and continued walking on without saying anything.

"Hey!" Nora called, alarm rising in her voice. "How did you know I was trying to get away from the city?" she asked again.

"I've been following you," Mabon said, turning to her but not able to meet her gaze. "At first I thought you were the police, and I wanted to make sure you weren't going to double back and find me. And when we got farther away from the city than any insider police officer would ever venture, I guess I just got curious." He blushed a deep crimson and continued making his way through the trees.

"Why would the police be looking for you?" Nora asked cautiously, slowing her gait to let the distance between her and the outsider grow.

"They think I harmed an insider."

"Are you the one accused of killing the woman who fell?" Nora asked.

"I didn't kill anyone. I helped her."

"I know," said Nora. "I heard all about it. You're the cleaner."

"Yes," said Mabon. "Or I was. I can't go back to that now."

"No," said Nora. "You can't. They're looking all over for you. You broke the law of contact. They'll terminate you if they find you."

"I know."

They continued walking in silence for a long time. The afternoon sun was above them in the sky, and Nora was starting to tire. But she kept on following the young outsider, not wanting to display any weakness in front of him. Her legs were heavy now, and she was starting to feel dizzy and nauseous. She knew she couldn't go on like this much longer. When Adam awoke and started to cry, she was relieved. "I'll have to stop and tend to the baby," she said.

Mabon didn't say anything. He just nodded and led Nora into a clearing. When he reached the middle of the open space, he held a finger to his mouth. He stood stock still for a moment, listening to the sounds of the wild. "We're safe for now," he finally said. "You can relax and take care of the baby."

"How do you know we're safe?" Nora asked.

Mabon watched as the insider took fresh diapers, cleaning supplies, and nutrifier from her bags and knelt before the baby. It made him nervous to have her here so near to him. He'd never been this close to an insider in daylight. This insider was lovely, but in a different way than the woman who fell. The other was like a small bird. This one was stronger, but in a softer, more pleasing way than an outsider. Her shape made him uncomfortable.

"The wild talks. All creatures have to listen to hear what it says if they want to stay alive in it. Anything moving inside the wild raises alarm: birds flushing and calling, squirrels chattering and scolding, the leaves and grasses whistling and rubbing together. If you listen now, you can hear the birds singing. Their song is peaceful and happy. If they go suddenly silent and the squirrels begin to chatter and chide, we'll know someone or something is near."

Nora felt the outsider's eyes on her as she removed the baby's clothes and unfastened the diaper.

When Mabon caught sight of the naked child, he gasped. "That's an outsider!"

Nora nodded and continued to wipe the baby clean. She hadn't really wanted to reveal her secret to this strange young man. She still wasn't sure she could trust him. But she didn't really have a choice. "This is Adam."

"I thought insiders were forbidden from bearing outsider children?" Mabon asked, stepping closer to look at the child.

"We are," said Nora.

"So how did you do it?"

"I didn't," said Nora, lifting Adam up and placing a fresh piece of cloth under him. "He's not my baby. His mother is the insider who fell from the wall."

"*Her baby*," Mabon said, sitting down on the trunk of a fallen tree. This was a lot for him to take in. "She said something about a baby, but I thought she was just delirious. She made me promise I would help him."

Nora fastened the fresh diaper around Adam's waist. When she was finished, she picked up the dirty diaper.

"I can take care of that," Mabon said, reaching out to take the bundle. Their fingers touched as he did so, and Mabon pulled away instantly. Even after his encounter with the fallen woman, touching an insider still felt wrong.

"Do you want to keep the rag?" Mabon asked, holding it up by a corner.

"Yes," said Nora. "You'll have to wash it out, though. It really stinks."

"That doesn't bother me," said Mabon. "I'm used to much worse. I'll go take care of it." He grabbed a bottle of water and disappeared into the trees.

While he was gone, Nora thought about running. But then she remembered the pack of dogs and started wondering what else might be out in the wild. She realized that even though she didn't know Mabon, and she certainly couldn't trust an outsider, she felt safer when he was around. And he seemed to know things about the wild that might be useful. She decided to stick with him for now.

When Mabon returned a few moments later, he was carrying

the clean diaper, a full water bottle, and a good-sized fish.

"Where did you get that?" Nora asked, gesturing at the fish.

"I found a river nearby. There was a young bear there and he was tossing fish up on the bank. He ran away when I got there, so I borrowed one." He beamed. "We'll cook it later."

He handed Nora the clean diaper and the water bottle. "Can I ask you something?" he said.

Nora gulped the fresh water down. "I guess so," she said, shifting Adam in her lap and picking up a tube of nutrifier.

"So this baby is a boy. He looked complete. Is this why you are out in the wild?"

"Yes," Nora said, holding the nutrifier up to Adam's lips. "My companion and I found him inside Aahimsa, near the wall. I knew that if the police found him, they'd terminate him. I couldn't let them do that. I managed to smuggle him out of Aahimsa, but now I don't know where to go or what to do."

"What happened to your companion?" asked Mabon. "Where is she?"

"She's back in Aahimsa," Nora said, her heart tightening as she though of Alice. "She doesn't know where I am. She didn't want anything more to do with Adam."

"Oh," said Mabon. "I think I understand."

"Can *I* ask *you* something?" Nora said, wiping a dribble of nutrifier from Adam's chin.

"Yes," said Mabon. He sat down on the ground across from her, but made sure to keep his distance.

"What happened with the insider woman, Minn? Why did you help her?"

"Minn?" Mabon asked. "Was that her name?" He was glad to finally be able to put a name to her face. It somehow made the whole situation seem less like some strange dream. "She was hurt very badly, and she asked me to hide her. She was so fragile and so desperate, and I just felt this deep urge to protect her. I took her to my hut and let her rest on my bed. There was nowhere else. She was so sad and lovely. She begged me to help her baby if I ever found him. When she said it I thought she was crazy... but here he is."

"And you broke the rule of contact knowing what would happen to you?"

"Yes, I knew. I couldn't leave her there in the filth of the dead zone to die alone." Mabon cocked his head to the side suddenly and put his fingers to his lips. He listened for a moment. "We have to go!" he exclaimed, jumping up from his seat on the ground. "Hurry!"

"What's the matter?" Nora asked, scrambling to her feet and placing Adam in his basket.

Mabon picked up his gear and most of Nora's, then led her out of the clearing and into the woods.

"What's happening?" Nora asked, starting to panic.

"The birds have stopped singing. There's something wrong. I'm not sure what."

Mabon led Nora deeper into the woods, trying to be as quiet as possible so he could hear any changes in the sounds around him. Suddenly he stopped and signalled for Nora to be quiet.

Nora listened hard. She thought she could hear some rustling in the woods behind her, where they had just come from.

"I think something's following us," whispered Mabon, stooping down and picking up a large stick. "Or maybe some*one*." He stepped in front of Nora and took up a protective stance.

Nora clutched Adam's basket closer to her and took a couple small steps back, trying to be as quiet as possible.

A pathetic yelp broke the silence, making Nora jump. It came from a tall stand of ferns nearby. Nora waited while Mabon investigated, his stick raised and at the ready.

Mabon used his stick to part the ferns, and looked down among them. Then he turned and gestured for Nora to come over. She stepped cautiously toward him and looked down. There, lying at the base of a gnarled apple tree, was the young dog that had defended Nora back when the pack attacked her. The dog's brown fur was matted with blood, and he could barely lift his head to look up at them.

"He must have followed us here," Mabon said.

"Poor thing," said Nora, bending down to touch his head. The dog whined and blinked up at Nora.

"Step back," Mabon said. "I'll have to finish him. We can't leave him here like this."

"Why not?" asked Nora.

"Because there are too many other creatures out here to come and find him. He'd be eaten alive, just like the leader of his pack."

"But he's hardly more than a puppy," said Nora, looking up at Mabon. "Couldn't we take him with us?"

Mabon stared hard at her. Her face was drawn and pale, except for her fiery red cheeks. He had noticed that she and the baby were breathing with a heavy wheeze and that her voice was raspy and tired. She was in no condition to go much farther on her own, let alone with a baby and a wounded dog. But something in her gold-speckled eyes told him that she was determined to take the dog with them, no matter what he had to say. "I'll have to carry him," he said finally. "He won't be able to walk on his own. But that means you'd need to carry your own bags. Could you manage that?"

"How much farther will we have to go?" Nora asked, stifling a cough. "Couldn't we just stay here and rest awhile? It's not like we know where we're going anyways."

"We can't stay here," Mabon said, bending down and tearing a strip of cloth from his tunic. He picked the dog's leg up and carefully wrapped the cloth around its wound. "We're too out in the open, and the rangers will be looking for us. We'll have to find somewhere safe to stay for the night."

"And what happens after that?" Nora asked. "Do we just keep walking forever?"

"I don't know," said Mabon. "I've been thinking we could go to the Manuhome and see my old friend Dr. Ueland. I'm not sure what, if anything, he'd be able to do to help. Maybe he could hide us there, though I can't see how. But I don't know where else to go."

"What's the Manuhome?" Nora asked.

"It's the main facility for both the agricultural and manufacturing homelands. It's where many of the outsider workers live, and the rest are trained before they're sent to their postings. I lived there when I was younger, before I was banished to the dead zone. Dr. Ueland is the head of the Manuhome. He trained me himself, and he was good to me."

"How far is it?" Nora asked.

"I'm not sure," said Mabon. "Maybe another's day's walk. Maybe more." He stood up and brushed the dirt from his trousers. "We should get going. It will be getting dark soon."

Nora's grunted as she picked up her own bags. She tried to lift Mabon's as well, but they were too heavy. "Don't worry," Mabon said, picking them up and slinging them over his shoulder. "I'll take them. You just carry Adam and your bags." He stooped low and gently raised the dog up. It whined, but settled into the young man's strong arms without a fight.

Nora picked up Adam's basket and followed Mabon deeper into the woods.

Chapter 14

"You're much too young. I won't hear of it."

Alice had never seen her mother so angry. The stress of the past few days was obviously grating on her.

"I'm sorry, Mother. But I know my rights. I turned eighteen today. The law says that I am ready. It's my choice, not yours."

"That may be true," said Blanchefleur, "but there are other factors to consider. You know that the law exists to encourage insiders to bear children. It was never intended to be used by spoiled children to threaten their parents. You are free to make your own decision, but I am under no obligation to continue my support for you if I disagree with your choice."

"You could never throw me out, Mother," Alice said, taking her mother's hand. "I know you better than that." She looked up at her mother with wide blue eyes, eyes that could conquer a world. "Come on. This is important to me."

They were standing in the huge washroom adjoining Blanchefleur's bedroom. Alice sat down on the closed seat of the sculpted toilet and watched as her mother carefully removed the makeup from her eyes.

"I don't want to fight, Mother," she continued. "My life has been empty since Nora disappeared. Now that she's gone I need someone of my very own to love."

"Now isn't that just the point? Without Nora, you have no one to share the difficult job of parenting." Blanchefleur turned and looked her daughter square in the eyes. "You are aware that partnership is one of the main elements of the temple ceremony?"

"You never had a partner."

"I had my reasons. In a position like mine, partners who will be a support and not a burden are difficult to find. And even the most supportive of partners can be a drain on one's resources at certain times." Blanchefleur shifted uncomfortably on the bench of the marble vanity that spanned almost the full length of the wall.

Blanchefleur's fury failed to intimidate Alice as she knew it ought. When she was little, Alice had loved to sit in this washroom and watch her mother put on her face. Now, years later, she was still her mother's girl, and the pleasant scent of the perfumes and powders lined up on the vanity still made her feel secure and happy.

Sometimes, when she was younger, Alice would say that she wanted to live with the mayor as her companion always. When her friends spoke of their mothers' partners, Alice had told them that she was the only partner her mother would ever need. It never occurred to her that Blanchefleur might be lonely. Blanchefleur had never expressed even a hint that she was missing anything as she'd raised her child. It really hadn't been until Alice had met Nora that she'd begun to understand there was another sort of love.

"I have my own reasons for doing what I do, too, Mother…"

"All right, Darling, let me ask you just one question." Blanchefleur paused while she patted her face with a towel.

"What?" asked Alice, looking up impatiently. She had her foot propped up on the edge of the big tub and was applying a soft pink polish.

"My question is one directed to your heart," she said. "Does this have anything to do with Nora's sudden disappearance?"

"Of course not, Mother. I just want a baby. That's all." Alice put the put the lid back on her nail polish, placed it in the drawer of their vanity, and closed the drawer firmly.

Blanchefleur turned and put a hand on her daughter's shoulder. She focused intently on Alice's almond-shaped eyes. She spoke slowly and deliberately. "Nora disappears. A woman dies after giving birth to a child, possibly an outsider, who also disappears — from right near the summer home. And suddenly my daughter is feeling maternal urges. Forgive me if I sound paranoid." She looked at her daughter long and hard. "Even before I heard about the dead woman or about Nora's disappearance, I began to have a sense that something bad was afoot in Aahimsa," she continued. "My intuition was sounding the alarm. It has never failed me in the past, and I've never felt it so strongly.

Alice tried to move away, but Blanchefleur grabbed her other shoulder and held her fast. "Something tells me that this time, the problem will not be solved easily. When a mother tries to tell her daughter not to make stupid mistakes based on impulse, it is my experience that the daughter doesn't often listen. But maybe this time will be different. I hope so."

She turned around and looked at their two faces side by side in the mirror. "Oh, Alice, you know how much I love you. But what if something happens to me? Will you be ready to fill my shoes? Soon you may discover the terrible burden that power brings. You'll also discover how something very small — a foolish decision, perhaps — can do great damage."

Alice paused a few moments, and then stood up. "I'm going to have the baby," she announced.

Blanchefleur sighed. "Then there's nothing I can do. You know the law well."

"Thank you, Mother."

"I'm not sure I was complimenting you."

"One more thing, Mother."

"Yes…"

"I want my baby to live here with us right from the start. I don't wish for her to be sent to the Palace of the Caretakers. I want her nearby so I can watch her and hold her and take care of her myself."

Blanchefleur stood up so she was at eye level with her daughter. "I want you to know that I am convinced of two things," she said. "First, I am certain that I was correct when I told the rangers to search for Nora in the wild. She found the baby and fled with it, didn't she? She couldn't possibly still be inside the city — we've searched every square inch."

Alice stayed silent.

"What possessed her to do such a thing?" Blanchefleur continued. "Never mind, I already know the answer. The power they hold over us is unending." She put her hands on Alice's shoulders and squeezed hard. "You had better pray to the Goddess that Nora and the baby are found in time."

Alice still said nothing. There were no words to describe her feelings. Tears coursed down her cheeks like summer rain painting the windows of her room. Her mind and her heart were running across the wild, frightened and lost. "I don't know where she went," she finally said. "That's the truth." She wiped her eyes and wrapped her arms around her mother's neck.

Blanchefleur pulled Alice into a deep embrace. "I'm not sure you would recognize the truth if you saw it. You are aware, I'm certain, that you are somewhat immune to my wrath. Anyone else would suffer for treasonous behaviour like this. I can't believe you could be so selfish as to keep this secret. I fear for the future of Aahimsa unless you learn to control your self-indulgence."

Alice sniffed. "I'm so sorry, Mother. I just wanted to protect Nora." She wiped the tears from her eyes with the sleeve of her shirt. "If she is in the wild like you think, and the rangers find her, what will they do to her?"

Blanchefleur paused an instant and looked hard at Alice. "If there is a child with Nora, it will be terminated quickly. You understand that?"

"Of course! But what about Nora?"

"I don't know," Blanchefleur said gravely. "The matter would have to go before Council." She paused, then released Alice from her grasp. "What would you wish to happen?"

"I would like to have her back," Alice said matter-of-factly.

"That might not be possible," said Blanchefleur. "She wouldn't be the same. She might not even wish to return. Something powerful occurred in her mind to allow her to make the decision she did. The moment she decided to flee, she also decided to give up her life with us. The child became more important than you and me and the world we have built." She brushed a blonde lock from her daughter's tear-stained face. "The bond between woman and child is a powerful one once accepted."

"I don't care," said Alice. "I miss her. I may be angry and hurt, but I will forgive her. I know it. I will have my baby and she will come back and help me raise it."

"Alice, Darling," Blanchefleur said softly. "The decision concerning Nora's fate is not yours or mine to make. No matter how much we love Nora, if she has gone over to the outside — to the wild — she may no longer be fit to dwell with insiders again. Even worse, she can never be trusted again. When your child is born, she must be taught to follow the way of the insider. If she is to rule her people, like her mother and grandmother before her, she must be raised with the values of our society. Nora's ideas may have been changed by this episode, and it would be dangerous to raise a child with a wrong-minded influence. This is why I believe that Nora must be permanently out of your life, no matter the final outcome."

Blanchefleur's words only served to deepen Alice's sobs.

Alice cried for a long time. When she finally started to compose herself, she spoke through her tears. "You said you were convinced of two things. What was the second?"

"The second is that you are out of your mind," Blanchefleur said with a smile. "You have no idea how hard it is to raise a child at home. Nor do you appreciate why the practice is discouraged."

"And why is it discouraged?" Alice asked.

"You see, my dear," Blanchefleur said, turning her daughter around to face the mirror. "When you don't give the initial care of your child over to the caregivers, a deep bond forms between you and your child."

"What's wrong with that?"

Blanchefleur spoke softly into her ear. "It becomes impossible for some of us not to give in to our daughters' foolish ideas." She kissed her daughter on the cheek.

Alice beamed. "I love you, Mom."

"I'm sure you do, my dear."

Blanchefleur glided out of the bathroom, leaving Alice standing alone in front of the mirror. Alice couldn't help smiling at herself in the glass.

Chapter 15

Mabon showed Nora how to find hard ground, bare of plants, in order to leave little sign of their passage. When they walked through grasses, he showed her how to pass so as not to bruise or bend a single stem. He kept his eyes peeled, looking for a hiding place, and eventually he found what he sought — a huge circular stand of prickly ash, amidst which stood several huge spruces with massive drooping branches whose heavy ends rested on the ground. He made his way in through the thorny ash trees and set the sleeping dog on the ground, then came back and helped Nora work her way past.

"Climb in there," he said, lifting one of the heavy spruce branches inside the thicket.

Nora obeyed, carefully dropping to her knees and pushing Adam's basket along as she dragged herself and the bags under the low-hanging branches. Mabon hauled his gear into a hollow space off to the side before returning outside to clean up any signs that might betray their presence, and then, satisfied, made his way back into the sweet earthly hiding place.

Nora was breathing heavily now, and her face was flushed a bright crimson. She moved the softest of the bags up behind her and, gathering Adam close, lay down and fell asleep almost instantly.

Mabon was concerned about her health. She was rasping heavily, and he could feel the heat of her fever from where he was sitting a few feet away. He rummaged in his bag to see if he had enough water left in his bottle to wet a cloth for her forehead.

Then, ever so faintly at first, he heard the approach of a nearing ranger party. By his estimation there were four of them, with perhaps more in the background observing. It was hard to tell by the sound of their footsteps. He wished they were speaking out loud, but he knew they'd be using inner speak. He could still remember the strange sensation of communicating via inner speak from when he was a ranger — the feeling of a hundred voices in your head at once, and everyone being able to hear your thoughts. At first, it had felt like torture, like being stuck inside a crowded room with the walls closing in. But after he'd learnt to control it, it hadn't been so bad.

The footsteps grew louder. Soon they would get to the prickly ash trees. He hoped the thorns were menacing enough to deter the rangers from trying to pass through.

The dog must have heard the approaching footsteps too, because he stirred and growled softly, deep in his throat. Mabon reached back and clamped the dog's jaws shut. *Had they heard?*

If these had been the growls of the entire pack, he knew that the rangers would give them a wide berth. He could recall a few serious incidents between a pack of dogs and the rangers, and no creature on either side had escaped totally unscathed. Yesterday had been a surprise to him. The pack must have really hated the leader to attack him so ferociously when he was down and wounded.

There was the unmistakable sound of someone pushing through the prickly ash, the rasp of thorn on canvas.

"Ouch!" one of the rangers whined aloud, breaking the ban on speaking aloud. Then more sounds of fabric being raked by thorns, leaves, and branches. *Was another ranger coming through to help in the search, or had the first ranger been called back?* Mabon waited for the slash of the machetes against the trees, but there was only deafening silence.

Mabon looked over to Nora and saw that she was awake now, aware of the threat, and frightened. Adam was still sleeping soundly, but she had her hand over his mouth just in case. Mabon gave her a nod and held eye contact with her while they waited to see what the rangers would do.

The long silence was excruciating. After what seemed like forever, Mabon signalled for Nora to remain silent as he slowly lifted his head up among the branches overhead and looked around. His heart leapt with joy as he saw that the area was clear. He hunched back down and smiled.

"We'll wait a while longer, but I think we'll be able to leave soon," he said.

Nora said nothing but wondered how much farther she could go.

When they decided that they'd waited long enough, Mabon found a solid branch of fallen hardwood and fashioned himself a club, which he used to break a passage through the ring of prickly ash trees.

"If the rangers had used their machetes to do this, they could have come through the trees easily," Mabon told Nora as he thrashed at the thorny branches. "It's a good thing they're trained to fight and not to think." He grinned boyishly and playfully pushed a red-brown curl out of his eye.

They had only travelled half an hour into the lowering sun when Nora began to cough heavily. She stopped and leaned against a tree for support, and then slipped down to the forest floor. Somehow she'd managed to hold Adam's basket upright as she fell, and it now lay quietly on the needled ground beside her.

Mabon, who had been walking ahead, put down the dog and his kit and moved to her side. He found her lying on the ground, sweating heavily and struggling for breath.

"I can't go on," she said.

"You can make it," he said, taking out his water bottle and pouring the last drops into her lips.

"I can't," she said, closing her eyes. "Just leave me here. Take Adam. Protect him."

"I'm not leaving you anywhere," Mabon said. He reached down toward her, then suddenly pulled back. "May I...would you mind if I...carried you?" he asked.

Nora looked up into Mabon's bright blue eyes. There was a softness to them that she hadn't noticed before. It dawned on her that she barely knew him. She'd always been taught to fear outsiders and the violent urges they couldn't control. She'd seen this side of Mabon already, when he'd fought the pack of dogs, and it had scared her. But for some reason — a deep feeling in her heart that she couldn't explain and didn't fully understand — she trusted him. She nodded. "What about Adam?" she asked. "And the dog? And our things?"

"Do you think you could hold onto Adam if I were to carry you?" Mabon asked.

Nora nodded.

Mabon lifted Adam out of his basket and placed him in Nora's arms. "Is it all right if I touch you?" he asked.

She looked him in the eye once more, searching for some hidden malice, but saw nothing to fear. "I guess there's no other way," she said at last.

Mabon bent his knees and lifted her into his strong arms. He thought of the woman who fell.

Nora rested her head against Mabon's right shoulder. She was close enough to smell his wild animal scent. It was unpleasant, but strangely comforting. She somehow felt safe in the arms of this outsider, the sworn enemy of her city, of all her sisters.

"We won't go far," he said. "We'll just walk until we find somewhere safe to stop for the night."

"All right," she said, her voice barely a whisper.

The feeling of Nora's breath on his ear sent shivers along Mabon's spine. "Hold the boy tight," he said.

Nora pulled Adam closer to her chest. Her throat burned and her legs ached, especially where they rested against Mabon's arms, but she refused to complain.

Mabon moved cautiously in the dying light as he searched for a safe place to rest for the night. He made his way up a hill and found the easiest paths he could through a dense grove of full-grown giants and then a maze of fallen rocks and crumbled shale. At the end of the rock field, he reached a towering limestone cliff. He skirted its base for a long while before he found what he was looking for: a small cave set into the rocky bluff. He lay Nora and the babe on the cave floor in the darkness and covered them as best he could with his time-worn khaki jacket. Nora stirred as he lay her down.

"I'm going for our things and the dog," he told her. "Will you be okay until I come back?"

"I hope so," she said. "I have a flashlight in my pocket. Do you want it?"

"Give it to me for a minute to look around and make sure this place is safe. I won't need it outside. There will plenty of moonlight tonight."

Nora handed Mabon the flashlight and he turned it on and shone it around the cave. The cave floor was dry, except for a small pool of water upon a natural stone shelf in the rear. There were no animals inside the cave, and no sign of recent usage by any animal or human. He handed the light back to Nora. "Don't waste it," he said. "I'm going now. I'll be back as soon as I can."

"You promise you'll come back?" Nora asked weakly.

"What do you think?" Mabon said, smiling down at her. He hated to leave her in such a state, but he needed to get the dog and their supplies before the rangers found them.

"Thank you," Nora said after a moment of silence.

Mabon gave her a strange look. "Don't thank me. For the first time in years, I'm not alone. I'd be crazy to not come back." He bounded out of the cave and into the wilderness.

Nora sat in silence, except for the irregular drip, drip, drip of water falling into the pool. The sound comforted her, like the ticking of a tired clock, and in a few minutes she fell into a comfortable sleep.

Chapter 16

Without his cargo, Mabon was free to travel quickly. Carrying Nora and Adam had been exhausting and painful, but in many ways he had liked it. After so many years alone in the dead zone, it was comforting to have people close to him again, even if he wasn't exactly sure what to make of them.

The air was dry and cool, and it felt refreshing on his face as he jogged toward the spot where he had left the dog and the bags. He kept waiting for the dog's growl as he approached, but he heard nothing. When the stopping place was only a few paces ahead, Mabon slowed down and moved warily, wondering if the dog had survived. He had half expected it to be on its feet, as it had seemed to be improving earlier as he'd toted it along. Perhaps it had found shelter somewhere nearby, he thought. As Mabon drew close he saw the bags on the ground, but they were no longer exactly as he recalled leaving them. The contents of one of his bags were strewn all about the ground around it, but it looked like most of his belongings were there. The only thing he couldn't find was the fish he had been looking forward to cooking and eating — all that remained were a few bones and the tail.

Off to the side he found the body of a large raccoon, its neck broken. Nearby there were some small, dark stains that Mabon recognized as blood. He inspected the dead raccoon. There were deep bite marks around its neck, but there were no signs of it having bled very much.

Mabon could guess what had happened to the small dog, and he felt an immense sadness. It was clear to him that the little mutt had transferred its loyalty from the pack to Mabon, Nora, and Adam, and had guarded their gear from the raccoon. And it had paid the price.

Mabon skinned the raccoon, which was heavy with fat, and removed what edible meat he could with his knife. He wrapped the meat in the animal's skin and placed it in one of the bags. Next he searched the area for signs of the dog. He looked under the skirts of the trees, calling gently and whistling for it to come out, but he couldn't find the dog anywhere. He spent longer than he should have before remembering that Nora and Adam needed him far more than the dog did. So he loaded up the gear and made his way back to the cave.

He entered the cave quietly. He could hear Nora and Adam coughing and rasping, and he knew he couldn't go to sleep yet. He searched his pack hoping that the raccoon hadn't damaged his medicine bundle, and was pleased when he found it intact.

Mabon took out the medicine bundle and some matches and set them up at the rear of the cave, near the small pool of water. He stepped outside and returned a few minutes later with an armload of dried branches and bits of browned grasses stuffed into his pockets. He lit a small fire and looked through his things for a pot. He found a small metal one and set it aside.

Mabon unrolled his medicine bundle and carefully selected

some dried herbs, then scooped some water from the pool and tasted it. It was cool and clean. He filled the pot with water, added the herbs, and then set it over the coals of the fire and left it to boil. He returned in a few minutes and removed the pot from the heat. He would wake Nora and the baby so they could have some medicine, but not before the liquid cooled.

As Mabon waited in the glow of the small fire, he thought about his situation. This was a strange business in what was becoming a world of strange businesses. Even though he was fully aware of the threat of the rangers appearing and terminating him at any moment, being here in the cave, watching the warm firelight dance over Nora and Adam as they slept, he could only feel happy. The last time he'd felt this content was when he'd helped the dying insider back in the dead zone. And that's what had got him into this trouble in the first place. But he knew he wouldn't trade any of it, whatever it was or what it became, for any amount of what had been his previous existence.

When the medicine had cooled, Mabon poured a small measure into a used infant nutrifier tube and the rest into Nora's water bottle. He carried both over to where Nora lay in fitful sleep and woke her up, being careful not to touch her.

Nora started when she woke. It took her a moment to remember where she was and whom she was with. "What's going on?" she asked.

"I have medicine for you, to help your breathing," Mabon said. "You can go back to sleep after you take it."

Nora rubbed her eyes and sat up a bit. Mabon handed her the bottle and she held it up to her nose and sniffed it. "Smells terrible," she said, wrinkling her nose.

"It works," said Mabon.

Nora took a sip of the warm liquid and coughed violently. "Tastes terrible, too!"

Mabon smiled. "But it works."

"You lit a fire," Nora said, looking around. "Isn't that dangerous?"

"Yes," said Mabon. "But I had to mix the medicine and heat it. We won't get very far if you're sick...or dead."

"Oh," Nora said, embarrassed. She swallowed the rest of the bitter tonic. "Are you sure this will help?"

"I'm sure. It's a mixture of yarrow, swamp willow bark, and other things. It always works for me."

"Then maybe we should give some to Adam."

"Here," he said, handing her the nutrifier tube.

Nora held the tube up to Adam's mouth and squeezed some of the liquid into it. His face scrunched up and turned bright red, and he let out a terrible howl. Nora desperately tried to muffle his cries, but Mabon just laughed. "Looks like he doesn't like it, either."

Nora managed to get Adam to settle down and take a few more drops of the medicine. A minute later, he was fast asleep again. Nora could hear his breathing starting to relax and get deeper. She lay him down on the ground and curled up next to him.

As she settled back down, she thought about Mabon. He was an outsider. He was tall and strong, fearless and determined, but also fierce and violent when he had to be. The scene with the pack of dogs kept playing over and over in her head. She'd never seen anyone so much as lay a finger on another living creature in a menacing way, but the way he'd defended himself against those dogs had seemed almost natural to him, as if violence was part of his genetic makeup. She knew he had the power to hurt her if he wanted to. And everything she'd ever been told about outsiders had taught her that he would, the second he had a chance. But she was no longer as afraid of him as she'd been when she'd first met him. In his own way, he seemed gentler and kinder than many insiders she had known. She didn't understand. She drifted into sleep with these questions playing in her mind.

Sometime during the night, Mabon woke up to a rustling sound coming from outside, near the cave entrance. He was on his feet instantly. He picked up a small chunk of broken granite, crept closer to the entrance of the cave, and braced himself. The fire had gone completely cold, and it was pitch dark now. Even so, he knew anyone venturing close to the cave would be able to smell that there had been a fire inside recently.

He listened intently as who or whatever it was made its way closer to the cave entrance. Mabon could hear laboured breathing now, as if the prowler had just completed a difficult climb. He lifted the chunk of granite over his head, ready to bring it down at any moment.

Suddenly, he heard a small, mournful whine. He saw the silhouette of an animal slip inside the cave, sniffing around as it drew nearer. His heart lifted and he smiled warmly as the creature stepped into a patch of moonlight. The young dog was all right. It had survived and it had come home. Contented that it must not be hurt too badly if it was able to track them here, Mabon patted the dog's head and then went back to sleep. He would see to it in the morning.

Chapter 17

When Nora opened her eyes the next morning, she was startled to see Mabon sleeping only a few feet away, facing her. For the first time since she'd met him, she took a close look at him. His reddish-brown curls were dishevelled, and they formed a fiery halo around his sun-browned face, almost fully obscuring a wound on his neck, just behind his ear. Nora wondered who or what could have caused an injury in such a strange place. Her gaze followed his neck over his well-defined jaw and across his straight nose. Mabon's eyes were closed, and she watched his long, dark lashes flutter as he slept. He was wearing dirty orange coveralls that fit snugly against his solid body, accentuating his lean but muscular physique. His two large fists were drawn up against his full mouth, which was set in a crooked grin, as if he were amused by the world around him. On his left wrist was a tattoo with an identification code: FR065419XK.

It was a strange sensation, watching this outsider as he slept — just intimate enough to make her feel equally uncomfortable and inquisitive, repelled and compelled. His large, rough, masculine features were alien to her, almost unpleasant, but somehow she felt herself drawn to him at the same time. She looked down at Adam, who was lying on the ground between them, and tried to imagine what he'd look like when he was grown. She wondered if he could grow as tall and as strong as Mabon. But no matter how hard she tried, she couldn't picture him as anything but the sweet, gentle child he was.

Nora sat up, and was surprised to see the dog dozing on the floor on the other side of Mabon, close to where he slept. She was happy to see it.

Nora cleared her throat quietly. This morning it felt less scratchy and sore, and she was thankful for Mabon's medicine, as unpalatable as it had been. She picked Adam up and listened to his breathing. It was much steadier now. Adam whimpered and suddenly Mabon sat up, instantly alert. His eyes focused on Nora and the child and then the dog. He relaxed and his crooked smile returned.

"Sorry I slept so long. I wanted to be up ahead of you."

"You were exhausted," Nora said. She wondered if he could somehow sense that she'd been watching him, and blushed. "You needed the sleep."

Mabon rose from his bedroll and reached for the black and tan dog. It growled and then let out a yip as the young man rubbed its ears. The dog got to its feet, its tail wagging happily.

"Lie down and let's see your wound," Mabon cooed softly to the dog. He inspected the pup's underbelly and flanks. There were several small cuts, but none that were serious. "You're not hurt too bad. You're a tough guy. But you're lucky to be alive." He turned to Nora, "We should call him Lucky."

Nora smiled and nodded.

Nora fed Adam while Mabon brought his belongings to the rear of the cave and washed his face with water he scooped from the pool.

"The medicine's working," she said. "I feel much better this morning, and Adam's breathing is stronger."

"I'll make a fire and heat some more for both of you. We'll go once you feel better."

"Is that wise?" Nora asked. "Adam and I are both just starting to feel better. I'm not sure how long either of us will be able to travel."

Mabon laid out a few small bits of wood across a fistful of dried grass and lit them. "We can't stay here. If we stay too long, the rangers will find us."

"Do you know how to get to this Manuhome place?" asked Nora.

"It's been a long time. But I think I can find the way. I just hope Dr. Ueland is still around. If he is, he'll do what he can to help us, I'm sure of that."

"What if he isn't there?"

"Then we'll have to keep going, as far into the wild as we can. Away from Aahimsa, and out of the rangers' reach."

"The wild's a terrible place. Everything's trying to kill everything else."

Mabon watched the grey smoke rise and disappear through a gap in the rocks overhead. "All my life, I dreamed of going to the wild and being free," he said. "I dreamed I'd disappear into the wild like this smoke," he pointed to the opening overhead.

"Why didn't you ever try to get away?" Nora asked.

"I couldn't. I was always watched." Mabon instinctively placed his hand on the wound under his ear. "Until Minn fell from the wall, I was controlled by a device that had been implanted in my neck when I was a small child. It could read my thoughts and hear my voice. If the controllers didn't like what they learned of me, they would make the device explode and terminate me."

"Are all outsiders controlled by devices like that?" Nora asked.

"Only rangers," said Mabon. "Unlike other outsider workers, the rangers need to be controlled in a way that doesn't destroy all their masculine instincts and powers, even though, like most other outsiders, they're still not able to make babies." He blushed.

"Who was watching you?" Nora asked. She'd never known that the outsiders were watched so closely. She'd never really known much about the outsiders, actually, aside from the fact that they were violent and dangerous, but that their labour was necessary for the continued success of Aahimsa's society. Or at least, that was what Blanchefleur had always said.

"The insiders," Mabon said, shifting his eyes down to his pack. He pulled the medicine roll from his kit and silently made his preparations. "The wild is a good place," he said after a while. "You'll see. There are dangers, it's true, but that's nature. The real danger for outsiders like me always came from inside the wall."

Nora didn't say anything. She didn't know what dangers exactly he was speaking of, and she didn't really want to ask. She'd always known Aahimsa to be a safe and peaceful place, and the thought of danger coming from within the city walls seemed almost absurd to her. Hearing this outsider, who had just yesterday killed another creature, talk of the insiders as the dangerous ones was just ridiculous.

"You're in danger, too, aren't you?" Mabon finally asked.

Nora looked him square in the eye. "The baby is the one in danger," she said icily. "I'm not scared for myself."

"You should be," he said. "What will the insiders do if you get caught?" he asked. "Will they kill you, like they will Adam?"

"No," she said, her face reddening. "I might lose my job and my privileges. I might be sent to do a job I'd hate. Or I might be just told off. Who knows? But they'd never terminate an insider. It's forbidden. Insiders are safe within the wall." She turned away, set Adam on the ledge, and made a business of checking his diaper.

Her head was spinning.

"You're sure?" Mabon asked, his voice rising. "You're outside the wall now, you know," he said, stepping closer to her. "The rules could be different out here. You may know what the insiders' laws are now, but do you not know the past? Insiders killed all kinds of their own back then. Many women were murdered for siding with outsiders. They were told to choose. Those who refused or chose wrong were killed along with their husbands. Is it so hard to believe they could do it again?" He crossed his arms.

The tone of Mabon's voice scared Nora, but she was too angry to back down. Her eyes flashed with gold as she turned to face him.

"That was long ago," Mabon continued, "but nothing changes. You're an outlaw who stole an outsider child. You know what that means. You broke a mortal law, and there is danger for you and the child, whether you believe it or not." By now, his voice was shaking with anger and resentment.

Nora took a step backward and held Adam close to her chest. The gold anger had faded from her eyes, and been replaced with deep green fear.

Nora's frightened eyes reminded Mabon of Minn's, and he instantly felt sorry for being so blunt. He'd never meant to scare her. When he spoke again, his voice was soft and conciliatory. "Minn told me about Adam before she died. She was terrified, for herself and her baby. She made me pick her up and she made me promise to help her and Adam. What would frighten her so much that she'd leave her baby and jump from the wall?"

"She knew that her baby would die and she couldn't stand knowing it or seeing it happen, I guess," said Nora, relaxing just a tiny bit.

"Do you know how she managed to have him in the first place? I don't know much about how things work on the inside, but I'm assuming insiders aren't allowed to bear outsider children without being closely monitored."

"She had illegal relations with a temple donor," Nora explained, sitting down on the cave floor and bouncing Adam on her knee. "When she found out she was pregnant, she disappeared from her job at the Palace of the Temple Donors. She hid out underground in an abandoned church until after she'd had Adam, and then she tried to find a way to smuggle him out of Aahimsa. She died trying." She looked up at him. "But you would know more about that than I would."

Mabon nodded, and a faraway look came over him. He sat beside the fire, stirring the medicine, for a long time before he spoke again. "What are temple donors?" he asked.

Nora felt awkward talking to anyone, especially an outsider, about temple donors. It felt somehow unsuitable. She took a deep breath, and turned her green eyes to Mabon. "The temple donors provide the fluids used in the temple ceremony to start pregnancy and birth." She paused, then stared at the baby. He gurgled happily.

"But how do they get the fluids?" he blushed. "I've heard something about that, but I don't know if it's true."

Nora sighed and looked at him. "What did you hear?"

Mabon felt trapped in her eyes. His cheeks turned an even deeper crimson. "One of the rangers said they came from young outsiders who hadn't been...changed."

"That sounds right," Nora said. "The fluids come from young donors and they're stored in the freezing chambers at the temple. This is how babies are begun in the City of Aahimsa. In all other cities, it's different now. Outsiders don't exist anywhere in the whole world except for the lands of the city of Aahimsa. The other cities use cloning."

"What's cloning?" asked Mabon.

"I don't know how it's done, but it doesn't require fluids. It makes a baby out of a woman's body without a man."

Mabon tipped the medicine from the pot into Adam's nutrifier tube and Nora's bottle. "Your medicine's almost ready. It just has to cool. I'll put the fire out in case someone smells the smoke." He paused. "No one in Aahimsa uses cloning?" he asked.

"A few insiders from Aahimsa go to other cities to make children by cloning. But only the rich have money for that. Blanchefleur says they're biting the hand that feeds them. She hates cloning and discourages it. She says it hasn't been properly tested and she thinks we'll lose what she calls 'half of human evolution' forever. She'd rather wait and see how things evolve. She swears that there will be no cloning in Aahimsa. She's a practical woman, and she knows that Aahimsa's manufacturing, and its wealth, need the cheap labour of outsider workers. And the replacements for depleted workers come from those temple fluids."

"Who conceives these workers?" asked Mabon.

"The poor do this as service for the community. They are paid well for it."

"I think the medicine is cool enough," Mabon said, carrying it over and sitting down next to Nora.

Nora again noticed his sharp animal smell. She felt an odd sort of comfort as they sat together. He handed her the warm cup. She tasted it, then drank it down. Mabon took the empty cup from her and handed her the nutrifier tube. She began to feed Adam his medicine, a happy tune she couldn't name playing in her head.

"Where did you learn the history of the insider?" she asked.

"At the ranger headquarters, when I was a boy and at the Manuhome with Dr. Ueland. The old workers told stories about the world before the walled city was built. We all know that outsiders ruled the earth, and that the insiders took our power away."

"That's true," Nora said, taking the empty nutrifier tube from where it had fallen on Adam's blanket. "Outsiders were always fighting about something or other and the world was always at war. Women, children, and the elderly suffered terribly and saw no hope for change. After a few wars too many, the planet was ruined."

Mabon turned toward her, his side against the wall, his long arms around his knees, and listened as Nora continued telling him the history of the world as she knew it. He heard her words, and the sound of her voice relaxed him.

"Women knew something had to change. A few met and planned secretly, and eventually, after a great struggle, they convinced other women to join them. The leaders were patient, and they waited and planned and educated themselves until they had the political and economic power to change things. And then they did — quickly and effectively."

Mabon rose to see to the fire, which had rekindled itself and begun to smoke again. He broke up some of the longer bits of tree branches and worked on building a kind of a frame to go above the fire.

"Do you still want to hear this?" Nora asked, lying a now-sleeping Adam back in his basket.

"Yes," said Mabon. "Go on."

"Slowly but surely, your fathers lost their rights and powers. There was no turning back. Women took control of the courts and legislatures, and then the military. There were revolts, of course, but with the help of the military, these were put down quickly and brutally. When it was all over, the women in power divided the world into insiders and outsiders and rebuilt the ruined cities to ensure their safety and security. For the first time in centuries, the world knew peace."

Mabon turned from the fire. "Yes, a lot was taken away. The women must have been very angry. But the insiders haven't fixed the problems. Insiders and outsiders are not different animals. They are different parts of the same one, and they are meant to live together." He broke a few of the smaller bits of wood and added them to the fire, then continued, his voice low. "We were moved outside the walls. We were taught only what we needed to do our jobs. But we learned from our fathers before their time was up, and their knowledge has been passed down through the generations. At the Manuhome, I learned to read enough to do my job and to do numbers in bookkeeping. But most outsiders can't read. We know that listening and remembering is important and we have found ways to pass learning along."

He paused and looked into Nora's soft green eyes. He was still nervous around her. The old rules about not touching and staying away were difficult to forget. Yet her closeness warmed him in ways he couldn't explain. The present feeling was a sort of comfort and pleasure, like what he felt in a forest glade on a warm spring day, or what he'd felt when he had helped Minn.

Mabon removed the parcel of raccoon meat from his pack.

"What's that?" Nora asked, her slender nose crinkling in disgust.

"Lucky killed a raccoon that tried to get into our supplies. The raccoon ate that big fish I stole from the bear, and then wounded Lucky as they fought, but I think the little guy will be all right. His wounds are already healing well. This meat is a gift from the raccoon to replace the fish he stole. I'll feed some to Lucky, and we can cook the rest for ourselves."

Nora looked at the hunks of red flesh with disgust as Mabon began cutting them in strips and suspending them over the frame he'd built to go above the small smoky fire. When he was done, he scooped some water into the small pot, added a fistful of oatmeal from his bag and a few small chunks of the meat, and placed it over the fire.

"We should get going as soon as the food is cooked and eaten," Mabon said, stirring the contents of the pot. "If the smell of the meat doesn't attract the rangers, the smoke definitely will."

"What exactly do these rangers do, anyways?" Nora asked. "What are their jobs?"

"They're caretakers of the lands outside Aahimsa — sort of like a police force or an army — and they also work for the controllers. The controllers can hear their every word, every thought. They always know where the rangers are and what they're doing. If they lose control or contact with a ranger for some reason, they'll terminate him. If they don't like the ranger's behaviour, they'll terminate him. If a ranger disobeys them or breaks one of their rules, they'll terminate him."

Nora was speechless. All she could think about was how horrible Mabon's life must have been, his every thought and move controlled by someone else. Nora had loved Alice, but she'd also felt smothered and powerless as her companion. But that was nothing compared to what Mabon had dealt with every day of his life.

Mabon emptied the contents of the pot into two bowls. He gave one to Nora and kept one for himself.

Nora smelled her stew and took a tentative taste. "It's really hot," she said. "But it's actually pretty good. Where did you learn to cook?"

"I had to cook to feed myself," Mabon said between mouthfuls. "I was given basic food rations as a cleaner, and I learned to cook by doing it. There was no other way."

There was a long pause in the conversation as Nora and Mabon devoured their stew.

"So, who actually controls the controllers?" Nora asked when she was finished her stew.

"Blanchefleur, I guess," said Mabon.

"That can't be true," said Nora, the gold specks returning to her eyes. "I lived in Blanchefleur's home and was companion to her daughter, and I never saw any sign of that. From what you've told me, the controllers are capable of doing some pretty terrible things, violent things. Blanchefleur isn't like that."

Mabon shrugged. "Somebody has to control the controllers. And if not the mayor, then who? I saw myself how the insider controllers mistreated the rangers who disobeyed them. 'Obey or die.' Most of us would never have done what we did if there were any other way. It's not the rangers who are the violent ones; it's the controllers. And the insiders who control the controllers."

Mabon's smile was gone and his blue eyes looked hard and angry. He took Nora's empty bowl from her hands and carried it to the ledge at the back of the cave, where he rinsed it with water from the pool. He then did the same thing with the pot. When he was finished, he stuffed both into his bag.

Nora could see how upset he was, and it scared her. She didn't know what he was capable of when he was angry. She watched as he wet several handfuls of grass and dropped them onto the fire coals, which began to smoke.

Mabon calmed himself little by little as he worked. When the fire was smoking well, he placed the frame overtop it and then covered the frame with one of his blankets. Most of the smoke was trapped under the blanket, but some of it escaped into the cave before rising to the ceiling and disappearing outside.

"Now I'm free," Mabon said gently as he sat down beside Nora on the floor. His eyes had softened and he smiled to reassure her he was no longer angry. Nora smiled back, relieved that his temper had subsided so quickly.

"I think I understand," Nora said, thinking back to her life with Alice. It seemed like years had past since she'd left Alice back at the summer home.

Mabon whistled to Lucky and the dog sidled over. Mabon fed Lucky some chunks of the smoked meat and gave him some water.

"You know," Mabon said, looking Nora in the eyes, "I could take Adam into the wild and protect him. If saving him is all you want to do, and if you believe the insiders would take you back, you could say I somehow caught you and forced you to take Adam out of the city. If you could find your way out of Aahimsa, then I could've found my way in. They would believe you." He watched her pretty face carefully, trying to figure out what she was thinking. He wanted her to stay. He was sure of that. But he also wanted her to be safe.

Nora was stunned. The possibility had never crossed her mind. She realized she could probably do this and get back to her life with Alice and Blanchefleur. And Adam would be safe. She suddenly felt a confusion that challenged everything that she had assumed about herself. Why was there any question of what she would do? This was what she really wanted, wasn't it? To get back to Aahimsa? But what about Mabon? What would happen to him?

For the first time since she'd left, Nora admitted to herself that she didn't want to go back to Alice and Aahimsa and the life of servitude, and that she didn't want to hand over Adam's care and upbringing to anyone else, even Mabon.

"No," she said finally. "Adam stays with me. He's my responsibility. Where he goes, I go."

Mabon worked hard to restrain his happiness.

"Let's leave now," Nora said. "I'm ready."

Chapter 18

Nora was tired already. They had climbed rapidly as they'd made their way through the wooded area beside the Humble River. It wasn't easy going; the pathway was choked with weeds, bracken and tall grasses. Her arms were scratched and bruised from pushing through stiff evergreen branches. But they had finally found an abandoned walking path to follow, and it wound more easily through the trees along the river.

Mabon moved easily, flowing like a human river ahead of Nora, turning every few moments to make sure she was still with him. Nora watched him closely to make sure he didn't get too far ahead. She didn't want to lose sight of him for a single moment.

When a ribbon of moonlight penetrated the murky sky, they paused to feed Adam. Mabon sat facing Nora and prepared a tube of nutrifier while she changed Adam's diaper cloths. They worked together wordlessly. When they were finished, Adam happily accepted the tube of nutrifier from Nora, while Mabon batted away the insects that buzzed around his head as he ate.

Mabon felt a warmth spread through his heart as sat with Nora and Adam. Being here with them was such a change from the hopeless isolation he'd felt when he'd been on his own in the dead zone.

"Why is it called the Humble River?" Nora asked in a quiet voice. She, too, was oddly contented.

"It really isn't," said Mabon. "We call it by its old name."

"Old name?"

"It used to be called the Humber River. The insiders changed it to Humble. The outsiders don't know why. Do you?"

"Humber was probably an outsider name," said Nora. "That's usually why name changes were made. But how would I know? I've never even heard of it before."

Adam had now finished drinking and was sound asleep in Nora's lap. He seemed perfectly content now, and his breathing had become quiet and regular. The fresh air obviously agreed with him. Mabon moved closer to them to support Nora as she held the child. She noted how closely they were sitting, and self-consciously moved away. Mabon coughed and stood up. "We should go," he said gruffly.

Nora stood up and wordlessly gathered her things, then followed Mabon down the path. They continued down the narrow trail, picking their way through the darkness as quietly as they could. Suddenly, out of nowhere, a pair of dark forms slipped from the shadows and crossed the path ahead. Mabon stood still as a tree. Nora stopped in her tracks. She looked toward the dog, expecting him to bark, but he was as still and quiet as his companions. They stood like that for what seemed a long time as the shadowy figures beat their way through the trees, making far too much noise.

"Rangers, two of them," Mabon said when they were gone. "That was close. Too close."

Nora shivered. "How far is it to the Manuhome?"

"Not too far from here, I think. But we should stop and rest until first light. It's not safe travelling when we can't see."

"What were those rangers doing?"

"Looking for us, I imagine. Come on. We'll find a comfortable place under one of these trees. Once there's enough light to see our way, we'll go. An hour or two should take us to the Manuhome."

They found a large spruce and Nora got down on her knees to try to climb under. It was too difficult to squeeze through while holding Adam's basket, and she was afraid that if she took him out and tried to climb under the trees with him he'd be scratched by the low-hanging branches. "Could you hold Adam while I crawl under?" she asked Mabon.

He hesitated. He had never held a baby. Nora passed Adam to him and he carefully lifted the child in his rough hands, trying awkwardly to manoeuvre him while supporting his head and neck. Adam was heavier than Mabon expected, but he still seemed so fragile, like one of the birds in the dead zone. Like his mother.

Mabon held the baby close against his broad chest and smiled as Adam nestled his head in the space between the young man's shoulder and neck. He watched as Nora and the dog climbed under the skirt of a large spruce tree.

Nora lifted a heavy branch as high as she could and Mabon slid under, making sure to protect Adam's head as he passed under the prickly branches and found a spot near the tree's trunk.

"We should get some sleep," Mabon said, lying down on a patch of soft spruce needles and positioning Adam carefully beside him.

"Yes," said Nora, smiling in the darkness. "We should."

Chapter 19

Mabon awoke to a warm, wet, sticky sensation on his face, and was only half surprised to find Lucky licking him. Morning was working its fingers of light through the needles of the spruce.

It only took moments to get everyone up and moving. Mabon, Nora, Adam, and Lucky began their short journey to the Manuhome under a clear blue sky. They were closer than Mabon had figured — within minutes, the tall walls of the manufacturing homeland were looming up ahead of them.

"I'll try to get a message to Dr. Ueland," Mabon said as they got closer to the walls. "You, Adam, and Lucky will have to stay here, out of sight."

"How will you do it?" asked Nora.

"Dr. Ueland used to send me on outings into the woods beyond the Manuhome, where I wasn't officially allowed to venture," Mabon said. "He was the one who taught me about the healing powers of plants and herbs, and sometimes he'd send me to go look for them. The insiders were never willing to provide as much medicine for the Manuhome infirmary as was needed — the outsiders were expendable to them. Dr. Ueland had a secret code for when I got back to the Manuhome walls and needed to be let in. I just hope he still remembers it." He gave Nora his crooked grin and disappeared into the woods.

Sometimes you just have to try your luck, Mabon thought to himself as he made his way toward the Manuhome. Dr. Ueland didn't much care for change. Mabon was counting on that.

Mabon located the window that used to belong to Dr. Ueland's bedroom. He hoped Dr. Ueland was still living in the same apartment, and that he still liked to sleep in. Mabon tried his aim with a pebble, but it ricocheted off the side of the Manuhome wall. *A little rusty*. The second pebble struck too low. The third pebble he tried bounced off a neighbouring window. Mabon ducked behind a bush and waited a few minutes before he peeked out and made sure no one was looking.

The fourth pebble Mabon threw hit Dr. Ueland's tall window dead centre. Mabon ducked back behind the bush, but kept an eye on the window this time. He was just about to venture out and try another pebble when Dr. Ueland's pale, thin face appeared in the window. Mabon raised both his arms straight overhead and slowly lowered them, the signal he and Dr. Ueland used to use. He could just make out the sight of Dr. Ueland's face breaking into a wide grin. Dr. Ueland gave him a quick wave, then disappeared from the window.

Mabon hurried back to get Nora, Adam, and Lucky, and led them to Emergency Gate Three. They only had to wait a few minutes before they heard the heavy lock slide across and the door swung open. Behind it was a small man wearing grey flannel pyjamas. His face was thin and severe, and he was wearing wire-framed glasses over his intense black eyes. Nora was afraid of him for a moment, but then he erupted into a wide grin that instantly changed his appearance from stern to friendly, almost childlike, putting her at ease.

"Mabon!" Dr. Ueland whispered excitedly, shaking Mabon's hand and patting him on the shoulder. He was a full head shorter than Mabon, and could barely reach.

"Dr. Ueland," Mabon said.

"Come in, quickly!" said Dr. Ueland, looking around furtively and gesturing them to enter. "It's not safe out there." He gave Mabon a questioning look as Nora followed him in through the gate carrying Adam's basket, but didn't say anything.

The corridor they entered was dimly lit, and obviously not regularly used. Dr. Ueland put his fingers to his lips and turned, gesturing for them to follow. He led Mabon, Nora, Adam, and Lucky through a maze of dark tunnels and up a concrete service stairway. When they reached the fourth floor, he poked his head out the door, then waved for them to follow him quickly. He led them across a bright hallway and through another door, which led to a large office. Dr. Ueland closed the office door firmly behind him and locked it.

Dr. Ueland turned to Mabon. "Is this who I think it is?" he asked, nodding toward Nora and Adam.

"This is Nora," Mabon said, turning to Nora and giving her an encouraging look. "She's from Aahimsa. She escaped under the wall with the child of another insider."

"Then she is who I thought she was," Dr. Ueland said, turning to Nora. "I've heard a lot about you over the last few days. Blanche-fleur is making quite a fuss about your disappearance."

Nora blushed.

"It's nice to meet you," Dr. Ueland said, smiling. "I'm glad that you're safe." His gaze fell to Adam, who was asleep in his basket. "Is it true what they say about the baby?" he asked. "Is it an outsider?"

"It is," Nora said. She put the basket down, then picked Adam up and held him so Dr. Ueland could see his face.

"Lovely boy," Dr. Ueland said, admiring him. "Does he have a name?"

"Adam," said Nora and Mabon, almost together. Dr. Ueland's eyes widened and he nodded appreciatively.

"You two must be starving," Dr. Ueland said. "I'll get you something to eat." He unlocked the door, slipped out, and relocked it from the other side.

While he was gone, Nora tended to Adam's diaper while Mabon took a seat at Dr. Ueland's desk and looked around the office. Even when he'd been Dr. Ueland's assistant, he'd never seen the inside of this room. It was large, but sparsely furnished, with only a battered old wooden desk, a few mismatched chairs, a large table covered in paperwork, and a few filing cabinets. There was a small washroom off the side, and another door that Mabon guessed opened into a closet. There was nothing on the walls of the office except for a round, industrial-looking clock and a control panel. A small red light on the panel was flashing, and Mabon wondered if it always did that, or if it was alerting Dr. Ueland of a problem somewhere in the Manuhome.

Dr. Ueland returned to the office a few minutes later with a jug of water and a basket containing three mugs, a metal bowl, a loaf of bread, some cheese, and a few apples. He set everything down on the desk, then pulled a small kitchen knife from his pocket, and began slicing the bread and cheese.

"Thank you," said Mabon, passing Nora an apple and taking another for himself. They bit into the fruit hungrily.

"Happy to help, Mabon," said Dr. Ueland. "When I heard what happened with the insider woman who fell, I feared the worst for you. I'm glad you've managed to make it this far. But I'm a bit curious how you did it, and how you three have managed to end up here together." He glanced down at Lucky, who was stretched out in front of the door, seemingly guarding it. "Or you four, I should say." He poured some water into the bowl and carried it over to Lucky, then returned and poured the rest of the jug's contents into the three mugs.

As they ate their breakfast, Mabon and Nora told Dr. Ueland all about how they'd come to arrive at the Manuhome — Mabon talked about his encounter with Minn and explained how he'd lost his controller device, Nora spoke of finding Adam and escaping under the wall through the church basement, and they took turns describing their scuffle with the pack of wild dogs and journey through the wilderness.

When they were done, Dr. Ueland nodded, but remained silent for a long time, deep in thought. "It's an incredible story," he finally said, standing up and pacing back and forth across the room. "Almost as if it were fated." He stopped in front of Adam's basket and looked down at the child, who gazed back up at him with big brown eyes. "Would I be correct in assuming that Adam is...*complete*?" He turned to Nora, who hesitated and looked at Mabon. Mabon nodded.

"Yes," Nora said.

"Then this is more incredible a story than I could have hoped," said Dr. Ueland. He bent down and touched Adam's cheek. "I wonder if you two have given any thought to the gravity of the situation you're in," he said, looking at Nora and Mabon. "Just how important this escape of yours is, and how much is riding on its success..."

There was a long, uncomfortable silence. Neither Nora nor Mabon wanted to admit that they hadn't given much thought to the wider implications of what they were doing. They were aware of them, certainly, but they'd been so focused on just surviving and escaping the immediate danger threatening them that they hadn't thought much about what could happen if they did.

"Well," said Dr. Ueland finally, returning to the desk and sitting down across from them. "I assume you came here to see me for a reason. What can I do for you?"

"I was hoping you could help hide us for a while," said Nora. She blushed. "Mabon told me that you were kind."

"Mabon is the kind one," said Dr. Ueland, taking his seat across from them at his desk. "I'm practical. It isn't often in my power to be kind." He frowned. "I'm sure that Mabon already knows what I'm about to say. I have a lot of power here in the Manuhome, but there are severe limits to what I can do. If Adam were older, I might be able to hide him here with certain difficulties. But we have no babies here — we never have and we never will. There are many outsider workers here who would remember Mabon, and therefore it would be nearly impossible to hide him here without someone informing Blanchefleur and her rangers that he was here. And there are no insiders at the Manuhome, so a beautiful young lady like yourself would certainly be noticed."

"So you won't help us?" said Nora. Her head felt like it would explode. Tears were welling up behind her eyes, but she was determined not to cry.

"I didn't say that," said Dr. Ueland, smiling slyly. "I have a plan, and I think you'll like it."

"What is it?" Nora asked.

"Mabon will remember that while he was training with me, I began a practice of helping to cure some of the older workers who had been injured from years of manual labour and were slated for termination," said Dr. Ueland. "In fact, that was ultimately why he was stripped of his ranger status and banished to the dead zone. He was caught doing one of the errands I sent him on, gathering medicinal herbs, and he very selflessly took the blame for it. He said he'd been acting on his own to help an elderly friend and, by doing so, he allowed me to continue helping the old ones after he'd left."

The doctor turned to Mabon. "But you will see that your punishment has not been in vain, Mabon. Not only was I able to help cure some of these old ones of the injuries they suffered, I was able to help them escape. For several years now, I've been helping some of the older workers disappear into the wild once they've had a chance to recover from their lifetimes of hard work. I've been falsifying their termination papers, and letting them go free. And they've managed to build quite a life for themselves out in the wild. They've set up a whole community, hidden from the reaches of the insiders, where they live and work to support themselves. It's really quite amazing."

Dr. Ueland turned back to Nora. "And so you see, I do have somewhere I can hide you, it just isn't here."

"Where is this place?" asked Mabon. "How would we find it?"

"I have a way of communicating with the old ones, using pigeons — a method our forefathers used long before the revolt. I should be able to get a message to them quite quickly. I'll ask them to send someone to guide you." He stood up and headed toward the door. "I can keep you here until he comes. No one should bother you, as long as you stay in this room. My staff knows not to interrupt me while I'm working in here." He reached down and patted Lucky's head when he got to the door. Lucky stood up on his feet and stepped out of his way.

"Let me get dressed while you finish up your breakfast," said Dr. Ueland. "I'll gather up some food and supplies for your journey, and I'll be back soon." He looked at Mabon. "If anyone knocks on the door, don't open it. I'm the only one with a key, so I'll let myself in when I return." With that, he slipped out the door and locked it behind him.

Chapter 20

It was hours before Dr. Ueland returned to the office, and even then, it was just to bring Nora and Mabon some dinner and some pillows and blankets so they could rest for the night. He was gone almost as quickly as he'd arrived. He popped in again the next morning to bring them some breakfast and a few things to keep for their lunch later on, but wasn't able to stay then either. It wasn't until late that night that he entered again. This time he had someone with him — a thin, elderly outsider dressed in a brown homespun cloak and tunic. His legs were bare and his feet were shod in leather sandals. He had long white hair that curtained his watery eyes and fell all about his leathery face, which broke into a grin when he saw Mabon and Nora.

"Mabon, Nora," Dr. Ueland said, "I'd like you to meet Aesop, the leader of the old ones."

"So happy to meet you both," Aesop said. "The good Dr. Ueland has told me all about you." Lucky wagged his tail and jumped up on the old man. "And who is this?"

Nora thought it was a good sign that the dog immediately took to this lively old man. "That's Lucky," she said.

"He's certainly lived up to his name so far," Aesop said, patting Lucky's head. "You two are lucky to have made it this far, with the rangers combing the woods for you." He walked over to where Adam was lying in his basket and bent down to get a better look at the child. "This must be Adam." He tickled Adam's toes. "You're the cause of great excitement throughout our happy little valley, little one. You'll be well taken care of there."

Aesop sat down to rest and had a bite to eat while Nora and Mabon packed up their belongings. Dr. Ueland had brought them some supplies for the trip to the valley of the old ones, and they'd accepted them gratefully and packed them up as well.

When they were ready to set off, Dr. Ueland poked his head out the door, and, when he was convinced the coast was clear, led them back across the hall, down the service stairs, and through the maze of dimly lit corridors to Emergency Gate Three. He stopped before he opened the gate for them.

"Safe travels, my friends," he told them. He turned to Mabon and Nora and that stern look travelled back across his face like a thundercloud rolling in. "Protect that boy, no matter what the cost. His life is worth more than all of ours combined."

Nora thought she noticed Dr. Ueland and Aesop share an almost imperceptible nod.

"I'll send a pigeon to let you know that we've arrived safely," Aesop told Dr. Ueland.

"Please do," said Dr. Ueland. "I'll be in touch again soon."

Dr. Ueland unlocked the gate, and the group of travellers disappeared into the night.

Chapter 21

Nora and Mabon followed Aesop for hours through the dense forest, stopping occasionally to tend to Adam, eat, or rest. Just as the sun started rising in what Nora now recognized as the east, they reached a large field. Here and there in the distance she could make out the remains of ruined offices and apartment buildings.

Aesop stopped and turned to them. "From here on, there's an extra danger." He pointed to a rusty old sign at the edge of the field with a picture of a skull and crossbones on it. "There are many unexploded land mines in this area, left over from the ancient wars," he explained. "They're very dangerous and very unpredictable. Stay close to me at all times and follow in my footsteps exactly. You'll need to carry the dog, Mabon. And stay close together."

"All right," Nora said. "We will."

Aesop led them up a path and then turned suddenly to the left. Nora wondered how close they had come to stepping on land mines. They continued to zigzag through the field, slowly making their way to the other side. When they reached the edge of the field, Aesop pulled back a branch, and they stepped into a majestic pine forest whose interior reminded Nora of the pillared cathedral dedicated to the Mother Goddess.

The trees grew in parallel rows and Nora concluded that they had been intentionally planted this way. More and more light defined the woods as they walked, and Nora was astonished at the natural beauty and variety of the plants and flowers that grew up from the springy carpet of brown pine needles. The ground rose slowly and steadily upward, but the light and the pine-sweet air helped increase their speed, and they covered the ground quickly.

Before the hour was out, their surroundings abruptly changed again. They left the pine forest and travelled across a section of barren ground that was littered with rocks and the scattered debris from broken concrete buildings. Gradually they approached the remains of a more intact cluster of damaged stone buildings, which loomed above them like forgotten giants. Every few feet they passed painted wooden signs showing rangers being blown apart by explosions. At the top in red letters were the words:

DANGER
EXCLUSION ZONE
KEEP OUT!

Nora moved closer to Aesop and wondered if such grave dangers existed everywhere in the wild, or just in pockets like this one. It was hard to believe that wars so long past could still have such an effect on the land around them.

"We'll have to be particularly careful now," said Aesop, slowing down. "The rest of the way is riddled with landmines." He turned to Nora and looked at her apologetically. "I'm sorry, Nora, but for the rest of the journey, you'll need to be blindfolded." He ripped a narrow strip of cloth from the base of his tattered cape and held it up to her.

"Why do I have to cover my eyes?" Nora asked. She looked up at Mabon, who appeared just as alarmed as she was.

"You may have rescued Adam, but you're still an insider," Aesop explained. "We don't know anything about you, and we can't be sure that you haven't been sent by Blanchefleur in some secret insider plot to find us and terminate us. Forgive me, but the insiders have never given us any reason to trust them, so even though you appear to be different from the others of your kind, we have to take precautions."

"That's crazy!" Nora said, the gold flecks flashing in her eyes. "We've walked most of the way here in darkness, and we've been marching through a maze of minefields for hours. I have no idea where we are. And I'm certainly no insider spy."

"She's speaking the truth," Mabon said. "I've been travelling with her for days. There's no way she's anything but what she says she is."

"I'm sorry," Aesop said, looking genuinely pained. He held the blindfold up to Nora again. "But if we are to go any farther, you must cover your eyes."

Nora looked across her shoulder at Mabon. He nodded. "It will be all right," he said. "I won't let anything happen to you or to Adam."

In spite of Mabon's reassurance, Nora shuddered as Aesop tied the rough cloth across her eyes.

"You'll have to spin around a few times," Aesop directed, "so you don't know which direction we're heading in."

Nora put Adam's basket down, and then followed Aesop's instructions. When she'd finished spinning, she was dizzy and unsteady on her feet. She tried to take a few steps forward, but stumbled and just barely managed to catch herself. "This is stupid," she said. "I can't walk like this. I'll trip and set off a landmine and kill us all."

"Here," Mabon said, lifting Adam's basket and placing its handle in her palm. "Take this in one hand. I'll hold your other hand and guide you…if that's okay?"

Nora didn't answer at first, and Mabon was glad she couldn't see the crimson stain that he could feel creeping into his cheeks.

"Okay," she said finally. She held out her hand and Mabon took it.

Nora's hand was smaller than Mabon had expected, and much softer. It reminded him of the smooth leather gloves he'd worn when he was a ranger. He held it tightly, but took care not to squeeze too hard. "Don't worry," he said. "I won't let you fall."

Aesop led Mabon and Nora on a walk that took much longer than Nora had anticipated. After several minutes, Adam began to squirm in his basket, causing it to shake in Nora's hand. As she fought to keep it steady, Nora realized how cramped and tired the muscles of her arms and shoulders had become. Her back ached. Her feet were sore. She was about to give up and ask for a break when Aesop's voice came from ahead of her.

"We're almost there. Watch yourself, now. In a moment you'll be climbing down a wooden ladder and into an underground passage." His voice cracked asthmatically. "Stay still until I open the hatch, Mabon."

"Is the ladder okay?" came Mabon's voice. "The steps don't look safe…"

"It'd better be. We use it all the time. But there's always a chance of it breaking, so hang on, everyone!" He started to chuckle, but it quickly turned into a coughing fit. Once he had regained control of his breathing, he continued. "I'll go first and light a torch. Mabon, you pass the dog down and then follow, and Nora will pass Adam to you, then come down last. Nora, I'm sorry, but you'll have to use both hands to climb. We won't be able to guide you."

Nora heard some commotion as Aesop climbed down the ladder, and then a small yip from Lucky as he was passed down. She felt Mabon let go of her hand.

"Don't worry," he whispered to her. "I'll be there to catch you if you fall."

Nora heard Mabon's heavy steps down the ladder and then the sound of his feet crunching against the gravel below.

"Okay!" he called up. "You can pass Adam down now."

Nora bent down shakily and slowly lowered Adam's basket to the place she thought the hatch would be. She felt it bump against the ground lightly.

"A little to the left!" Mabon's voice came from below.

Nora slid the basket to the left, and felt the ground cut out from underneath it. She gasped for a moment as the weight of the basket pulled her down, but then felt the basket being supported from below.

"I've got him!" Mabon called.

Nora let go of the basket and waited for Mabon to put it down.

"Okay," Mabon called. "Now it's your turn. Take a small step to your left, and then reach your foot down behind you."

Nora followed Mabon's directions and found the hole where the top of the hatch was. She searched below with her left foot for a few moments before she found the top rung. She bent down and braced herself against the side of the hole with her arms, then stepped down with her right foot. She carefully made her way down the ladder toward Mabon.

"That's it!" he called to her. "You're doing great."

The blindfold made Nora feel unsteady as she descended into the hatch. She caught a whiff of damp earth and burning oil, and it reminded her of the church basement where she'd hidden with Adam. She suddenly felt trapped, and she stopped moving and clung to the ladder in a panic.

"It's okay," Mabon's voice came, smooth and reassuring. "You're almost there. You can do this."

"I can't!" shouted Nora.

"Yes you can," said Mabon. "I won't let you fall. Just take two more steps and I'll be able to grab you."

Nora closed her eyes under the blindfold and focused on the sound of Mabon's voice. She gripped the rung of the ladder tightly with her hands and slowly shifted her left foot down, searching for the next rung. She found it, and stepped down gingerly. She followed with her right foot, and then repeated the motion one more time.

Suddenly she felt two strong hands on her waist. Mabon had reached up and grasped her, and she loosened her grip on the ladder so he could lift her down. She felt herself float through midair, and suddenly there was solid ground beneath her feet.

"There," said Mabon letting her go. "You're safe now."

"Good job," said Aesop. "The worst is over now. It's not much farther."

Nora felt Mabon place Adam's basket in her left hand and then take her right in his own.

They left the rougher section of the tunnel and moved onto a solid floor. Nora could hear their footsteps echoing down the corridor ahead of them. The hallway smelled of concrete, as if they were in the basement of a building. They walked what seemed a long way and then came to a set of stairs that led upward. "Be careful," Mabon whispered as he led her up. These stairs were solid and wide, and Nora didn't have trouble climbing them. When they reached the top, she could feel a cool breeze. The air was fresh and she could smell delicious cooking scents, which made her realize how hungry she was.

Mabon gasped.

"What is it?" Nora asked. "Can someone take this blindfold off now?"

"Yes," said Aesop. "We can uncover your eyes now."

Mabon untied the strip of cloth and pulled it from Nora's eyes. She was immediately blinded by the bright afternoon sun. She blinked until her eyes adjusted, then took a look around. What she saw amazed her.

They had exited onto a grassy terrace on the side of a small cliff, one of many dozens of terraces connected by narrow paths that ran all around the west bank of a lush green valley. Below them was a beautiful village nestled beside a sparkling blue lake. The verdant land was divided into many fenced-in orchards of fruit trees, which were separated by vast fields of grain and massive vegetable gardens. A dozen or so cows and goats grazed lazily in a pasture beside the fields. There were stables and other outbuildings, small huts scattered here and there, and the remains of a larger building built up against the side of the cliff below her. All around the valley rim, dozens of elderly outsiders worked with wooden-handled hoes or smaller metal gardening tools, planting and weeding the vegetable beds.

"Welcome to Happy Valley," Aesop said, grinning and disappearing down the narrow path.

Nora picked Adam up out of the basket and held him close while Lucky skirted her heels excitedly. She turned to smile at Mabon. For the second time since she'd escaped the church basement, she felt a great surge of hope, a rush of almost pure joy. Adam must have sensed her relief, as she felt him gurgle with happiness as well. He seemed to be laughing, and soon both Mabon and Nora had joined him. They stood there a long time, the hopeful young woman and her child, the lucky dog, and the joyful, free young man.

Chapter 22

"May I have the honour of seeing him?" an old one asked in a cracked and respectful voice.

Nora and Mabon had descended down into the village with Aesop, and they were now completely surrounded by small, hunch-backed outsiders with long white hair and homespun tunics, each jostling for a view of Adam. There was an almost mystical respect for the child from this crowd of old and extremely odd outsiders.

"Yes, you may all see him," said Nora. "But please remember that we are tired and hungry, as is the child. We've walked a long way. Could you find something for us to eat and somewhere safe for us to change and wash him? Then everyone can see him as much as they like. He'll be here for a while."

There was a buzz of conversation amid the crowd, which began to move along with the travellers as they followed Aesop into the main building.

The guests were led to a well-lit dining area, where chubby

elders ambled about in front of a huge stone fireplace. The arrival of the travellers caused an uproar, which quickly changed to festive joy. The gathering erupted into gleeful conversation and spontaneous music.

The leader of the kitchen crew welcomed them and led them to a huge table in the centre of the room. He was short and very fat, with the ruddiest cheeks Nora had ever seen and large, moist eyes that bulged like those of a fish. As he motioned for them to sit, he rocked back and forth from large foot to large foot. Nora chuckled as he almost toppled over in his excitement.

They were given carved wooden bowls of steaming porridge sweetened by something Nora had never tasted in Aahimsa. "What are we eating?" she whispered to Mabon, who sat opposite her.

"Porridge. It's made of oats, like the ones I added to our raccoon stew."

"No! I know what porridge is. I mean the sweet stuff on top of the porridge."

"It's maple sugar," he said. "It is made from maple tree sap. Have you never had it before?"

"No, never. It's amazing. It even makes porridge taste good."

Next they were served platters of sliced bread with bowls of pale butter. Brin, the leader of the kitchen crew, placed a jar of something pale and yellow in front of Nora.

"Is this more maple sugar?" she asked.

"It's honey," said Brin. "There is honey in Aahimsa. I know because I saw it shipped from the agricultural homelands to the city. But not honey like this. This honey was made by Brin the Engineer's bees from the pollen of the sweet clover of the Humber Valley. There is no honey in the universe that can match its wonderful flavour."

"You're an engineer?" Nora asked as she spread a thick layer of honey on her bread and took a bite. She didn't know if it was the fresh air, or her hunger, or if it truly was the best honey in the universe, but it tasted fantastic.

"Was an engineer. Old titles die hard here. In the time before we came here, we were only known by what we did. We had no personal worth back then. Now that we've finished installing electric power in our buildings — power we're stealing from the Manuhome wind farm," he added slyly, "I'm done with engineering. I'm more interested in my bees and my herd of lovely goats." He looked down at Adam in his basket. "Would the child like some warm sweet goat milk, perhaps?"

"I still have some infant nutrifier left," said Nora. "He'll be all right. But thank you."

"I know of nutrifier. It's the fake milk used by the poor of the city. The milk from my goats is real. It will please him like my honey pleased you. You can taste the sweetness of the clover, can't you?" He waited, knowing she would answer in the affirmative.

She didn't disappoint. "It's delicious, Brin. Thank you." She picked Adam up out of his basket and sat him on her lap. "Maybe we'll try your goat's milk, after all."

Soon Nora and Mabon were so full of the wonderful food that they felt uncomfortable. Adam slept full-bellied and satisfied in his basket on the bench next to Nora.

"I can hardly keep my eyes open," Nora whispered to Mabon. "Adam's asleep and I promised the old ones they could see him. But do you think they could they wait for the morning?"

Brin must have either overheard her or anticipated her fatigue, because he came up behind her and said, "You must be exhausted after your long journey!" He gestured for them to follow him. "I'll take you up to your rooms, if you'd like."

The round little man once again bounced from foot to foot as he led them through the winding corridors of the main building. Nora was too tired to laugh, but she smiled at the happy motion as they passed several large storage areas — former parking garages — that were full of wooden barrels and crates. "What are those?" she asked drowsily.

"We keep grains and vegetables in storage," explained Brin. "We've managed to relearn many of the old ways. Our pickles and jams are wonderful, if I do say so myself. I know it isn't polite to boast, but when one gets to my age there is no harm in indulging one's ego."

They climbed a set up stairs up to a hallway lined with numbered doors. Brin motioned for Nora and Mabon to follow him into the first of the rooms. "Mabon can use this one. It has been vacant for a few weeks. It belonged to Narn the Gardener. You will sleep well in here, Mabon. Narn was a good spirit. He rests now with his god."

The room was dry and cozy, with a small bed of hand-worked pine. It was topped with a brightly-dyed wool blanket. A multi-colored braided rug covered the stone floor beside the bed. On a squat wooden side table on the other side of the bed sat an earthenware pitcher and bowl and a thick, woven hand cloth and towel. A small lamp in the corner cast a halo of light across the warm, tidy room.

"Thank you, Brin," said Mabon. "Compared to my hut in the dead zone, this is heaven."

Brin led Nora and Adam into the adjoining room. Nora spied a wooden cradle on the floor beside the huge bed and guessed that special preparations had been made while they'd eaten. She was moved at the gentle thoughtfulness of these outsiders. "Where did you find the cradle?" she asked.

Brin laughed. "There's no place to *find* anything among us. But we are very handy. Cable the Carpenter apologizes for the crudeness of his work. He didn't have time to do it well, but he promises to improve upon it once the child wakes tomorrow."

The huge bed intended for Nora was similar in design to Mabon's single bed in the adjoining chamber. Its white sheets were covered in thick furs and there was an enormous fluffy pillow at its head. The room was also furnished with a table and a much larger braided rug. An oil lamp, the twin of Mabon's, burned with a yellow flame on top of the side table. The room was basic, but it manifested a simple elegance.

"Goodnight, good woman," said Brin as he backed from the room.

Nora didn't know why she felt so moved by Brin's calling her a good woman, but she was definitely touched. She walked over to the cradle and was about to set Adam inside, but then she decided she wasn't ready to separate herself from him. She carried him up into the bed and placed him close to her among the soft furs. He stirred for a moment and his big eyes looked up into hers. He smiled. She closed her eyes and pulled him close.

"Goodnight, angel," she whispered, thinking how nice her words had sounded, and wondering just exactly how angels really looked. Before she fell asleep, she had a feeling that something was missing. She thought about Alice a moment, but she realized it wasn't Alice's presence she missed. It was Mabon's. She had grown used to his being close. It was an odd feeling, missing him, but she smiled in spite of herself and fell soundly asleep.

Chapter 23

When the anticipated day finally dawned, sunny and warm, the autumn colors had painted the trees golden in the dense stands around the manor. The workers at the city stables had spent hours grooming their finest matching pair of fillies, which were adorned in shimmering silver buckles and brightly buffed harnesses. Their manes were brushed and fluffed and they were ready to lead the polished ebony carriage, with its inlays of silver and gold, through the narrow cobbled pathways leading to the sacred fertility temple.

The carriage ride had been the mayor's idea. After her initial hesitation over her daughter's plan, Blanchefleur had finally accepted Alice's choice as inevitable, and had thrown herself into the preparations headfirst, insisting on only the best for her daughter's temple ceremony.

Alice was radiant as she stepped out the manor house doors and headed down to her carriage. She was wearing a shimmering gown that seemed fashioned of the same material as the snow-white orchids in her flowing blonde hair. A pair of simple white leather ballet slippers completed her outfit.

The ceremonial route was lined on both sides by hundreds of well-wishers and admirers, who waved and cheered enthusiastically as the mayor and her daughter drove by. Upon their arrival at the temple, the entourage was greeted by hundreds of exuberant children, dressed in garments as bright as garden flowers, who sang to the spectators and scattered soft, fragrant petals all the way up the temple steps.

As Alice stepped across the threshold and into the exterior lobby, the entire temple began to hum and vibrate with the heavy notes of the mighty pipe organ playing Aahimsa's city anthem. As Alice stepped into the main chamber, the crowd rose to its feet and gasped in awe and appreciation of her magnificent gown.

When the anthem had ended, the organ adjusted its button stops and began to play the opening bars of the magnificent "Life-Giver March," which praised the earth and its wondrous bounty and celebrated the wonders of birth and renewal. The huge temple choir joined in, and Alice and Blanchefleur began their slow walk down the long aisle of Aahimsa's Temple of Life.

At the altar, the holy women of the temple waited for Alice to arrive. Today they wore the blood-red robes of the Holy Creation ceremony. Behind the women stood a series of carved figures depicting the many races of insiders within Aahimsa. Each carved figure represented fertility and the miracles of pregnancy and birth. The statues stood forming a circle, within which a tent of translucent white silk was suspended. This was the Tent of Acceptance, where the private portion of the ceremony would take place.

When mother and daughter arrived at the marble gate leading to the altar, Blanchefleur stopped and kissed Alice's forehead. "May the mother of all the earth be with you, my child," she whispered into Alice's ear. "You are so young to be undertaking this journey. I wish you well. Are you certain this is what you want?"

"I am."

"You know you can change your mind without shame. It's the law."

"I love you, Mother. I'm doing what I wish to do. Don't worry, I'll do you credit yet. Someday you and the whole city will be proud of me." Alice smiled at Blanchefleur, turned, and walked up the stone steps to the altar, where she stood calmly and confidently before the three women.

The nearest placed a hand on Alice's shoulder. "I, Eros, am here to serve and love you. What is your wish?"

Alice knew the ceremony well. She was not supposed to answer until all three women had spoken their opening remarks.

The second of the women turned to her. The first woman's voice had had the quality of satin. This next was the voice of steel. It rang in Alice's ears with great assurance. "I, Frigga, am here to serve and watch over you. What is your wish?"

The third woman spoke with a voice that fluffed the hairs on the back of Alice's neck. It had a comforting quality to it. "I, Mab, am here to serve and guide you. What is your wish?"

Alice felt the pressure and the pleasure associated with knowing every eye in the room was now fixed on her. She waited as long as she could before beginning the slow rotation that would bring her around so that she was facing the huge crowd.

She allowed her eyes to scan the multitude of faces of the assembly before seeking out that of Blanchefleur, who was crying discretely and wiping away her tears with a silk handkerchief.

Alice waited until she was certain all eyes were on her. Then she began: "I come before you to offer the greatest gift of all. I come offering my body as a gift for the new one. I come requesting a gift from you all as well. I am asking you to entrust me with the task of bringing that new one into the world and guiding her in her search for the truths that we have been given by our mothers."

The three holy women moved forward. Eros spoke for all of them. "It is for you to decide. Your gift is acceptable to all of us. We entrust you with the task." Eros looked over the heads of the crowd. "Do all of you who gather here promise to do all you can to help this lone insider make her way through life?"

The crowd answered in unison, "We do."

"Enter, then, Alice, and partake," said Eros. She lifted a flap of the white silk tent and Alice stepped through. The three sacred women followed.

The conception ceremony was brief and efficient, and over far sooner than Alice had imagined. When they were finished, each of the three attendants spoke in turn the traditional words: "May you become one with all the mothers who have come here before you."

Alice answered each with a sincere "thank you."

Eros placed a blood-red sash over Alice's left shoulder, and then led her back outside the diaphanous walls of the tent.

As they emerged, the organ filled the hall with jarring bass notes and then dropped to a softer background as the crowd began to sing "The Mother of the Earth is Good." Alice led her glorious procession to the rear of the great temple and out the great temple doors.

Outside, to the delight of the ordinary citizens of Aahimsa, Alice climbed back aboard her coach and rode triumphantly along the path to the manor home, radiant in her new status as a mother-to-be.

Part III

Chapter 24

"Come, Adam. It's time to work on your lessons." Nora watched her boy hurry over to the bookshelf, with Lucky following at his heels.

Nora was astounded at how quickly they had both grown. Lucky was now well past middle age — a tall, broad-shouldered dog with a massive head and jaws reminiscent of the leader of the hungry pack that had attacked them almost nine years ago. And Adam was no longer a small boy, enthusiastic about climbing into her lap for comfort and security. Their major physical contact now came during the hours when they sat close together at work on Adam's studies.

Time was such an odd thing, Nora mused. In some ways her life with Alice seemed like only yesterday, but in other ways it had become hard to imagine living any place other than here in Happy Valley with Mabon and the old ones. Despite all her fears and uncertainty about leaving Aahimsa, she had grown to love her new life.

Reading was her and Adam's common joy, but Nora still shook her head and frowned when she saw the book he had chosen to carry away from the dusty stack on the bookshelf. "Oh, no, not that old thing again!"

"I like this book," Adam answered, handing the faded volume to his mother.

Nora turned the worn copy of *A World History* over and sighed. She detested the book, but by now had learned that she only had so much influence over the developing tastes of her adopted son.

Several of the old ones were excellent readers, as well, but only those for whom the skill had been a necessity to their former occupations in the homelands. The rest had never been taught to read, and had to rely on others to read aloud to them. Nevertheless, the old ones had made a habit of saving any books they found in their infrequent salvaging missions to the various ruined towns and cities nearby, and had placed particular importance on finding and collecting books that detailed what life was like before the revolt, when outsiders ruled the world. Nora hated most of these books, but she figured Adam was better off reading them than nothing at all.

Adam sat down beside Nora and pulled his legs up onto the wooden bench. Nora listened as he read aloud, stroking Lucky's soft head as she sat. The sweet cadence of Adam's voice lulled Nora into a thoughtful trance, and she began to wonder if Mabon would be coming to join their lesson today. The times when Mabon came to sit close to her and Adam and listen while they read had begun to happen more and more often recently, and Nora had grown to cherish the young man's close presence, and even the way he sometimes challenged her to question her own beliefs about the world and its history.

Nora reacted predictably to the world history book every time. Mabon would always sense her lack of interest, but there were times that her reaction to the words was downright hostile. She would read a chapter such as "From Java Man to the Present," and tell Adam that the old world the book spoke of no longer existed, if it ever really had.

"What kind of history *is* this?" she asked regularly. She gave her opinion that these were just stories of overgrown boys scurrying across the face of the planet, leaving behind paths of destruction wherever they travelled, and pointed out that they ignored the lives of every woman who had ever lived.

She had once read a chapter called "Columbus Discovers America" to Adam and Mabon. By the time she'd finished, she'd been absolutely incensed. "This Columbus man was sent out by a woman known as Queen Isabella of Spain," she ranted. "It was all *her* idea, but this book is giving *him* — a hired sailor! — the credit. These outsider writers seemed to want to credit the males for everything ever achieved by their society. It's so confusing. Isabella was the queen, the leader. But she was the leader of the men, and they did what she told them to do. So shouldn't the chapter be called 'Queen Isabella Discovers America'? I don't understand!"

Mabon sat and smiled, listening to the fire in her voice and loving the sound of it. "In a way," Nora continued, "Columbus and these other men were like the rangers of the wild. Mabon, in your training as a ranger, including the time at the Manuhome and even your punishment in the dead zone, you were doing the bidding of the controllers, who — according to you — were doing what Blanchefleur told them to do. The mayor of Aahimsa is, in a way, like the Queen of Spain. But it's not the rangers who decide what they do. It's Blanchefleur. So it was Queen Isabella who really discovered America."

"Does that mean it's Blanchefleur who's doing the killing when outsiders are terminated?" asked Mabon.

"Ugh!" Nora had shouted, the gold specks flaring from her eyes. "You don't understand!" And with that, she'd stormed from the room.

Nora had found it frustrating at first to talk to Mabon. Aside from the odd critique of the insiders, he didn't have much to say. He had spent the last few years alone, doing a horrible job he didn't want to talk about.

"What did you *do* every day in the dead zone?" Nora had asked one day, just to make conversation.

"I was a cleaner," Mabon had said. "I cleaned."

"What does that mean?" she'd asked.

"The insiders didn't want anything alive from the outside to get into Aahimsa. The electronic moat over Aahimsa's walls prevented birds and bats and bugs from flying into or over the city. Most flying things learned to avoid the force field, but every day there were a few that were knocked down and killed. They fell into the dead zone, and it was my job to get rid of them. I did it." He'd crossed his arms and looked at her pointedly. "Do you want to hear more details?"

"No," Nora had answered. "How did you stand doing that every day?"

"I just did it. I had to, or I'd be terminated. I hoped some day they would move me somewhere better, but they never did. When you have no choice, you either learn to play by the rules and find good things to think about or you let yourself die."

"Were you that unhappy?"

"Sometimes. Mostly, though, my heart lived out in the wild. I imagined I was somewhere else and I was happy. And I *was* someplace else and happy then, in a way."

"What did you do when you were a ranger?"

"At the headquarters camp, we played war games or watched old movies about sports in our off time. Sometimes we heard stories about ranger history. It made us feel like we were important." He'd told Nora some of the stories and she'd laughed. Mabon had looked hurt, which had surprised her.

"I'm sorry, Mabon," she'd said, still chuckling. "But you must realize that the stories you loved were lies, made up by your controllers?"

Mabon had been shocked to hear Nora say this. "I don't believe you," he'd said. "Why would you say that? Are you trying to make me feel bad?"

"No, not at all!" Nora had said, her smile fading. "When we want to think something good about ourselves, people can make us believe all sorts of things. I was also taught things that aren't true — not completely, anyways."

"What things?"

"I was taught that all outsiders are dangerous and cruel — and that isn't true."

"How can you know that for sure?" Mabon had asked.

"Because I know you, and I know Adam, and I know the old ones. And none of you are any of those things. That's how I know."

"But it's still true that life before the insider cities was crueller than the worst of life is now. You and Adam have read from the old history books. They tell of armies of men that spread like poison clouds across the face of the planet. People's lives were worth nothing. It was the men that did this — to one another, to women and children and the old. And these were men who had children of their own, men who loved their own women and their own old ones. How could that happen, if they weren't inherently dangerous?" Mabon had shook his head in dismay. "There are things in us that I'll never understand."

While Nora had been half-listening to the sound of Adam reading and half-daydreaming, Mabon had slipped into the room. He stood at the doorway, smiling at the sight of the two of them cuddled up together at the table. Nora looked up and noticed him, and signalled for him to be quiet even though she knew he wouldn't interrupt.

Mabon walked over and sat down at the table across from them. Adam looked up and gave the young man a quick wave, and then continued until he finished the section he had set out to read, which was about a powerful outsider from a place called Germany who had murdered many innocent insiders and outsiders.

"You're a good reader, Adam," Mabon said when the boy had finished.

"Thanks," Adam answered. "I like this book."

"Perhaps someday we'll find more of them," said Mabon.

"Mom," Adam said, looking at her pleadingly, "can I go out to the ruins with Mabon sometime to look for more history books?"

Nora gave Mabon a hard look. "Someday when and if it's safe, perhaps. But not for a long time." She turned to Mabon and her voice took on a tone of exasperation. "Mabon, please don't encourage him. You know it's not safe for him to go far out into the wild, with the rangers constantly on patrol. It's bad enough that you take him out at all." She stood up and brushed off her rough hempen skirt. "Besides, I'm sick and tired of hearing about all the nasty things outsiders did to the world and to one another."

Nora knew nothing she said could make Adam less fond of spending his free time outside with Mabon and the old ones. Adam was interested in every aspect of life in the valley. He loved the grain fields and the vegetable gardens. He loved the animals that roamed the pastures. He loved every inch of ground, every blade of grass. But mostly he just loved spending time with Mabon, who he looked up to with blind adoration.

Mabon had more than fulfilled the promises he had made to Nora almost nine years ago when he had asked her to trust him. She didn't have a single regret over her choice to follow him into the wild. Well, perhaps one. Mabon had always been good to her, and he'd been like a father to Adam in almost every way, doing his share of caring for the child and giving him all the attention and affection he could ever ask for. But sometimes Nora still felt lonely, and missed the love and companionship she'd felt when she'd been Alice's partner.

"Can Lucky and I go outside to the gardens with Mabon?" asked Adam. "I want to go down and see the new goats. I'm done my lessons for today."

"I guess so," Nora said, walking over to stand behind Mabon at the wooden table. He shifted over slightly, increasing the distance between them. "Just don't go filling his head with nonsense, Mabon," she said, stepping back a step or two.

Adam and Mabon left the room like two happy children. Adam tagged Mabon on the shoulder and began to run, the big old dog on his heels. Mabon glanced back through the doorway at Nora and grinned, then ran out in pursuit of the boy and dog.

Nora watched them go, and sighed.

Chapter 25

"Where's Mabon?" Aesop asked, popping his bushy white head through Nora's open door. "I haven't seen him today." He looked at Nora expectantly with his colorless, watery eyes.

Aesop and Mabon had become extraordinary friends in the years since she, Mabon, and Adam had arrived in Happy Valley. The rest of the old ones were used to seeing the tall young man walking slowly alongside the sun-bronzed old one with the wild hair. The two friends made regular excursions outside the valley, checking for signs of danger. Aesop had the eyes of a hawk in spite of their faded appearance, and the hearing of a deer. Along with Mabon's formidable strength, agility, and speed, they made a powerful team when it came to preserving the safety of their sanctuary.

"He walked down to the animal shelters with Adam," Nora replied. "Adam wanted to see the newborn goats."

"Okay," Aesop said, winking at her. "I'll come back later." He turned and continued down the hall.

Aesop always made Nora smile. He was always pleasant and calm, but he had a quiet intelligence that commanded respect. The old ones had been right to choose him as their leader.

"See you later, Aesop," she called to him as he left. "If I see Mabon, I'll tell him you stopped by."

She decided then that she, too, would like to see the baby goats. All babies were lovely, in her mind. She put down her book and headed outside.

The valley teemed with life. Goats and sheep and a dozen cattle roamed free, munching on the wild grasses. Vital areas — places like the large gardens, the grain fields, and the orchards — were fenced off to keep the livestock out, but many acres of pasture remained accessible to them, including most of the grassy area where the old ones lived and worked. There was a certain charm to this practice, Nora thought as she walked, though it made navigating the paths without sullying one's shoes a bit of a challenge.

Nora arrived at the barns and walked around quietly, keeping an eye out for Adam and Mabon. She wanted a chance to catch Adam's reaction to the baby goats without butting in. When she arrived outside the last barn, she heard Adam inside laughing happily. She stepped up on a bale of hay and peeked inside through one of the dusty barn windows. Below her in the stall, a mother goat stood while her two babies alternately poked their faces into her small udder.

As she wondered what had happened that had made Adam laugh so happily, she looked down to see that Lucky was below her, merrily wagging his tail. She stepped down before he started barking and patted his big head to keep him quiet. Lucky licked her hand for a moment and then, satisfied, left her side and returned to the barn.

Nora climbed back up on the bale and peeked through the window again. She could now see Mabon inside. He was bare-chested, and his shirt was draped over the top rail of the mother goat's stall. Nora watched the muscles of Mabon's back ripple as he forked up the manure and straw mixture from the stall floor. She felt a fuzzy warmth flow through her and her heart started beating noticeably faster.

"Mabon," she heard Adam say. "Did you see the goats being born?"

"I got here in time to see the second one birthed," Mabon said, throwing a forkful of manure on the pile. "It was exciting."

"Have you ever seen a human baby being born?"

"Nope," Mabon said, ruffling the boy's hair. "You're my only baby. Mine and Nora's. You were pretty tiny when I first met you, though."

"Mom told me about the wild dogs and how you saved us. You were very brave."

"I did what I had to." Mabon picked up some dirty straw and threw it out between the rails.

"You met my real mom, though, right?" Adam asked, sitting down on a bale of hay. "What was she like?"

Mabon stopped what he was doing and leaned on the handle of the fork. "She was very pretty and she loved you very much. She was a good mother."

"Did I have a father, too? Like the baby goats do?"

"Yes," said Mabon. "Your mother loved him. But I don't know who he was. I think he died before you were born."

"Would you ever want to be a real father to a baby?" Adam asked, picking at a piece of hay sticking out of the bale. "Like he was?"

"I would," Mabon said. "Very much. But it isn't possible." He picked up a bale of hay, broke it, then scattered it across the floor of the stall.

"But you love my mom, don't you? The way my real parents loved each other?"

Mabon's cheeks flushed crimson and he looked away as he pulled his shirt back on over his head. "What do you think, Adam?"

"I think you do," the boy said.

Mabon smiled his crooked smile, turned, and headed out of the barn. Adam followed close behind.

Nora, her green eyes moist, jumped off the hay bale and hurried to get out of sight. She didn't want them to see her right now. She hustled around to the end of the barn and hid behind a hay wagon with banded wooden wheels.

"So you'd like to go and get more books someday," Mabon said.

"Yeah," said Adam, "but my mom doesn't want me to."

"Your mother is smart. We can't risk it. We can explore closer to home, but we'll have to be careful."

Nora had something to say about venturing outside the valley for any reason. But now wasn't the time. She waited until the boy, the dog, and the man had disappeared from sight before she ventured out on the path that led back up to the main building. The day was pleasant and the uphill climb was a joy.

"Mom!" Adam called as he came running up behind her a few minutes later. "Are you and Mabon going to get married, like the insiders and outsiders in my history books did?"

Nora stopped him and put her arm around his neck, pretending to put him in a headlock, and laughed. "Where did that come from?" she said.

"I think Mabon loves you," Adam said, his dark brown eyes as sincere as she'd ever seen them.

Nora didn't want to make light of his question, but she wasn't sure how to answer it.

"Don't you love him?" Adam asked.

"I guess I do, in a way," Nora said carefully. "We're good friends. I'm very fond of him." She was aware that she wasn't telling the exact truth. She didn't know about marriage. That seemed like a foreign idea to her, but it was one that warmed her heart when she thought about it.

Nora sat down on a grassy knoll beside the path and Adam collapsed on the ground beside her.

"What if you and Mabon had a baby?" Adam asked. "You'd like to have one of your own, wouldn't you?"

"I don't think that's possible," Nora said, running her fingers through Adam's curly brown hair.

"That's what Mabon said," he answered. "How come?"

"I can't say," she said.

"Why?"

"You'll understand when you're older. Run along, now."

Adam hugged her and ran back in the direction of the main building.

Nora continued on her way, thinking about what Adam had just said. Until she had left Aahimsa, the idea of loving an outsider as a partner would never have occurred to her. But here in this place, where wild things and farm animals had these relationships, it seemed almost like a natural thing to do. She blushed to think about it.

She passed by one of the huts where grains were stored and several of the old ones, including Aesop, were inside loading wheat and other grains into buckets to carry to the kitchen. She waved at the old ones and they waved back. She wondered if they would be surprised to know what she had been thinking as she'd walked toward them.

"Did you find Mabon?" she asked Aesop.

"Yes, just a moment ago. I told him I'd seen you earlier. How were the goats?"

"Exciting," she said. "Come on, and I'll tell you about it."

Aesop picked up his bucket and joined Nora on the path. Nora told Aesop all about the adorable baby goats as the two of them followed the walkway up into the main building. As they navigated their way through the corridors toward the kitchen, they passed the village infirmary. This was where community members were taken when they were ill or approaching their final days. It was always warm, both physically and emotionally, and it was kept spotless. It smelled of clean floors, clean walls, and clean bedding and laundry. Nora had been a regular visitor to the infirmary during her time in Happy Valley, reading stories to the old ones or helping them pass into the next world with dignity.

Today as they walked by, they found Adam and Mabon inside with Brin. Brin was doing something with a light socket while Mabon and Adam worked on a carpentry project. Mabon had one knee on the end of a pine board and was sawing it while Adam struggled to hold the other end steady.

"Hi, Mom," said Adam. "Hi, Aesop."

Mabon looked up from what he was doing and grinned, pleased to see them. The gold specks flashed in Nora's eyes when they made contact with Mabon's, but this time they didn't appear out of anger.

"We're making a shelf to hold sheets and stuff," Adam said.

When Mabon finished sawing the piece of wood, he carried it across the room and applied glue to both ends, then held it in place between two uprights. He handed Adam the hammer, and winked.

The boy's brown eyes sparkled as he tapped four finish nails in place.

Mabon inspected the shelf carefully when he had finished. "Good job," he said, roughing up Adam's brown locks.

"We'll leave you men to your work," Nora said, waving and

continuing down the hall.

"Mabon and Adam have a good friendship," said Aesop as they walked away. "Mabon is a good father to the boy. He teaches Adam things."

"Yes," Nora agreed. "Mabon's taught him things that I never could. Even after all these years here with you, I still don't fully understand the ways of the outsider."

"I wonder if Mabon truly does, either," Aesop mused.

"What do you mean?" Nora asked.

"It won't be too many years now before Adam comes of age," said Aesop. "When that time comes, he will have many questions, questions about what it is to be a man. I'm not sure Mabon will be equipped to answer those."

Nora blushed and lowered her eyes, but Aesop continued.

"Have you told Adam how special he is?" he asked. "Does he know that he's different from all the other outsiders? That he has a special...ability?"

"No," said Nora. "He's still so young..."

"But he will grow up, faster than you think," Aesop said. "And he needs to know why he's so special, what he could do with his gift." Aesop's voice was becoming more intense, more passionate with every word he spoke. "He's our only hope for the return of the old ways, where man and woman lived together side by side. He's the last chance to save our world, the world as our ancestors knew it... He's the last wild boy."

Aesop stopped and turned to Nora, his glassy white eyes boring into hers. When he spoke again, his voice was calmer, but heavy and serious, almost pleading. "You know they've never stopped looking for him, Nora. You've heard about all of the ranger sightings over the years, about Dr. Ueland's reports from the Manuhome. Blanchefleur hasn't given up on finding him, and she never will. One day, those rangers of hers are going to show up on our doorstep, and we're going to have to get Adam away to safety. We have to be prepared for when that day comes. And so does Adam."

And with that, Aesop turned and headed off to the kitchen, bucket in hand.

Chapter 26

"Have you ever had yearnings for an insider?" asked Mabon. The deep crimson stains rose up in his cheeks as he spoke.

It was a warm summer's day, and Mabon, Aesop, and Adam were on one of their security patrols just outside the entrance to the valley. Adam was playing with Lucky nearby, but out of earshot.

Aesop sat down on a grassy knoll close to where Mabon was leaning against a tall, tattered paper birch, and laughed his light, soft laugh. "I'm told that such attractions were once a normal ambition for outsiders, but that desire was taken from me shortly after I was born. I've always wondered what it feels like."

"It's a strange and powerful wanting," Mabon said. "Sometimes I feel a stirring down below my belt. My controllers trained me not to feel things like that. But now that they're gone, the feelings are coming back. Sometimes when I look at Nora, all I can think about is how much I want to lie with her and hold her close. I'm always afraid she'll guess my thoughts."

Aesop stood up and pulled at his snowy whiskers. "Why are you afraid of her knowing how you feel?" he asked. "Those are the normal feelings of a complete man, even a nearly complete man like yourself. It is the natural yearning of the wild to want to mate."

"I'm afraid because in my head she's still an insider and I'm still an outsider."

"Do you wish to be with her, Mabon? To be a real partner to her?"

The young man blushed. "What do you mean 'be with her'?" he asked.

"Surely you have seen how sheep and goats make their young. You've seen them breeding."

Mabon looked horrified. "I can't make children. I was sterilized as a child, like all rangers. Even if I could, I wouldn't do that with Nora!" He cast his eyes down at the ground in front of him, picked up a pebble, and tossed it from hand to hand.

"Why not?"

"Because I feel too much for her. And I can't give her a baby, anyways."

"Perhaps she'd *like* you to do such a thing with her, Mabon. Being in love isn't only about having babies. I've seen the way she looks at you. She has feelings for you. Even an old fool like me can see that."

"I don't think I could do it," Mabon said, his eyes following the pebble as it bounced from hand to hand. "I've been trained to serve the insider, to protect her. I was taught never to touch her." He put the pebble down and looked down at Aesop. "Sometimes when Nora and I are sitting close together, I get an urge to reach out and touch her. It feels wrong. It *is* wrong. Those were the sins of my fathers, and I must atone for them."

"The sins of your fathers?"

"The sins of *our* fathers, Aesop."

"Don't be foolish, Mabon. What are these sins you speak of?"

"I've been listening to the old history books. The men did terrible things — to themselves, as well, but especially to the women. I understand these sins better now."

Mabon stooped to pick up his quiver of arrows, slung it over his shoulder, and picked up his long bow. "I'm afraid I can't ever be a real mate to an insider." He cocked his ear and listened for a moment. It seemed to him that the forest had gone suddenly silent.

"Do you care for Nora?" Aesop asked.

"Of course!" Mabon answered. "More than the world, more than my freedom. But it doesn't matter. It isn't possible. After what our forefathers did, no insider could ever love an outsider again." He stepped to the centre of the clearing and listened.

"Perhaps you're right," said Aesop. "But maybe you should tell Nora your feelings and let her decide what is possible and what is not. You already share a child together. That's a bond that can't be broken."

"Adam will soon grow to become a man, Aesop. He can't be happy forever here with me and Nora, whether we're together or not. He can't bind us to each other."

"That's true," said Aesop. "He'll want a mate of his own, and he should have one. Maybe you can show him how to be a good partner so he can find someone for himself — an Eve for his Adam. He's our future. He and his mate can start up a new world that will not make the same mistakes as the old one."

"That world is gone, Aesop. It can never come again. You know what happened. You've read the history books, too." Mabon pulled back the string of his long bow and released it with a loud twang. "You know of the bombs falling on women and children and the old. Even I don't wish for the return of such a world. Our ancestors were evil."

"They weren't all evil, Mabon. Some of our ancestors were innocent. Many were good. I know it."

"How do you know?" asked Mabon.

"Because I have known many who were good, Mabon, and I have come to know you. Your controllers tried to turn you into something evil, but you're anything but. If you are good, then there must have been many others who are too. Besides, I don't think the killer is any more evil than the ones who send him to kill. And in the books it is evident that some of the killers were sent by insiders. So it is still today. Are your rangers more evil than their controllers? Are those who rule the controllers less evil than they are?"

"You are wise, Aesop," said Mabon, scanning the foliage nearby to see if he could catch a glimpse of Adam or Lucky. "Nora told me the same thing — that I was good. I've learned a lot from both of you. I never dreamed that there was a way of living where you could plant seeds in warm soil and watch them grow into something useful or beautiful. There's a lot about this place that's like the heaven many of the old ones speak of — the heaven from the ancient religion. But there's a lot that lies in wait to destroy what's here. I fear for Adam and for Nora. They're not a part of this world or anywhere else. She comes from Aahimsa, and he comes from a world that's lost inside the ancient books. Neither of them can ever go back."

Suddenly they heard loud male voices shouting "Stop! Stop!" and then the fierce barking of Lucky. For the first time since Mabon had known the dog, he sounded as nasty as the other dogs in his pack had on the day they had attacked Nora and Adam. Mabon tried to move his legs, but terror paralyzed him. His heart was ready to explode. All he could think of was Adam and what might be transpiring beyond the trees.

He felt a tugging on his homespun shirt and heard an anxious voice say, "Let's go, Mabon. We have to hurry!"

Suddenly he was running straight at the sounds of snarling and screams of anger ahead of them. When he reached the edge of the clearing, he stopped abruptly, then swung himself up into a nearby tree.

Mabon grabbed his bow and quickly notched one of his arrows. "I can see the whole clearing," he whispered down to Aesop. "Adam's stopped and there's a ranger with him. Lucky is running back and forth barking in both directions, so I figure there's at least one more ranger in the trees close by. Adam is trapped between them."

Mabon could see the silver blade of a machete glinting in the ranger's hand. At the moment, the ranger was far enough away from Adam that the boy wasn't in immediate danger. Mabon felt his panic easing as he focused his arrow on the ranger. He didn't recognize the man, but he looked dangerous.

Mabon watched Lucky move toward the big tree he was hidden in. He must have picked up my scent, he thought. Adam slowly edged his way in that direction, as well, poised to run.

"Stop!" the ranger called. He raised his machete and started running toward the boy. Lucky turned around and lunged at the ranger, who yelled and swatted at the air with his machete. Lucky harried the ranger from side to side until Adam was halfway to the tree. Mabon could see the fear in Adam's dark eyes as the boy bent down, picked up a fist-sized rock, and threw it at the ranger. The ranger blocked it with his arm, crying out angrily in pain.

Just as Mabon drew his arrow and prepared to shoot, the second ranger stepped out of the trees. Mabon recognized this one as a commander from his days in the squad. He remembered him being particularly cruel and violent. Mabon pulled back on the bow and steadied his arrow. The ranger had a large knife in his hand, and he ran at Adam, knife poised. Mabon didn't hesitate. He released an arrow, which buried itself in the ranger's shoulder. The ranger dropped the knife, fell to his knees, and tugged at the arrow, screaming for help.

The first ranger raised his machete and ran at Adam. Adam stood stark still, frozen. Mabon trained his arrow on the ranger's right thigh and plunged it into its thickest point. The ranger yelled in pain and tumbled to his knees. Adam startled into action and ran in the direction of the tree where Mabon and Aesop waited.

"Over here!" Aesop said. "Let's go home!" he called out loudly enough for the rangers to hear. Then he whispered, "Follow us! We're heading east, away from the valley. After a bit we'll turn around."

"Why?" asked Adam quietly. "I want to go home."

"Come on, Adam," Mabon said, climbing down from the tree. "We'll explain later."

Behind them they heard the rangers announce to their controllers that they'd found the wild boy, but they'd lost him and that he was heading to the east to get home. Then came the sound of two small explosions. Mabon had heard those sounds before, and he knew the rangers wouldn't be coming after them. They turned for home, and the birds of the wild began to sing once more.

Chapter 27

"What's happening today?" asked Nora, sitting down at one of the tables in the dining hall. Mabon and Adam were already there, eating a breakfast of hard-boiled eggs and bacon. "Everything's in an uproar, and everyone's running all over the place. I've never seen the valley so busy."

"We're having a special visitor," said Brin, coming up behind her. He took a large bite from a thick, buttered slice of toast as he swayed toward them with a tray for the table.

"Who is it?" Adam asked, taking two slices from the tray Brin offered him and setting them on his plate.

"Mabon and Nora know him," said Brin. "You do, too, but it was a long time ago when you met him, Adam. You were just a baby. You wouldn't remember." Brin set the tray down in the middle of the table and sat down beside Adam.

"Dr. Ueland?" asked Mabon, picking up the tray and holding it out to Nora. "Is Dr. Ueland coming here?"

"Yes," said Brin. "A note came by pigeon last night."

"When will he get here?" asked Nora as she peeled the shell from her egg.

"Soon," said Brin.

"Will we get to see him?" asked Mabon.

"I imagine you will. I expect he'll want to see you all again."

They rushed to finish breakfast and clean up the table and dishes. When they were done, Nora, Mabon, and Adam headed back up to their rooms to get ready. Nora changed quickly and splashed some water on her face. She hadn't even had a chance to finish combing her hair when Mabon knocked on her door to let her know that Dr. Ueland had arrived. They hurried down to the dining hall to meet him, with Adam following along behind them.

"Mabon!" Dr. Ueland said as they approached the table where he sat. "It's so good to see you again." He stood up and happily shook the man's hand. "Nora, you look more beautiful than ever," he said, turning to give her a hug. "The valley life has been good to you." His eyes fell on Adam, who had been lingering behind Nora, and he grinned at the boy. "And this must be Adam," he said, holding his hand out. Adam took it and shook it gingerly. "You've grown into quite a young man, son."

Adam nodded and then took a step back, behind Mabon.

"I'm only here for a short visit," Dr. Ueland continued, looking at Mabon and then Nora. "But I have much to talk to you two about."

Mabon could sense tension in the doctor's voice. "Adam, why don't you go back and help Brin?" he said. "He's making bread for tonight's dinner."

Adam ran off in the direction of the kitchen, happy to be freed from the adult conversation.

"I'm afraid I don't have much time," said Dr. Ueland, sitting down at one of the tables. "So I'll have to dispense with the pleasantries for now. I'm sorry to say that I don't bring cheerful news."

Mabon and Nora sat down opposite him.

"I'm guessing the worst," said Mabon, his strong hands balled in white-knuckled fists.

"You're right to do so," Dr. Ueland said, shifting around on his bench uncomfortably.

"I'll keep this brief. I'll be telling most of this to the others soon and then I'll be getting as far away from here as fast as I can." He paused and took a deep breath, then began. "Blanchefleur and her controllers are on to us. Apparently they've known for some time that some of the older outsiders have been escaping termination. I'll be in trouble over that, though I'm not sure whether Blanchefleur knows I was involved. I'm safe for the moment, however, since no one else has the training and skill to run the Manuhome — I've seen to that." A serious look came over his face, and he continued. "They know you two disappeared, and that an unaltered male child left Aahimsa about the same time. They may even believe that you're together, but I have no way of knowing that for certain. I do, however, have reason to believe that they've also very recently discovered the general location of this happy hideaway of yours."

The blood drained from Nora's face, and her fingers grasped the edge of the table. "How do you know all this?" she asked.

"Our manufacturing branch was asked to produce instruments for locating ancient explosive devices in the ground," he explained, "like the ones just outside the valley. It was a rush order, and the controllers were quite insistent that we have them ready as soon as possible. They also ordered us to make more machetes and knives — lots of them. We actually had several detectors in storage from mine clearances decades ago, and a stash of various weapons, but we're telling the insiders that it will take a several days to make what they need." He looked at Nora apologetically. "We should have been better prepared for this. I'm sorry."

"But how could they possibly know?" Nora asked. "How could

they have found us?"

"I'm sorry," Dr. Ueland said. "I don't know."

"I do," said Mabon quietly. He told them about the run-in he, Aesop, and Adam had had with the rangers a few days before. When he finished his story, he looked at Nora abashedly. "I'm so sorry, Nora," he said. "I didn't want to tell you until I had to. I didn't want you to worry."

Nora was silent for a moment, but then she turned on him, her green eyes flashing gold. "How could you, Mabon?" she screamed. "How could you let that happen? And how could you not tell me! Adam is *my* son. I had the right to know!"

Mabon had never seen Nora so angry before. He wasn't quite sure how to respond. "I'm sorry," he finally said. "But Adam is my son, too. I love him just as much as you do. And you know I will always do everything I can to protect him."

"And not telling me about this was supposed to *protect* him?" Nora spat.

"No," Mabon said sadly. "It was supposed to protect you. I just didn't want you to worry if it turned out to be nothing."

"Look," Dr. Ueland said, cutting through the tension. "Placing blame isn't going to help anything now. What's done is done. We just have to move on and figure out what to do next."

"What *can* we do?" asked Nora.

"It may be possible for you to get away from here safely," Dr. Ueland said, "but I don't know where you can go. There are huge expanses of uninhabited wilds out to the west and south, but no one has any idea what you can expect to find out there. It may not be pretty or safe. But it could be your only hope." He reached out and took Nora's hand. Even after all these years of living amongst the old ones, she still flinched just the tiniest bit at the outsider's touch. "Adam's probably of an age now that I can hide him at the Manuhome for a short time, pretend he's a trainee. I can't promise how long. Some of that will depend on him. He'll have to be a quick study at blending in and learning the ways of the outsider. The rest will depend on whether Blanchefleur discovers that I'm the one who's been letting the old ones go free."

"When would he have to go?" Nora asked.

"As soon as possible," Dr. Ueland said. "I'll need a few days after I return to the Manuhome prepare for his arrival and set up an appropriate cover story, but you'll need to send him as soon as you can after that. The rangers will be here at your doorstep before the week is out."

"We can't stop them, can we?" asked Mabon.

"I doubt it," said Dr. Ueland. "But you might be able to slow them down, if you can motivate the old ones to take part. Even with our manufacturing sector working full time, there won't be a lot of weapons for them to use. Thank goodness the Central Council hasn't lifted the ban on guns. That means the rangers will have to use caution and discretion in their attack. Believe me, if they all came armed with guns, the battle would be over before it even began." He looked at Nora, who was blinking back tears, and patted her hand tenderly. "I'm sorry," he told her. "I wish there was more I could do."

"Thank you," Nora said. "For everything you've already done."

Dr. Ueland nodded and stood up. "I have to get going now," he said. "There's lots more to be done yet." He shook Mabon's hand and patted him on the back. "Good luck, my friends," he said. And then he left the village as quickly as he'd arrived.

Chapter 28

Alice sat happily on the grassy bank of the pond behind her house and watched as her daughter played. Tish was squatting down, the hem of her lacy pink skirt soaking up muddy water while she made tiny spiralling swirls in the clear water in front of her.

Tish clearly had a mind of her own. Even Tish's birth had been on her own terms. Alice had planned to deliver the child naturally, though her doctor had warned her that due to her youth and her small size, natural birth could present problems. As her labour had progressed, it had become evident that her doctor had been correct. However, Alice had still insisted on trying it alone. Her doctor had been terribly concerned and had finally informed Blanchefleur, who ordered a surgical delivery. Alice was carried under protest to the operating theatre. She recovered rapidly, and quickly got over her anger at her mother once she saw her child. As soon as she was physically able, she claimed complete control of Tish.

Breast-feeding had proven to be much less romantic than Alice had imagined. The soreness and discomfort had been a real disappointment. However, she'd had something to prove, and prove it she would. She had gradually grown accustomed to the routine, and the joys and sensations of motherhood had begun to compensate for her early disenchantment.

"Tell me again how you used to come here when you were a girl," said Tish.

"I'm still a girl," said Alice. "I still feel like a girl inside, and don't I still look like a girl?"

"You're still pretty, Mom. I mean when you were a young girl like me."

Alice had aged well, and was now a beautiful woman of twenty-six years. She had gained a few pounds, giving her figure a bit more softness. If anything, though, she was even lovelier than she had been when Nora had known her.

"Did you and Grammy ever come out here?" Tish asked.

"Yes. We came here every summer."

"Just the two of you?"

"Sometimes. For a while my friend Nora would come with us as well."

Tish moved closer to her mother and nestled her head just below Alice's chin. Her summer-white curls smelled like air-dried laundry and flowers.

Alice closed her eyes and remembered Nora. She wondered if her friend would have run away if she'd been kinder to her.

"Did you ever come here to the pond with Nora? Did you ever sit here with her?"

Alice coughed and cleared her throat. She had difficulty speaking. "Yes, we did," she managed finally.

"Was it fun?"

"It was fun. It was lots of fun. But nothing is as much fun as being here with you and Grammy." Now that Tish was older, Alice and her mother had become inseparable. The summer house was alive with love once again, something she had thought would be impossible in the months following the disappearance of Nora and the outsider child.

Alice hugged her daughter and looked down on her. "We should head in soon, darling." When she caught herself using certain phrases, it was like listening to Blanchefleur speak to her in childhood. She expected their voices sounded the same to others. She stood up and brushed the grass and dirt first from Tish and then herself.

"Do you still know her?"

"Who?" asked Alice, still thinking of her mother.

"The girl who came here?" said Tish, taking her mother's hand and walking close enough that she could feel her mother's warmth through their summer dresses.

"No, she's gone away."

"She died?"

"I don't know," Alice said. "She's just gone away somewhere."

Aahimsa had settled down into its normal routines over the past few years, and so Tish had never heard of either Nora or Minn. Everyone had forgotten them. Everyone, that is, except Alice and Blanchefleur. Alice thought about Nora often, but she'd almost completely forgotten the outsider child. Blanchefleur, on the other hand, had become obsessed with her fears, and was convinced that he was still out there, threatening to undo everything the insiders had worked so hard to achieve. She continually spoke of her premonitions that dangerous dark clouds were forming over Aahimsa.

Alice wondered where Nora was at this moment. Were her bones lost somewhere out in the vast spaces of the wild? Or was she alive somewhere? And if she was alive, was she happy?

Tish walked over to the low bank at the edge of the pond. She was carrying a stick she had found on the ground and she swung it from side to side. "Can we stay here forever, Mom? I want us to build a pretty house, and you and I can live by this pretty pond."

"Would you like us to do that?" Alice asked.

Tish nodded agreement. She stared hypnotically at her mother with massive blue eyes.

Alice smiled. "I'd like that, too. For now, though, let's pretend that the summer house is it. It would do, you know. After all, it's only you and me."

"And Grammy," Tish added. "She can come visit us sometimes too."

"Okay," said Alice. "Just you and me and Grammy."

"Can we go for a walk in the trees, Mom?"

"I'm afraid we can't do that right now, dear. Your grandmother is expecting us for lunch, and we had better not be late. Grammy Blanchefleur and I have things we need to talk about."

"But, Mom! I want to go look in the trees now."

"Next time, dear. Let's get going."

Several hours later, in the manor house, Tish sat alone playing her favourite card game. Blanchefleur had taught her to play memory one evening a few weeks ago and was now hard-pressed to beat the girl. Blanchefleur had poured two glasses of wine and led the way into her private den. Alice had followed, surprised to be invited to enter her mother's most private sanctuary. Alice wasn't sure what her mother wanted to talk to her about, but she had an uneasy feeling about the upcoming conversation.

Blanchefleur took a seat in one of the heavily stuffed leather armchairs and gestured for Alice to take the other. After years of solitary service in this room, Blanchefleur's chair was showing its age, while Alice's still had a new feel about it. It appeared to never have been sat upon. Blanchefleur sipped her wine and stared fixedly at her daughter.

Alice waited as long she could before speaking. Finally, she could bear the silence no longer. "You said something urgent needed my attention, Mother. Does this concern me?" She held her mother's eyes and sipped from her glass.

An evening glass of red wine together was a ritual that they'd begun following Tish's birth. It had been a concession on Blanchefleur's part, acknowledging that Alice, as a new and responsible parent, was clearly now an adult. But even after all these years, Alice had never drunk her wine in Blanchefleur's study.

"I believe it very much of direct concern to you. How much of a concern, I can only guess. As I told you the last time we spoke, I've changed the strategy concerning the deployment of the rangers. I put an end to the sloppy random and endless search patterns. They were too ineffective. Instead I ordered the rangers to concentrate in the area where the verified contact recently occurred. And the controllers began to keep careful and detailed records of even their most inane observations. The results have been surprising and informative. We have discovered that there is a sizable community of old outsiders who were supposed to have been terminated that are instead living out in the wild. Someone has most certainly been issuing false documentation from the Manuhome."

"How does this concern me?" asked Alice. Her cheeks were mildly aflame, but she decided not to worry, since it would only make matters worse to panic. She knew where her mother was going with this, but chose not to say anything on the matter until she had to.

"Well, my darling. You know how much I rely on intuition. I've burdened you enough with my worries recently. But tonight I feel certain about what happened all those years ago. Recently two of our more intelligent rangers chanced upon an outsider child about nine years old in the wild. For a long time I felt that Nora might somehow have survived in the wild with that child. Now I know how she did it. I'm so positive that I'm ready to make my move."

"You think Nora's alive?" asked Alice. Her chest tightened and her heart felt as if her mother had seized it between her hands and crushed it. Alice had long pushed her feelings for Nora into the depths of her subconscious, and now they had been suddenly and brutally yanked back to the surface.

"I not only think that Nora's alive, but she has a healthy and complete outsider child with her. I might as well be frank, my darling, and tell you that I'm still simmering over your refusal to be truthful about what happened at the summer house when Nora left."

"What difference does it make now?" asked Alice, her voice shaking.

"Possibly none. I'll get to the point. Two of our diligent rangers discovered a well-worn pathway near the place where the boy was sighted, a valley along the upper Humble River where there were once large buildings. Hotels, I believe. I've ordered surveillance of the area. We think that the old ones have been living in the derelict buildings, which they've renovated — quite ingeniously, I might add. It appears that they have somehow even connected their residences to the power grid. Of course, you have no idea what I'm talking about, do you?"

"No, I don't. First of all, who are these old ones?"

Blanchefleur chuckled. "The valley retreat was created by those who the rangers refer to as 'the walking dead,' old outsiders who were past their serviceable years and were supposed to have been terminated, but somehow managed to escape into the wild." The mayor's eyes were locked on Alice, who, in spite of her efforts to show no emotion, was breaking down in front of her angry mother. All she could think of was Nora, and where she fit into all these plans.

"So how will it be solved?" Alice asked, although she could see only one possible outcome.

"I'm about to send the rangers in to retrieve Nora and the child."

"And what about the old ones?" Alice asked. "The rangers will kill them, won't they?"

"Of course they will," said Blanchefleur. "There are certain realities that are difficult to accept. However, it is best to remember that these outsiders are legally already dead. They've just managed to slip by their termination date and steal a few extra years in the wild."

"But that's murder!" said Alice, aware how the remark would upset her mother.

"Alice, you know perfectly well that these outsiders are not being murdered. Murder is an illegal act. We do not commit illegal acts. We obey all of the federation's laws. The healthy, useful parts of these workers' lives are over, so they are gently terminated for their own good. It isn't pleasant to get old and useless. In many ways, they're the lucky ones."

"Why not just let them go free? They're not hurting anyone by living out their last days in the wild."

"To be perfectly honest, darling, I've suspected that this was going on for some time. I thought that the old ones were wandering off into the wild to die. If they survived, so what? But it has suddenly become a problem. The Central Council has learned of the situation and they have determined that this dangerous outsider community must be destroyed. Their logic makes perfect sense. We cannot allow an unregulated outsider society to operate completely beyond our control. They make it possible for persons who threaten us to survive and flourish in the wild. If we do not remove all trace of them, the Central Council will move in and occupy our city and we will face severe discipline. It would mean the end of Aahimsa and the destruction of our way of life. Our homelands would be shut down, and everyone who works there, young and old, would be terminated, including the rangers. All reproduction would be carried out by cloning, and all of our city's rituals and ceremonies would no longer exist. All traces of half of the gene pool of our species would be eradicated."

"Can't you convince the Central Council to back off?"

"Are you worried about the old ones, or about your friend?" Blanchefleur asked bluntly. "Or is it the child that you and Nora found back at the summer house that you stand up for?"

"I don't care about him!"

"Ah, then you admit you harboured the child, and that it was a *him*. Please, Alice, I must be sure."

"What will happen to Nora?"

"Nothing, I hope. Of course, there's always the possibility of an accident, but we have extraordinary controllers, and there have been few problems with the rangers. The Forest Rangers is a well-trained frightening force, however, and it's difficult to maintain control of them sometimes. The controllers have warned the council that there is a high likelihood of a killing frenzy in a large operation like this. There have been incidents recorded in the distant past of such occurrences. Blood tends to cause a sort of insanity among the rangers." She paused and took a sip of her wine. "I'll ask you again, Alice. Did Nora escape with an outsider child?"

Alice thought before she answered. She wanted to do everything she could to see that Nora had every chance of survival. If she lied about the child, would it matter? The rangers were going into the valley either way. If she told the truth, they could be warned what to expect. Perhaps they could be instructed to separate Nora from the boy without hurting her. But what if it had been her and Tish? she wondered. How would she have wanted Nora to act in her stead? Could the rangers ever tear Tish away from her without hurting her? Of course not. She knew then what she had to do. "Yes," she said, lowering her eyes.

"Was this outsider child complete?"

"Yes," she said, and began to sob.

"Then we have few choices. The rangers will continue to muster below the valley and clear the land mines blocking them from the valley entrance. When they have gathered there in sufficient force and the land mines have been cleared, the attack will begin. The child will be terminated and things can finally return to normal."

"How long before it all begins?"

"A few days. I'll give the final directions to the controllers tomorrow. I'll tell them about Nora and the runaway child. The rangers will be ordered to bring Nora out of there alive and treat her with the respect due to any insider, under penalty of death. There will be no mistakes this time — I'll see to that myself. The mistakes of yesterday must be corrected so that I may sleep again."

Alice gazed at her mother. She didn't look like any simple military operation would make her sleep better. She was getting old and tired, and she was letting her paranoia and exhaustion get the better of her.

Alice rose from her chair and walked over to her mother. She sighed deeply, and then bent and kissed the older woman's cheek. "I know you're only doing what you think must be done," she said.

"Of course!" Blanchefleur said.

Alice started to walk out of the room, then paused and turned back to her mother. "Were there no outsiders ever who were good and kind?" she asked.

"Certainly! There were many, but that didn't stop the suffering. There were enough who were neither good nor kind, and there was no way of determining one from the other."

"Can Tish and I stay in the Manor House with you until it's all over?" Alice asked.

Blanchefleur rose from her chair and wrapped her powerful arms around her daughter. "Well, of course you can." She stepped back and looked her daughter in the eye proudly. "Perhaps my little Alice will be ready to serve her city when her time comes, after all."

Chapter 29

Nora sat at the big head table in the dining hall, between Mabon and Aesop. In front of them, seated on wooden chairs around smaller tables, sat Brin and those other old ones who were well enough to attend, about three dozen in all.

They had decided that Aesop would be the first to speak. Nora watched as Aesop rose to his full height, his leathery face stern and his white hair wild, emphasizing his mood. After a moment the small crowd fell into a stony silence. "Dr. Ueland has warned us that our days here in the valley have grown woefully short," Aesop began. "Blanchefleur's rangers have found our little hideaway, and will be attacking soon." There were murmurs of shock and dismay throughout the crowd. Aesop cleared his throat to silence them, and then continued. "We have gathered you here to construct a plan. But first you have to decide between two options: either to flee or to fight."

Nora looked around the room, scanning from face to face and noting the alarm and fear on each of them. There were rumblings of speech, but no single voice emerged from the crowd. Finally Brin, who had been rocking from side to side in his chair, stood up. He waited in silence until the room settled again into stillness. Brin smiled his broad smile. "Can any of you imagine me running away from these rangers?" There were pockets of nervous laughter. "Can you imagine me running anyplace?" he continued. This time the laughter was widespread, softening the tension somewhat. Brin joined them in their laughter. He began to shift slowly from foot to foot in his usual way. "I don't expect any of us old ones, except maybe Aesop, could get very far. If we run, we'll be in the open wild. At least here there is shelter. If we are being attacked, it had better be here, where we can do something or other to defend ourselves."

A few of the old ones laughed at the idea of defending themselves. Someone said, "That's a laugh, us defending ourselves against rangers."

Someone else said, "What's the point, if we're going to die anyway?" There was an embarrassed silence and almost everyone shifted their glance to their feet.

Aesop stood up again. "So your plan is to simply give up? If we quit, then we all die like helpless cattle in a slaughterhouse. Even the death of a cow has a purpose; it gives us food to eat. What will our deaths mean? Nothing. They will mean nothing. We will suffer pain and outrage and it will all be for nothing. We will be dead, and so will Mabon and Nora. And Adam, with all the hope he promises for the future, will die as well. What will be next? Ueland and the rest of the outsider workers? If that's the case, then our entire half of the species will be gone forever."

"We may not be able to save ourselves," said Brin. "But we have to at least try to save our future. Mabon, Nora, and Adam should leave now, and get as far from here as possible before the rangers come."

"No!" shouted Mabon and Nora, almost together.

Nora stood up and looked hesitantly over the crowd. But when she spoke, it was with a quiet confidence. "If we go now, they'll find us. They'll use all the rangers gathered here to hunt us down. Then they'll return to slaughter you and destroy the valley. We can't let that happen. We have to try and stop them, or at least slow them down and reduce their numbers. Maybe we can even beat them!" There were a few guffaws from the crowd. "It *is* possible," Nora continued. "I truly believe it. But even if it isn't, we'll at least be giving Adam a better chance. And if we die, we die with honour and self-respect."

Mabon stared at her. He couldn't believe what he was hearing. Nora, who abhorred violence and had always believed that there was a peaceful solution to any conflict, was advocating for war. He wasn't sure why, but he couldn't help feeling proud of her.

"Nora's right!" shouted Aesop, his eyes full of fire. "This valley was our first real home. *Ours.* Before this, we'd never had anything that was ours in our lives. We're free here. Nora and Mabon brought us Adam, the only complete male outside of Aahimsa, the last city where any man continues to exist. Perhaps soon he will be all that remains of our half of the once powerful and proud human race. We have no choice. We have to fight for what little there is that is still our own."

"But we can't win," one of the old ones said. "No matter what Nora says."

Nora spoke again. "I left Aahimsa because I couldn't let my own kind kill an innocent baby. I fled the only world I knew. Now that baby has grown up strong and healthy. I love Adam like a son. But he is also your son, the only son you will ever be able to claim as your own. I rejected the world of women and found another world, a world of gentle old men. But neither world is complete, neither is as it was meant to be. As long as Adam lives, there is a spark of hope that we can return to a world where men and women complete the human circle."

"That's all well and good," came another voice from the crowd, "but how are we supposed to stop these trained, well-armed fighters?"

Mabon stood up beside Nora. "We may not be able to stop them," he said. "But if we put our heads together and use the advantages we have here, we can at least slow them down. Are you at least willing to try?"

"I will not die for nothing!" shouted Brin. "If we die, let it be with dignity."

"Yes!" shouted voices in the room. Everyone cheered and applauded.

When the cheers died down, Mabon spoke again. "I'm no military commander, so I'm hoping you will all help me. First, everyone needs to go back to their rooms and workplaces and find as many things that could be used as weapons as they can. I've made a few makeshift bows and arrows for you, and I'm hoping you can help make more. These bows are not powerful, but they should be easy to pull."

"But we're not archers," said one of the old ones. "I couldn't hit the broad side of a barn."

"You don't have to be an expert. I'll teach you how to send the arrows up in a high arc. If enough of you are doing this at once, the arrows will come falling like rain on the rangers. You will slow them down and confuse them enough for me to get a decent shot at them."

"Will you kill them?"

"Maybe. We'll be trying to hurt them enough that they can't fight any more. But if they have to die, they will. They'll certainly kill us if they get to us."

Nora watched Mabon from her seat. He seemed so sure of

himself, so courageous. She could almost see the confidence of the old ones building. She was bursting with pride and affection.

"And as for weapons," Mabon continued, "use anything heavy or sharp, blunt or pointed: axes, hoes, hay forks, shovels, carving knives attached to poles, sharpened sticks, even pots and pans. Dress in your heaviest clothing, leather if you have it. Boots and gloves, hats, anything that can absorb a blow or deflect another weapon."

The old ones nodded vigorously.

"As you know, our valley is shaped like a bowl, with very steep, hard-to-climb walls. The rangers could probably climb them, but I don't think they will. They won't expect you to fight them and so they'll come in the easy way, by the sloped entrance we regularly use for coming and going. That's where they've been removing the land mines. We'll set up obstacles on the top of the slope and barricades inside the valley, where we will be waiting."

Mabon walked over to where Nora was sitting and stood behind her. "Nora and I and Adam will stay to fight for as long as we can. When the time comes, we'll slip out and use ropes to descend the steep wall to a landing very near where the rangers are now encamped. I expect we'll be safe there, as most of the rangers will have joined the battle by then. We would stay until the end, but we must get Adam away from here if he is to have any hope of survival."

"Are you sure you shouldn't just leave right now?" Aesop asked, standing beside Mabon. "Hide out in the wild until Ueland is able to take Adam in at the Manuhome?"

Nora rose and stood next to them. "We already owe you our lives," she said, "Adam, Mabon, and I. We have decided we want to say and fight, for as long as we can."

"You're brave, but very foolish," said Aesop, his watery eyes pinched and serious.

"Not foolish, nor brave," said Nora. "We think it will be much safer to leave while the battle is going on. The rangers will be distracted then."

"How much time have we got to get ready?" asked Brin.

Nora looked toward Aesop and Mabon and raised her eyebrows in question. Aesop gestured to Mabon, who simply shrugged. "A day," he said. "Maybe less. We need to get started right away. Those of you who are still able to will need to start moving bales of straw up to the valley entrance and more down near the tunnel. Bring up all the wagons and equipment —anything that will move — and use it to build a strong barricade at the entrance. Pile on boards, wooden crates, fence posts, furniture and beds, anything large and heavy. Keep the drum of gasoline nearby so we can soak the straw and set it on fire at the right moment. Drive nails through planks so they stick out like porcupine quills and set them up across the valley entrance. The more obstacles we make, the more we slow them down. Everyone put on their thinking caps, and let's get to work."

Chapter 30

After the meeting, Mabon and Nora returned upstairs. They found Adam sprawled out on Nora's bed, slowly turning the pages of a book called *Gulliver's Travels*. Lucky was napping on the floor beside the boy.

"What's your book about?" Mabon asked Adam.

"It's about a man who travelled in lots of different lands," said Adam. "It has giants and small people. It's a fun book, but it's serious too."

"I'm glad you like it," said Nora. "But you'll have to put it away for now. Brin asked me to send you down to help him prepare the dinner."

"But he has kitchen staff for that," Adam answered. "Why do I have to do it?"

"His staff is busy with other things," Nora said. "Run along, please."

"Okay," Adam said reluctantly. "C'mon, Lucky." He gestured to the big old dog, who, in spite of his stiff joints and the white hairs around his snout, still followed the boy around like a puppy.

"I still can't believe our time here is almost over," Mabon said after Adam was out of earshot.

"I know," Nora said, sitting down on the bed. "I don't want to go."

"None of us wants to leave this place. Sometimes there's no choice."

"I just can't stand the thought of leaving Adam," Nora said, her eyes filling with tears. "I know the Manuhome is the safest place for him right now, but I'm not sure I can let him go."

Mabon sat down beside Nora and put his arms around her. He'd barely ever touched her before, let alone held her, and he was surprised at how right it felt. He pulled a clean cotton handkerchief from his trouser pocket and quietly dabbed her eyes one at a time. He half expected her to take the handkerchief from him and finish by herself, since she was usually so headstrong and self-sufficient, but this time it felt different. He could feel her helplessness and her need for tenderness.

Nora ever so slowly moved her face closer as Mabon wiped her cheeks and the damp corners of her lovely, full mouth. She nestled her head against his strong shoulder and he kissed her forehead as he had kissed Adam's as a baby. He felt a warm flush of pleasure as he watched her watching him, and he felt a surge of confidence in her love for him, a love that had been his for the asking for a long time. He kissed her soft, full mouth, his lips landing on hers, lightly at first, as a butterfly on a rose, and then, tasting her warmth and the salt of her tears, he felt her respond with urgency and their need for each other grew in intensity until they could no longer hold back.

When Adam returned in later that evening to call his parents down for dinner, he noticed that many of the furnishings in their rooms were missing. He found Mabon and Nora sitting side by side on the one remaining sofa, holding tightly to each other's hands. In spite of their damp, red eyes, they looked unmistakably different — stronger, and somehow content.

"Everybody's going nuts outside," announced Adam. "What's going on?"

Nora looked at Mabon, who gestured for the boy to sit between them.

When he was settled, Nora said, "What exactly is happening?"

Adam looked at them with worried eyes. "A bunch of the old ones tipped a wagon over at the entrance to the valley, and then they started piling stuff on top: plows, carts, wooden troughs, even beds and dressers and tables from the kitchen. They're wrecking the place!"

"Do you know why they're doing all this?" asked Mabon.

"I heard somebody talking about a fight with the rangers."

Nora looked toward Mabon. He nodded at her. She took Adam's hand in hers. "Do you know that you are special?" she asked.

"Yes," he said "And you and Mabon and Aesop and Brin are special, too."

"Yes," she said, "We are. But we're not special in the same way you are. Someday you'll be a man and you'll find somebody you love. You'll have children together, girls and boys like you. Your children will grow up and find others they can love, and they'll have children of their own. But right now, you, Adam, are the only boy in the world who is free to do that."

Adam glanced at her and then at Mabon. He looked confused.

"Someday you'll understand better," she said.

"Why do the rangers want to hurt us?" asked Adam. "Is it because I threw a rock at one of them?"

Nora turned to Mabon. "No," Mabon said. "Blanchefleur, the Mayor of Aahimsa, ordered them to find us. She's looking for you. She knows you're special, and she wants to make sure you don't have a chance to grow up and have children."

"So we have to fight them," said Adam.

"Yes," said Mabon. "That's why the old ones are building the barricade at the entrance."

"But what happens if the rangers catch me?" Adam asked.

"We won't let them," said Nora. "After we fight the rangers we'll escape and take you to the Manuhome. Dr. Ueland, the man you met, will hide you for a while so Blanchefleur and the rangers can't hurt you."

"Can I help fight the rangers?" Adam asked.

"Yes, you can help," Nora said. "But you will have to stay close to us at all times. We have to be ready to run at any moment. Do you understand?"

"Can I use the bow and arrows Mabon made me?" Adam asked, his dark brown eyes bright with excitement. "I've been practising really hard!"

Nora gave Mabon a stern look. He shrugged and smiled. "Yes, you can," he answered. "But you heard what your mother said. You have to stay close to her and to me. We have to get you to Dr. Ueland safely so you can have a chance to grow up to be a man."

"Will you both be coming with me to the Manuhome?" Adam asked.

"We'll take you there, but we aren't allowed to stay there with you," Nora said, biting her lip. "You'll have to be brave and do whatever Dr. Ueland tells you to. He's a good man. We'll come back and get you as soon as we can."

"But I want to stay with you guys!" Adam said.

"We want you to stay with us, too," said Mabon. "But it won't be safe where we're going. You need to stay with Dr. Ueland until we can find a place that will be safe for us all to live."

Adam forgot about his excitement. He hugged Nora tightly and began to blubber and then to cry. Nora took him in her arms and rocked him like she had when he was a tiny baby, and Mabon in turn put his arms around Nora. The three of them sat there a long time, locked in their embrace, trying to hold on to one another while their world collapsed around them.

Chapter 31

Adam was right, thought Mabon as he arrived at the main valley entrance, where the old ones were busily preparing the barricade. They really were wrecking the place.

"Heartbreaking, isn't it Mabon?" Aesop said, throwing a chair on top of the pile. "All those years of building and improving this place and now we're ruining all of our belongings in a futile attempt to stop Blanchefleur from killing us all. What a waste."

Mabon couldn't think of anything to say. Maybe it was a waste of time to try and fight the rangers. Maybe it had been a waste of time to try to save himself and Nora and Adam all those years ago. But it hadn't been a waste for him. The years he'd spent here with Nora, Adam, and the old ones were the best of his life. In a way, it was the only part of his life worth fighting for.

"Everything ends," said Mabon finally. "Our time in the valley wasn't a waste. Even if it ends today, it was worth trying. This was a happy place for you and the others."

"I'm sorry, Mabon," said Aesop. "You're right, of course. It's just that seeing all of this stuff piled here — our lives' work — hurts. But all the more reason to fight. We may not succeed, but we have to try. And we will."

Mabon and Aesop watched the old ones as they brought carts full of their possessions and added them to the barricade. A ways off, there was another group of outsiders sorting through all the items others had brought to serve as weapons — garden tools, scythes, axes, long-handled pitchforks, hammers, all manner of knives, crow bars, boxes of nails, old barn boards, jars of cooking oil, and rolls of barbed wire. The drum of gasoline stood nearby, next to several boxes of empty glass jars filled with liquid and strung with cotton fuses.

Closer to the main building entrance a group of the feebler old ones was sitting on the ground, stringing bows. Mabon and Aesop walked over to admire them. Mabon picked one up and tested the tension of the string. "These are well made," he said to Aesop, nodding in approval. "Do you know whether Brin finished the arrows?"

"Yes, he did. He's pretty proud of them. He used feathers from the chickens for the fletching and flattened nails for the points. The old ones may not take out many rangers, but they'll certainly be able to distract them."

"When do you think the rangers will come?" asked Mabon.

"Soon, I hope. Everything we could add to the pile — beds, chairs, cook stoves — is there, which doesn't leave us much to get by with while we wait. But not too soon, either. Not until we're ready to defend ourselves."

Mabon nodded. "There's still lots to be done. I should get back to work." He gathered all the bows together, and then headed off to find Brin's arrows. When he had everything he needed, he took a few of the old ones aside and demonstrated how to shoot the arrows high in the air.

Mabon, Nora, Adam, and the old ones spent the rest of the evening and much of the night training and preparing for the battle ahead. By the time the sun started to rise, the entrance to the valley was completely barricaded, and obstacles were set up all over the area.

Just as the morning dews began to dry, Mabon, Nora, and Adam stashed their packs and a coil of rope at the cliff they were planning to descend from when the time came to make their escape. With Lucky chasing at their heels, they walked back down toward the valley floor hand-in-hand, each trying to enjoy what they knew might be their last morning together as a family.

As they neared the barricade, Lucky began to bark wildly. Everyone stopped and listened, and soon they could hear the sounds of loud shouting and cheering in the distance.

The valley erupted with motion as the old ones prepared for battle. Mabon, Brin, and Aesop began breaking hay bales and scattering the dried grasses over the area, carefully avoiding the tangled barbed wire and the jumble of old boards bristling with sharp nails that lay at their feet. Nora helped some of the other old ones pour a mix of gas and oil all over the freshly strewn hay, and Adam secured Lucky in a nearby hut. All this time the voices and the chanting of the rangers grew louder as they approached the valley rim.

"Everyone get ready!" Mabon shouted suddenly, slinging his bow and quiver of arrows over his back and grabbing a handful of oil-soaked arrows to carry with him.

Adam led the way up and over the tangled pile of their belongings to the top of the barricade. Brin was one of the last to climb up, and it took a bit of pushing and propping on the part of some of the old ones, but he made it to the top. Everyone took their positions and waited with bows and arrows at the ready.

Nora watched as the rangers began to climb boldly over the

mounds of straw and hay, machetes brandished high over their heads. Several of them stepped on the nails below and cried out in pain, while others cursed aloud as they found themselves tangled in the sharp coils of the barbed wire.

"Ready!" shouted Mabon. The old ones at the sides of the barricade took arrows from their quivers, notched them, and drew back their strings as best they could.

"Now!" called Mabon. Several dozen arrows flew high up into the sky and fell down like vicious rain on the hoard of rangers below. The rangers cried out in surprise and pain.

Mabon chose two oil-soaked arrows and struck a match. He lit one and then the other and sent them directly into the straw, which burst into a wall of roaring flame. The rangers caught in the blaze screamed in agony while the others struggled frantically to save them.

Two of the rangers managed to break through the burning straw and run toward the barricade. Mabon notched an arrow and was ready to fire at the first ranger when the man fell, an arrow jutting from his shoulder. Mabon looked over to see Adam behind him, still in position, and startled by the effect of his own shot. Mabon shifted his aim and brought down the second ranger with an arrow to the chest.

The ranger Adam had wounded came suddenly to his feet and, after breaking the shaft of the arrow in his shoulder, clambered up the barricade furiously, his machete raised high in his good hand. He was heading straight for Adam. Mabon reached for an arrow, but before he could get it strung Nora aimed her own at the frenzied ranger and released. It glanced harmlessly off the man's shoulder. Mabon followed hers with a shot that struck the man directly in the neck. His lifeless body tumbled to the ground.

The fire had died down quickly and the rangers were now working on stamping out the remaining flames. Several of their party were badly burned. Nora was sickened by the violence — the stench of burning oil and the screams of pain made her nauseous. Nonetheless, she continued to contribute to the steady rain of arrows that found their mark often enough to eventually send the attackers fleeing back down the slope and out of sight.

"They're gone!" shouted Adam. There was a loud cheer from the old ones behind the barricade.

"They'll be back," said Nora, "and next time there'll be nothing to slow them down. They'll be coming straight at us."

"Nora's right," Mabon said. "How's our supply of arrows?"

"Plenty left up here, and several other buckets down at the bottom of the barricade," said Aesop.

"Refill your quivers and prepare yourselves," said Mabon.

"We'll head down and drag the wire back across the entrance and scatter more hay and oil," said Brin, speaking for himself and a few of his kitchen crew. They clambered down the barricade to the entranceway and began tugging at the mangled clump of barbed wire. They had only managed to pull it halfway across when someone up above shouted, "They're coming back!" The kitchen crew took off, tugging Brin along with them.

"You three had better clear out now," Aesop called to Mabon. "This could be the end. We'll take over from here."

"Help!" someone cried from below. Mabon looked down to see Brin, who had fallen as he'd tried to climb up the barricade. Three large rangers were almost upon him. The other old ones were forced to retreat and were scrambling to the top of the barricade. Brin managed to get to his feet, and backed up toward the barricade, slowly shifting from foot to foot.

Mabon let fly an arrow that struck one of the attacking rangers in the arm. It slowed him down, but the other two carried on at full speed.

Brin reached into his loose cloak and pulled out a sizable

cleaver and a large carving knife. "Which one of you wants to be carved first?" he said, swiping the knives out in front of him and trying to look as deadly as he could.

One of the rangers swung his machete and Brin ducked to avoid the blade. As he did, he fell to the ground, but on his way down he somehow managed to drive his cleaver into the ranger's thigh. The ranger howled in pain and bore down on Brin.

"No!" Nora screamed.

She, Adam, and Mabon sent a flurry of arrows down at the ranger as he attacked, but not enough to save their friend's life.

As the battle waged on, Nora thought about the world history book she hated so much and knew that if someone wrote the story of what was happening around them right now, it would be just as horrible and cruel as the outrages from the past. It was fight or die for both sides, and most would probably die.

Just as Nora thought they might be making progress, a second battalion of rangers came barrelling up the hill, yelling and shouting as loud as they could. Nora leaned down to grab an arrow, but her bucket was empty. She looked around her and saw that many of the others were depleted as well.

"Go! Now!" Aesop screamed at her. "Save the boy!"

Mabon, Nora, Adam, and Aesop scrambled down from the barricade and took shelter behind it. Nora's heart was aching from the loss of dear Brin but she still wasn't ready to desert her friends. She looked over at Mabon and managed to catch his eye for the briefest of moments. That was all she needed to know he was thinking the same thing.

"Form two lines to hand up those gasoline jars," Mabon instructed the old ones. "Two of us will stand on each end of the barricade, one to hold a lighted torch and the other to light and toss the jars. These are very dangerous, so be careful." He pointed to one end of the barricade. "Adam and I will take this side. Aesop, can you and Nora take the other?"

Aesop nodded. "I'll toss," he told Nora. "You hold the torch." He looked at Mabon and Nora sternly. "You really should get going."

"We will, my friend," said Mabon. "But not yet."

Mabon and Adam climbed to the top of one side of the barricade's end, while Nora and Aesop mounted the other end. The rangers were now coming through the entrance in large numbers, easily skirting the blackened barbed wire and nails. Some had already started to climb the barricade.

"Light the torches!" Mabon yelled. "And fire when ready!" He lit the wick on his bomb from Adam's torch and whispered, "Don't look." He threw the jar so it would land just ahead of the attackers. The second it hit, a huge fireball knocked the rangers to the ground. Mabon glanced across the barricade and saw Aesop throw a bomb farther back, among the now-fleeing attackers. A few survivors beat at their clothing and that of their fellow rangers as they hurried to retreat, but many others lay on the ground, lifeless.

Mabon was shocked at the damage the bombs had wreaked in spite of his knowing what to expect. The reality of their effects far exceeded his imagination. This was something he'd only heard about, not something he'd ever experienced before.

As he surveyed the wreckage, two rangers peeked out from below the horizon of the slope and began to edge forward slowly. He tossed another bomb, which erupted violently at a distance from them, and they turned and ran back to the shelter of the trail.

"Aesop!" someone called from behind them. One of the old ones had come to the base of the barricade and was shouting up. "There's a party of rangers climbing up the east wall! Some of them are already inside, and they're killing everyone in their path!"

Another voice called out, "And there are more climbing the

back wall. What do we do?"

"It's time to abandon the barricade!" Mabon shouted. "They're outflanking us. Spread out as best you can and find shelter. The worst thing you can do now is to be in one clump where they can attack you all in a body. Grab as many weapons as you can — bows, arrows, knives, forks, axes, bombs — whatever you can carry away — and get out of sight. If any rangers get close to you by themselves, attack them as quickly as you can and then get away and hide. If someone gets in trouble, help if you can. Now go!" The remaining old ones scrambled down the barricade, gathered whatever weapons they could, and scattered in all directions.

Mabon threw one last bomb near the gate before he and Adam climbed down the barricade. When they reached the bottom, Aesop and Nora were there, waiting for them.

"This is the end," Aesop said. "It's time for you to go."

Mabon nodded.

Chapter 32

Alice hurried along the hallway toward the control room. She flattened her palm against the identifier and waited for the door to open. Alice had been inside the mysterious room within the manor home a few times as a child, but her mother had been increasingly private about it in recent years. Blanchefleur never mentioned it — that is, until she'd invited Alice in this morning — and there was an unspoken understanding that Alice would never ask about it. All Alice could remember about it was the flicker of the viewers and controls and the old-fashioned metal microphones on heavy bases.

The door slid open and Alice stepped inside. It took a few moments for her eyes to adjust to the dim lighting. The room was silent, aside from the muted audio leaking from around Blanchefleur's earphones.

"What's happened so far?" Alice asked, her voice faltering slightly.

"They rangers have gone into the valley. We have the old ones hemmed in."

"Are the old ones cooperating?"

"There has been considerable resistance up to this point, far more than what we would have expected from a sad group of old outsiders. It looks like somebody, perhaps that cleaner, or your Nora, has been acting the general. But that's over now and I don't anticipate further problems." Blanchefleur looked at her daughter intently for a moment before continuing. "You can listen to the audio feed from the rangers' control devices, but it's rather gory. Perhaps I'd better just relay the important details to you."

"Do we know what's happened to everyone in the valley?" asked Alice. She was worried about Nora, but didn't want to admit it to her mother.

"There have been some casualties on both sides, but so far I don't have any news of Nora or the boy."

"I'd better listen, then," said Alice, her voice determined but breaking ever so slightly at the mention of Nora's name. "It's time I grew up."

"If you wish," Blanchefleur said, nodding in approval. She removed her headset and switched on the control room speakers.

Alice was overwhelmed by the feed. Nothing could have prepared her for what she was hearing. She had stepped inside the minds of the rangers. She heard blood roaring through their frenzied bodies, the cries of pain and of war, the impact of sharpened steel butchering flesh and bone. She screamed for her mother to turn off the audio.

Blanchefleur rose, hit the mute button, and then put her arms around her daughter. "I was the one who ordered this. It's my duty to witness the horror I've created. I'll do the listening. Go back and be with your little girl. I'll call you if there's news of Nora or the boy."

Alice nodded, then left the room without a word.

Chapter 33

As Aesop, Mabon, Nora, Adam, and Lucky made their way across the valley, doing their best to avoid the rangers, all they found was death and destruction. Everywhere they went, buildings were burning down and men were dying. Most of the bodies they passed belonged to old ones, but there were a several rangers who had been bested as well. A few times along the way, they'd been surprised by rangers, but they'd managed to take their enemies down and continue on.

When they reached the top of the cliff, they threw their weapons down and stopped to survey the valley below. Thick black smoke was pluming up from several buildings, darkening the sky. The crops had already been burnt down, and all that was left of the fields were scorched squares of earth and some smouldering embers. There were a few frightened cows and chickens roaming around, but otherwise the valley seemed eerily quiet.

"Where is everyone?" Adam asked. "What happened to all the rangers?"

"They're probably inside the main building, searching it," said Mabon.

"For what?" Adam asked.

"For you," said Nora, reaching out to wipe a smudge of ash from his face. "And it won't be long before they realize you're not there. We have to get out of here."

Mabon walked over to the edge of the cliff, and looked down over the precipice.

"It looks clear down there," he said. "We should go now, while we still have a chance."

Nora nodded.

Mabon turned to Aesop. "Come with us, my friend," he said, placing his hand on the old man's shoulder. "There's nothing left for you here."

Aesop shook his head sadly. "I can't," he said. "I'm far too old to be traipsing off into the wilderness with you. I'd only slow you down and put you in danger if I did." He looked out over the destruction below. Tears filled his cloudy eyes, and he didn't try to hold them back as they rolled down his wrinkled face. "This is my home. It's the only place I've ever truly lived. And it's where I will die."

Mabon nodded and wrapped his arms around the old man, pulling him into a deep bear hug. "Thank you," he said. "For everything you've done. You are my friend, my teacher, and my father." When he pulled away, his eyes were rimmed with red and his lashes were wet with tears.

Mabon turned, picked up the coil of rope, and carried it over to a large tree next to the edge of the cliff. He wrapped one end around it several times, and then fastened it with a strong knot. He pulled on it as hard as he could to make sure it was secure, then picked up the other end of the rope and dropped it over the edge of the cliff.

"I'll go down first," he said, picking up his bow and quiver and draping them over his shoulder. "I want to make sure the area below is clear before you two follow. When it's safe for you to come down, I'll whistle three times to let you know. Adam should come next, and Nora, you come last."

"Okay," Nora said, pulling him into a tight embrace and craning to kiss his cheek. "Be careful."

"I'll take Lucky down with me," Mabon said, scooping the dog up and tucking him under his arm. "Nora, you'll need to throw our packs down before you come. Just make sure Adam is clear of the rope before you do." He leaned down to give Nora one last kiss, and then took hold of the rope and stepped carefully over the edge of the cliff.

Nora, Adam, and Aesop watched as Mabon made his way down the cliff face, using his one free arm to anchor himself on the rope while he searched for footholds with his feet. His journey was slow, but he made it down safely. When he reached the bottom, he put Lucky down and disappeared into the forest, the dog on his heels.

After what seemed like an eternity, Mabon still hadn't returned. Nora stared down at the edge of the forest, willing him to appear. Her heart was racing and she could feel the panic taking hold of her. "Something's wrong," she finally announced. "I'm going down after him. Adam, you stay here with Aesop. Don't come down until I give you the signal."

"Are you sure that's wise?" Aesop asked. "What if something happens to you?"

"Then you'll need to get Adam out of here," said Nora. "Please, Aesop," she pleaded. "I have to help Mabon."

"All right," said Aesop. "Just be careful."

Nora leaned down and kissed Aesop's leathery cheek. "Thank you," was all she managed to say. She pulled Adam into a hug and squeezed him as hard as she could. "I'll see you again in a few minutes," she said. She kissed his head and breathed in his warm citrus smell, just like she had when he was a baby. "I love you."

"I love you too, Mom," Adam said, hugging her tight.

Nora reached down for the rope and grasped it tightly, then shimmied herself over the edge of the cliff.

Adam and Aesop watched as Nora picked her way down the rocky face, gripping the rope with all her strength as she did so. Suddenly there were the sounds of running feet behind them and a ranger shouted, "There he is!" Aesop and Adam turned around to see two rangers racing up the hill toward them.

"Quick, grab the bombs!" Aesop cried. Adam ran over to the tree where Mabon had left extra arrows and a few of the remaining glass bombs beside their supplies and retrieved the gasoline jars while Aesop fumbled through his cloak pocket for a match. He found one and struck it against a rock just as Adam returned with two jars. Aesop took one of the bombs and lit the fuse, then threw it with all his might at the approaching rangers.

The bomb hit the ground and exploded in front of the ranger closest to them, sending him flying backwards. They watched as his burning, lifeless body rolled back down the hill toward the valley.

"What's happening up there?!" Nora screamed from halfway down the cliff, desperately trying to clamber back up.

"It's the rangers!" Adam called, handing Aesop the second bomb.

Aesop lit the fuse and threw the bomb at the remaining ranger, but it missed and exploded in front of the attacker instead. The flames fanned out across the dry hillside and blocked the ranger's way, and he had to step back to avoid them.

"You have to go, Adam!" Aesop said scrambling to grab anything he could use as a weapon. Adam looked at the old man and hesitated. "Now!" screamed Aesop.

Aesop's order kicked Adam into gear. He raced over to the packs, grabbed them both, and dragged them to the edge of the cliff.

"Watch out, Mom!" he yelled down to her. He pushed the bags over the side of the cliff, as far away from his mother as he could. They bounced off the cliff face as they fell and landed on the ground below with two thuds.

When Adam turned back around, Aesop was standing in front of him, holding a pitchfork, and the ranger was bearing down on them.

"Get out of here!" Aesop cried.

Adam grabbed the rope and was about to slip over the cliff when the ranger reached Aesop. Aesop stabbed the pitchfork at the ranger, but the ranger easily deked out of the way and got hold of the long wooden handle with one of his strong hands. He tried to wrench it out of Aesop's grasp, but the old man's strength surprised him. They ended up in a tug of war, with Aesop pulling and stabbing while the ranger tried to grab hold of the fork with his other hand. The ranger finally won out, and he threw Aesop off the fork with one strong sweep. Aesop landed heavily, his head cracking against a large rock with a sickening thud.

"Your turn, wild boy," the ranger said, turning to Adam with a cruel smile. He took a step toward the boy, holding the pitchfork out in front of him menacingly.

Adam leapt out of the way, toward the spot where he'd left his bow and quiver. He scrambled across the ground on his hands and feet, trying to make it to his weapon, but the ranger was on him before he could get there. The ranger kicked him down, and he fell to the ground face first. He rolled over just in time to see the ranger rearing back with the pitchfork, ready to strike.

"No!" came Nora's desperate voice from behind the ranger. She'd managed to climb back up over the top of the ledge, and was running toward the ranger as fast as she could.

The ranger turned toward Nora in surprise. She lunged at him with all her strength and knocked him over. The pitchfork went flying from his hands and landed a few feet away.

"Run, Adam!" Nora screamed as she wrestled with the ranger. The ranger overpowered her easily, and pinned her to the ground.

"You take one step, boy, and I'll slit your mother's throat," said the ranger, pulling a long knife out from his boot.

"Adam, go!" Nora said. She kneed the ranger as hard as she could and he winced in pain.

Adam didn't hesitate. He reached behind him, grabbed his bow and an arrow from his quiver, and fired as quickly as he could. The arrow caught the ranger in the shoulder and the man howled in pain.

The ranger stood up and charged toward Adam, his knife at the ready. Adam fired again, and this time he hit the ranger straight in the chest. The ranger staggered backward and then fell, landing hard on the rocky ground. This time he didn't get up.

"Are you okay, Adam?" Nora asked, running over to him and inspecting him for wounds.

"I'm fine," Adam said. "But Aesop..."

They looked over to where the old man lay on the ground, still and silent. Nora went over to him and gently touched his wrinkled face. His eyes fluttered open and he gazed serenely up at her. Nora lifted his head and shoulders into her lap. He coughed, cleared his throat, and spoke in a choking voice. "Did you get him?" he asked.

"We got him," said Nora.

"Good," he said, smiling. "Now get that boy of ours out of here, and go find Mabon."

"I can't leave you like this," said Nora, reaching down to hold his hand.

"I'm already dead," said Aesop. "Don't make this all for nothing." He coughed once more and winked at Nora.

"You've been a great friend to all of us," Nora said, bending to kiss his forehead.

"Thank you, Aesop," said Adam, reaching down to hold his other hand. "I'll make you proud. I promise."

Aesop moved his eyes from one to the other. A look of peace and happiness filled his old face and his eyes focused somewhere far away. A moment later, he was gone.

Chapter 34

When Nora and Adam reached the bottom of the cliff, there was no sign of Mabon anywhere. They picked up the two packs from where Adam had thrown them down from the cliff and headed into the dense evergreen forest, entering at the same spot where they'd seen Mabon disappear.

Nora tried to look for signs of which way Mabon might have headed, inspecting tall grasses to see if they'd been broken and searching the ground for footprints, but Mabon had been too good at covering his tracks. When they reached the edge of the rangers' encampment, Nora stopped and put a finger to her lips. The camp was eerily quiet. The only signs of life were the smouldering embers in the fire pit. Nora and Adam skirted the perimeter of the camp as quietly as they could, keeping an eye out for rangers and for Mabon, but there didn't appear to be a soul around.

There was a rustling in the trees behind them. Nora stepped in front of Adam to shield him from the intruder and assumed a protective stance. "If I tell you to run," she whispered. "Run.

Don't worry about me, and don't look back. Just get as far away from here as you can."

"Okay," Adam whispered.

They stood for a moment, waiting, their hearts beating through their chests. Suddenly a bush nearby shook wildly, and then Lucky's head appeared from the foliage.

"Lucky!" Adam cried. He ran over to the dog, who jumped up on Adam and wagged his tail excitedly.

Nora came over and patted Lucky on the head. She noticed that there was blood matted in his fur, but when she inspected him, he didn't appear to be wounded.

"Where's Mabon, Lucky?" she asked the dog.

Lucky whined at the sound of his master's name.

"Lucky!" Adam said. "Can you take us to Mabon?"

The dog didn't move.

"Find Mabon, Lucky!" Nora tried.

Without any warning, Lucky bounded back through the bush and out of sight. Nora and Adam raced after the dog, trying to keep up as he skirted around trees and under bushes. Finally he reached a clearing. The bodies of three large rangers were splayed across the ground, but there was no sign of Mabon. Lucky ran over to a large fir tree at the edge of the clearing, stopped, barked once, and then crawled underneath. Nora and Adam followed him into the shadowy shelter.

They found Mabon inside, propped up against the tree trunk. There was a deep wound on his leg, and he was bleeding heavily. With his good arm he held up a bloody knife, ready to attack.

"Mabon!" Nora said, rushing to his side.

"Nora!" he said, dropping the knife. "Adam!" He smiled his crooked grin. "You're okay! I was so worried."

"We're fine," said Nora. She pulled a blanket from her pack, tore two long strips from one side of it, and wrapped them tightly around Mabon's wound to stop the bleeding. "What happened to you?"

Mabon winced as Nora knotted the course bandage around his leg. "I was checking out the ranger camp, making sure it was safe for us to pass through. It seemed empty, so I went in for a closer look. While I was there, the three guard rangers came back and spotted me. I ran into the woods, but they chased me and caught up to me in the clearing outside the tree. I managed to fight them off, with Lucky's help, but not before one of them got me with his machete."

"Are you going to be okay?" Adam asked.

"I'll be fine, now that your mother has patched me up," Mabon said. "I'm so sorry. I should never have left you on your own. Did you have trouble getting away?"

Nora shook her head. "One of the rangers found us before we had a chance to get down the cliff. Aesop held him off as long as he could, but…"

"No," Mabon said, clenching his teeth.

"I'm sorry," said Nora.

Mabon squeezed his eyes shut and took a deep breath. He sat silent for a long moment. "We have to get out of here," he finally said. "They'll be looking for us."

"Will you be okay to walk?" Nora asked, pulling a bottle of water from her pack and passing it to Mabon.

"I think so," he said, taking a sip. "But I'll need some help."

Nora and Adam helped Mabon crawl out from under the enormous fir and get to his feet. He tried putting all his weight on his bad leg, but it was too painful, so Nora put her arm around him and let him lean on her as he walked. They found they could move along this way at a fairly steady pace. Adam picked up the packs and followed along beside them as they walked.

The three travellers and their dog headed back toward the cliff face, and then followed the edge of the cliff toward the western side of the valley. When they arrived at the western side, they left the protection of the cliff and struck out into the dense forest and headed south, in the direction Mabon hoped would eventually lead them to the Manuhome.

They moved slowly and cautiously under the leafy canopy of the forest, aware that they were now vulnerable from all sides. It had started to rain lightly, and the sound of the raindrops dripping down from overhead meant that they wouldn't be able to hear anyone approaching. Rain drowned all the voices of the wild but its own. But it wasn't all bad. That same shower also washed away their tracks, so they were able to move quickly, if uncomfortably, along. Even so, they were constantly looking over their shoulders, aware that danger could find them at any moment.

They walked for hours, but in spite of Mabon's painful leg and Nora's fatigue from supporting his considerable weight, neither complained. When darkness came and their exhausted bodies could take them no further, they found shelter under a large willow, whose drooping branches formed a curtain around them and protected them from the drizzling rain.

They were gone again before the sun rose, and by lunchtime Mabon started to recognize signs that they were nearing the Manuhome. The rain had stopped by then and their progress had slowed slightly, since they kept needing to stop and cover their tracks. When they reached a tall, grass-covered mound of loose gravel that looked back toward the distant valley, Mabon dragged himself up it, with Nora's help, and looked out over the surrounding lands, searching for signs of the rangers. They could just make out a plume of smoke rising like river fog above the trees a few hundred feet away, in the direction they'd just come from.

"They're close," Nora said.

"They must have caught our trail and followed us," Mabon said, holding her tight. "We have to get out of here. We've got to make it to the Manuhome before they catch up to us."

Mabon turned and looked toward where Adam and the dog had been standing at the bottom of the hill a few minutes before and realized they were no longer there. His heart sunk to the pit of his stomach.

"Where's Adam?" Nora asked, alarm registering in her voice.

They scrambled down the gravelled incline, frantically searching the area for any sign of Adam or Lucky. It took Nora everything she had not to scream out Adam's name, but she knew that would just put him in more danger. They reached the bottom of the hill and paused, trying to figure out which direction Adam went.

"Halt!" a voice snarled from close behind them. "Don't turn around. There are machetes poised at the back of both of your necks. Drop your weapons. Now!"

Mabon felt the urge to push Nora aside and take his chances, but he knew there was too great a possibility that she'd be hurt. He cursed himself for not being more careful.

Nora took Mabon's hand and squeezed it, silently trying to tell him that he and Adam were all she cared about. "Do as he says, Mabon," she said as she stooped to drop her bow and quiver on the ground. "We have no choice." She thought about Adam, and hoped he was getting farther and farther from them every moment.

Mabon reluctantly unslung his bow and quiver and dropped them to the ground.

"Step back a few paces, away from your weapons, and then you can turn around slowly," the voice ordered.

Nora glanced at Mabon, looking for some sort of sign on his rugged face. He was smiling, but she could tell from the tight set of his crooked lips, his version of a grimace, that he was nervous. He was trying to reassure her, she knew, but his attempt at calming her down was only succeeding in making her more frightened.

"Step apart now and raise your arms high as you turn around. Move slowly and don't try anything stupid."

Mabon and Nora let go of each other's hands and slowly raised their arms, turning reluctantly until they were facing a tall ranger holding two machetes, one in each hand, each weapon clearly trained on one of them.

"I'm going to ask you a question and I want an answer. Where is the wild boy?"

"I don't know," said Nora, her voiced pinched but unwavering.

"What about you?" the ranger said, turning to Mabon.

Mabon's voice was angry and curt, full of disgust. "He's not here," he said.

"So you want to play tough, do you, cleaner?" the ranger said, placing the blade of his machete against the side of Nora's neck. "How about this? You either tell me where the boy is, or I kill the insider."

Chapter 35

"You can't let him do this, Mother!" Alice screamed. When day and night had gone by and her mother still hadn't sent any word of Nora, Alice hadn't been able to take it any longer. She'd barged back into the control room intending to demand an update. Instead she'd arrived just in time to hear the ranger capturing Nora and her outsider friend.

Blanchefleur said nothing. She just flipped a switch on the console and continued as if she hadn't heard Alice at all.

"Mother!" Alice yelled hysterically. "You can't do this to Nora! She's an insider, a woman like you and me. You may have been able to explain away the deaths of the outsiders, but you won't be able to do that with Nora. This is murder, and you know it."

"Murder?" Blanchefleur stood and faced her daughter, the white flower on her lapel drooping and crushed flat. Her blue eyes were cold and hard. "It's Nora who's the murderer. You heard what happened with the old ones. None of this would ever have happened if she hadn't stolen that outsider child. The blood is on her hands, not mine."

"You don't really believe that, do you?" Alice spat. "You're just as bad as the outsiders before the revolt, aren't you, Mother? You and all those women from the council, talking about how horrible life was before the city. I listened to the slaughter in the valley. You were right. It sickened me to my stomach. All those old ones were already dead, you said. But they weren't dead, were they? I heard their screams of pain. And I heard the screams of pain from the rangers. They were people, too. When you use other people to do your dirty work, it's still your dirty work. It's you who's the murderer."

"You ungrateful brat!" Blanchefleur screamed. She drew back and then slapped her daughter across the face, hard enough to leave five red finger marks across her porcelain cheek. "You think it's easy for me to do this, but it's not. I don't enjoy sitting here, listening to the horrors of war, but I have no choice. I do it because it's my job. I do it to protect the world from the will of the Central Council. I do it for the great city of Aahimsa. And I do it so you can enjoy the privileges of being the mayor's daughter."

"Don't put this on me," Alice said, holding her hand to her smarting cheek. Her icy eyes flashed with anger. "This is your mess. You're the one who ordered the attack. And you're the one who has to live with the consequences."

"Fine," said Blanchefleur. "I will. And since I no longer have to worry about what you think, I guess I can just go ahead and tell the ranger to do whatever's necessary to find the boy."

"You don't have to do this!" Alice pleaded.

"But I do," said Blanchefleur. "If I don't, the Central Council will take control of Aahimsa. And the first thing they'll do is terminate your precious Nora, and the rest of the outsiders, too. It's too late, Alice." She picked up the microphone and lifted it to her lips.

"No!" Alice shouted. Before she knew what she was doing, she had pounced on her mother and knocked her out of her chair. The two women wrestled wildly on the floor, each trying to gain control of the heavy metal microphone.

"Get off of me!" Blanchefleur screamed.

"I'm sorry, Mother," Alice told her through heaving breaths. "I can't let you do this!"

"I have to!" Blanchefleur said, panting. Blanchefleur wriggled and kicked and somehow managed to overpower her daughter. She pinned Alice to the floor and held the microphone over her head, ready to strike.

"Mother, no!" Alice screamed, her eyes widening into saucers.

Blanchefleur looked down at her daughter's terrified face, and paused. A look of horror crossed over her. "Holy Mother," she whispered, putting the microphone down beside her and releasing Alice. "I'm sorry. I'm so, so sorry, Alice. I don't know what came over me." She curled up in a ball and started rocking back and forth like a child. Tears filled her eyes, and she let herself cry for the first time in as long as she could remember.

Alice crawled over and put her arms around her mother. She held her tight, like she held Tish when she was frightened or hurt. When Blanchefleur had calmed down, Alice picked up the microphone. "Let them go," she told the ranger. "Tell them to run, and to hide themselves well. And tell the insider that Alice says she's sorry."

Chapter 36

"Don't tell him anything, Mabon," Nora said defiantly.

The ranger didn't say a word as he waited for Mabon's answer, but it looked like he was concentrating hard on something. Mabon knew how it worked. The ranger's control device worked the same way his had. He was probably communicating with his controllers using inner speak, waiting for their approval before he struck.

They waited what seemed like an eternity, but the ranger held his ground, his eyes set firmly on Mabon. Mabon remained stone silent the entire time, ready to attack the ranger if he made a move toward Nora.

Nora reached down, took Mabon's hand, and squeezed it hard. "I love you," she whispered, realizing that this was the first time she'd ever said it out loud. The ranger pressed his machete harder against her neck and she felt the blade pierce her skin. She braced herself for the impending blow.

Suddenly a confused look came across the ranger's face, which quickly turned to anger. He raised his machetes threateningly, then, without warning, dropped them on the ground. They bounced off the hard-packed dirt and settled a few feet away.

"You can go," he said coldly. "My controller said to tell you to run, and to hide yourselves well." He paused and looked at Nora with disgust. "And someone named Alice says to tell you she's sorry."

Nora nodded and smiled. She turned to Mabon. "Let's go find our boy."

Nora and Mabon picked up their packs and weapons and ran off into the forest, leaving the ranger, alone and confused, in the clearing.

"What just happened?" Mabon asked. "Why did he let us go?"

"I'm not exactly sure," said Nora. "But I'm not about to stick around to find out."

There was a rustling of leaves and branches near the place where they had entered the forest, and the sound of running footsteps approaching. When they looked up they saw Lucky run out from the trees, followed by Adam, carrying his pack in one hand and his bow in the other.

"Adam!" said Nora, pulling him into a big hug. "Where have you been?"

"Lucky ran into the woods, so I chased after him," Adam said. "By the time I caught him and we got back to the clearing, the ranger was there. I didn't know what to do. He was too far away to hit with an arrow, and I knew if I ran out to you he'd probably kill you. I was so scared!"

"You did the right thing," Mabon said, ruffling his hair. "Everything's going to be okay, now, I think. We just have to get you to the Manuhome and get you hidden before they come after us again."

Chapter 37

When Mabon threw the pebble at Dr. Ueland's window this time, he hit it on his first try. Dr. Ueland must have been waiting right there, because his face appeared behind the glass almost instantly.

He met Mabon, Nora, Adam, and Lucky at Emergency Gate Three, and within moments they were back up in his office with the door locked behind them. The room still looked exactly as it had nine years before, and Mabon smiled when he saw it. "Still not one for change, I see," he chuckled.

Dr. Ueland smiled wanly, but the stern look he usually wore didn't leave his face. "There isn't much time for catching up, I'm afraid. We've just been informed that the Manuhome has been put on high alert. Blanchefleur has ordered it locked down, but she won't tell us why, other than to say it has something to do with the Central Council, and that it's for our own safety."

"What does she mean, 'for your own safety'?" Nora asked. "Is it dangerous here?"

"I'm not sure what she means, but once we're in lockdown it's probably the safest place you can be. No one will be able to get in or out, not even me."

"How long is this lockdown supposed to last?" Nora asked.

"I'm not sure," Dr. Ueland said.

"So if we leave Adam here, we may not be able to get him back out?" Nora said, alarm registering in her voice.

"It's possible," said Dr. Ueland, "though I don't imagine you'll be back for quite some time, and I've never heard of a lockdown lasting for more than a few weeks."

"It'll be much more dangerous out in the wild than it will be in here, Nora," Mabon said, putting his hand over hers. "We have no idea what to expect beyond the borders. This is the best place for Adam right now."

Nora nodded. "What time is this lockdown supposed to happen?" she asked.

"I was supposed to order it immediately," Dr. Ueland said, "but I wanted to give you a chance to get Adam here before I did. I was just about to give up and lock the doors…" He smiled again, this time a genuine grin. "I'm so glad you all made it here safely."

"Thank you, Dr. Ueland," Mabon said. "So are we."

"Unfortunately, I can't hold off much longer," said Dr. Ueland. "I'll have to order the lockdown soon, and you need to get out of here before I do. We have a lot to discuss, but we'll have to do it quickly."

Dr. Ueland opened his desk drawer and pulled out some bread, a jar of Brin's honey, and a few bottles of water. "I figured you'd be hungry," he said. "I'm sorry I wasn't able to do more."

"This is plenty," Mabon said. "Thank you."

"Poor Brin," Nora said, looking at the jar of honey. It was the first time since the battle that she'd had a chance to mourn her fallen friends, and the weight of their loss hit her like a ton of bricks.

"He didn't make it," Dr. Ueland said. It was more of a statement than a question.

Nora shook her head sadly. "None of them did."

The serious look washed back over Dr. Ueland's face, and he let out a sad sigh, hanging his head. "What a waste."

As Dr. Ueland stared down at the floor, he noticed Mabon's bandaged leg under the desk. "Mabon, you're hurt!" he said.

"It's not so bad," said Mabon, giving Dr. Ueland a crooked grin.

"I'll get some bandages and we'll change your dressing," the doctor said. "You can't go back out there like that."

Dr. Ueland swept out of the room, and was back in no time with a pile of bandages and a bottle of pills. He sat down beside Mabon and changed dressing with expert skill. When he was finished, he handed Nora the stack of clean dressings and the bottle of pills. "These are antibiotics," he said. "Make sure he takes one every day until his wound heals over. And try to make sure he keeps a clean bandage on his wound at all times."

"I will," Nora said. "Thank you."

Dr. Ueland turned to Adam, who was sitting quietly in the corner, stroking Lucky's soft fur pensively. "I have clean clothing that I think will fit you, Adam. Once Nora and Mabon leave, you can shower and get changed into your uniform. It should be easy enough for you to blend in, physically speaking, for now, but there are other problems that we have to face."

"What sort of problems?" Nora asked.

"Adam will be entering a very different and challenging world. I'm going to take him in and train him as an office administrator, as if he would be managing one of our operations here at the Manuhome. He'll have to live here under a false identity — no one must know who he is. Lucky for us, a young worker recently died in our infirmary. I haven't issued the death certificate yet, and I won't, now that Adam is here. The boy who died was a worker out in the agricultural homelands. No one here knows him here, so there shouldn't be any suspicion."

He turned back to Adam. "It must appear to everyone that you belong here. You'll have to do everything you can to fit in. You'll have to take on a new name, and you'll have to pretend to be older than you are — the minimum age for new trainees is twelve. You'll also have to learn about the culture of the Manuhome — the rules of living here, the sports that are watched and played, the common knowledge and common attitudes of the place."

"I can do that," said Adam.

"Good," said Dr. Ueland. "The worker who passed away was named Ned. That's your new name, okay, Ned?"

"Okay," said Adam. "I'm Ned."

"Perfect," said Dr. Ueland.

"You'll be staying in a private room close to mine for the first few months. At least, until I'm satisfied that you are ready to be part of the general crowd. It's very important that you learn quickly. Most importantly, you'll need perfect control of your emotions. This won't be easy. You'll have to appear eager and happy, even if you're not. One mistake and the game is over. There will be times when you will have to disappear from sight, especially in the next little while, until the present crisis slows down."

"Okay."

"Now here is our biggest problem: Do you know the difference between you and the other outsiders?"

"Yes," Adam said. "I'm special."

"And why is that?"

"Because I can have children and the others can't."

"That's right," said Dr. Ueland. "Do you know why they can't?"

"No."

Dr. Ueland turned to Nora. "How much have you told him about his situation?" he asked.

"Not much," she said. "He's still a child."

"That stops now, I'm afraid," said Dr. Ueland. "He has to understand, no matter how hard it is. It's a matter of life and death for him."

Nora nodded.

Dr. Ueland kneeled down in front of Adam. "The reason the other outsiders can't have children, Ned, is because after they were born they had an operation where the possibility of making children was taken away."

"Oh," said Adam. "That's sad."

"Yes," said Dr. Ueland. "The reason I'm telling you this is that, physically, you're different from all of the other outsiders here. That's why it will be hard for us to hide you here. You'll have to shower in private. Your voice will change when you get older. It will be deep like Mabon's voice is, and we'll have to teach you how to hide it when the time comes. You'll grow a beard, too, but we'll have to keep it shaved very smoothly."

"Okay," said Adam. "I think I understand."

"Good," said Dr. Ueland. "Now what's your name again?"

"Ned," said Adam.

"Good boy." Dr. Ueland smiled and patted Adam's back.

Nora had promised herself she wouldn't cry, but she couldn't help herself. The thought of leaving Adam in this place, not knowing when she'd see him again, was too much to bear.

"Don't cry, Mom," Adam said, walking over and wrapping his small arms around her. "You'll have to be brave," he said. "Just like me."

Nora lost control for a moment and then gathered herself. "I'll try," she said.

"I'm afraid I'll have to take you two back down now," Dr. Ueland said, looking from Nora to Mabon. "I've already waited much longer than I should have to lock this place down."

Dr. Ueland picked up a cloth bag and two rolled sleeping bags from the floor near the door and handed them to Nora and Mabon.

"The bag contains some survival supplies and some food. It will help a bit, I hope."

"Thank you," said Mabon, shaking the doctor's hand. "For everything you've done. I hope one day I'll be able to return the favour."

"You already have, Mabon," Dr. Ueland said, pulling him into an embrace.

Dr. Ueland poked his head out the office door and, when he was sure the coast was clear, led Nora, Mabon, Adam, and Lucky back down through the bowels of the building to the security gate.

Nora and Mabon stepped out into the dark night, but Adam stayed inside. Lucky stood beside him, tail wagging.

"Can Lucky stay with me?" Adam asked.

"No, Ned," said Dr. Ueland. "It's not possible. We aren't allowed pets here. Not even me."

Adam's eyes brimmed over with tears. "When will I see him again?"

"I don't know," said Nora. She glanced at the dog, who had a mass of white hairs around his eyes and ears and whose brown coat was beginning to fade. He was getting old, and Nora knew there was a good chance the boy would never see him again. Somehow this thought made the impending separation from her boy more real, and she was overwhelmed by the feeling of loss that washed over her. Her entire body started to shake involuntarily as she struggled to fight back her tears.

Mabon knelt next to Adam and pulled him close. Adam was looking away from him, but the shudder of the boy's thin shoulders and back betrayed the depth of his misery. First one large tear and then a second slipped from Mabon's eyes. He squeezed them shut tightly, as if to stem the tide, as he rocked Adam gently from side to side.

Nora could hold back no longer. She sobbed openly and without restraint. She sank to her knees, kissed Adam's wet face, and ran her fingers through his unruly hair.

Even Lucky joined in. He stood on his hind legs he joined the grieving mass of his family, licking the salty tears from their faces.

"I wanted to be brave for you," Adam told Nora and Mabon, his head hanging. "I'm sorry."

"You have been brave," said Mabon.

"We'll take care of Lucky for you, Adam," said Nora. "I can't promise when, but we'll do everything we can to get you back with us as soon as possible. Until then, listen to Dr. Ueland and do as he says so you stay safe."

"Whenever you are settled, come and get him," Dr. Ueland said.

"Thank you, Dr. Ueland," Nora said and hugged him.

"Where will you go?" asked Adam.

"There's a cave nearby we can stay in until things die down a bit and my leg's healed enough for me to walk," said Mabon. "We stayed there with you when we fled Aahimsa all those years ago. After it's safe to travel, we'll head west and then south, where it's said the land was good long ago."

"When we find a place that is safe and can provide for our needs, we'll be back to get you," said Nora.

"It won't be long," said Mabon, ruffling Adam's hair one last time. "You'll see."

There were more hugs and kisses and repeated good-byes, and then Dr. Ueland said gently, "I'm sorry, but it's time. We have to go now, Ned."

Adam hesitated and looked from Mabon to Nora to Lucky, and then joined Dr. Ueland behind the door. Nora and Mabon held each other tightly and waved to their boy as the door swung shut behind him.

Epilogue

When Alice finished tidying up the summer house, it dawned on her that Tish had been outside playing on her own much longer than usual. Usually by this time, her daughter would have found a dozen excuses to make her way back inside. Today, there had been no thirst, no hunger, no burning question that just couldn't wait for an answer.

Alice was on the verge of going out to investigate when she heard the door open and close again. She waited for Tish to appear in the kitchen. When she didn't, Alice went out to the living area. The bedroom door was open and Tish was seated on her bed, playing with a doll. She had a dazed expression, and was obviously preoccupied. Alice sat down beside her, and draped her arm around her daughter's shoulders.

"Who is Nora, Mom?" Tish asked.

Alice was thunderstruck. She struggled to control her voice as she answered, "Why do you ask, darling?"

"The woman I was talking to beside the pond said her name was Nora. She asked me who I was and who my mother was."

"Did you tell her?"

"Yes. She said she used to know you a long, long time ago."

"Is she still out there?"

"I think so. She stopped talking and went really quiet and I got nervous so I came inside."

"Can you show me where she is?" Alice asked.

Tish nodded. She took her mother's hand and led her out to a spot in the grove beside the pond.

Nora was no longer there. There was no sign that she'd ever even been there.

"Mom?" Tish asked.

"Yes, darling."

"The woman said to tell you something."

"What was it, darling?" Alice sat down on a rock and gazed out across the pond. The great wall around Aahimsa loomed in the distance across the water, casting a dark shadow over its rippled surface.

"Thank you."

THE END

Acknowledgements

I'd like to thank Terrilee for believing in this
book from the start and to Caitlin Drake Smith
for her amazing editorial advice.

I'm so grateful for The Acorn Press which has
been so important to the development and encouragement
of writing on Prince Edward Island.

ST. MARTIN'S PAPERBACKS TITLES BY
STEPHEN J. CANNELL

The Tin Collectors

King Con

Riding the Snake

The Devil's Workshop

Final Victim

The Plan

THE

VIKING

FUNERAL

STEPHEN J. CANNELL

St. Martin's Paperbacks

THE VIKING FUNERAL

Copyright © 2002 by Stephen J. Cannell.
Excerpt from *Hollywood Tough* copyright © 2002 by Stephen J. Cannell.

Cover photograph of badge by Tim Bradely.
Digital treatment of photograph by James Wang.

Library of Congress Catalog Card Number: 2001048654

ISBN: 0-312-98343-3

Printed in the United States of America

St. Martin's Press hardcover edition / January 2002
St. Martin's Paperbacks edition / December 2002

St. Martin's Paperbacks are published by St. Martin's Press, 175 Fifth
Avenue, New York, NY 10010.

10 9 8 7 6 5 4 3 2 1

DEDICATION

I was sitting having lunch in a Hollywood restaurant with my friend Bill Gately, a lean, dark-haired, intense man who often speaks in whispers. Suddenly Bill leaned forward and said, "Hey, Steve, you ever hear of the parallel market?"

Bill had recently pulled the pin after a distinguished career at the U.S. Customs Service, where he ended up as the Assistant Special Agent in charge of the Los Angeles office. The year before, he had supervised the now-famous Casablanca bank sting. In that covert operation, which was run inside Mexico, he ended up busting dozens of Mexican bankers who had been secretly laundering billions of dollars in Colombian drug money, escaping detection by wiring funds bank to bank.

In my opinion, Bill Gately is one of America's heroes. He has spent his life holding the fort against international crime syndicates, often risking his career and life, to bring dangerous criminals to justice. So naturally, when Bill talks, I listen.

I told him I had never heard of the parallel market.

What he explained to me at that lunch two years ago eventually became the basis for this novel. Without Bill, I would not have been able to write *The Viking Funeral*, because I would have been just as blind to the devastating effects of the parallel market as I'm sure the rest of you are.

While this is a work of fiction, it is based on fact. These facts have been overlooked or scrupulously hidden by our own government.

The stated reasons for this oversight defy logic.

When you read this, I hope you will become as outraged as I am.

For

WILLIAM GATELY

Friend, Colleague,

American Hero

Police officers must agree on a certain set of philosophies, because there cannot be a rule for everything.

L.A.P.D. Management Guide to Discipline

1

JODY

Looking back, it was pretty strange that just the night before, they'd been talking about Jody Dean. Shane and Alexa had been in Shane's bedroom in the Venice house; Chooch was in the front room doing his homework.

Here's how it happened. . . .

It was six in the evening, and the conversation took place after they'd been making love, Shane draping his arms protectively around Alexa's narrow waist, smelling the sweet scent of her, feeling her soft rhythmic breathing on his neck. He was still inside her, both of them trying to sustain the afterglow of lovemaking for as long as possible, staring into each other's eyes, communicating on levels much deeper than words could convey.

He'd been building up to it for months, but it was right then, at that particular moment, that Shane decided he would ask this incredible woman to be his wife, to share his life and help raise his son, Chooch. All he needed to do was determine the timing of the proposal. Maybe Sunday night, after the awards ceremony. But soon, because he now knew he had to add her to his life . . . to his and Chooch's.

A swift series of connect-the-dot thoughts followed, and his mind was suddenly on Jody: Jody Dean, who wouldn't be at the wedding, standing at Shane's side, as they had both once promised each other. Jody wouldn't be standing up for Shane as Shane had for him, his raucous humor making everything funnier and more exciting, pouring insight and personality over Shane's special day. "Jodyizing the deal," he would have called it. And then, tumbling over this thought, a tidal wave of sadness and loss.

Alexa was looking into his eyes and must have seen his gaze gutter and dim, because she suddenly asked him what he was thinking, and that was how his best friend's name came up the day before Shane's whole world changed.

"I was thinking about Jody," Shane said, not explaining how Jody had entered his mind during postcoital sex, when his thoughts should have been on her. She lay in his arms and nodded, maybe frowning slightly, but it was hard to tell because they were so close together. He could see only her eyes and they had not changed, still soft with love.

"Oh" was all she had said, but she shifted slightly and Shane came out of her.

"I was thinking how he would have been happy for us," Shane had tried to explain, still not confessing his real train of thought.

Alexa hadn't known Jody, not really . . . station-house war stories, mostly, and opinions; there was certainly no shortage of either where Jody was concerned. Jody had been assigned to the Special Investigations Section—SIS—when . . . when he . . . well . . . when he did the unthinkable.

Alexa had been running the Southwest Patrol Day

Watch back then. Of course, she knew how the event had busted Shane up, how it still deeply affected him. After all, Jody had been like a brother. Jody's family had been like Shane's family. The Deans, with their wealth and position, never once made Shane feel like what he knew he was—a socially inept, unclaimed orphan from the Huntington House Group Home. They had cared about him when Shane had nobody who cared. Jody had been like a brother all through elementary school, high school, and the Marines. Actually, if you wanted to be absolutely accurate, all the way from Little League through the Police Academy.

But there was something else about Jody, something even harder to define, which Shane had often thought about but never completely understood. He had finally come to accept it simply as Jody's aura, or Jody's "mojo"—some force of personality that made his ideas seem better, his jokes funnier, his world slightly brighter. It had even been there at the very beginning, when they were only seven or eight, back at the very start, from that first day at Ryder Field, that first Pirate Little League practice.

Shane had been dropped off by the volunteer driver of the Huntington House van and had joined the team. He didn't have a father or mother to cheer him on, or a family to buy his uniform—Jody's father stood in on both counts. Jody had had a startling effect on him from that very first day. He had it on everyone, children and adults alike—almost hypnotic. You knew that if you did it his way, it would just be more fun, more exciting and that in the end it would come out all right, even though sometimes it didn't. Sometimes Jody's way produced disaster. But with Jody, even disaster could be an E-ticket event, where if you held on tight, you could come off the ride, adrenalized and miraculously unhurt. Shane had been Jody's best friend, right next to all that pulsing, hard-to-define excitement; ringmaster of the Jody Dean Circus. Everybody always came to Shane, trying to get him to do their commercials, to sell their ideas to Jody. Everybody knew that Jody was destined for greatness, until that August day in the police parking lot, when . . . when it . . . well . . . when the unthinkable happened.

Alexa rolled away from him and sat up on the side of the bed, cutting off that string of painful recollections. "Jody's dead, honey. He's been dead for three years." She said it softly, but there was concern in her tone, as if no good would come of this.

"I know. . . . It's just . . . I was thinking he'd be happy for us, that's all," eager to change the subject now, almost popping the question right then, to refocus the energy in the bedroom. If he had, it all probably would have come out differently. But something . . . maybe all those dark memories, stopped him.

"It's enough for me that *we're* happy for us, and that Chooch is happy."

"I know. . . ." But his voice sounded wistful and small. He knew that she was jealous and frightened of these Jody thoughts—feelings and memories that she had never been a part of, that had once led Shane to the edge of a dangerous crack in his psyche, then to his spiraling depression in the months just before they met. It was hard to explain to her what Jody Dean meant, what an important part of Shane's personal history he was. She couldn't understand what the loss of Jody had done to Shane and how it had changed him. Until Chooch and Alexa came into his life, he'd been ticktocking along, heading slowly but surely toward his own dark end.

Alexa got out of bed and started to dress. Her suitcase was open on the bedroom sofa, and she had already finished packing her things, getting ready to move out of Shane's house for the week that her brother was in town.

"Buddy comes in on American Airlines tomorrow morning," she said, changing the subject.

"I'll be there, ten o'clock. Then dinner at the beach at seven. I got it all down," his tone still hectored by a confusing recipe of Jody thoughts that he couldn't completely decipher, even after all these years.

She turned and looked at him. "You all right with this?" she suddenly asked, picking up on his sharp tone, but not the reason for it. He knew she wasn't talking about Jody now or picking up her brother, but rather the awards ceremony this coming Sunday afternoon. She was going to receive the LAPD Medal of Valor for a case he'd originally discovered, then ended up working on with her. He was not being recognized. Of course, during that investigation Shane had broken more rules than the West Hollywood Vice Squad. The case and Shane's misconduct had been written up in the *Los Angeles Times*—twenty-five column inches, with color photographs describing all of his transgressions. In the face of that, the department couldn't award him the medal.

During the week they worked the case, Shane had taken a confusing emotional journey from pure hatred of Alexa Hamilton to grudging respect, to finally knowing that she was the most special person he had ever met. The case had turned his life around. Not only had he fallen in love, but Sandy Sandoval, a beautiful police informant he had once managed, confessed just before she died that her fifteen-year-old son, Chooch, was Shane's love child. Suddenly, his life had new meaning. In the end, the mayor and the police chief had both been arrested, along with a famous Hollywood producer and a real-estate tycoon. That was why Alexa was getting the M.O.V. on Sunday and why her older brother was coming to town to watch her receive it.

"I've got to get the budget review for DSG wrapped up before the end of the week." She was talking fast now, quickly getting dressed, inserting her small, department-approved brass stud earrings while trying to switch off the dark energy of Jody Dean.

She was referring to the annual budget for the Detective Services Group, where she had just been assigned as the executive officer. Normally the XO at an Administrative Operations Bureau would be a lieutenant, but Alexa, though still a sergeant, was on the lieutenant's list, third tier. She was probably less than a month away from getting her bars.

Shane got off the bed, his thoughts of Jody Dean left drifting in the wake of this new conversation.

"I'm gonna go say good-bye to Chooch," she said as she ran her fingers through her shoulder-length black hair, then turned and snapped her suitcase shut, presenting him with her classic profile for a moment. His heart clutched. . . . *God, she is beautiful.* Then she carried the suitcase out and set it down in the hall next to the front door. A moment later Shane trailed her out of the bedroom.

Chooch was not studying for his final exams at the desk in the den, where he did his homework. Shane looked out the back window and saw that Alexa had already found him in the backyard, seated in a metal chair, going over a vocabulary list for tomorrow's test. Shane watched through the window as Chooch stood and Alexa reached out and took his hand. His sixteen-year-old son was tall and had his deceased mother's Hispanic good looks. The waters of the Venice, California, canals dappled late-afternoon sunlight across their features. Alexa was looking up at the six-foot-tall boy, who seemed intense and serious, nodding at whatever it was she was saying. As he watched them, he thought they seemed perfect together, standing, talking earnestly in the backyard of his little Venice canal house. He liked what he saw, what he felt—liked the sense of calm that all this laid against his once turbulent interior. Then Alexa leaned forward and kissed Chooch on the cheek, and he hugged her.

Shane's mind flipped back once again. *Too bad Jody isn't here to see this*, he thought.

Then he opened the door and went out into the yard to join them.

2

THE IMPOSSIBLE
HAPPENS

" . . . So Coach Fry says that they have this camp every year. It's up by San Francisco, and he says he's gonna call and find out if there's still a place. That is, if it's okay with you," Chooch said, looking over at Shane, wondering which way it was going to go. They were in Alexa's powder blue Subaru, on the way to Harvard Westlake School the next morning, the morning it happened—Friday morning.

"How long is the camp?" Shane asked.

"Coach said it's about a month. It starts next week, June seventh. After school gets out."

Shane nodded. He was worried about expenses, but Sandy's estate had left money in trust for Chooch, and part of his new responsibility as a parent was to provide enriching life experiences. On the other hand, he wasn't sure that the Jim Plunkett Quarterback Camp in Palo Alto, California, qualified as life enrichment. But Chooch had a great arm, and the football coach said he would probably start at quarterback his sophomore year.

Shane had spent afternoons after his therapy sessions

standing on the sidelines at Zanuck Field, watching spring ball. Chooch in practice pads, his silver helmet shining in the afternoon sun, taking his five-step drop, setting up, rifling passes to streaking wideouts on long fade or post patterns. He had to admit that his son looked good, but he was hesitant to let him go, to lose him for even a few days, let alone a month. Sandy had raised him for the first fifteen years of his life, and Shane had no idea he was the boy's father. Now, after Sandy's death, Shane was Chooch's sole parent. The newness of this obligation produced a degree of anxiety. Indecision enveloped both of them, swirling around in the front seat of Alexa's car like a sandlot dust devil.

"Why don't you ask him to make a call, find out what the deal is?" Shane finally compromised.

"Solid." Chooch grinned at him.

Shane had just transitioned to the 101 Freeway and edged Alexa's car into the right lane to get off at Cold-water, where Harvard Westlake School was located. Sandy had enrolled Chooch there, and Shane was now paying the tuition—more than ten thousand dollars a year—from Chooch's trust account.

"Bud," he said softly. "Not to change the subject, but I need to get your take on something."

"The Chooch Scully Store of 'Sagacious' Advice is open," he said, using one of his new "vocab" words Shane had tested him on last night, after Alexa had left.

"I know you like Alexa. I know she's important to you, right?"

"She's the other level, man, you know that."

"Yeah," Shane said. "I was wondering . . . how would you feel about putting her into our deal, full-time?"

"You mean you're gonna knock off this light-house-keeping thing you've been doing and finally give her a long-term contract?"

"That's the idea," Shane said, smiling. "But I don't

want to ask her unless you're okay with it."

"If you can get her to say yes, then get after it, dude. 'Cause you an' me won't ever do any better."

Shane smiled and looked over at Chooch, who was grinning openly.

"Okay, okay, good deal," Shane responded with relief.

Soon they were in the line of cars in front of Harvard Westlake. As they pulled up to the drop zone, Chooch grabbed his book bag from the backseat, then hesitated. "Don't screw up the proposal," he said. "Get a good ring, no zirconias. And I wanna preview the pitch. I wanna hear how you're gonna say it. You can practice on me, y'know, so you don't boot it."

"Come on, whatta I look like?"

"Like you're in over your head." Chooch grinned. "I don't want you t'blow us out on some whack move."

Shane raised his right hand and Chooch high-fived it. "Good luck on your English final," Shane said, and Chooch nodded his thanks. Then he was out of the car, still smiling as he walked up the path toward the classroom. He was instantly joined by two friends, both girls.

Shane pulled the Subaru back onto Coldwater, got on the 101 heading west, on his way to the 405 South. He would probably arrive at LAX an hour early to pick up Alexa's brother Bud, but Shane figured he could get some coffee at the American Airlines terminal amid the passenger rush, and plan this new part of his life. He was breezing along in the middle lane up over the hill, passing Sunset. He had his left arm on the open window, feeling the warm June air in his face, hidee-hoeing along, his mind freewheeling, when he glanced over and saw the Al Capone Ride—the lowered orange and black muscle car with a strange, thin layer of black dust all over it. The car was tracking along next to him in the fast lane. The man behind the wheel was looking straight ahead, up the freeway, his curly blond hair and short beard whipping in the slipstreaming wind.

Shane's heart actually stopped . . . like when you're about to get very lucky or very dead. The driver looked over at him.

It was Jody Dean.

They stared at each other for almost ten seconds, racing along, door handle to door handle, at sixty, sixty-five miles an hour, both of them frozen by the complicated moment.

Shane was filled with thoughts too mixed up to fully deal with, thoughts that started out as questions but boomeranged back as unbelievable dilemmas. His dead best friend was ten feet away, speeding along, staring over at him from the fast lane. Jody Dean, who had committed suicide, shooting himself in the Valley Division parking lot three years ago, leaving his fly-specked, stiffening corpse sprawled in the front seat of a Department L car for the shocked officers of SIS to discover. Shane's mind double-clutched, missed the shift, and redlined dangerously. How could Jody Dean be alive? It was impossible. Jody had eaten his gun, put it in his mouth and pulled the trigger, turned his brains into blood mist. Shane Scully, his best friend, his Little League catcher and soul mate, had carried the coffin, watched it go into the furnace, cried over the urn as he handed it to Jody's grieving widow. In the months that followed, before Alexa saved him, Shane had started circling the drain himself, getting closer and closer, following Jody into the same suicidal vortex.

So how could Jody be in the fast lane of the 405, driving a dirty black and orange '76 Charger, not ten feet from him? Suddenly, Jody's expression changed, became hardened with recognition and resolve. Shane's attempt at a logical explanation was unhinged by that determined look on Jody Dean's face.

You see, Shane *knew* that look. There was no mistaking it. He'd seen that look a thousand times, going all the way back to Little League. Ten-year-old Jody, on the mound staring in at nine-year-old Shane behind the plate. *That look on his face, and in his eyes, stone cut and insistent.* Shane, crouching behind the plate, clad in his catcher's gear, each sending the other thought vibes. A silent conversation nobody else could hear. *We gotta give him the rainbow curve, man . . . or give him the slider. . . .* Jody, reading these thoughts and shaking his head even before Shane's fingers flashed the sign. *Nothin' doin', Hot Sauce . . . gonna throw the heater,* he telepathed back as clear as if he had walked up and shouted it at Shane. That was what was happening right now. Jody's thoughts shooting across the painted lane dividers from the Charger's front seat, shooting a vibe . . . a warning, plain as if Jody had shouted it: *Forget this, man. Forget you ever saw me.* And then, some kind of good-bye: *See ya. Sorry. . . .*

Suddenly, Jody floored the dust-covered Charger, shooting ahead, changing lanes around a slow-moving truck.

"No!" Shane's voice was a strangled plea. "Don't go! Not again!"

Shane pushed the pedal all the way to the floor, but Alexa's Subaru was underpowered, winding up slowly like a twenty-year-old air-raid siren, taking its time to reach full power, its thin whine lost behind the Charger's four-barrel roar. Finally, Shane was going almost a hundred, chasing the vanishing muscle car between semis and soccer moms, businessmen and airport taxis, weaving dangerously in and out amid a chorus of blaring horns and unheard curses.

The Charger was ahead, gaining ground, its loose but empty chrome license-plate holder winking morning sunlight back at him.

Suddenly, Jody cut off a Ryder van and the top-heavy

rent-a-truck, with its inexperienced driver, started pin-wheeling across all four lanes. In seconds, it was directly in front of the Subaru. Shane had a scary two seconds as he tried to avoid death at a hundred miles an hour. Alexa's car broke loose, swapping ends. Then he was carouseling wildly down the freeway: the landscape strobing past his windshield—dangerous, disembodied glimpses of trees, guardrails, and concrete abutments. A kaleidoscope of images on spin cycle . . . Around and around the Subaru went, metal lint on the busy L.A. freeway, until he saw the end coming. A bridge abutment spun into view like a huge concrete iceberg.

Shane fed the little Japanese car some gas, trying to straighten out the spin. He caught some traction, and the car made a try at straightening out, but he was still crooked and sliding sideways when he hit the wall of concrete, slamming into it hard. He felt the whole right side of Alexa's car explode, as door handles, side mirrors and paint all disintegrated or flew free, followed a second later by the whole left door—all of this accompanied by the scream of tortured metal. Shane was staring at blurred concrete graffiti and tagger art grinding and strobing past the doorless opening like the scenery wheel in an eighth-grade play.

The Subaru finally shuddered to a halt, and then it was over. He was sitting in the car, stuck in the fast lane, facing the wrong way, his heart jackhammering in his chest.

Shane spun around and looked out the back window. The black and orange Charger was nowhere to be found.

Jody Dean was gone as suddenly as he had reappeared.

YOU'RE OUTTA THERE

Okay, so how do I bullshit my way out of this one? I'm a police officer, trained to make split-second observations but also regarded by the department as something of a head case. I'm forced to sit in a cracked vinyl La-Z-Boy three times a week while an overweight, balding therapist looks across at me over templed fingers, saying, "Uh-huh," "I see," and "How does that make you feel?"

His career was already in big trouble. This little story about seeing a dead man on the 405 Freeway would make him look as though he'd started carrying his shit around in a sock.

Shane sat in the office of the towing company, waiting for the cab he'd called, looking out the window at a crumpled gallery of traffic mistakes, the latest of which was Alexa's little Subaru. Aside from the destroyed right side, the car looked badly torqued to him. If the frame was bent, it was a total. Right on top of this sobering realization, his cell phone rang. He dug it out.

"Shane, where are you? Bud just called, and nobody

was at the airport. He had to take a cab." Alexa sounded annoyed.

Shane had completely forgotten about Bud, the breakfast-food salesman. Shane had never met Bud but had talked to him once or twice on the phone. His booming "Hey, pal" voice always seemed jovial while still managing to convey displeasure.

"I'm sorry, honey. I hate to tell you this, but I had an accident in the Subaru."

"Are you okay?" Instant concern.

"Yeah, I'm fine." But of course, he wasn't. He was close to hysteria, his whole body shaking, his nerves buzzing like a desert power line. "I'm great," he lied, then added, "I need to talk to you. We need to sit down. I'm taking a cab over to the Glass House. I should be there in half an hour."

"Shane, I—"

"Look, I'm sorry about Buddy and the car. I'm afraid I really boxed it."

"I don't care about the car, Shane. As long as you're okay, that's all that matters."

Through the fly-specked office window, Shane saw the Yellow Cab pull into the tow company's parking lot. A round-shouldered Melrose cowboy, wearing a plaid shirt and a silver buckle the size of an ashtray, got out and started looking around for his fare. Shane motioned to him.

"Cab's here. I'll be there in forty minutes."

"Shane, you know I'm swamped getting this financial review finished."

"I need help. Something just came up. I can't go into it on the phone."

"Okay, then let's try meeting at the Peking Duck. It's fast. We can grab something while we talk, but gimme at least an hour."

"Okay," he said, and closed the phone. He heaved himself up and walked on stringy, oxygen-starved muscles out of the tow-service waiting room, then got into the Yellow Cab.

They were on the 405 heading back to L.A., Shane sitting quietly in the backseat behind the driver, looking for his bridge abutment, finally seeing the crash site sliding by across six lanes of traffic at Howard Hughes Parkway. A pound of rubber and a powder-blue slash of paint. His accident, like a thousand others, was now immortalized on freeway concrete, insignificant as a sauna-room butt mark.

A block from Parker Center was the Peking Duck, which was actually now called Kim Young's. It had been sold by the original owners after an armed robbery attempt, but the old sign was still hanging out front. Kim Young had bought the restaurant from his cousin, who retired, giving up his American Dream after four dust bunnies in ski masks had tried to take the place, unaware that half the LAPD Glass House Day Watch lunched there. This criminal brain trust of highwaymen had just pulled their breakdowns out from under cool street dusters when they were surprised to hear half a dozen automatics trombone loudly behind them. They spun around and in seconds ate enough lead to qualify as the second-largest metal deposit in California. It took a crane to lift them into the coroner's van.

Shane took a booth in the back. The restaurant had linoleum floors and was always noisy. He sat alone, waving at a few friends who came in but not over.

He thought about Jody—or more correctly, how he would explain what he had seen to Alexa. His mind was already hunting for a way out: shifting details to make them seem more acceptable, eliminating facts, pulling them this way and that. Piece by piece, he was trying to arrange the event so that it would become at least digestible, removing one crumb at a time, working to make it disappear, his thoughts like ants struggling to carry away a picnic. However, this was too big. He had to deal with it. But how? What should he do? How could he explain it?

Ten minutes later Alexa entered the place, and Shane heard the volume of conversation dip as forty or fifty guys whispered her arrival across tables stacked with egg rolls and dim sum. Then again, maybe that was just his jealous imagination—he wasn't sure. She walked toward him, her hips swaying slightly, her slender calves flexing.

She slid in, reached across the table, and squeezed his hand. "You sure you're okay? No whiplash?" she asked, concerned.

"Yeah, but your car is junk. A sea anchor."

"If it saved your life, it did its job." She smiled. "I'll cash the insurance and get a red one. I was tired of powder blue anyway."

Then, almost without knowing how he started, he was telling her, talking about seeing the Charger, seeing Jody Dean looking back at him across a lane of traffic, the heart-stopping moment of recognition . . . And then, Jody, taking off, leaving Shane in the dust; the Ryder van pin-wheeling in front of him until the Subaru finally ground to a halt under the bridge on the Howard Hughes Parkway.

Alexa didn't say anything while he was telling it. "Shane," she said after he had finished. "Jody is *dead*. We talked about it last night. What is it? Why do you insist on . . . ?" She didn't finish, but instead, let go of his hand.

"His suicide never made sense to me. . . . I couldn't believe he'd kill himself," Shane said. "He wasn't the kind of guy who eats his gun."

"Yet cops who seem normal do it all the time. . . . When it's a good friend, it's just harder to accept."

"Alexa, I may be going through a psychiatric review, but I'm not a psycho."

"Jody is dead," she repeated. "You carried his box to the furnace—gave his ashes to his wife. You *know* he's gone."

"Then who did I see on the freeway? He ran, Alexa. Took off. I crashed because he cut off a truck and it almost hit me. Why would he run if it wasn't Jody?"

She sat there quietly, looking at him, for a long time, trying to find the right thing to say. Then she lowered her voice and leaned toward him. "I want you to let this go. Okay? I want you to keep quiet about it and let it go."

"Don't think it'll look good in my package? Help dress up my psychiatric review?" he said sarcastically.

She smiled a tight smile. "I'm sure there's some explanation. Jody's body was identified by his wife and by his commander at Detective Services Group . . . who was it back then?"

"Captain Medwick."

"Right. Carl Medwick. He and Lauren wouldn't identify the body if Jody wasn't dead."

"Yeah . . . yeah . . . of course. Probably not." The conversation stopped, but these ideas lay between them, festering malignantly.

"You just saw somebody who looked like Jody," she added.

Ants working hard, tugging at crumbs, still trying to make this untidy idea go away.

"Of course, you're right," he said, with more enthusiasm. "That's gotta be it. Gotta be. And he ran because . . . because . . ." He looked up for help.

"Because, sometimes, Shane, when you stare at people, you can look very ferocious. The driver of that Charger just got scared."

A big piece, an important piece, dragged . . . hauled,

actually, to the edge of the blanket, but not gone . . . not quite yet.

"You're right," he said. "Shit, I probably scared the poor guy, whoever he was, half to death."

"I've seen you do it."

"He probably thought I was some lane-change killer about to pull a gun and start blasting."

They both sat there anxiously, trying to buy it, hoping for the best, like family members waiting for a biopsy.

"Yeah . . . God, what was I thinking? The guy sure looked like Jody, but it wasn't him. Couldn't've been," Shane said.

Alexa nodded.

But as he sat there in the Peking Duck trying to convince himself, he remembered that look again—Jody's look. In his memory he saw little ten-year-old Jody, standing on the mound, shaking off signs in frustration, sending Shane his own brand of telepathy . . . Jody-thoughts coming in on their special frequency. With this realization, the self-deception ended. It *was* Jody in that Charger, talking to Shane without having to speak, just like in Little League. *Stop screwing around, man. . . . I'm gonna throw the heater.* Rearing back, going into his windup, burning it in there . . . Shane, knowing the pitch without even flashing the sign. Cowhide slapping leather. Fastball. Right down the old pipe.

Strike three, asshole. . . . You're outta there!

4

QUESTIONS

What happened next made no sense at all.

Since Shane had missed his psychiatric appointment because of the accident, he decided to kill the early afternoon pursuing this dilemma. He'd promised Alexa that he'd forget about Jody, forget about seeing his dead best friend tooling along on the San Diego Freeway instead of doing what he was supposed to be doing—gathering dust in an antique urn.

Shane broke his promise to Alexa because he had to. He got Jody's old commanding officer's address from the department newsletter mailing roster, then cabbed home to Venice and picked up his black Acura. Chooch's last spring practice wouldn't finish until six P.M., and Alexa had agreed to pick him up in a department car. Shane had lied, telling her that his shrink appointment had been pushed back and that he'd be late getting out of the psychiatrist's, freeing himself to go see Jody's old captain.

Captain Carl Medwick lived in a *Leave It to Beaver* neighborhood in the West Valley: maple trees, picket fences, tricycles parked unattended in the driveways, as if

L.A. hadn't become the bike-theft capital of the world, not counting Miami and Singapore.

Shane parked out front and looked at the wood-frame house painted a light blue—Subaru blue. He was beginning to loathe that color.

He rang the front doorbell and then, after the door opened, found himself staring into the bloodshot, tear-filled eyes of a handsome middle-aged woman wearing a loose-fitting cotton-print dress and comfortable shoes.

"Excuse me, ma'am. Is Carl Medwick home?" he asked. The question caused the woman to bring a lace handkerchief up to her eyes. It fluttered there and landed hesitantly, like a delicate white butterfly. She didn't answer. He tried again.

"I'm looking for Carl Medwick."

"We all are," she said, her voice weak, almost a whisper. "He's not here. He didn't come home last night."

"Didn't come home?"

"He went to the store and didn't come back. We talked to the police, called all his friends, checked the places he goes, we even checked the hospitals." Rambling all this at Shane, not even knowing who he was but needing to say it to somebody . . . to anybody . . . ticking off the details of her search to convince them both that nothing had been forgotten.

"I'm Shane Scully, a sergeant in the department," he said, stretching the truth. He was really suspended Sergeant Scully. Psychiatrically disoriented and temporarily unassigned Sergeant Scully. But the fib worked, because the woman reached out and clutched his hand. "I'm Doris Medwick, his wife. Please tell me you found him."

Shane held her hand, looked into her bloodshot eyes, and shook his head sadly. "I'm afraid I'm not a part of the Missing Persons Bureau," he said.

"Oh . . ." She hesitated, then went on. "He . . . he was in his woodshop, working . . . building a birdhouse for our granddaughter. He said he needed some materials and would be back in twenty minutes. Then he drove to the store. They found his car in the parking lot at the Hardware Center, but he didn't . . . he wasn't . . ." The handkerchief came up again, fluttering around her face, wiping her eyes, blowing her nose. She was a stout but attractive gray-haired woman in her late sixties with almost translucent white skin.

According to information Shane had collected from several of Medwick's friends, the captain had retired, having pulled the pin two months ago.

"Could I take a look at his shop?" Shane asked.

"What possible good could that do?"

"I'm a detective," he fudged. "Sometimes I find it's a good idea to study the events that occurred just prior to an incident."

"Oh," she said. "The other policemen didn't ask about that." She led him through a house filled with discount furniture. Despite her husband's disappearance, the room was freshly vacuum-tracked and dusted. Shane had witnessed this behavior before. The families of a victim often busied themselves with chores, as if the mere performance of those everyday acts restored order and normalcy. *Look how nice the carpet looks for when he gets home, and I've polished the furniture. Everything is all right.*

Doris Medwick turned on the garage lights and left him alone. Shane found himself looking at a very professional woodshop area. He moved to Captain Medwick's workbench and glanced down at the skill saws and jigs, the power sanders and drills. In the corner, vise-clamped to the bench, was an almost completed prefab birdhouse. The box it came in called it a Squirrel-Proof Robin's Roost and Feeder. The sides were glued and the screws countersunk. The roof had been assembled but not attached, and a plastic water dish was fitted into a wooden feeding tray. It was made of fresh-smelling, unpainted pine and was about two feet square, not counting the pitched roof. It was easy to confirm what had happened: Carl had run out of brass screws. The empty box was on the bench, and two drilled holes in the underside of the birdhouse remained empty. The project lined up with Doris Medwick's story.

Shane stood there, looking down at the unfinished birdhouse while a feeling of deep-seated unease swept over him. Carl Medwick had been Jody's commander at Detective Services Group. Carl had identified Jody's body. He'd finished his tour on the LAPD, pulled the pin, and, thirty-four months after Jody's suicide, had started his retirement. Then yesterday, the day before Shane saw Jody on the San Diego Freeway, Carl runs out of screws, goes to the hardware store, and mysteriously disappears.

The timing of these two events, like the unfinished Robin's Roost, was for the birds. He turned off the lights and left, pausing at the back door to say good-bye.

"You will call if there's anything, anything at all? . . ." the distraught woman pleaded, still not registering the fact that Shane was not part of her husband's missing-persons investigation. He had a strong feeling that Carl Medwick was going to stay lost.

"Absolutely," he said, adding, "Who did you talk to at the Missing Persons Bureau?"

"A woman, Detective Bosterman."

"Thanks. If I get anything, I'll be in touch."

He left, in a hurry to get away from there, lickety-splitting down the trimmed driveway, past the gardening shack by the garage with its neatly stored rakes and hoes and top-folded bag of Lawn-Grow. Mrs. Medwick tracked him from the back porch until he got around the corner. He could feel her bloodshot eyes on him, steady as government radar, pinpointing a spot directly between his shoulders.

*   *   *

It took Shane half an hour to get Lauren Dean's new address, finally finding it through his old Homicide Division, getting Sergeant Bill Hoskins to grab it off the computer for him.

Lauren had moved since Jody died and was now in a small, one-bedroom duplex in a run-down section of Downey.

By the time Shane pulled up, it was already three-thirty in the afternoon and he was scheduled to be at Moonshadows restaurant in Malibu by six forty-five. It was going to be tight.

Shane parked in front of an old, weathered-concrete two-story building with paint-chipped shutters and tried to come up with an approach. How would he tell Lauren that he had seen her dead husband on the freeway just that morning? He sat there, trying to find a subtle opening, finally realizing there just wasn't one. He decided he had to ask straight-out if she'd viewed her husband's body as everyone claimed she had. He could see Jody's old green Chevy Malibu in the drive, so he figured she was home.

Shane climbed out of the car and walked into the courtyard. The building was badly in need of maintenance. The drainpipes were broken at the gutter spouts, the wood trim unpainted and termite-eaten. *What the hell is Lauren Dean doing living in a dump like this?* But in the next instant, he realized the answer: because Jody had committed suicide, the widow wasn't entitled to any Department loss-of-life death benefits.

He rang the bell and stood there while fear swept over him. *What am I afraid of? This is all going to make sense eventually.* It had to. There are no ghosts, no paranormal events. Facts were just missing, and those missing facts were creating a distorted picture. When he filled in the blanks, it would all make perfect sense. . . . *It better start making sense,* he thought.

Lauren Dean opened the door. Since he'd last seen her

two years ago, she'd gained forty pounds and looked twenty years older. Cynicism and disgust had pulled the once happy curve of her mouth down into a permanent scowl that she seemed completely unaware of. Once beautiful—stunning, in fact—Lauren Dean was now plump and used up: her skin mottled, her clothing dirty, her fingernails a nerve-frayed war zone of nibbled cuticles. It was as if he were looking at somebody else—the ghost of Lauren Dean, or her ugly older sister.

"Shane?" she said, and he could smell scotch on her breath.

"Lauren, I need to talk to you about Jody."

She looked at him for a moment, not moving or breathing. "Jody?" she finally said.

Again, he could smell the liquor. "Could I come in?"

A hard question for her. He could see indecision seesaw back and forth in her pale green eyes. Then she stepped back reluctantly and let him into the apartment.

The place was a mess. Round pizza boxes dotted the living-room furniture like giant tomato-stained mushrooms. Shane picked a spot on the sofa and sat across from Lauren.

"What about Jody?" she challenged.

"Lauren . . . I need to find out something. It's gonna sound a little strange, so hang with me here, but I think I saw someone today on the San Diego Freeway who looked a lot like Jody. In fact, exactly like him."

"Oh, Jesus, gimme a fucking break." She snorted a puff of stale scotch at him.

"I know . . . I know . . . but it's bugging me and I just wanted to get clear on this. When they called you after he . . . after he . . . did the . . . did the . . ." Shane couldn't say it, even now, almost three years later.

"You mean after he blew his fucking head off?" Lauren finished the thought for him, bitterness and anger stretched across her face, pulling her mouth down farther, flattening her features like a nylon stocking mask on a drugstore bandit.

"Yeah, after they found him. They called you down to the ME's office. Did you get a good look at the body? Was it him? Were you absolutely sure? 'Cause the guy I saw . . . I didn't talk to him, but it looked like he recognized me. . . . I could sorta read it in his eyes."

"I always used t'wonder about you two guys finishing each other's sentences, like you were hooked together by cable," she said, not answering his question. "After I first married him, before Jody ate the nine and turned my whole life to shit, he used to say he thought you and he had both been the same person in another life, said he could tell what you were thinking, say it before you said it."

"He could—sometimes he could."

"And now . . . it's hard for you without him, you miss him. So subconsciously you're trying to bring him back."

Shane started to answer, but stopped. Was that what he was doing?

"Let him go, Shane. Let Jody go. He's dead. Believe me, I know. D-E-A-D. Dead." And then she smiled at him. A ghastly smile it was, too. Her teeth were tobacco-stained, and her new double chin quivered. "Let the motherfucker go. Hasn't he done enough to the both of us? Hasn't he?"

"Did you identify the body like it says in the death report?" he persisted.

"Yeah. Yeah, I looked at him. The back of his head was gone, but it was him. It was our precious, go-to-hell Jody, no doubt about it. I don't know who you saw on the freeway, but it wasn't him. Jody walked out on us, babe. The selfish prick put that cannon in his mouth and blew all three of us away with one shot."

Shane looked at the wreckage that was now Lauren Dean. He wondered how she could have let this happen.

"I'm sorry, but you can't stay," she said abruptly. "I was just going out. . . . I have an appointment." She slurred the word *appointment,* missing most of the consonants.

She stood and led him to the entry, anxious to have him out of her house. She opened the door and stood by it as he walked behind her in the underlit hallway.

As he was about to pass by her, he saw something that stopped him, made him reevaluate everything she had just said. Jody Dean had zeroed himself out—taken a pine box retirement. Yet there, on the table in the hall, was an unopened envelope just like the one Shane got every two weeks from the City Payroll Department.

She led him out into the late-afternoon sunlight and closed the door without saying good-bye. He stood there on the porch, his mind reeling. "What the fuck is going on here?" he whispered softly. One more in a series of unanswerable questions. *If Jody committed suicide like everybody says, why is his widow still getting paychecks?*

5

DINNER

Moonshadows sat above the rocky beach in Malibu. Waves rolled under it in sets, crashing on the rocks below, throwing a fine sea mist up into the air that refracted in the setting sun.

Buddy, the breakfast-food sales and marketing executive, was already there with Alexa and Chooch, telling a story. Buddy was round-shouldered and pear-shaped with a bushy head of hair, which salt-and-peppered his massive head. ". . . so the sales rep is telling me he can't sign up the tri-state area, 'cause the little guys, the minimarkets and such, won't compete with the huge category killers—the chains like Ralph's or Vons—on new product lines. I tell the guy: Stop crying, this is a candy store problem, 'cause our money is just as green as theirs, and all you gotta do is find the right palm to grease. Give the local rack-jobber his blood money."

Alexa looked up and saw Shane approach, jumping to her feet to give him a hug.

"Buddy, I'd like you to meet Shane." Alexa was trying to orchestrate everything.

Shane shook Buddy's big fleshy hand. Buddy was soft and out of shape, but he was big, almost six-four.

After the introductions, they all sat down to a tense meal where Shane felt more and more like the main course.

"So how bad did Alex's car get mashed?" Buddy asked, getting the conversation rolling. He seemed to call her Alex instead of Alexa, as if it somehow made her one of the boys.

The evening crawled by like a half-crushed bug dragging itself across a four-lane highway. By nine o'clock, Buddy had eaten his main course and half of Alexa's and was just finishing the third basket of complimentary bread, ordering his sister to get a new basket after each one was emptied.

When Buddy wasn't treating Alexa like a servant, he was patronizing her. Never once did he bring up the Medal of Valor award she was going to receive on Sunday. His sister was being given a huge honor, the LAPD's highest, yet he didn't seem to care. It was hard for Shane to believe that someone he loved and looked up to would allow herself to be so overrun by this loud breakfast-food salesman.

Chooch stayed quiet, trying to keep out of the cross fire, while Buddy switched from the subject of Alexa's car to questions about Shane's medical leave.

"So, it's like some kinda shrink deal?" he asked, a concerned frown pulling two caterpillar-shaped eyebrows toward each other. "But, you're okay, though, I hope?" Smiling now. "You're not gonna snap and start comin' at us with a razor?"

"I'm fine. It's no big deal," Shane said, choking back several more confrontational replies.

"In police work, psychiatric reviews are standard," Alexa explained less than truthfully.

"But it's with a shrink, right? A psychiatrist," Buddy

persisted. "The LAPD *makes* Shane go and see a head doctor. That's what got me worried, 'cause you don't see that happen in business unless the guy's parked out in the ozone, where the buses don't run."

By ten o'clock, it was mercifully over. Alexa drove Buddy to his hotel. Shane drove Chooch back to their house. Alexa showed up half an hour later and met them in the backyard.

"So, what did you think?" she asked anxiously, wanting his approval.

"Quite a guy," he said evasively.

"But did you like him?" she persisted.

"More to the point, do you think he liked me?" Shane said, hedging.

"He's a little judgmental sometimes, I admit. But you'll learn to love him. He just wants what's best for me."

"He sure orders you around a lot," he finally contributed.

"I'm used to taking care of him. Mother died, so by the time I was ten, I did all the housework, all the cleaning, for Dad and Buddy. I guess he just got used to me doing things."

"Alex, can you get us tickets to *The Producers*?" Shane mimicked. "Can you go ask the waiter to get us more bread? He doesn't have a broken leg, does he?"

"So, you didn't like him?"

"Yeah, I liked him. It's just . . . He treats you a little like hired help."

Then Chooch saved him: "What Dad is saying is, we're used to seeing you be in charge. You're everything around here for us, and we always want to do stuff for *you*. It's a little different seeing you with your brother . . . but we think it's neat the way you take care of him. That's what he meant."

"Exactly what I meant." He smiled at her.

Chooch went inside to do his homework while they sat in the backyard, looking out over the Venice canals.

Venice was located halfway between Santa Monica and Marina Del Rey. It had been built by Abbot Kinney in the thirties, to resemble the canals and bridges of Venice, Italy, but the eight-block area had gone downhill. Just two blocks from the ocean, it still managed to retain a sense of quaint, rustic charm, but the once grand houses and reproduction gondolas had been replaced by fiberglass rowboats and a mixture of stucco houses and wood-frame tilt-ups.

Regardless, Shane loved his little house. It spoke to him in ways he found hard to describe. He and Alexa sat in his metal lawn chairs, watching the moonlight waver on the still waters of the shallow canals.

"Aside from wrecking my car and seeing Jody's ghost," she said, trying to be lighthearted about it, "how was the rest of your day?"

"Fine."

"I hope you didn't do something else—start running around investigating the Jody thing."

He didn't answer.

"I'm just interested," she said softly. "And a little worried."

"Captain Medwick is missing. He was building a birdhouse for his granddaughter, then went to the hardware store for brass screws yesterday and didn't come back."

She sat quietly, her cop instincts buzzing with this fact, just as his had. "Doesn't have to be connected," she finally said.

"I know."

After that they both fell silent awhile. Then he gave her the rest of it: "I also went to see Lauren Dean. She says that it was definitely Jody on the coroner's tray. She said the back of his head was blown off."

Alexa didn't say anything.

"Only thing wrong with that is, I think she's lying," he said.

"Why would she lie about something like that?"

"Because she's still getting paid by the city. There was a City Payroll Department envelope on her hall table. If Jody shot himself, why would the city be paying her death benefits?"

"There could be lots of reasons. She could owe money to the credit union and be getting statements, or it could be tax material . . . or she . . ." Alexa stopped and looked over at him critically as he leaned down and pulled out a blade of grass, then stuck it in his mouth.

"You're not gonna give up on this, are you?"

"I'm just telling you what I saw."

"I'm gonna set up a meeting for you with Commander Shephard."

"Why are you gonna do that?" Shane asked, instantly wary.

"I want him to show you Jody's autopsy report and crime-scene pictures. He could get those for you. He heads the Detective Services Group. They supervise SIS. Jody was in Special Investigations when he died, so Commander Shephard can pull all that stuff from the custodian of department records at the Personnel Division. He can get it for you without turning it into a three-act play. You've gotta get this off your mind."

Shane sat there, chewing on the grass stalk, turning it between his teeth, feeling it tickling his tongue. "Good idea," he finally said. "Thanks. I'd really like to see all that."

"How soon do you want to go see him?" she asked.

"How 'bout tomorrow?" he answered softly.

THE GOOD SHEPHERD

"After you get used to it, it's not so bad here," Jody said. "It's not heaven, but it's not hell. You'd like it, Shane. We got everything we need." Jody was talking to Shane, but he was lying in his casket. The back of his head was missing and he had on his old Pirates' Little League uniform. It was stretched tight over his adult body, his pitcher's mitt laid ceremoniously across his chest.

"Everything you need?" Shane asked. He was wearing his old catcher's gear but was having trouble keeping the mask on straight. It kept sliding around on his head, blocking his view.

"Everything we need, 'cept one thing . . ."

"What's that?"

"Coca-Cola. Can you beat it? No Cokes here, and me with my sugar jones raging all the time."

"No Coca-Cola?" Shane asked, dumbfounded. "I never thought about the hereafter not having Cokes. You'd think they'd have 'em if you asked."

Then Jody sat up, leaving his brains behind. "Dammit,"

he said, looking down at the bloody mess on the white satin pillow. "That keeps happening."

Suddenly Shane woke up. He lay in his bed, staring up at the ceiling. It took him two hours to get back to sleep.

Mark Shephard's office was on the sixth floor of Parker Center—the administrative floor.

Shane and Alexa got off onto the seafoam-green carpet, then walked down the corridor, past the blond-paneled doors, where the four deputy chiefs and the super chief had their offices.

The Detective Services Group, which Shephard commanded, was in the Office of Operations and supervised five detective divisions: Bunko-Forgery, Burglary–Auto Theft, Detective Headquarters, Robbery-Homicide, and the Detective Support Division, which included the controversial Special Investigations Section (SIS), where Jody had been assigned when he took his life.

SIS had come under a lot of fire in the press recently because it was a super-secret section, with a very unusual operating technique. Their critics claimed they would target predicate felons, usually parolees just out of some Level 4 institution. All of their targets had long, violent criminal histories. It was alleged that they would set up surveillance on the scumbag, often lying back and just watching while the ex-con bought illegal street artillery at some gun drop (a fresh felony and parole violation) or hung out making criminal plans with some other "yoked" and "sleeved" ex-cell soldier (also a parole violation). They wouldn't bust the target for these violations but would wait until he and his ex-con buddies finally pulled some major Class A felony: a holdup, armed robbery, kidnapping—you name it. The members of SIS would follow the targets away from the crime and exercise their patented car-jamming maneuver. This consisted of speeding up in two or three department plainwraps, then jamming the target vehicle to the curb . . . whereupon six or seven adrenalized, heavily armed cops would do high-risk takedown. As a result, SIS had bought a large percentage of these assholes seats on the ark. Because of the high body count, and growing number of incidents where civilians were accidentally injured or almost killed by stray gunfire, city activists were constantly gunning for the unit, and SIS was always in the pot, on slow boil.

Jody had been in SIS for almost a year before he ate his gun in the division parking lot. A lot of people said it was the pressure of the unit that brought him to suicide, but Shane knew that Jody relished the work there. He said he loved the rush, the adrenalized risk taking. But most of all he loved "capping assholes."

They had discussed SIS a month before Jody died. It had turned into one of their few really bad arguments. Shane hated the unit and everything it stood for. SIS was holding court in the street and, to his way of thinking, was little more than a death squad. Shane had left Jody's house moments before the argument got violent.

Alexa's office was down the hall, on seven. She was the XO of the Detective Services Group and the only sergeant officed there. She'd been given a small room, with no window and a shared secretary. As Shane and Alexa waited in her office, they heard Mark Shephard come in and get his coffee. They were told by his secretary that he would see Shane after he went through his mail.

"What'd you tell him about why I wanted to see the file?" Shane asked while they waited.

"I told him the truth, that you saw somebody who looked like Jody on the freeway and that you wanted to set your mind at ease."

"Jesus, Alexa, I'm in the middle of a ding-a-ling review. That's all I need right now."

"What else can we tell him?"

"I was gonna say Lauren asked me to look at the file. That she needed some information for his life insurance or something and couldn't bear to see that stuff again."

"He's not a moron, Shane. He wouldn't go for that. Besides, we can trust him. He's a friend."

"He's *your* friend. I barely know him."

"They don't call him the 'Good Shepherd' for nothing," she smiled. "He's good people; he won't blow you in."

A uniformed lieutenant in her late twenties appeared in the doorway. "The commander is ready now."

Mark Shephard was a climber in the department, but he was an unusual mix—a uniform-friendly commander who also had Glass House suck and deft political skills. He reminded Shane a lot of his first Boy Scout leader: tall and good-looking, with a tan complexion and blond hair. Mark Shephard's blue eyes crinkled with what seemed like ever friendly amusement.

"Sorry to keep you waiting, Sergeant," Shephard said. He wore his blue-steel revolver on his belt in a Yaqui slide holster, the flap snapped down over a black checkered grip. A lot of Glass House politicians, who had done the minimum amount of street work, packed chrome-plated, custom-gripped artillery—but not the Good Shepherd. This was a no-nonsense piece. He had his coat off, and Shane could see that he stayed fit.

"Thanks for seeing me," Shane said.

"Any friend of Alexa's . . . I'm really proud about the ceremony, her getting the MOV. As her commander, I'm honored to be reading the citation this Sunday, before Tony gives her the award." Tony was the new chief of police—Tony Filosiani—a street cop from New York who had applied for the job of top cop in L.A. after Chief Brewer was arrested. He had been chosen over other candidates because of his record of turning around morale in troubled departments. Los Angeles had had a string of police crises, from Rodney King to the Rampart Division scandal to the Naval Yard disaster.

Chief Filosiani was short and round and talked out of the side of his mouth in New York Brooklynese. As a result of this and his penchant for large pinky rings, he had been dubbed the Day-Glo Dago.

"I guess the best thing is to just take a look at Sergeant Dean's death package," Shephard said, interrupting his train of thought.

Shane nodded.

Commander Shephard pushed the folders over. Shane sat down in the chair opposite the desk and opened them.

Shane had never seen Jody in death. He'd pictured it in his mind, of course, but his subconscious had neatly sanitized it. His imagination was nothing like the photographs. As he opened the folder, his stomach lurched. His throat constricted. It was worse than he expected. In the pictures, Jody was sprawled in the front seat of a department plainwrap.

The details were graphic: the puckered blood-drained lips, the huge hole blasting away half of the back of his head, the green flies feasting on heavy arterial ooze. Shane could see Jody's gun, the big Israeli Desert Eagle he'd been using at the end. The .44 magnum automatic was light in weight but 30 percent bigger than the old army .45. It dangled in death, at the end of Jody's broken finger, like a child's forgotten toy. The recoil had obviously snapped his index finger, and as a result, the gun hadn't flown from his hand as was normal in most suicides.

Shane went through the autopsy and crime-scene pictures carefully, forcing himself to study them: Jody slumped in the front seat leaking fluid fatally; Jody on the coroner's table. The clinical labeling screamed from the bottom of each photo: anterior angle, medial angle, proximal and midline photos; right side, left side, overhead. Jody, naked on a steel autopsy tray, bathed in sterile lighting and antiseptic brutality.

Finally Shane went to the autopsy report itself. The ME's phrases jumping up, posting themselves forever on his memory: "massive trauma," "self-inflicted gunshot wound," "destroyed distal portion of the cerebellum." Then the death terms: "cadaveric spasm," "adipocere," and "acute cyanosis."

Shane read it all, finally closing the folder. He looked up at Commander Mark Shephard, who had turned his attention to the mail on his desk but now felt the gaze and lifted his friendly blue eyes to meet Shane's. "Well?" the Good Shepherd said. "What do you think?"

"I must have been wrong," Shane answered softly.

7

NIGHT MUSIC

The phone screamed in his ear. He clambered up out of a restless sleep. *Where's the damned clock? What the fuck . . . ? What time is it?* Focusing now on the lit dial, trying to read it: a few minutes after two in the middle of the night. *You gotta be kidding.* He grabbed the phone, fumbling it out of the cradle.

"Yeah?" his voice raspberried.

"How they hangin', bro?" Jody's voice was grinning, having fun with this back-from-the-grave moment.

Shane bolted upright in bed, his heart immediately slamming with adrenaline, banging unevenly, a four-barrel engine with a bad cam. He was gripping the receiver hard, his knuckles turning white, his palm instantly slick on the instrument. "Jody? Is this Jody?"

"Back from the Great Department in the Sky. Thought you and I needed a little night music," his term for the late-night talks they had during sleepovers as kids.

Shane was wide awake in less than thirty seconds; sleep was quickly broomed away like corner cobwebs. He swung his feet off the bed. Got them down onto the floor for stability.

"Why? . . . Why? . . . Why did you do it? Why did you make us think you were dead? I cried, man. It really fucked me up."

"Hey, it's just police work, Salsa. I'm doin' a job." Jody had nicknames for everyone; nicknames were a "Jody" thing. He'd called Shane "Salsa" or "Hot Sauce" almost from the beginning, because in the old days when they were children, Shane had a short fuse and often couldn't control his temper.

"You're still on the job?" Shane said, trying to pin down that fact. "With the department?"

"Yeah, but you didn't hear it here. I'm working UC."

"You're undercover?" Astounded, still trying to find the edges of it. In his heart he had known that Jody was alive from that first moment he saw him on the freeway last Friday, but hearing his voice was different—spooky, surreal.

"It's a big laydown, so a few of my old road dogs and me been bustin' moves and doin' doors on some serious assholes." "Doin' doors" was an old term referring to cops stealing from drug houses but more recently had come to mean any activity where cops cheated to get busts. Shane took a deep breath to settle down. It was unbelievable . . . Jody on the phone, in the middle of the night, talking trash, sounding wired. "We found out there are a few moles in the Clerical Division who would've given us away if we got regular paychecks. This is a big hustle, Salsa. Lots of chips on the table. We needed to work the bust from the inside."

"What bust?"

"Hey, come on . . . You know better than to ask that."

"Jody . . . I . . . Look, Jody, I have to see you."

"Ain't gonna happen. Can't happen. Reason I called is, I know you'll pull on this thread till you unravel the whole sweater, and that could fuck me up. You gotta chill, brother. You gotta leave this behind. Forget you saw me. Don't plex up on me, Salsa."

"Plex up"—a prison term meaning to get complex. *Why is he using con lingo?*

"Does Lauren know?" Shane asked.

"No, I cut a deal with my CO. . . . Told 'em she wasn't solid . . . she'd give us up. I needed to get out of that. It took a while, and I had to pull some juice downtown, but in the end, the department went along. She thinks I'm dead." But he said all of this slowly, as if considering it a word at a time. Shane figured it could mean anything.

"She's not doing well, Jody. She's gained weight. She's become an afternoon drinker."

"Hey, Salsa, shit happens. I made a mistake with her. I thought it was love, but it was just my dick. She's okay. She's got my police pension. I got a medical pass on the suicide. They said it was caused by psychiatric stress, so it protects my death benefits. 'At's the best I can do. After this job, I'm gating out . . . gonna get small, shake off the drag line."

More prison lingo. "Gating out" was release from custody. "Drag lines" were prisoner restraints, linking cons together.

"So, Shane . . . I called 'cause I didn't want you to mess me up. A lot of people could get fucked unless you keep this to yourself. I hadda eat some shit to get my people to stay frosty. A few guys wanted to send you some GBH." More prison talk: "grievous bodily harm."

"Jody, is this sanctioned?" he heard himself ask. But he knew it didn't matter how Jody answered. He knew he couldn't trust anything he said.

"I'm not working off my badge, Hot Sauce. I'm just working off the books. Do yourself a favor and forget you saw me. Forget we were both on the 405. It didn't happen. Do that, and everything stays right side up."

"And if I don't?"

"Don't even suggest it, man. I Jodyized this deal! Make me a hero with my troops. I told 'em you'd see it my way—*our way*. I told 'em you were good people. And, Salsa, don't tell anybody about this call. With your current problems, those squints in the Glass House are gonna black-flag what's left of your career."

"Where's Carl Medwick?" Shane asked suddenly.

"How the fuck should I know? Home in bed, I guess."

"He disappeared the day before I saw you."

"Now you're acting like a complete asshole. If you keep this up, it won't come out good."

"So you're threatening me now?" Shane said, his voice turning cold with anger and betrayal.

"I'm just passing along information. Use it, or don't."

Then there was a long, tension-filled pause. Shane could hear Jody breathing. Both of them were waiting to see what would happen next. Finally, it was Jody who broke the silence.

"So, that's all I wanted to tell you. Miss you, man. Sorry we can't lay in together."

"Lay in"—prison lingo for a meeting.

"I'll see ya, Salsa. You're still my catcher, like always. Dig this pitch outta the dirt for me. Go Pirates!" And then he was gone.

Shane sat on the corner of his bed for a long time, stunned. The receiver finally started beeping in his hand. He dropped the handset back in the cradle, got up, walked out, and sat in one of the white metal chairs in the back-yard. He felt the cool ocean breeze drying the sweat on his face. He stared at the moonlit canals, trying to sort out what Jody had told him.

Is it possible? he wondered. Could the LAPD be work-ing a deep sting so dangerous and sensitive that they would fake the deaths of Jody and several other officers? Would they take them off the books, so some criminal snitch working in the Clerical Division wouldn't spot a paycheck coming through and sell the information to a crime syndicate? Was it possible that these guys would leave their wives and that the department would arrange for their families to be paid with death-benefit checks and then just let them disappear? It was almost too bizarre to contemplate. Except for one thing . . .

Shane was pretty sure the new chief wouldn't have anything to do with it. The Day-Glo Dago might talk out of the side of his mouth and wear a New York pinky ring, but his reputation for honesty was well known.

Burleigh Brewer, the old chief, whom Shane had caught with his hand in the money jar, was a rule bender, and rule benders always hired people who go along and don't ask questions—people like Deputy Chief Mayweather. Only Mayweather was dead—a suicide after Shane broke him on the Naval Yard case. Chief Brewer was still alive; however, he was on trial and wasn't going to admit to putting an illegal unit into deep cover, paying their wives with death checks. Even if Brewer was in on it, which he may not have been, and even if Shane could prove it, Brewer would blame it on Mayweather or some other cop who wasn't around to argue. The old chief wouldn't say anything that would adversely affect his case in court. That door was closed. Even so, it was possible that the corruption that spawned the Naval Yard disaster could have also given rise to this.

He sat there, his mind chewing it over. What should he do? How should he play it?

Tomorrow afternoon Alexa was getting the Medal of Valor. Maybe after the celebration dinner, after he had taken Buddy back to the airport, maybe then he could ask her advice. Alexa had political savvy without being a politician. She'd know what to do.

Shane had no evidence of the call from Jody. He'd get AT&T to print out his phone records, but he knew Jody would have used a public booth—a number that was un-traceable.

Don't plex up on me, Salsa, his old friend had said.

"Well, fuck you, Jody," Shane whispered into the night wind, the anger and betrayal so intense that acid reflux burned in his throat. *If you didn't love me enough to say good-bye . . . if you could let me carry your coffin and cry into your ashes, if you didn't trust me or Lauren, the people who loved you, then bring on the GBH, buddy. . . .'Cause I'm gonna find out what the hell you're up to. . . .*

He was still sitting in the metal chair, churning and making plans, when the sun came up Sunday morning.

8

MORE THAN THE EYE CAN SEE

Chooch and Shane went shopping for Alexa's ring on Sunday morning. Murray Steinberg opened his store in the Jewelry Mart on Spring Street at ten, turned on the lights, and began showing them diamonds. Murray was tall, rail-thin, and nerdy. He always seemed to be rubbing his palms together like a huge skeletal insect but had a heart the size of Minnesota.

Shane had been the primary on Sharon Steinberg's rape/murder. She was Murray's sister and only living relative. It had been a particularly gruesome crime that had happened almost three years ago. Shane had promised Murray that he would never let it slide to the back of his too-crowded homicide folder. Sharon Steinberg had been tied up, mutilated, and raped in her own bed before she finally, mercifully died from loss of blood.

The twenty-four/twenty-four-hour rule dominates most homicide cases. This unwritten rule states that the last twenty-four hours of a victim's life and the first twenty-four hours after the murder is committed are the two most important time periods in the investigation. The reason being that a victim's actions just prior to the crime are just as important in determining the killer as mistakes the perp makes in the first twenty-four hours after the murder. If nothing happens during these two time spans to help solve the investigation, chances are good that the crime will go uncleared.

Because of the vast workloads in L.A. Homicide, with two or three fresh murders hitting the duty board every day, most homicide detectives put old, unsolved cases on the back burner. Because of administrative pressure to keep clearance percentages up, cops always focus on the fresh crimes, where the likelihood of success is higher. The unsolved cases are technically still active, but not actively policed.

In the case of Murray Steinberg's sister, Shane had become so incensed by the level of perimortem violence that he refused to stop working the case. He knew that the perp was in the psychiatric category of "sadistic rapist," a man who had tortured and humiliated Sharon Steinberg before her death, dehumanizing her during the rape, making her an actress in his sexual fantasy. Shane had given up his days off for almost six months, working without overtime. Finally, he had managed to turn a witness that eventually led to the arrest of a thirty-year-old carpet cleaner and weekend dust bunny named Grady White. Grady was a hot-prowl burglar who cased his jobs when he cleaned carpets. He had entered the house to steal appliances but, after seeing Sharon asleep, had descended into glazed sexual rage, finally torturing, raping, and killing her. In Grady's house there were Polaroids neatly pasted into a memory book of not only Sharon's rape-murder but ten others. Shane got him prosecuted and convicted on six of the ten. Four women pictured in his book remained unidentified. Grady was currently awaiting a July 10 execution at San Quentin.

That was why Murray had opened his store on a Sunday and was now showing Chooch and Shane VS-1 diamonds at wholesale prices. Technically, Shane probably should have refused the bargain, but somewhere in the back of his head, he reasoned that it was the right solution. Murray was finally paying Shane back for months of tireless work on Sharon's murder, and Shane was getting a ring he could otherwise not afford.

Shane finally settled for a perfect stone at slightly over two carats, which would have retailed for around five thousand dollars. Murray refused to take a cent more than cost, which he maintained was thirty-four hundred. The old jeweler left the showroom with a platinum setting to make up the ring so Shane could take it with him.

Chooch and Shane sat silently, looking at the other diamonds glittering on the black velvet show cloth. They looked like stars in a cloudless night sky.

Finally, Murray returned with Shane's ring, now twinkling in a classic setting with two diamond baguettes on each side, which Shane had not paid for.

"My wedding gift," Murray said when Shane asked about them.

Shane thanked the embarrassed jeweler, who said, "Acht, is nothing. I'm wishing I could do more, my friend."

Soon Shane and Chooch were back on the street with the box burning a hole in Shane's pocket, the ring inside waiting to be slipped onto Alexa's slender finger.

"When you gonna give it to her?" Chooch asked nervously.

"At a romantic dinner tonight, after Buddy leaves."

"Good move," Chooch agreed. "Wait'll he's outta town. That guy could sink a Carnival Cruise."

"You don't think it's too soon?" Shane asked, suddenly nervous. "The Medal of Valor and this ring, all in one day?"

"Go for it, man."

*   *   *

The Medal of Valor ceremony took place at three in the afternoon, in the Jack Webb Auditorium at the Police Academy, where the LAPD had their biannual graduation ceremonies. The academy was a cluster of Spanish-style buildings located in Elysian Park in the foothills, at the end of a long, two-lane drive. Shane always thought the Police Academy looked like a Spanish hotel or a Franciscan mission, sprawled on its ten landscaped acres, including a full athletic field, swimming pool, and shooting range.

Shane and Chooch got there half an hour early and parked in the reserved-parking lot, already almost full with TV news vans. The annual awarding of the Medal of Valor was always a big deal in L.A. Besides Alexa, there were four other officers receiving the honor, but it was Alexa the press had turned out to see.

The high-profile case that she and Shane had broken eventually made the cover of *Time* magazine, a full picture of an LAPD shield with a black ribbon across it. The article was titled "Grieving the Police."

There were stories in the issue about the Detroit and Philadelphia police scandals as well as NYPD's problems, but the Long Beach Naval Yard case turned out to be the granddaddy of them all. Alexa's picture was in a sidebar describing her incredible heroics.

Shane and Chooch walked into the auditorium, which was already almost full. He saw Buddy up near the front. Shane waved at him, but Buddy either pretended not to see him or had decided to ignore him.

A tall, good-looking lieutenant in plain clothes from Press Relations grabbed Shane moments after he arrived.

"Sergeant . . . good. I was hoping I'd spot you. We have a special place for you," the lieutenant said. His ID was in a badge holder hanging upside down in his suit pocket like a Spanish leather bat.

"What about my son?"

"He can sit here. We thought you'd want to be up close."

"Go ahead, Shane," Chooch said, grinning. "I'm cool." Then he plopped down in the back.

Shane was led out of the auditorium, along a side corridor, and into a small room with a TV monitor that showed a picture of the empty podium.

"You can see it better from here."

"Whatta you kidding me, Loo?" Shane said, using the nickname reserved for all lieutenants while glowering at the handsome recruiting-poster officer. "I'm supposed to watch it back here, on TV?"

"Look, Sergeant." The Press Relations officer was now talking slowly, as if addressing an irritating child. "The last thing we need today is to have the press make *you* the story." He looked at Shane hopefully. "I'm sure you want Sergeant Hamilton's day to go smoothly."

Shane knew in his heart that the man was probably right, so he finally nodded, but it still pissed him off. Shane was being hidden away like a leper. He reached into his pocket and secretly wrapped his fingers around the jewelry box containing Alexa's diamond ring. "Okay," he finally said. "But will you tell Alexa I'm here?"

"Of course. Absolutely." It sounded like bullshit rolling smoothly out of the handsome press officer's mouth.

"Hey, Loo, no kidding . . . she needs to know I'm here."

"I wouldn't kid about this, Sergeant. I never kid about anything," he said, revealing a shred of his humorless personality. Then he turned and left Shane alone in the room.

That was when the third strange thing happened.

Shane watched on the color TV in the isolation room as the event was postponed for almost fifteen minutes. He slipped out of his makeshift holding cell and found out that Commander Shephard, who was scheduled to read Alexa's citation, had not yet arrived.

As a result, the award ceremony began half an hour late, and the other four officers received their MOVs first. Their commanders all read their commendations, then the chief awarded the medals. Then it was Alexa's turn. Since Mark Shephard had still not shown up, Chief Tony Filosiani stepped to the microphone and ad-libbed some remarks:

"Obviously, I was still back East, running da Rye, New York, department, when all dis happened," he said in Day-Glo Dago Brooklynese. "Now dat I'm here in Los Angeles and have had the opportunity of dealing with all of you, I wanna say, I'm humbled by the extreme bravery Sergeant Alexa Hamilton displayed in the completion of her assigned task. We all should take pride in her profound dedication to her duty, and to the people of dis city." He turned from the podium and faced her.

"Sergeant Hamilton, you are among the finest officers I have ever been privileged to command, an it is with great pride dat I present you wit' dis, our department's highest honor."

Alexa blushed, standing at attention in her blue pressed and starched uniform, her black hair shining.

Shane had not returned to the Press Relations room; he was standing in the auditorium's wings, looking out at her. He, like Chief Filosiani, was also very proud of her, while at the same time experiencing a sinking feeling of concern for the missing Commander Shephard.

Has he disappeared like Captain Medwick, his predecessor at DSG?

Chief Filosiani read the citation. It described how, while she was at Internal Affairs, Alexa became aware of a high degree of police malfeasance involving a Hispanic gang named the Hoover Street Bounty Hunters, whose turf was located around the L.A. Coliseum. She discovered that arrested gang members were easily escaping from the police cars in that division. They were often not Mirandized, so their cases were thrown out of court. On one occasion, an arrested Bounty Hunter had been left unattended and just got out of the back of a squad car and walked away. The citation explained that these police screwups had been sent to IAD, where Alexa had noticed that police officers in these incidents were all involved with Shane's dead ex-partner, Ray Molar. Alexa had followed the trail of this investigation to a huge real-estate scam involving the defunct Long Beach Naval Yard. LAPD Chief Burleigh Brewer and L.A. Mayor Clark Crispin had been silent partners in that venture and were arrested two weeks later. The citation further stated that in the apprehension of the criminals, Sergeant Hamilton had been severely wounded. Of course, Shane, who had originally brought all of this to Alexa's attention and had helped solve the case, was not mentioned in either the citation or the chief's portrayal of her heroism.

As he stood in the wings, Shane had a fleeting moment of jealousy and anger directed at Alexa. How had it come to pass that no matter what he did on the job, he always seemed to come out a loser? He knew the answer as soon as he asked the question. He tended to grate on his superiors. Shane had, on occasion, tried to be politically correct, to kiss ass, but it never came off right; plus he hated the taste it left on his lips. Alexa, on the other hand, never kissed ass but seemed to have the ability to get her points across without rancor. She was tough and uncompromising; somehow, unlike Shane, she didn't irritate everyone in the process.

He ultimately had to admit that his failure had been more a question of style than substance. He stuffed these ungallant thoughts away, then watched as Alexa stepped forward after the citation was read and the chief hung the medal around her neck. It glistened there, shining in the

TV lights, as the room full of people applauded.

A press and media buffet in the Police Academy cafeteria followed. In its typical killjoy fashion, the department served soft drinks instead of champagne. People stood around in clusters, stealing looks at their watches and saying what a wonderful ceremony it had been. Shane hugged Alexa, then, while she accepted congratulations from staff rank officers, he moved through the room, again looking for Commander Shephard, who had still not arrived.

The Press Relations lieutenant worked Shane like a sheepdog, screening him from the media, herding him here and there, trying to keep him away from anybody holding a mike or a camera. Shane, of course, obliged willingly, not wanting to begin another round of negative press coverage on the case or embarrass Alexa.

Finally, Shane and Chooch were back in the Academy parking lot, looking at the rear door of the Jack Webb Auditorium, waiting for Alexa to come out.

"That was cool," Chooch said, not realizing that Commander Shephard's no-show was a potentially dark omen.

"Yeah," Shane said, holding the leather ring box inside his pants pocket, gripping it, feeling the corners digging into his palm. "Listen, Chooch, I'm gonna go for the quarterback camp. I think that's a good deal. I called the coach, and he's setting it up."

"You sure we can afford it, man?"

"Yep. Gotta do it."

"It starts in two days. I could probably go up a few days late."

"Nope. You gotta be there when it starts. I'll figure out the plane reservations when I take Buddy to the airport." Shane let go of the ring box, reached out, and put his hand on Chooch's shoulder. "But I'm gonna miss you, man."

"Maybe you can come up and watch."

"I'll try," he said, but he already knew what he was going to be doing. The quarterback camp would put Chooch in Palo Alto, safely out of Jody Dean's reach, because he didn't know how ruthless Jody had become. Right now, Shane wouldn't put anything past him.

Alexa walked out of the Jack Webb Auditorium and over to the car. She had changed out of her dress blues and was wearing a plain black skirt, white blouse, and heels, carrying the uniform in a hanging bag, smiling as she approached the car. The MOV was in a gold-lettered leather box stuffed under her arm, significantly larger and more elegant than the box in Shane's pocket.

"Great ceremony," he said giving her a hug.

Chooch did the same. They stood in the Police Academy parking lot, all shifting their weight awkwardly.

"Next stop, dinner with Buddy," she said. Buddy had left the ceremony shortly after it was over. "He had to go back to the hotel and get packed," she alibied.

"So what happened to Mark Shephard?" Shane finally asked. "That was strange, wasn't it?"

"I don't know. I called his office and his house, but there was no answer," she said.

A heavy cloud passed overhead, further darkening the parking lot and the moment.

"Listen, I think on the way to dinner, we should swing by Shephard's house," Shane said. "There could be more here than the eye can see. This guy is a Glass House commander. I doubt he'd miss a chance to make the six o'clock news."

"It *is* pretty strange," she agreed.

"So, let's do it." Shane said. And that decision took them one step further down the road to disaster.

9

DUTCH TREAT

Shane and Chooch followed Alexa's department-issue
Crown Vic to Commander Mark Shephard's house in the
Valley. It was strange, Shane thought, that Alexa knew
exactly where he lived. They pulled up in front of a small
Spanish-style bungalow—typical L.A. construction from
the mid-forties. The house had a red-tile roof, arched
doorways, and a small, neatly trimmed front lawn. A spill
of purple bougainvillea garlanded off a garage trellis.

"This is it," she said, exiting her car and joining them
at the curb.

Shane stole a glance at her. "How many times you
been here?" he asked with forced casualness, trying not
to come off like a stiff-necked jealous boyfriend.

"Had to drop some budget stuff off once or twice," she
said, not looking at him.

"Okay, let's go see if he's home." He got out of the
car, and Chooch scrambled out of the backseat. "Stick out
here by the car, will you, Chooch?" Shane asked.

"How come?"

"Just wait by the car, okay? I'm not sure what we're gonna find."

"I think you're being overly dramatic," Alexa said, but her voice seemed guarded.

They left Chooch and moved up to the front door of the house. It was locked, so they rang the bell. No answer. No key under the pot, over the jamb, or in any of the other no-brainer hiding spots.

They rang the bell three more times.

Shane moved around to the garage and looked in the side window. A dark green, department-issue Crown Victoria staff car was parked inside. "Car's here," he said. *Not a good sign.*

Next they tried the back door—also locked. He decided he'd have to break in, so he took out his small set of lock picks.

"Those things again?" she said, wrinkling her nose at them.

"We could just stand out here until the neighbors report us," Shane said.

She nodded, so he slipped the picks out of the little leather case. The set contained half a dozen slender needles with widened ends, and one larger shaft piece. The trick was to work the pick's wide shaft into the lock, then slip the needles in under it, twisting them so they'd fill up the spaces inside the tumbler lock. Once he had enough purchase inside the dead bolt, he could turn the collection of picks to throw the lock. Shane had seen several newer-style lock-picks used by state-of-the-art B&E men. The most recent consisted of long strips of a new metal alloy attached to a heating coil. They were first slipped into the lock, then heated up by the coil until the soft metal melted into the lock. The alloy dried quickly, hardening and allowing the bolt to be turned. But Shane liked his old-fashioned Sam Spade set better. It took a little longer, required more skill, and appealed to his sense of police noir.

He got the door open and smiled tightly at Alexa; then they moved into a small, white-tile-and-wood-trimmed kitchen.

Mark Shephard lived alone. For a bachelor, he was uncommonly neat: dishes washed and stacked on the drip tray, washcloth folded neatly over the goosenecked faucet that hung over an old-style metal sink. They passed out of the kitchen, into the dining room.

Shane could smell him before he saw him. The sweet, sick odor of flesh decaying in a self-liquefying bath of butyric acid.

The Good Shepherd wasn't looking so good today. He was sitting in his Archie Bunker armchair, directly in front of the TV, wearing gray slacks and a white dress shirt, his shoes laced neatly on his feet. His head was thrown back with his mouth wide open, as if he had fallen asleep in front of the tube. Except for two green flies crawling in his mouth, he looked peaceful. His .38-caliber Smith & Wesson was halfway across the floor behind him.

He had shot himself in the temple, or so they were supposed to believe. The entrance wound was round and neat. Purple-black blood and cerebral spinal fluid had oozed from the hole, staining his shirt collar and shoulders. There were what looked like second- or third-generation maggot larvae festering inside the wound. Shane knew that each generation represented approximately twelve hours, indicating that he had been dead somewhere around thirty-six hours, or at least since yesterday evening.

"Oh, my God," he heard Alexa whisper. "No . . . no . . . please, no."

Shane glanced at her and saw a look of shock and pain tightening her features. She seemed pale and frightened— not exactly Medal of Valor crime-scene behavior. How-

ever, Mark Shephard was her friend, he reasoned. The
Good Shepherd had arranged for her to be his XO at Detective Services . . . arranged it early, even before she had
made lieutenant. So they were close. It was hard to witness a close friend *in terminus situ*, oozing blood and
hosting fly larvae. Even though they were cops and had
seen it before, she would find this difficult; that's why she
seemed emotionally wrought.

He reached out and touched the body. It was loose, the
flesh jiggled . . . rigor mortis had already come and gone,
confirming his rough estimate of TOD.

"Suicide. Why would he commit suicide?" he heard
Alexa say.

"Yeah," Shane said, now noticing some more disturb-
ing pieces of the crime-scene puzzle. Shane was a homicide detective, so right off, three things bothered him—
two small, the other large. First, and least important, was
the fact that Mark Shephard had his shoes on. Most suicides, approximately 80 percent, remove their shoes before killing themselves. The why had never been
adequately explained to him, but they did it nonetheless.
It was troubling only in conjunction with his two other
observations. The large event was the bullet itself. It had
entered Mark Shephard's right temple, but had not come
out again. The gun was on the floor where it had supposedly been thrown from his hand by the recoil after the
shot. It was the same checkered-grip .38 that Shane had
seen on his belt in Shephard's office Friday morning.
Shane knew that a full-load, 110-grain .38-caliber slug
traveled at a velocity of 995 feet per second and had 240
foot-pounds of muzzle energy. These were manufacturer's
stats. So the big, hard-to-explain piece was why the bullet
had not exited the other side of Shephard's head, taking
half his skull with it like it was supposed to?

The third thing Shane noticed was that at the edge of
the wound, there was "tattooing" from the exploding gun-

powder coming out of the barrel. Most tattooing from guns held close to the head made a tight pattern around the wound. The tattooing around Mark Shephard's wound, however, was about an inch from the exterior circumference of the bullet hole, indicating that the bullet Commander Shephard had used to take his life was most likely a standard-police-issue, light-load cartridge. Light loads were the hated ordnance of all street cops because they contained half the gunpowder of a full load. The reasoning was that if a police officer got into a gunfight in the street, the bullet would carry only half as far and not kill an innocent civilian feeding a parking meter a mile away. It also had damn little velocity, so when fired close-up, it left this wider tattoo.

Mark Shephard was a cop. Cops were issued light loads. A light load wouldn't necessarily go all the way through Shephard's head and out the other side. It would cause this wider tattoo. That's physics. That's the way the cartridge is designed. So what's the problem? What's wrong with this picture?

Only one thing.

Shane had been on the job for almost twenty years, and in all that time he'd seen or heard of hundreds of cops screwing their service revolvers into their mouths or ears and doing a Dutch Treat. But in all of those cases—every single one—the cops used full loads. Not one of them had tried to kill himself with a light load, and the reason for that was obvious: there was a high degree of probability that a half load wouldn't get the job done, like in the street, where it sometimes failed to even slow down an enraged assailant. Half loads, most of the time, managed only to maim or cripple.

Why had Mark Shephard used the underpowered cartridge? Was this a suicide, or could it be a murder? Had somebody used the commander's gun to kill him, unaware that it contained Remington Lights? While these thoughts were going through his mind, the situation became even more complicated when he heard Alexa sobbing.

He looked over and saw her sitting on the sofa, her head in her hands, crying. He'd only known her well for half a year, but she was not a weepy woman. Why was this street-trained police officer who had witnessed the worst of man's inhumanity to man sitting on the sofa crying like a heartbroken relative?

Shock? Yes.

Dismay? Of course.

Anger and depression? You bet.

But tears, uncontrollable tears, at a crime scene?

What the fuck is going on here?

10

AFTERMATH

They didn't get out of Mark Shephard's house for hours.
Buddy had to take a cab to the airport, and Chooch drove
the Acura home. Shane and Alexa stood on the Good
Shepherd's neatly trimmed lawn while the ME and lab
techs did their gruesome work: bagging the corpse's
hands, photographing the body with its growing colony
of fly larvae.

Alexa watched in silence. Somewhere around six, the
body was wheeled out and put into the coroner's wagon.
The windowless, black Econoline van pulled slowly away
from the little Spanish house, taking its resident away for
the last time.

Shane looked at Alexa, who had regained her compo-
sure but seemed drained, almost shrunken, standing in
front of Mark Shephard's house, watching his corpse
leave.

"Tough, huh?" he finally said.

She nodded but didn't say anything.

"Listen, I think we need to go someplace and talk
about this," he suggested softly.

She looked at him, her gaze unfocused, her features pulled tight in an expression that seemed trapped somewhere between a frown and a squint, reflecting her emotional devastation. She nodded but still didn't speak.

"You hungry?" he asked.

This time she shook her head.

Jesus, for the love of God, say something. I'm dying here. But Shane said only: "I could use some food. Lemme buy you some coffee."

She finally spoke. One word, only two letters; sounding hesitant and unsure.

"Okay."

Shane had told the ME that he suspected the fatal shot was a light load. The ME concurred, also referencing the wider tattooing and the lack of an exit wound. Shane told the ME they were leaving and left his pager number, then drove Alexa's Crown Vic back toward Venice while she looked glumly at the passing neighborhoods.

They hadn't spoken about it, but with her downer brother safely out of town, Shane had intended for her to move back in, to spend the night in his bed at 874 East Canal Street. He stopped a block away from his house at a small restaurant on the beach.

The place was called the Hungry Termite, which always struck Shane as an unlikely, unappetizing name. He had never been able to find out why it was called that, but the cover of the menu had a stick drawing of a termite eating a sandwich. They sat at a patio table and listened to the surf crashing on the sand a few hundred yards away.

"I'm sure Buddy got to the airport okay," Shane offered, to get the conversation rolling.

"Good . . ."

"I'm afraid I didn't turn out to be much of a taxi service for him."

Again she just nodded.

"Alexa, we need to get the needle off deep grief for a

62

minute and start thinking more like cops," he said, angry
at the way she was behaving. It was almost as if she'd
been sleeping with the guy.

"Christ, Shane, gimme a little time to deal with this.
He was a good friend."

"Right. He was a good friend. I get that, but I'm not
so sure this isn't somehow connected to Jody being back."

"*Jody?*" She seemed appalled at the suggestion. "Good
God, Shane, Jody again? We're still on that?"

"I don't think Commander Shephard killed himself,"
Shane said, and the remark sat there between them, a big
unwashed idea with absolutely no hard evidence supporting it.

"I beg your pardon?"

"I'm just doing police work here, okay? I'm trying to
make sense of this."

"Right. Jody is alive. Got it. Makes great fucking
sense."

"Alexa, you've been with me during a pretty intense
investigation. In fact, it was a good enough investigation
to win *you* the Medal of Valor." *Shit*, Shane thought, he
was now sort of bitching to her about not sharing the
award. But she didn't react, so he went on: "You know I
can look at facts and construct truth, or at least sometimes
I can." Hating the way this was going, sitting here, doing
his own dumb-ass commercial while she swirled her coffee around in a chipped Hungry Termite mug using a
stainless-steel spoon. "There's a lot of stuff on this
unnatural death I don't like the look of."

"Let's call it suicide since that's what it is," she said.
When he didn't answer, she added, "I'm listening." But
there was a dead, listless quality to her voice.

"Okay, why would he shoot himself with a light load?"

"Distraught."

"Come on, I don't buy it. He's gonna take a chance

on coming out a vegetable? You ever see a cop do a Dutch Treat with a light load?"

"Shane, people do stupid things in times of stress. Mark was obviously stressed. He . . . he . . . God. . . . Do we have to talk about this?"

"Yes, we have to. Jody is alive, Alexa. He called me last night. He told me he was working UC on some high-profile case, said he was 'doing doors' on predicate felons and that the department had supplied him with a new ID and faked his death so that his crew wouldn't get busted by moles in the Clerical Division. In Payroll. They're actually paying death benefits to the wives of the guys in his unit. That's how they're getting their police salaries."

She sat there, with anger in her eyes. At least the dead indifference had disappeared. Anything was better than that. "How would they ever pull that off?" she said. "The department isn't going to be involved in cops doing felonies, committing crimes to get criminals, then faking death payments, Shane. That's the most insane thing I've ever heard."

"Not Tony Filosiani, but the old department. Chief Brewer might have done it, or Deputy Chief Mayweather, before he killed himself to avoid jail. This thing predates Filosiani. It started back with Chief Brewer. Mayweather was head of Special Investigations Section. He was supervising the Criminal Intelligence Group and the Organized Crime Division. Do you, for a minute, put it past him to recruit a buncha walk-alones out of SIS or some of those testosterone cases from SWAT, guys who wouldn't mind scoring points the old-fashioned way? You know Mayweather might have sanctioned a group like that."

"And put it under Mark Shephard, a decent, honest cop?"

"Yeah, maybe," Shane said softly.

"No fucking way. Mark wouldn't do that."

"Okay, Alexa, we also need to talk about you and Mark. I know this is a shitty time for it, but I'm sensing more than professional respect here." His hand was back in his pocket, tightly gripping the little box containing Alexa's perfect VS-l, two-carat engagement ring. He knew she wouldn't lie. The answer to this question might determine whether the ring would ever end up on the third finger of her left hand. "Was there more going on there?" he asked, his voice tight.

Alexa sighed, and took a sip of coffee. She seemed to be steeling herself in preparation for Shane's reaction. "You're right. Mark and I were more than just friends," she said quietly.

The sentence arced around inside him like loose volts of electricity. His right hand flinched; his stomach rumbled dangerously, threatening to erupt.

"We used to date. Nobody in the department knew, because he wanted it that way. He was a commander; I was a sergeant . . . and two years ago he asked me to marry him. I turned him down, but I came close, Shane. I almost said yes."

"And why didn't you?" He was numb with this, not thinking, just reacting.

"I didn't marry him because something told me not to. . . . Something told me that even though I found him extremely attractive and sexy, even though he was sweet and considerate, and had a great sense of humor—"

"Okay, okay. I get the point," he interrupted. "Go on."

"Something told me that he was close, but not the one. In the end, I respected him a lot but didn't love him quite enough."

"And so, when he asked you to take over as his XO at Detective Services Group, that was his chance to be around you so he could get the romance going again."

"Maybe he saw it that way. I can't speak for him . . . but I told him I was seeing you and that I wasn't looking to have an affair with my commanding officer. I wouldn't consider sleeping with the boss on management principles alone. Mark said he understood but wanted me there anyway because I was the best person for the job. And, dammit, Shane, I think I am."

Shane sat there, inert, unable to find the right words to express his emotions.

"I won't deny I had strong feelings for him," she went on. "I still do. I'm sorry I lost it at the crime scene. That was unprofessional. It just hit me hard. I wasn't ready to see him that way."

"It's okay," Shane said, but it wasn't. He had almost crushed the little box in his pocket. He didn't expect Alexa to be a virgin, but the idea that she'd recently been so close to marrying another man agonized him. "Look, Jody is alive," he said finally, to get his mind off it. "I know 'cause I talked to him. SIS was Jody's division when he disappeared. My guess is that this secret unit, whoever they are, is being run out of Special Investigations, because I get the feeling from what Jody said that he's in charge."

"How do you know that?"

"Because Jody was always in charge. It's just his way. He wouldn't be in the unit unless he was running it."

She nodded. She'd heard enough stories about Jody Dean to know that was probably true.

"If this crew was being run out of SIS, then Mark Shephard would have been the unit supervisor, their administrative division commander. Most of these deep-cover units have only two or three contact people, staff officers who know they exist. My guess is Mayweather was one, but he's gone. Medwick ran Detective Services until two months ago, and now he's missing. And trust me, he won't be coming back from the store with his box of brass screws. . . . He's in a shallow grave somewhere, curled around a bag of lye."

"And now Mark," she said.

"Yeah, Commander Shephard completes the trio. So if these three are gone, who's the department CO? Who's running this bunch a' kazoonies?" When she didn't answer, he answered for her: "You are, Alexa. Whether you know it or not, you're the XO, so you're now in charge. I think they're constituted under some subgroup in SIS under DSG. You're acting head of Detective Services until Chief Filosiani appoints a new head."

"You're serious about all this, aren't you?"

"Alexa, he's *alive*. Jody is alive. I don't know who doctored those crime-scene photos and the death report Shephard showed me, but with computer-generated imaging, you can do almost anything with photographs today. I'm telling you, Jody's death was rigged. Lauren Dean is either in the dark or lying, but either way, she's so screwed-up about it, she's turned into a lush. Everybody else who knew about this unit at DSG is dead or missing. I think we've got a huge problem here."

She sat looking across the table at him, taking all of this in. "If you believe that, then you need to take it to the chief. . . . You need to tell Filosiani."

"The Day-Glo Dago? This guy talks out of the side of his mouth like a Brooklyn cabdriver. You're acting head of DSG. . . . I'm telling *you*."

"I'm just a sergeant. If you believe all this, you need to go to a staff-rank commander or above, and for reasons of security, I suggest the chief. Filosiani didn't get to the LAPD in the front seat of a cab. He was one of the best street cops in New York. He's cleaned up three departments and has been honored at the White House. He's a smart, tough, in-your-face police officer, so if you think Jody is running a criminal conspiracy and is killing his commanders, then you better take it to him and not just your girlfriend because you don't trust anybody above the fifth floor at the Glass House."

They sat there looking at each other, chewing on this for a long time.

"If I decide to do that, would you go with me?"

"I don't think Jody is alive. I think you're—"

"What?" he interrupted. "Making it up?"

"Why do you want me to go with you?"

"Because it's your responsibility as XO and because you've got heat. Today you won the Medal of Valor . . . and because you owe me." *There. He'd finally said it, but he knew it had come at some cost to their relationship.*

She looked out toward the ocean, her beautiful profile to him. Finally, she turned back, but she didn't answer. She sat there, pondering thoughts too difficult for him to read or for her to relay. Loss and despair completed the mask of confusion on her face.

TOMATO FARMING

Alexa came back to Shane's house with him, but she was quiet most of the way. He pulled her Crown Vic into the garage next to his Acura. They got out and went into the house, where they found Chooch asleep on the living-room sofa, his algebra book across his chest. Alexa slipped out the door to the backyard while Shane shook Chooch's shoulder.

"Hey, bud," he said.

Chooch opened his eyes and looked up as if Shane had just beamed down from the teleport room of the *Enterprise*. Then recognition dawned as he yawned. "Just resting my eyes," he said. "Last final tomorrow."

"I think you should rest the whole machine," Shane said, taking the book off Chooch's chest. "You know this stuff. Once you've got the formulas, you can't study for algebra. You should get a good night's sleep."

Chooch cocked a wary eyebrow. "Yeah?" he said. "And just what'd you get when you took this course?"

"Doesn't count." Shane grinned. "Statute of limitations ran out on that crime." Shane helped Chooch to his feet.

He glanced out the window and saw Alexa on the lawn, her back to the house, staring at the canals, both arms wrapped around her as if she were cold on that warm June night.

"You give her our rock?" Chooch asked, following Shane's gaze out the window.

"No, not yet. Something came up. It didn't seem like the right time."

"Don't screw this up."

"Don't worry. Now get to bed," he said, and Chooch shambled off to his room.

Later that night Shane and Alexa made love in his cluttered bedroom. It started off well enough: some gentle caressing at the beginning, with Shane moving his hand over her soft, tight body, finding the place between her legs, rubbing her while her arms encircled his neck, her breath warm on his ear. But somewhere between the beginning and the end it turned competitive, with both of them on top of the sheets, bathed in sweat, thrusting their hips at each other, climax finally coming in a ferocious moment that more closely resembled anger than love.

Instead of closeness, loneliness followed the event.

"I've been thinking about it, and I changed my mind," Shane said as they lay on his bed in the dark room. "I can't go to Chief Filosiani. If I do that, my career is over. I have zero evidence. I can't prove that I saw Jody or that he called me. If I try and bring all this up—Medwick and Shephard—I'm gonna look like a jerk."

She rolled toward him and looked at him carefully. "I think that's the best way to handle it," she said, softening as he held her. "Honey, if you insist on pressing this Jody thing, it will turn out bad. . . . You're almost through your psychiatric review. Once that's done, you're back on the job. Maybe then, if you still feel this way, you could look into it. But if you do it now, you could get pushed into forced retirement."

"But let's suppose I'm right. Let's just say, for the hell of it, that I did see him, and let's suppose he *is* doing doors. Don't we need to stop him?"

"It's a matter of timing, Shane. Now is the wrong time."

"I'm not going to the chief anyway," he said, knowing that she was right. A move like that would be an event Filosiani couldn't ignore. Without a shred of evidence to back up what he saw, his career would be over. He didn't trust the Day-Glo Dago, despite all the stories going through the department about the legend of Tony Filosiani, the "policeman's policeman." Shane wasn't yet ready to put his entire twenty-year career into the hands of the short, round-faced man who talked out of the side of his mouth and looked as though he should be in the corner market, cutting up flank steak.

Chief Filosiani had hit the LAPD like a shaft of white light from the first day he took over four months ago. His first day on the job he had witnessed four cops trying to wrestle a crazy old homeless man through a metal detector at West Hollywood Division. The man had been arrested for walking naked down Santa Monica Boulevard, wearing only a silver biking helmet. He said that he was from the planet Argus and wanted an audience with the President. There were four large uniformed cops fighting with this deranged and panicked old man in front of the booking cage, trying to force him to put on a city jail jumpsuit and go through the metal detector into the holding-cell area. The four uniforms were rolling on the floor, trying to cuff him, when a short, balding man in a shiny suit stepped forward and gave a space salute, slamming his fist onto his chest.

"Welcome to the planet," Filosiani bowed. "It is with great honor and respect that we welcome visitors from your galaxy." The man jumped to his feet and returned the salute, standing naked in front of the four sweating cops.

"I am the interplanetary ambassador for Earth people, and I will be your escort while you are a visitor here. Is this your desire?" the new chief continued in Brooklynese.

"Yes," the old man said.

"It is our custom that visitors to the Earth Senate and Presidential Chamber wear the honored robes of the Interplanetary Guest Council. Would this be acceptable?" Filosiani bowed again.

"Yes . . . I will wear your robes," the man said, bowing in return. Filosiani reached out and took the orange city jail jumpsuit out of a startled cop's hands. The old man shimmied into it, pulling up the zipper. Then Tony bowed once more to the old man, who bowed back.

"Now, as is our custom, it is necessary to take you to our Interplanetary Medical Center where you'll be screened for diseases and bacteria from the planet Argus that may be harmful to the people a' Earth. Will this be acceptable?"

"Yes . . . I understand."

"Our galaxy medical officer here will escort you," he said. Tony gave the old man another space salute, which was returned, then they bowed a fourth time, looking like two Japanese businessmen. One of the cops led the homeless man quietly through the metal detector guarding the entrance to the West Hollywood Division booking cage. He walked peacefully into the holding cell, wearing his new orange Earth clothes and silver biking helmet.

The old man was booked without further incident and taken to the mental ward at County Hospital.

The four cops had by now figured out who the short, round man in the shiny suit was. They stood and listened as Tony gave a lecture on how to handle deranged or disoriented people: "This old man is sick," he told them.

"You guys don't fight or wrestle with a sick person. Y'buy into his fantasy and he'll follow ya anywhere. Do it right, fellas," he said, smiling. "Save all this rough-and-tumble stuff for the hard cases."

The story spread like wildfire. After Chief Brewer, L.A. was ready for a top cop with a shrewd streak of humanity. But still, Shane wasn't ready to go in front of the little man with his Jody Dean story, at least not yet. Not until he had something more—one piece of concrete evidence.

Alexa elected not to sleep over, and Shane didn't try to stop her. She took her car back to her apartment in Santa Monica. They were badly out of sync and needed time to get past it.

Shane put the little leather box containing her engagement ring inside the top dresser drawer and finally went to bed.

He didn't dream of Alexa and he didn't dream of Jody. Strangely, he had a dream about tomato farming. He was sitting on a huge green tractor, trying to plow a straight furrow so he could plant his tomato seeds. But the tractor kept going its own way, despite his efforts to steer it. The huge green machine left a wavy, drunken furrow behind him. "Dammit," Shane kept saying, as the tractor wavered. "Dammit, stay straight, will ya?" It was a difficult night of farming.

THE CANOE FACTORY

The next morning Shane went to Mark Shephard's autopsy. The ME performing the examination was Dr. Clyde Miller, a notorious civil-service character. He wore tie-dyed T-shirts under his white medical smock and sang old Beatles tunes while he cut up corpses.

"It's been a hard day's night, and I been working like a dog," he warbled at ten A.M. to the accompanying screams of a bone saw in the autopsy room. The procedure was taking place in operating theater three of L.A.'s huge medical examiner's facilities. The next-in-line corpses were on rolling gurneys in the narrow basement corridor, all waiting under ironed green sheets, with red name tags wired festively to their bloodless toes. They were bumper to bumper under the fluorescent tubes, surrounded by the throat-clogging cologne of the newly departed—formaldehyde mixed with preserving chemicals. It was a sad little parking lot of last night's traffic and gun mistakes.

Commander Mark Shephard was the only self-inflicted gunshot death that morning. The physical inspection of the body was just getting under way as Shane arrived.

"Hey, Sarge, welcome. Another opening, another show," Miller caroled, switching momentarily to Cole Porter as Shane entered the room. "Was this poor guy a friend?"

"No, I found the body."

"Hard way to go," Miller grunted, and switched back to the Beatles, altering a lyric here and there as he continued his physical inspection of the lower extremities. "Hey, Jude, don't make it bad / Take a sad song and make it better / Just don't hide the reason you're gone, and this Doc will find the answer, answer, answer, answer." He broke into the "na, na, nas" as he went over Commander Shephard's legs and feet, inch by inch, looking for any exterior abnormalities before making his Y-cut at the sternum, then emptying and weighing the Good Shepherd's heart, liver, and kidneys.

Shane was standing at the head of the table when Dr. Miller suddenly stopped singing and turned to his medical assistant, a black woman Shane had never met, who was functioning as his "diener" during the autopsy. "Whoa, Nellie. Whatta we got here?" he said, raising an eyebrow.

Both Shane and the tall African American woman moved to the foot of the table to see what he had found. There, on Commander Mark Shephard's left ankle, on the inside just above his medial mallealous bone, was a small, two-inch, hand-drawn tattoo of a Viking head in profile. A horned helmet dominated the artwork.

Shane looked at the tattoo, then took a small camera out of his pocket that he always brought to autopsies to photograph anything of note for his case folder. He carefully shot the tattoo from different angles.

Two things about the tattoo bothered Shane: First, most police officers would rather cut off one of their fingers than get a tattoo anywhere on their body. They viewed tattoos as a mark of the criminal underclass. Cops who already had one prior to joining the force usually invested in laser surgery to remove it.

Common folklore on the streets was that if you were a criminal, always look to see if your cohorts in crime were tattooed—or "sleeved," as the cons called it—because any guy without a tattoo was immediately suspected of being the Law.

The "no tattoo" rule among cops was relatively inviolate, so it bothered Shane that Mark Shephard had this Viking on the inside of his ankle. But there was something else about the tattoo that bothered Shane even more.

About three years before, the L.A. County Sheriff's Department had discovered a band of rogue officers. This group called themselves "the Vikings," and they all had Viking tattoos on their ankles. They were suspected of forcing confessions, usually by administering a little chin music in some dark place. The Vikings were eventually broken up, but this tattoo looked exactly like the ones worn by that bunch of officers. It was in the same place on the body, low on the right ankle, where it could be covered by a sock.

When this rogue group of deputies was first discovered, Sheriff Sherman Block tried to stage an inspection. He wanted to examine every sheriff's deputy's right ankle in search of Viking tattoos. But the Sheriff's Department Law Enforcement Union filed a lawsuit, claiming that such an inspection without probable cause violated the officers' civil rights. It became a big deal, and eventually the sheriffs' union prevailed. The physical search never took place, but ten deputies were eventually terminated from the original core group.

Mark Shephard had the same tattoo, or at least one a lot like it. Shane wondered if the culture of the Vikings had somehow migrated from the Sheriff's Department to the LAPD. He made a mental note to try to get someone

to pull Shephard's file to see if he had ever been loaned
out to the sheriffs or had ever been part of one of the
cross-pollination task forces. There had been several over
the years, and a few were still operating: The Cobra Unit
in the Valley was one; L.A. Impact was another. Even
some of the big serial-killer task forces qualified. On the
Hillside Strangler Unit, the Sheriff's Department and
LAPD worked closely together because the murders occurred in both the city and county.

One other strange thing turned up as a result of the
autopsy, and also caught Shane by surprise. But it didn't
happen while Doc Miller was sawing up Commander
Shephard and singing selections from *Sgt. Pepper's
Lonely Hearts Club Band*. It arrived an hour later, when
the preliminary blood work came back from the lab.
Shane was stunned to learn that the Good Shepherd had
been stoned when he parked the Remington Light in the
central lobe of his cranial cavity. He had high traces of
marijuana in his bloodstream.

"Shit," Shane said as he stood outside the ME's office
in the hazy mid-morning sunshine, trying to decide what
to do with this new piece of information. How would he
tell Alexa, or should he even tell her at all? Since it would
eventually find its way into the press, maybe it would be
better to let the *Los Angeles Times* deliver the bombshell.
Shane didn't need to be the one to further distress Alexa
with negative facts about her old boyfriend.

He decided to take some time and think about it. He
went across the street and had a Heineken in a tavern
called the Canoe Factory. The place was a hangout for
medical examiners and their staff after long days of opening corpses and turning them into what they referred to
as "body canoes."

As he sipped his late-morning brew, he realized he had
no choice but to tell Alexa, even if telling her would drive
them further apart. She was acting head of DSG, and it

was her responsibility. She had to know about the tattoo, about Shane's suspicions. Furthermore, he was determined to find out if his old best friend, Jody Dean, was out there committing multiple homicides on his former commanding officers.

At eleven Shane left the bar and just barely made his rescheduled psychiatric appointment, only five blocks away.

He sat in the reclining chair while the psychiatrist asked him how his last four days had gone.

"Very well," Shane lied. "Exceedingly well, in fact."

"Uh-huh . . . I see. Go on," the fat doctor said.

MORE TROUBLE

Alexa got out of her department-issue Crown Victoria in front of Mark Shephard's house, where Shane was waiting. "I really don't have time for this," she said. "I'm trying to get the budget stuff finished and take over down there." She was dressed in a tan skirt and green blouse. Her lustrous black hair was pulled back, clipped with a barrette glinting in the late-afternoon sunshine.

He was standing by his Acura, which was parked nearby. In the backseat, jumping around with boundless enthusiasm, was Officer Krupkee, a one-year-old German shepherd he'd just borrowed from the West Valley Drug Enforcement Team. He let the dog out of the back of the car, took his leash, and led him toward the driveway.

"We need to go through the house. You need to be here," he said, ducking under the yellow crime-scene tape, which was still strung up, moving around to the back door so the neighbors couldn't watch him break in. He was walking ahead of Alexa so she couldn't stop him.

He was already on the porch, lock pick out, when she

finally caught up to him. Officer Krupkee was jumping around, barking and sniffing wildly.

"What's this about? Is that a drug-enforcement dog?" Alexa's questions were apprehensive.

"Meet Officer Krupkee, West Valley Canine Hall of Fame. He's discovered more drugs than Dow Chemical."

"Shane," she said ominously, "why are we bringing a drug dog into Mark's house?"

"You remember the Vikings, that old Sheriff's Department club, or whatever it was?"

"Yeah, sure. Guys who had tattoos on their ankles and held court in the street."

"I went to Commander Shephard's autopsy. He has one of those on his ankle."

"Not when I was dating him."

"Then it's more recent than that," Shane answered stiffly.

He pulled the photo he'd taken at the autopsy out of his jacket and gave it to her. He'd had it developed at a Photo-Mat an hour earlier. She gave it a quick glance, then handed it back without comment.

He stuffed it away and began feeding his picks into the back-door lock. He finally got them in, but his hands were sweating. When he tried to turn the lock, his fingers slipped, or maybe it was Officer Krupkee tugging and jumping in circles at the end of his leash; whatever the reason, the picks fell out of the lock onto the wooden porch. Shane bent down to retrieve them and started over again.

"What's the second thing?" she asked as he went back to work on the dead bolt.

"He had marijuana in his bloodstream," Shane said, avoiding eye contact while working on the door.

"Mark didn't do drugs."

"Go tell the ME."

She was silent, considering this. Then: "So, now we're over here with a DED to do what?"

"Alexa, I know this isn't going to go down well between us, and I really do regret it, but I think it's possible Mark Shephard knew Jody wasn't in that urn on Lauren's mantel, and that's why Shephard is dead. I think Jody's undercover unit may be going bad, and I think it's possible Mark knew what Jody was doing—maybe tried to stop it."

"Think, think, think . . . Isn't Shane a thinking policeman? Of course, a little evidence would sure be nice."

"And you can stow the sarcasm, okay? I'm not trying to run down the memory of your friend."

She was pissed; he could see it even in her sharp movements.

Mercifully, he finally got the back door open, and they walked into the house, Officer Krupkee leaping around at the end of his handler's chain like a demon possessed. Shane reached down and unhooked the leash. The dog took off, running around the kitchen, sniffing, pawing; then, unrewarded, he dashed toward the living room while Shane followed. Alexa was a few feet behind.

"We're looking for his stash, is that the drill?" she asked.

"If Shephard used drugs, he would probably have a stash here somewhere," Shane admitted. "When I used to work drug homicides, way back before I became the leading department kook-a-boo, I found that hypes would often hide confidential stuff with their works: hot merchandise, murder weapons, dirty pictures, right there next to their happy bag."

"And that's what we're looking for?"

"If somebody forced Mark to smoke a joint before killing him, this place will be clean. We need to know either way."

"Why?"

"Alexa, stop chewing on my foot, okay? I need a witness. You're it. If I turn up anything and I'm here alone, they'll probably say I planted it. My word is about as good as a junkie's promise right now."

Suddenly, Officer Krupkee started barking. Shane and Alexa went into Mark Shephard's bedroom and saw the dog sniffing and pawing at the heating grate in the wall down by the floorboards, across from the bed.

Shane looked at Alexa, whose face and features were tense. He dropped down on his hands and knees. The screws on the vent were loose, so he began pulling them out with his thumb and fingernails. One by one, he extracted them while the leaping, barking dog jumped and lunged around, eager to help, pawing and growling at the heating grate.

"Good going, Krup," Shane said. "Alexa, lock him in the bathroom, will ya?"

She grabbed the chain, dragged the dog off. Shane heard her give the dog a "sit/stay" command. Then he heard the bathroom door close. He waited for her to return before pulling the heating grate away from the wall. She kneeled and they both looked inside.

Shane could see something way in the back of the exposed opening. He put on a pair of rubber gloves, reached into the small hollowed compartment, and pulled the contents out of the wall. What came first was a large black metal box, about a foot long and six inches high. Shane set it down in front of them and glanced over at Alexa, who nodded. He opened it and inside found a very sophisticated high-frequency radio of some sort. It was set to 367.23 on the UHF band. The radio was turned off. Shane looked up at Alexa, who nodded again, so he turned it on. The batteries were working, but nothing was broadcasting: static hissed. He switched it off.

"Ever seen one of these before?" he asked.

"No . . . looks scrambled. I don't think it's department-issue."

Shane peered back inside the opening in the wall, took a penlight out of his pocket, and shined it inside. There was another box in the hollowed-out vent. He pulled it out. This one was mahogany, or some kind of polished wood, and was much smaller. He lifted the lid, and inside was what looked like a few rocks of cocaine, some marijuana, and a bag of pills.

"Shit," he heard Alexa say under her breath.

"I'm sorry," he murmured, but didn't risk a look at her. Instead, both of them just stared at the box.

When he finally looked up, he saw nothing on her beautiful face, no expression of any kind.

"I think we can go see Chief Filosiani now," Shane said. "I finally have something to show him."

"He's out of town until tomorrow, at a police chiefs' conference in San Francisco," she said softly.

"Tomorrow then, as soon as he gets back. Set it up." Shane took out his camera and photographed the heating grate. He and Alexa bagged the radio and wooden box, then loaded them both into the trunk of her Crown Vic. She got into the front seat, and after Shane put Officer Krupkee into the back of his Acura, he went to her driver's-side window and squatted down so he could look in at her.

"Alexa, we can't let this destroy us. I don't want this to wreck what we have."

"It's not you, Shane. . . . I love you. It's me." Then without saying another word, she drove off.

BLACK DUST

"And since I think this guy could be dangerous," Shane said, "I'm not going to take a chance on what happened last time happening again."

They were driving to the airport. Chooch was heading off to quarterback camp. His duffel was stuffed; his helmet and pads were on the backseat.

"No way what happened last time can ever happen again," Chooch said.

They were talking about the Naval Yard case, when Chooch had been kidnapped in an attempt to get Shane to back off.

"So why didn't you give Alexa the ring?" Chooch asked, to change the subject.

"Don't worry about me and Alexa. Things always happen for the best."

"Shane, you're screwing this up."

"Maybe, but you don't have all of it."

"So, tell me."

"No."

"Why?"

" 'Cause I haven't got it completely figured out myself yet. And you may be right. I may be screwing it up, but you've gotta let me and Alexa work it out. This stuff can't be forced."

"You know, I love her, too," Chooch said.

"I know. I know you do."

When they arrived at the airport, Shane left his car parked at the LAPD substation. He got Chooch's stuff out of the backseat, and they walked to the Southwest Airlines terminal. Security was intense since the World Trade Center disaster; it took almost two hours to get to the counter. Shane helped Chooch check in and get his seat assignment, then they sat outside the metal detector in the lobby while people milled around, full of their own lives' worries.

"Chooch, look, I'm not gonna mess it up. Okay?"

"She's the best person we ever knew, and I'm urging you—shit, man, *I'm begging you* . . . give her the fucking ring."

"Don't swear so much," Shane said. "Your mouth is getting terrible. Swearing doesn't make you an adult."

Chooch smiled. "Okay," he finally said. "I'll work on it, but give her the frickin' ring."

It was time for Chooch to go, and his son stood. Shane was surprised lately to see that he and Chooch were exactly the same height. At six feet, they were eye to eye when they gave each other a hug.

"I love you, man," Shane said.

"Me too, Dad." Then Chooch grabbed his pads and helmet, which he had elected to carry onto the flight, and walked to the end of the line. Shane stood and watched as he got through the entrance, then turned back. "Give her the ring, Shane," he said once more.

"Is that your last comment on the matter?"

"That's it." Chooch smiled, then he was gone.

*　　*　　*

After that a strange series of events occurred.

As Shane was standing in the parking lot by the sub-station, about to get into his car, he noticed that on the trunk lids of most of the squad cars was a fine black dust. It reminded him of the black dust he'd seen on the trunk and hood of Jody's Charger as he looked over and saw his "dead" friend speeding along next to him on the San Diego Freeway Friday morning. Most dirty cars had brown dust, not black.

A uniformed police officer, a sergeant, moved past him on his way out of the substation, and Shane stopped him. "Hey, excuse me, Sarge . . ."

The man turned.

"I'm Shane Scully, detective three at Robbery-Homicide," he said as the man turned and walked toward him. Shane dug out his badge and showed it to the man.

"I heard about you. You got a lot of ink last year."

"Right." Shane smiled, trying to disarm what seemed like a negative attitude. "I notice all these Plain Janes here have a black dust of some kind all over them."

The sergeant wrinkled his brow. "You working for the motor pool now?"

"No," Shane said. "I was just wondering what it is."

"It's burned jet fuel. These jets take off every minute or so, and they spew black exhaust. Gets all over the cars that live around here."

"No kidding," Shane said, looking at a plane that was just taking off, climbing out past the terminals, trailing dark smoke out of four huge engines. "Got it," he said. "Thanks."

Shane got into his car and pulled out of the parking lot. He didn't know what he was looking for, or even what he was doing. Maybe it was just the vast amount of free time he seemed to have on his hands these days. He drove aimlessly around the Los Angeles airport, picking neighboring streets, looking at cars parked at the curbs. The ones that looked like they'd been there for a while all had the same layer of black dust on their hoods, trunks, and windshields.

Then Shane saw the green-covered fence.

It was at the end of one of the streets near the airport and seemed to run for several blocks. He parked, got out, and moved up to the chain-link, which was covered with Highway Department green plastic so you couldn't see through it. He took out his pocketknife and cut a hole in the plastic.

Inside the fence was a vacant neighborhood, just like the one he was in, only there were no cars on the street, no tricycles or toys strewn around on the brown, unwatered lawns.

"Whatcha doin'?" he heard a voice behind him demand.

Shane turned and saw an old man with a long, stringbean neck. His Adam's apple looked like a ball bouncing up and down on the end of a rubber band when he spoke.

"What is this place?" Shane asked.

"Noise-abatement area," the old man said. "They condemned all a'them houses 'bout two years ago, 'cause they sit right at the end a'the runway and the people who lived in them was all the time complaining about jet noise. Not that it's any better out here," he said. Then, as if to make his point, a jet took off, rising overhead, its engines screaming, trailing black exhaust.

"See?" the old man shouted over the racket.

"Shit, that's loud."

"They say you get used t'it, but y'don't. Fuckin' drive y'nuts. Can't never sell these here houses 'cause only a deaf moron would buy 'em. We built here in the thirties, 'fore there was an airport."

"So, nobody lives inside this fence?"

"Nope," the old man said. "Three square blocks, empty as a hooker's heart."

"Nobody ever goes in there?" Shane asked.

"Once or twice, some cops. Showed us badges; said they was using the neighborhood to practice clearin' barricaded suspects house to house. Only seen 'em go in there a couple a'times."

"Any way to get in?" Shane asked.

"There's a gate right up the street on the Florence side, but it's all padlocked."

Shane nodded, thanked him, then got into his car and drove up the street to have a look.

What he found inside that fence defied all reason, as well as most of the core values he believed in.

CRIBBING

The fence was topped by barbed wire.

Shane slid the picks into the heavy Yale padlock and flipped the tumblers. The padlock jumped, clicking open in his hand. He removed it from the chain that was wrapped around the center posts, then pushed the gate open enough to get through. He could see recent tire tracks in the black dust at his feet.

Shane reached down, withdrew the Beretta Mini-Cougar from his ankle holster, chambered it, and repacked it, tucking the weapon into a handier place in his belt. He moved into the deserted four-block neighborhood, then closed the gate behind him and relatched the lock the way he had found it.

Every two minutes a low-flying jet screamed overhead, shaking the ground and the houses with a deafening roar.

Shane steeled his nerves against the racket, slipping into the fenced noise-abatement area. A broken sign announced the street he was on as East Lannark Drive. He was moving slowly, cautiously from house to house, staying out of sight of the few unboarded windows, seeking cover behind chipped, unpainted garden walls or dead hedges. The effect of the neighborhood was startling: the houses had long been unattended, the lawns brown—bone-dry from lack of water; hedges and trees were skeletal and dusty; only a few hardy weeds clung stubbornly to rock-hard flowerbeds. The entire neighborhood was covered with the same fine black exhaust powder, turning everything dingy and gray.

Another jet screamed over him. Shane jumped in response to the shrieking roar of its four huge engines passing just a few hundred feet above his head.

Shane followed the tire tracks on the dusty pavement, running from hedge to house to wall, his senses quivering, his eyes darting back and forth, searching for any movement—any sign of life.

Could this be where Jody and his undercover unit are cribbing?

The tire tracks he was following turned right into one of the driveways. The house was a standard forties woodframe, shake-roof number that had once been cheery yellow with white trim. But the yellow had faded to a dirty cream and the once-white trim was now gray and peeling. Shane sprinted across the dead grass to avoid leaving footprints on the dusty pavement; he pressed flat against the east wall of the house. Somebody had removed the plywood that covered the front bay window looking out onto East Lannark Drive.

Another jet took off and he jumped again, his frayed nerves unprepared for the earsplitting roar. "Shit," he muttered. This was going to take a little getting used to.

Shane crept up to the locked front door. He could see that it had a shiny new brass dead bolt. He felt exposed and didn't want to stand there trying to open the lock, so he left the porch and continued down the driveway, ducking under the kitchen windows, past the locked garage door, pausing to look in through the dirty windows. Cobwebs dominated the empty space inside. Nobody had been in the garage for a long time.

He turned and moved silently up onto the back porch, where he found another new Yale lock. He pulled out his picks and in a few seconds had the back door open. Shane moved silently into the kitchen, closing the door softly behind him.

Another plane screamed overhead, rattling his nerves and the kitchen cabinets.

Late-morning sunlight streamed through dirty windows. A lone drinking glass was sitting in the sink next to a large nozzled bottle of Arrowhead water propped up on the counter. Shane tried the sink faucet, but as he had suspected, the water in the neighborhood had been turned off long ago. He picked up the glass, placing his fingers on the inside to preserve any fingerprints, and held it up to the window. He could see some latents smudged on the surface, so he put it down, reached into his pocket for an ever-present detective Baggie, which all cops carry, then popped the glass inside, putting it in his jacket's flap pocket.

Shane crept slowly out of the kitchen. He could not hear any movement in the house but pulled the Mini-Cougar out of his belt as he slipped into the small dining room.

A large slab of plywood, which had probably come off the front window, was laid across two sawhorses, forming a crude dining-room table. It was littered with maps. Some were of a portion of South Central L.A.—the tangled narrow streets south of Manchester. In a separate box at the end of the table were half a dozen folded maps, all in Spanish. Shane picked them up. He couldn't determine what Latin American country the maps depicted. He hadn't heard of any of the cities. Somebody had written *San Andresitos* on one of the maps. Most of them appeared to be of rural desert areas. He opened them and saw two towns marked with a circle: Maicao and Culcata. He set the maps back down in the box where he had found them, then continued out of the dining room into the living room. It was almost completely empty, except for one small camp stool and two Coleman lanterns. A small hibachi for cooking was set into the hearth where the smoke would go up the chimney. There was a corner-hanging lamp. Shane tried the light switch, but the power was also off. Shane kept his gun handy as he moved silently down a dark hallway into the bedroom, where he found a sleeping bag laid out on the threadbare carpet. Nothing else was in the room.

The jackpot was in the bedroom closet.

When Shane slid the mirrored sliding door open, he was looking at an arsenal of illegal weapons propped up against the back wall: an Uzi, complete with a Grumman laser sight, and two Heckler & Koch fully automatic machine pistols stacked next to two fully automatic AK47s. On the top shelf were boxes of 9- and 7.62-millimeter ammunition and a collection of thirty-round banana clips. Also in the closet was a black radio identical to the one he'd found at Mark Shephard's house. Shane took it down, set it on the floor and examined it. The dial was set to the same high-band UHF frequency: 367.23.

He switched it on; a whispered voice immediately staccatoed in the small bedroom but was overcome by another takeoff. The jet engines rattled the windows in their frames as the plane screamed overhead. Once it was gone and silence returned, Shane heard:

"Copy, W-6. There's a bird in your attic." A man's voice, whispery and coarse, followed by a hissing sound. Then a second voice crackled: "I saw him. Tell Sawdust we're in and watertight. Move the truck to the tip of the triangle. Hot Rod is holding the Alley. Inky Dink, gimme an update." Then he heard a black-sounding voice, low and resonant: "Pimp Daddy's in the house. Where's he get the white disco boots and them funky purple hats? Man, I gotta get me some a'dat."

Then unmistakably, Jody: "Hey, Inky Dink, cut the cross-talk. Take care of business. We don't take these guys till they come out with the package."

"Affirmative," the African American replied.

"Hot Rod, gimme your twenty," Jody demanded.

This time, a man with a Mexican accent: "I'm parked in the gas station across from the house."

"Okay. Till the party moves, stay back. Everybody hold position. Be ready to jam."

"Roger that . . . I'm parked and dark and ready to bark." The black voice again.

Shane had heard this sort of broadcast hundreds of times on police tactical frequencies. It was some kind of field surveillance, probably on a drug deal. This radio, like the one in Shephard's house, looked as though it had some kind of scrambler attached. It weighed almost twenty pounds—too heavy to lug around while he searched the house, so Shane switched it off and put it back in the closet, placing it up on the top shelf with the ammo and banana clips. There he noticed several boxes of earplugs like the ones they handed out at the Academy shooting range, answering his question of how anybody could live in these houses with the constant noise pollution overhead. Shane momentarily debated inserting some to deaden the racket, but he immediately rejected the idea. It was better to have frayed nerves than a deadly surprise.

He took out his small digital camera and photographed the arsenal in the closet. In the back, way down at the end, were two suits of Kevlar body armor. He slid the closet door closed, then moved through the rest of the house, photographing it all. The bathroom contained another jug of bottled water and some toiletries. When he finished, he exited the house and relocked the back door.

Shane darted across the street, where he could see that

another set of tire tracks had turned into the driveway of
a house there. He walked toward the gray stucco Spanish-
style bungalow, again staying off the pavement to avoid
leaving footprints in the fine black powder.

The back door was unlocked, so he pushed it open and
walked into the pantry, then into the kitchen.

Just as with the first house, it looked to Shane as if
only one person was living here. But this place was a
mess: paper plates and plastic cups were thrown on the
floor; McDonald's wrappers and stale fries were kicked
into the corner. Again, no furniture, but another hibachi
was in the hearth. It didn't look as if these guys cooked
and ate their meals together. The same general setup existed, except in this bathroom Shane found a hand mirror
with what looked like a residue of powder on it.

"Shit," he said softly as he ran a finger over the white
dust, touched it to his tongue, experiencing the sharp, bitter taste of cocaine.

Shane left the house and, following more tire tracks
deeper into the neighborhood, found another, one block
over on Sutter Street. Then he found a fourth and a fifth
house. Crystal meth, cocaine, and uppers were in three of
the last four bathrooms; more weapons and Kevlar vests
were in the closets. He also found one more black UHF
radio. Several of the weapons he discovered still had
LAPD evidence tags wired to their trigger guards with old
case numbers on them, telling him that this ordnance had
been stolen from the munitions locker downtown, where
confiscated street weapons were held after being used in
court prior to being destroyed.

He lost track of time as he wandered through the last
house on Dolores Street. Every two minutes, without fail,
another plane took off, rattling windows, roofs, and
Shane's confidence.

Suddenly, out of the corner of his eye, he saw movement, then heard the sound of a car engine. He looked

out the side window of the house and saw a gray van pulling up the street, followed by several cars. One of them was the orange-and-black Charger he'd seen Jody driving on the San Diego Freeway.

"Damn!" he said under his breath, cursing his lack of vigilance, as one of the cars pulled into the driveway of the house where he was hiding. Shane crossed to the front door. Through the small glass eyehole, he saw a tall, muscular African American man wearing a baseball cap get out of a Chevy pool-cleaning truck. He was carrying an assault weapon and a Kevlar vest. The man moved slowly up the walk toward the house. Then he heard somebody yelling from across the street:

"Hey! Somebody's been inside my crib!"

Shane turned and ran toward the back door, flung it open, and sprinted into the backyard.

"Muthafucka's over here!" he heard the African American shout.

Suddenly an assault weapon let loose close behind him, and as Shane darted across the yard, he felt a stream of lead stir the air by his head just as he ducked around the garage. He spun back in time to see the entire rear corner of the wood building turn into chunks of flying debris and stucco dust as more automatic gunfire chewed into it. He fired three shots blindly in the direction of his assailant, to slow him down and give him something to worry about. Then Shane turned and ran between the garage's back wall and a ramshackle grape-stake fence. He leaped up, grabbed the top of the wood rail, and flipped over, landing in another weed-ridden backyard. This one was also deserted, except for a rusting swing set on a cracked concrete patio.

"Cut him off! He went over the back fence! Block the alley!" the voice behind him yelled. Shane heard footsteps slapping concrete in the driveway of the backyard where he was now trapped. He aimed his Mini-Cougar at a spot where he estimated the running man would appear, and waited. His heart was slamming so hard in his chest, he could see his gun pulsing at the end of his triangled grip.

In a moment a huge man came around the corner of the house. He saw Shane and quickly brought a MAC-10 automatic pistol up to fire, but Shane was ready and got his round off first. The muscle-bound man went down screaming, his right thigh blown open, now firing his MAC-10 wildly, bullets sparking off plaster and concrete.

Shane ran directly at him and kicked the man savagely in the head. Then he snatched the MAC-10 out of his weakened hand and sprinted up the driveway.

Surprisingly, despite the gunfire, there was nobody out on the street. A red Ford Fairlane was at the curb, still idling. The fallen giant must have just left it there.

Shane ran to the car, jumped in, put it in gear, and took off. He accelerated up the street just as three men appeared at the intersection behind him and opened up. The Fairlane bucked and shook as magnum-force weapons fire poured into it. Suddenly, his back window and two rear tires exploded. He spun the wheel, taking the corner at the end of the block, squealing on ruptured rubber and sparking rims. He was now heading toward the padlocked fence at Florence Avenue.

"SHIIIIIIT!" he yelled, flooring it. The car wobbled on blown, flapping tires. As it hit the chain-link fence, Shane was thrown into the dash. The car bowed the metal gate, then the tortured hinges popped free and the gate flew open. The Fairlane rumbled through, coming to a stop on Florence Avenue.

Shane was immediately out of the car and running toward his Acura. In the excitement, he realized he had left the MAC-10 on the Fairlane's front seat. Behind him he could hear several men shouting in confusion.

"What the fuck's going on?" the old man with the stringbean neck asked, still holding his garden hose.

"Get inside and call nine-one-one!" Shane yelled as he dove into the Acura, and took off in reverse. He shot backward down Florence, spun a reverse 180, then floored it again. The Acura's torqued engine and tires whined as he sped up the street, finally turning the corner at the end of the block.

THE DAY-GLO DAGO

"SWAT went through the houses," Filosiani said out of the side of his mouth. "Even called the Tech Squad to dust, but so far, it's clean as the board a'health."

Shane reached into his pocket and withdrew the memory strip with the digital photographs he had shot inside the airport houses. "You have my word, *and* these pictures," Shane said as he handed it to the short, round, balding police chief.

"Good going, Sergeant. This is what I like t'see." Filosiani was standing behind his desk in the chief's office at Parker Center.

Shane looked around for a place to sit down. The last time he had been here, the office had belonged to Burl Brewer and was decorated with classic antiques. An amazing array of expensive charcoal line drawings depicting police officers doing their duty had adorned the walls. Shane had been told that the artwork was done by a famous L.A. artist from the thirties and that Chief Brewer had described them as a PR expense, paying more than thirty thousand dollars from the Police Department Public

Affairs budget. Now they were gone . . . sold by Filosiani at auction. The money, Shane learned, had gone to the equipment fund to order new second-chance Ultima flack vests—the latest and lightest body armor on the market. Now there was only a metal desk placed in the exact center of the room, with a secretarial chair behind it. No sofa, no occasional chairs, no artwork. Filosiani had put his phone and computer on a metal rolling table next to the desk. The walls were empty except for two framed diplomas: one containing his doctorate in criminology from New York University, the other his night-school law degree. A large bulletin board was leaning against the wall with the five LAPD division crime-stat sheets and an array of Polaroid pictures of the five division commanders, as well as shots of the administrative staff officers with their name and rank printed neatly below each one. Shane had seen military barracks with more amenities. Filosiani was a no-bullshit guy.

The chief saw Shane looking for a seat. "No chairs, Sergeant. This ain't a place t'sit n'chat. Y'state your business and go."

Shane had heard that the chief was rarely in his office anyway, preferring to be out touring the department, making unscheduled stops. Filosiani had posted office hours for those seeking meetings, but he spent at least three hours each day in the trenches, available to his troops. At first, the Blues in the field had remained skeptical, but slowly, one cop at a time, the Day-Glo Dago was winning converts.

A buzzer on the chief's phone rang. He picked it up and listened, then said: "Send her in."

The door opened and Alexa walked into the office, carrying a manila file folder. She crossed the office and delivered it to the chief. "That was in a wall safe behind a picture in Commander Shephard's office," she said. "I thought a hidden office safe was sort of unusual, so I checked to see who authorized the installation. I couldn't find any record anywhere. I checked the Furniture, Equipment and Transfer Log, along with the Equipment Budget Request for DSG, even the Maintenance and Repair Log. . . . Nothing. The safe must have been put in on the sly, on a weekend or something. We had to drill it to get it open. That file was all that was inside."

The Day-Glo Dago rubbed his mouth with his right hand, inadvertently flashing his diamond pinky ring in the light streaming through his huge office windows. "Okay, then . . . ," he said, opening the folder, "let's see what we got here." He squinted at the first page, flipped a few . . . read . . . squinted again . . . flipped some more . . . Now he was frowning. Then he closed the folder. "It doesn't say nothin'; just a bunch of numbers," he growled, looking at her. "Gibberish."

"Yes, sir," Alexa said. "It looks like some kind of arithmetic code." She still didn't look over at Shane, not wanting to admit that he might have been right, that Mark Shephard had somehow been involved in an illegal conspiracy.

"You get this over to the Questioned Documents Division?" Filosiani asked, referring to the section of the Scientific Investigations Division that broke codes and did handwriting analysis.

"Yes, sir, I sent them a copy; they're looking at it now, scanning it into their computer. Captain Franklin over there said they would probably be able to break it, but he couldn't estimate how long it would take."

"Sir, this unit is going to go further underground," Shane said. "Jody knows I found his crib. He'll be twice as hard to find now."

"Where's the radio you two took outta Shephard's wall?" Filosiani asked.

"In my office," Alexa said.

"Bring it in," he ordered.

She turned and left the room. Shane and Tony Filosiani traded stares but didn't speak. A few minutes later Alexa returned with the twenty-pound black UHF radio. She lugged it in and put it down on Filosiani's gray metal desk.

The Day-Glo Dago looked at the dial. "You say this is set on the same frequency as the one you saw in the noise-abatement house?" the chief asked in his distinctive New York accent.

"Yes, sir," Shane said. "Same frequency."

"It's got a built-in scrambler . . . and a satellite transmitter—very expensive and almost impossible to triangulate on," Alexa added.

"Dusted?"

"Yes, sir. We got a right-hand index and thumb off the faceplate. They're over at Latent Prints with the ones we got off the glass Shane found in the kitchen," Alexa said. "We're running them against Jody Dean's file; then, if that fails, we're gonna see if we can get a cold hit from the Police Academy class records."

Filosiani nodded. He leaned over the radio and put his pudgy fingers on the ON/OFF button. After a moment, he flipped the switch. The radio hissed to life, but there was no one using the frequency. The radio was monitoring dead air, so after listening to the hiss for a minute, he shut it off.

"They probably have those radio units turned on only when they're on surveillance," Shane volunteered.

"Okay, I'm gonna assume the worst here," Filosiani said softly. "I'm gonna assume we got a rogue squad throwin' bricks and tryin' t'fly under the radar."

Alexa's expression told Shane that her defense of Mark Shephard was starting to crumble. "Sir, I'm not at all sure that—"

"Yeah, yeah," Filosiani interrupted her. "Me, either;

but if we assume the worst, then we ain't gonna get schmucked."

The phone on his desk beeped, and the chief picked it up. "Yeah . . ." He listened without speaking for over a minute. "Okay. Got it." He hung up and stared at them. "Latents just got a cold hit. The prints from the radio were Shephard's, but the ones on the water glass belong t' an LAPD sergeant named Hector Sanchez Rodriquez. He was a member a'Cobra, workin' special crimes in the Valley Division. He supposedly died in a drug-house fire two years ago. The story is, he was workin' a Mexican drug ring, undercover, and SIS didn't know he was ours, tried to take down a crack house he was in, lobbed some canisters, and the place flamed. Sergeant Rodriquez went up in the fire. Records is sending his file over."

"Sir, Cobra is one of the LAPD units interacting with the Sheriff's Department. The Vikings were originally Sheriff's Department rogues. Commander Shephard had a Viking tattoo. Jody was in SIS, and since I got that glass two hours ago, we know Rodriquez is still alive, just like Jody. This is a criminal conspiracy."

There was a strange silence in the underfurnished office.

"This ain't gonna be easy," the Super Chief said. "Matter a'fact, it's gonna be tricky and dangerous as hell. . . . But if you two are willin' t'play a little loose, I think maybe we can reel this bunch in."

"Let's hear it," Alexa said.

"I'd tell ya t'pull up a chair, but since I don't have one, how 'bout we all go across the street and get a cuppa coffee?"

So that's what they did.

Shane didn't get home until almost ten-thirty that night. His mind was picking up the dangerous pieces of Chief Filosiani's plan and then putting them back where he found them. Jigsaw pieces that had made a convincing picture an hour ago now didn't seem to fit. In theory it could all come together, but the plan was physically dangerous for both him and Alexa. But despite his nervousness, it seemed as if it might be the only way to lure Jody out—the only way Shane could get Jody to trust him enough to let him infiltrate his secret squad.

Shane had the black UHF radio under his arm as he entered his Venice house from the garage. He could feel the reloaded Mini-Cougar heavy on his ankle. He had filled the nine-shot clip with light loads that would protect Alexa when he eventually fired at her per Filosiani's plan. He set the radio down on the kitchen counter and switched it on. Shane had to wait until the rogue unit went hot again; then while they had the UHF satellite radio on, he would step on their transmission, trigger the mike, talk to Jody, and make his pitch. He hoped Filosiani had given him enough information to get Jody to agree to meet him. As the radio hissed softly from the kitchen counter, Shane fished a beer out of the refrigerator and held it up to his face, rolling it along his forehead to cool his throbbing brain.

Then he sensed movement behind him.

He spun around, but he was way too late.

COMING CORRECT

The first thing Shane became aware of was a fetid, throat-constricting stench. He was still unconscious; the smell had started in the middle of a confusing, kaleidoscopic dream. The odor filled his nostrils, becoming stronger and more unpleasant as consciousness gradually returned. Getting his eyes open was a little like prying up a manhole cover with his fingernails.

He was finally looking at a damp, rusting metal wall; his hands were locked painfully behind him. Finally Shane realized he was sitting on a metal floor, handcuffed to some kind of structural support . . . all of this drifting through his thoughts without making much of an impact. The back of his head throbbed where he had been hit, and a sharp pain pulsed behind his eyes, threatening to explode with each heartbeat. Suddenly a moment of panic and a surge of adrenaline. His thoughts focused; his senses returned.

Cold, bluish light hissing from a Coleman lantern hanging from a knotted rope on the ceiling; the radio he took from Shephard's house, on a nearby table, on the edge of his peripheral vision; three . . . no, two men, talking low.

"Was me, I'd come correct on the man." The sentence had a Mexican lilt. The second voice was deep and rumbling. Shane recognized the same African American speech rhythm from the UHF radio broadcast he had overheard from the house on Dolores Street. He had to concentrate hard to translate the rich ghetto idiom.

"We all be flossin'. You hear what I be sayin'? Jody's all'a time treating us like we just studio gangstas hangin' round, tryin' t'get served. He ain't da only one bustin' moves here. Know what I'm sayin'?"

"You a tough cabeza when Jody ain't in the room, but you just doin' fake jacks, nigger." A chair scraped.

"Ain't afraid a'Jody—fuck Jody," the black voice said, then added: "I think Casper's over there lyin' in the cut. Check him out."

Shane heard footsteps, then a face loomed into view. The man had tangled shoulder-length hair and a bushy black beard laid up against dark, swarthy skin. He looked Hispanic, but his eyes were an odd color for a Latin, a strange light gray—hooded eyes, set deep under massive, bony brows. He shoved his chin down in Shane's face and studied him.

Could this be the late Sergeant Hector Rodriquez?

When the man spoke, the Mexican idiom disappeared. Now his tone was condescending, more like a cop talking to a street criminal: "How's things down there in Shitsville, Scully?"

Shane heard another chair scrape, and a second face swung into view. This was the African American who'd exited the pool-cleaning truck when Shane was trapped in the noise-abatement house. He was ebony black, and now that the man had his baseball cap off, Shane could see that he had shaved his head. From his right ear hung a long chain with a cross dangling at the end of it. His tank top was ripped and dirty.

"How long you been listenin', Scully?" the African American said.

Shane could smell booze on his breath. "Where's Jody?" Shane's pinched voice echoed weakly in the windowless space.

"Ain't here," the Mexican said.

"Are you cops?"

The black man looked at Shane and gave his answer careful consideration before he spoke. "We was makin' weak-ass music, y'know? Hadda leave da jam. You come along and be tryin' t'collect for the trip. 'Cept now all you be doin' is waitin' on the big bus."

The confusing ghetto-speak made Shane's head throb. "Get Jody. I got something he'll want to hear, something important." Shane was trying to focus, to collect his scattered thoughts. He didn't know how long he'd been unconscious. He couldn't see outside and didn't know if it was day or night. As his senses cleared, he began to feel the gentle lapping of water against the outside of the metal wall he was cuffed to. He thought maybe he was on a big rusting boat, somewhere down by the harbor. "I got something important to tell Jody," he repeated.

"You don't tell nobody shit. You assed-out big-time, muthafucka," the African American said softly. "You shot Victory. Fuckin' guy is moanin' and cryin'. We hadda smuggle him down t'Mexico t'get him fixed."

"Victory?" Shane asked.

"Peter Smith. Man calls hisself 'Victory' 'cause he say he never loses. He's the—"

"Hey, Inky Dink," the Mexican interrupted. "Shut up. Yer mama ain't here, so who you tryin' to impress?"

"Don't matter . . . Fuckin' guy's dead anyway."

Then, either because he had been disrespected or to make his point, the black ex-cop stepped forward and grabbed Shane, jerking him up violently. Shane's hands were still cuffed to some kind of structural support, so his wrists exploded in pain as he came abruptly to the end of the chain. His head and torso were only three feet off the floor, his shoulders aching, barely able to keep his legs under him.

"I told Jody we shoulda capped you when you went to see his old lady . . . when you talked to the Good Shepherd," the black ex-cop said angrily. "But he says no. He's got some fuckin' issues with you. Like what you two white boys did in Little League makes a shitload of difference t'anything. But he ain't here t'cover ya, so guess what? We gonna come correct on yo' white-slice ass."

He hit Shane with a thundering right cross.

Darkness swarmed, and Shane was knocked back inside his head. For a second he was still conscious, peering out through a tiny hole of light that quickly narrowed.

Then he was swimming in black . . . dreamless . . . unattached . . . alone.

18

THE WINDUP

"You amaze me," the voice said.

Shane kept his eyes closed; his head was down on his chest. His jaw felt dislocated. He was trying to get his jumbled thoughts in order, standing on the front porch of a disaster, rehearsing opening lines like a teenager on his first date.

Jody's voice droned: "You runnin' all over, talkin' to Glass House brass. I always held your back, Hot Sauce. How come ya couldn't hold mine?"

Shane still didn't answer.

"Give it up, man. I can see ya thinkin' in there. I read you like the funny papers. Open yer eyes, or I'm gonna set your socks on fire."

So Shane opened his eyes and looked up.

Jody was still greyhound-lean, his stringy muscles flexed and bulged under an old LAPD T-shirt that read SIS . . . WE MAKE HOUSE CALLS. Copper hair hung in long, untended ringlets around his head. His tangled beard had not been trimmed. But Jody's X-ray eyes were drilling, piercing holes in Shane's paper-thin psyche.

"I was countin' on you, Salsa, but you didn't come through. It was all I could do to keep my crew from swingin' by your house and giving you a shiny new set of nine-millimeter nipple jewelry."

"You're hanging out with very frank company," Shane mumbled softly; his throat was sore, his jaw was popping cartilage painfully when he spoke. "Your crew thinks you're a piece of shit."

"Two weeks more and none a'that matters. I can hold it together." He smiled, and for a second, Shane saw the old Jody from Little League, smirking after a tough out, joy mixed with sarcasm, as if his charmed life were still just a practical joke on everyone.

It was time to make his pitch. Shane felt weak and dull, not up to the task, but he had no choice. He wondered what day it was . . . how long he'd been unconscious. . . . He wondered if he needed to adjust the Chief's carefully worked-out timetable.

"You got something you're about to lay on me, Hot Sauce. So, get to it." Jody was back inside his head, browsing, uninvited.

"What time is it?" Shane started. "What day?"

"Two A.M. Tuesday morning."

"Tomorrow at nine A.M., the department is gonna know all you guys are still alive."

"I don't think so."

"Commander Shephard had a secret safe in his office. He kept a file on your unit behind your back. Alexa found it. She's taking it to Filosiani tomorrow morning." Shane watched Jody for a flicker of interest or concern but saw nothing. "The whole thing is written in some kinda number code," Shane continued. "Once Filosiani gets it, he's gonna send it over to Questioned Documents. They're gonna scan it into their computer and they'll probably be able to break it in a day or two. Then everything you did to Medwick and Shephard is gonna be for nothin'.'"

"Medwick and Shephard?"

"You killed 'em."

"I what?" Jody smiled. "Why would I kill those guys?"

"Because they were the only two left who knew that you and this squad of yours exists."

Jody was squatting before him, Indian-style. Shane remembered that Jody could squat on his haunches like that for hours; his thighs, like steel, never seemed to tire. He was looking at Shane carefully, reading him like always but never giving away his own thoughts. Jody's face was granite, so Shane had to push his bet. He shoved more chips out. "If that file says you and these other guys aren't dead, then the department is gonna figure you killed Shephard and Medwick so you could disappear. Once they believe that, there isn't a town high enough up in the Andes or far enough out in the bush for you to hide."

A long, tense moment was punctuated by the distant moan of a foghorn. Shane was now pretty sure he was inside one of the old deserted freighters he'd seen chained to the docks in Long Beach or San Pedro.

"I think you still got something else you want to tell me. This ain't all of it," Jody finally said.

"Jody, I've been fucked over by the department." Shane repeated the lines they had all come up with in the coffee shop across from Filosiani's office.

"No shit."

"I made that Naval Yard case, not Alexa, but they gave all the credit to her, gave her the Medal of Valor while I got a psych review. While she makes lieutenant, I'm stuck in a basket-weaving class. At first I was pissed. Now I'm just looking to get paid." Jody didn't respond, so Shane pressed his bet again—threw in some more chips. "When I saw you on the freeway, I was hurt," Shane continued. "You should've told me what was going on—that you were alive. I was like your brother. That's why I went to Medwick's house and to see Lauren. I couldn't believe you'd do this to me . . . let me think you'd killed your-self."

"I had no choice, Shane. It was a department-sanctioned deep-cover op. Medwick set it up. Got the phony coroner and death-scene photos made. CGI, they call it—computer-generated imaging. He got us all un-dercover drivers' licenses out of ATD, where they bury 'em with high-security numbers. Only Medwick and May-weather could access them." ATD was the Anti-Terrorist Division; among other things, it supplied bogus IDs for undercover cops on deep-cover stings. "I couldn't tell you, Salsa. . . . It was a black ops case."

"Bullshit. You told Lauren."

"Right. And look what it did to her."

No turning back now. "Whatever it is you got goin', I want in," he said. "I know you're about to score, and I know it's gonna be big."

"Yeah?"

"Yeah. You're not doing doors for the department any-more . . . you're way past that. You're running some kinda high-dollar conspiracy. For you to be taking this big a risk, it has to be huge."

Jody was still squatting before him, elbows propped on knees, hands straight out, not moving, studying him in-tently. Shane tried to make his thoughts neutral so Jody couldn't crawl back inside his head and read the lies.

"I was gonna use that UHF radio I found at Shephard's to contact you," Shane continued, "to set up a meet . . . but you moved first. I wanted to tell you, I think I have a way to save this for you, but if I do, I want in. I want an equal share."

"You're dreamin', Salsa."

"Jody, the department is going to find me unfit to re-turn to duty and they're gonna take back my pension. Twenty years on the job goes in the shitter. . . . They're gonna gig me, I can smell it."

"I warned ya," Jody said. "In police work, it's all about CYA."

"Covering your ass. Yeah. . . . So you better listen to me and cover yours. Since Shephard died, Alexa Hamilton is the temporary head of DSG. I told her I saw you on the freeway. She's goin' to Filosiani with it tomorrow. Since she's just won the MOV, he's liable to believe her."

"Good goin', Salsa," Jody growled. "How's this supposed to help me?"

"I call her up, tell her I figured the number code that Medwick's file is using. Tell her the numbered file she found in his secret safe is not an arithmetic sequence but a key-book code and that I found the key book. I'll set up a secret meeting with her in some deserted spot, tell her if she brings the file, I'll bring the key book, so we can break the code together. She's an ambitious bitch. She'll come because she'll want to claim the credit."

" 'Cept it's probably not a key-book code," Jody said. "Medwick was in DSG, and DSG always uses alphabet number codes."

"She doesn't know what it is. If I say it, she'll assume I'm right," Shane answered, "and she'll know Questioned Documents will never be able to break a key-book code. She'll *have* to play ball with me to get the book."

A key-book code was a simple and almost unbreakable code developed by the Germans in World War II. In order for it to work, both the sender and receiver had to have the same book. If the word you wanted to send was *apple*, and it was the third word on page 200 of the key book, then you would write *200-3*. The person receiving the code would read the third word on page 200 in the same book, where he would find the word *apple*, and so on. Without the key book, the Scientific Investigations Division would never be able to break the code because it didn't correspond to the frequency of letters used in the alphabet, like most codes, but to a page in an unknown book. Shane could see this realization dawn on Jody's face.

"Without the key book, she'll know she's got nothing," Shane continued. "That secret file was originally set up by Medwick and Mayweather. Mayweather died during the Naval Yard case, leaving Medwick. He retired and turned it over to Shephard. If the department knows you guys are alive, they'll know you killed those two captains. Your picture will be at every airport and border crossing. You'll spend the rest of your lives running."

Jody's intense blue eyes kept drilling, compelling Shane to look away.

"She used me, man . . . fucked me over," Shane growled. "I hate her guts." Shane was aching all over. His head was throbbing even worse than before. This story had sounded foolproof when he, Alexa, and Filosiani had discussed it over coffee earlier that evening, but now, handcuffed in the dark hull of the rusting freighter, he hoped Jody would go for it.

"Lemme think about it, Hot Sauce," Jody finally said, then rose gracefully to his feet without having to put his hands down for balance or to push himself up.

"I can get her to meet me and bring the file before it goes to Filosiani. I know I can."

"Would you kill her for it?" his old friend asked softly.

"Yeah, I could kill her, you bet I could."

" 'Cause if I go for this, that's what you're gonna do."

"Jody . . . it could be like old times."

Jody stood over Shane. "I'll get back t'ya," he finally said, then turned and walked out of the cargo hold, closing the rusting hatch behind him.

The distant foghorn moaned, a morose note, low and dark, like Shane's plunging spirit.

THE PITCH

Shane had been dozing.

Somebody was touching him under the chin, pulling his face up. His eyes opened and he was looking at Jody. The Mexican with the gray eyes loomed in the background; the Coleman lantern hissed and sputtered.

"Make the call."

"Thanks, Jody."

"Shut up and listen. You lure her out; you take the file; then you light the bitch up."

The Mexican stared.

"Hot Rod, here, and Inky Dink wanted to pull your drapes. I still might let 'em, so you're on strict probation." Jody glanced at his watch. "It's just after three A.M. You call her at home around four and get her moving. I want this to go down before sunup. Gimme the cuff key, Rod," Jody ordered.

The big Mexican stood still, his gray eyes burning with contempt.

"I said gimme the fucking key, Rodriquez," Jody repeated. "You gonna make me take it from you?"

That confirmed it. *The gray-eyed Mexican was Hector Rodriquez.*

Reluctantly, Rodriquez reached into his pocket and pulled out the key.

Jody snatched it from his hand, reached behind Shane, and uncuffed him. "Get up," he commanded.

Shane's legs were weak under him as he rose. Jody spun him around and quickly recuffed him.

They led him out of the rusting cargo hold, clanging up a set of metal stairs, onto the deck of the old freighter. As he came out of the hatch, Shane saw a million stars twinkling in a windswept sky. He filled his lungs with fresh ocean air. They led him off the dank freighter, down a makeshift wooden gangplank, and over to the same gray, windowless van that had pulled into the noise-abatement area. Shane was shoved into the back, down onto the floor. Rodriquez got behind the wheel, and Jody, carrying the black UHF radio, slid into the passenger seat facing back, never taking his eyes off Shane.

"You got my gun?" Shane asked, noticing his ankle holster had been removed.

"Right here," Jody answered, holding it up. "Why?"

"If I'm gonna take her out, I wanna use it. I qualified Marksman with that piece."

Jody smiled but said nothing. Rodriquez put the van in gear. Shane heard the tires crunch on the gravel as they pulled away from the rusting freighter. Then they jounced along on the rutted, paved roads down by the San Pedro docks until they got on surface streeets.

They drove for almost forty minutes while Jody made him rehearse his call to Alexa, going over it several times, adjusting a word or thought here and there until he was finally satisfied.

Shane could not see out of the windows, but he knew from the speed that they were now traveling on one of the L.A. freeways. Occasionally, he could see a lit sign streak by overhead, but from his position on the floor he couldn't read them. He had no idea which way they were going. Rodriquez's cold gray eyes never left him for long, constantly frowning back from the oblong rearview mirror.

Shane wondered where the rest of the members of the unit were. Victory was in Mexico, getting his wound attended to, but where were the others?

Finally they came to a stop, and Rodriquez turned off the engine.

"Okay, Salsa, we get out of the van. Hot Rod, here, is gonna lead the way. You follow. I'm in the rear. We go single file . . . head down . . . no talking."

"Right," Shane answered.

Jody got out of the van and pulled open the sliding back door. As Shane exited, he sneaked a look. They were at some low-end motel in a shabby, half-built, one-story neighborhood. Fields of weeds and low cactus plants completed the rest of the landscape. It seemed to Shane that they were in the far West Valley, perhaps Sunland or maybe even as far out as Valencia.

"I said head down!" Jody said harshly, and slapped him hard with the palm of his hand in the exact spot where Shane had been blackjacked earlier. He winced but managed not to cry out.

They followed Rodriquez into a small motel room through a chipped red door.

The room was threadbare and decorated like Pee Wee's Playhouse: ratty orange drapes fought with faded olive-green club chairs and a yellow bedspread; the vinyl furniture had hosted a hundred forgotten cigarettes. Jody closed and latched the door, then spun Shane around and uncuffed him, stepping back to put a few feet between them. "Okay, call her. Use that phone. I'm gonna be listening from the bathroom extension."

"Okay."

"And, Hot Sauce . . . here's the 411. I love ya, but that horse don't happen t'be runnin'. You get cute, I'll kill you right here and let Rod piss on your corpse. You should also know I sent Inky Dink over to Santa Monica. He's parked across the street from her apartment. So if this is a setup, he'll spot a tail, and then it's lights out for everybody."

"I'm down, man. Stop threatening me." Shane was trying to manage both fear and anger.

After a second, Jody nodded and handed Shane a typed address. "That's where she needs to go."

Jody moved to the extension, unscrewed the receiver, emptied the speaker element into his palm, replaced the handset in the cradle, then nodded.

Shane picked up the phone and dialed Alexa's number. Jody waited near the second phone until Shane signaled that it was ringing, then Jody picked up the extension and pulled the cord out to a spot in the dressing area where he could watch Shane.

On the third ring, Alexa answered the phone.

"Hello." Her voice sounded clogged with sleep, but Shane knew she'd been waiting for his call.

"Alexa, it's Shane."

"It's the middle of the damn night," she complained groggily.

"Yeah . . . Yeah. Look, something just developed. I think I'm onto something here."

"Huh? What? Jesus, what time is it?" A pause for theatrics, then: "It's four-fifteen in the fucking morning!"

"I think I found 'em, Alexa. Better still, I think I maybe found the code they're using. It's a key book. If I'm right, we got a Class A collar here. These guys are cop killers. It'll be our bust."

"Key book?" She was sounding more awake now. "A key book can't be cracked by the computer." Pensive and cautious—reading her lines like Meryl Streep.

"Exactly."

"Okay . . . Okay . . . Where are you? Don't do anything till I get there."

"We gotta make a deal first."

"I don't make deals, Scully."

"You do if you want a piece of this. You jobbed me on the Naval Yard case and you gave me up to Shephard when I saw Jody. This time, we do it one hundred percent my way."

"You've turned into a complete dick, ya know that?" she snorted. Then there was a pause, and she added, "Okay . . . what's your deal, big shot?"

"You do this exactly the way I say. No arguments, no revisions. Right now we both have a bargaining chip, so you bring the file you got from Shephard's office; I'll bring the book."

"That file's evidence! I don't even have a copy yet."

"We need it to make sure I really found their crib. If my book decodes your document, then we know I'm right."

"Where are you?"

Shane looked at the typed sheet Jody had given him.

"I'll meet you at 1623 Glen Oaks. Near the old deserted airfield in San Fernando out by the wash."

After a long silence, she asked: "Where's Jody's unit now?"

"They're on a field op. It sounds like an all-nighter. I'm listening on the radio we found in Shephard's house— monitoring them. If you hurry, we'll be out before they get back."

"Okay, stay put. I'll be there in twenty-five," she said, then hung up.

"Let's go," Jody said. "It's only ten minutes from here. Tremaine will tail her from her place."

Shane figured that meant Inky Dink was Tremaine.

When they got back into the van, Rodriquez slid behind the wheel again. Jody sat in the passenger seat, Shane on the floor in the back as before. This time they left the cuffs off.

"Get rollin'," Jody instructed. Rodriquez put the van in gear and pulled away from the motel.

They drove for three miles to the old abandoned airfield. It was on a hundred acres, but had only a twenty-five-hundred-foot runway and was right next to the Van Nuys wash. The underdeveloped site had become too valuable for a "propeller only" landing strip, so it had recently been sold to a big developer. A sign on the rusting wire fence proclaimed it as the future site of the Dominico Gardens Condominium Project.

They parked near a culvert. Jody began fiddling with the radio, finally tuning in a rap station. Synthetic drums and black anger filled the van.

"When'd you start listening to this shit?" Shane asked. "You used t'like jazz."

"Funny, but now I puke when I hear jazz. I need some 'tude with my tunes."

"Can I have my gun?"

Jody looked at him for a long time.

"Hey, Jody, you want me to cap this bitch or not? If I'm gonna do it, I'm gonna need a piece, or am I supposed to just kill her with a rock?"

Jody just smiled. "Calm down, Salsa. . . . Here." He reached into his belt and handed Shane's nine-millimeter Mini-Cougar back to him. Shane nodded as he pulled out the clip and checked it. The Remington Lights glittered in the pale moonlight. He slammed the clip back, then stuck the automatic into his belt.

"Okay, we're in the bushes," Jody said. "And, Shane . . . much as I hate to say this: You take her, or I'm taking you."

Jody nodded at Rodriquez; they got out of the van and

walked across the road. Shane watched them until he lost them in the dark.

Twenty minutes later Shane saw Alexa's headlights pull up behind him.

COP KILLERS

Alexa arrived in her Crown Victoria, pulling around and parking in front of the van. Shane stood by the open driver's door, glancing off, trying to see, without luck, where Jody and Rodriquez were hiding. The rising sun was just beginning to light the edge of the horizon. Shephard's radio was on the seat near him, turned down low. Jody and Rodriquez had handsets and were planning to broadcast a phony surveillance.

"Whose wheels are those?" Alexa asked, nodding at the van as she got out of the Crown Vic.

"Rental. Didn't want to use my car—Jody knows it," Shane answered.

Alexa approached him with the manila file in her hand. She was dressed in jeans with a blue LAPD windbreaker and had skinned her black hair back and fastened it with a clip. She wore no makeup, and he could see tension pulling at the corners of her mouth.

Suddenly, Jody's voice came over the radio, startling both of them: "Snake, this is Gopher. . . . Hold your position. I'm comin' to you."

"Dick-brain is still in there with his dealer. They're probably gonna inhale the retail," Rod's voice answered. "If these assholes are chalked up, it could get screwy."

"Roger," Jody said. "We're holding the back door. Let 'em come out. We'll do the takedown on the street. Out."

Shane smiled at her. "Sounds like they're gonna be occupied for a while." She nodded. Jody and Rodriquez were doing the scam broadcast for Alexa's benefit, but she already knew it was bullshit. Shane and Alexa didn't dare break cover for fear that there was a mike hidden in the van—the ultimate game of cheating the cheaters.

The file in her hand was the original. The copy had been scanned into the computer and was in a safe at the Questioned Documents Division. Filosiani had wanted them to use the original in Shephard's ballpoint pen, so Jody wouldn't become suspicious.

"That it?" Shane asked, pointing to the folder and reciting his first line, not knowing whether Jody could even hear him, but taking no chances.

"Yeah. Where is this place you found—how far from here?" she responded.

"It's right on the other side of the fence; the blue and white hangar by the gas pumps. The whole place is deserted. I'm not gonna lug this thing," he said, and switched off the radio.

Then he led her a hundred yards up the road to the padlocked gate.

"There," he said, pointing through the fence at the hangar. "The big blue and white one. I've been through it. They got sleeping bags, Coleman lanterns, ice coolers. . . . Place looks like an ad for *Field and Stream*."

"That's private property. Did you even bother to get a search warrant?"

"No, where'm I gonna get a warrant in the middle of the night?"

"You need a warrant, dummy. We can't go on private

property without one. Anything you find there will be inadmissible."

"Fuck court. This isn't about court; it's about me an' Jody. That fucker lied to me. I'm gonna bring him down." Shane was almost screaming at her, hoping the argument would be overheard.

"That was it all along, wasn't it?" she said. "You don't care about prosecuting these guys; you just want revenge. You're a bleeding sore, Scully . . . no wonder you're going through a Pattern of Conduct Review. Gimme the book," she demanded.

"I left it in there."

"Why on earth did you do that?" she challenged.

"Because if they got back before you arrived and the book was gone, they'd know somebody tossed the place. Jesus, how many of these have you been on?"

"Okay . . . it can still work," she said. "We won't touch anything or leave our prints around. We'll check out the book together. If it translates, we'll back out, call for a warrant and SWAT. Nobody has to know we went in there illegally first. That way we can still use the evidence." Lines written by the Day-Glo Dago.

Shane and Alexa had now arrived at the chain-link gate. After Shane picked the lock, they moved onto the deserted airfield, past a windsock long ago eaten by the toxic L.A. air. It hung at the end of a rusting pole, like the shredded skin of a dead animal. They had agreed earlier to say nothing unscripted, to avoid surreptitious communication for fear they might be under high-powered directional mikes and a telephoto lens. Shane thought this choice of an open location might have been designed by Jody to give Shane and Alexa a chance to reveal themselves to some long-range listening device.

Once they got to the hangar, Shane picked another padlock. He swung the door wide, and they walked into the huge, seemingly empty space.

The timing was now very critical.

Filosiani's idea was simple but dangerous: Shane was to lure Alexa out and then shoot her with a light load. The Day-Glo Dago explained that she would be wearing Kevlar. Filosiani wanted to know who they were working for, what crime they were about to pull off, and how deep the corruption went inside the LAPD—from possible Glass House commanders all the way down to the suspected moles inside the Clerical Division. If Jody thought Shane had murdered another police officer to acquire Shephard's file, the hope was that he would eventually accept Shane into the conspiracy and give him its entire scope.

The critical part of the timing came right after Shane fired his light load into Alexa's Kevlar vest. SWAT was supposed to arrive immediately after the gunshot, before Jody would be able to check Alexa and see that she was wearing body armor. They were then going to let Shane and Jody escape amid a hail of nonfatal gunfire. It had to look good and go down fast.

Shane glanced around the hangar's interior, but because it was windowless and dark, he couldn't see if anybody was hiding in the blackness. He knew that SWAT had tailed Alexa's car from a distance, using a GPS sending device attached to her bumper. They should be a mile or more back, so Tremaine would not be able to spot them. Shane hoped that Jody had sneaked inside to witness the "killing."

"Hand over the file," Shane said.

"I want the key book first."

"There isn't one, you dumb bitch," Shane said, then pulled his gun, ominously aiming it at her.

"You piece of shit. You cut a deal with Jody, didn't you?" she shrieked.

"Gimme the file," he repeated, cocking the gun for emphasis.

"This is a dumb play, Scully. I called in SWAT. They

followed me. You didn't think I was gonna wander in here without cover, did you?" Alexa said. This sentence was supposed to keep Shane clean when SWAT did in fact arrive.

"Whatta I do, Jody?" Shane called into the darkness.

"It's bullshit . . . a bluff," Jody's voice called back from somewhere inside the hangar. "What the fuck you waiting for? Give her the pill."

Shane and Alexa gave each other tight smiles. The trap was set; Jody was inside the hangar with them, watching.

Shane stepped forward, snatched the manila file out of her hand, and checked it.

"Cap her!" Jody ordered. "Do it now!"

Shane aimed his gun at Alexa, but even though all of this was rigged and she was wearing Kevlar under her windbreaker, he was afraid to fire.

"Do it, man! Whatta ya stalling for? She's bluffing. . . . There's no SWAT team!" Jody screamed from somewhere above. "Blow the bitch away, or I will!" They heard him trombone the slide on his automatic weapon.

Shane had no choice. He fired.

The Mini-Cougar bucked powerfully in his hand, surprising him with its kick.

It felt like a full-load recoil. How could that be? The clip contained Remington Lights.

Alexa flew backward, blood spurting from her chest where his bullet had entered.

He couldn't believe what he was seeing: His round had punched through the Kevlar. "Shit!" he screamed.

Suddenly, all hell broke loose. A machine gun started chattering outside, then two others joined in.

"Let's go! Let's go!" Jody screamed. "She brought backup!"

Shane was standing over Alexa's dead body, looking down at a growing pool of blood spreading out around her shoulders. "No . . ." he murmured in shock. More gunfire outside. Jody's footsteps pounding down a set of stairs somewhere behind him. At least ten weapons were now working outside.

Shane was still looking down at her, dumbfounded, when Jody grabbed him and pulled him across the hangar. Shane stumbled over his feet while his stomach leaped toward his throat. He barely avoided vomiting.

A door flew open on the far side of the hangar, and Rodriquez appeared. "Let's go, man! It's a fuckin' SWAT meet out there—they got ten guys and a step van!"

Shane was dragged along by Jody as they followed Rodriquez through connecting doors into an adjoining building. He could see a red-and-gray Bell Jet Ranger with skids and no FAA numbers parked inside on a rolling platform under a center light. Both side doors had been removed from the chopper. A blond man Shane had never seen before was in the pilot's seat; he already had the helicopter whining to life. The big rotors began to turn slowly overhead. Jody snatched a garage-door clicker off a nearby table and aimed it at a huge set of electric elephant doors. He pushed the button. Immediately, the metal slats of the doors began rattling, creaking, and clanking as they went up. Rodriquez moved to the opening door and stood just inside, pouring lead into the predawn darkness. Hot brass clattered and chimed at his feet. Jody pushed Shane into the back of the chopper, then dove in behind him. They could hear a constant barrage of machine-gun fire as SWAT team officers and rogue cops swapped 9-millimeter ordnance.

"Pick it up!" Jody shouted at the pilot.

The helicopter, with its engine at full roar, lifted up slightly and hovered inches above the portable pad. The rotor wind set up a perilous cross-draft inside the hangar, buffeting the Bell Jet Ranger from all sides. It began rocking dangerously but crept forward. When it was halfway out of the building, Tremaine jumped onto one skid and the gray-eyed Mexican hopped onto the other. The pilot pulled the collective back, and the helicopter rose while both men stood on the skids firing MAC-10 pistols at the SWAT officers below.

They were climbing rapidly, crossing the dirt taxiway. Shane could see three police cars and a black SWAT van falling away quickly beneath them as they pulled up. He could see sparks of gunfire aimed at them, but the chopper was moving too fast and SWAT was aiming low. Then they were heading north, leaving the police gunfire behind.

"Fuck you!" Jody yelled triumphantly out the open helicopter door at the distant line of black-helmeted police.

Tremaine and Rodriquez, still hanging on the skids, emptied their clips until the slides locked open. The airfield was now far away, out of sight.

"Mexico," Jody said, grinning at the pilot. The helicopter turned south to meet the Pacific coastline.

Shane sat numbly in the backseat wedged beside Jody, who suddenly grabbed the file out of his hand.

"We're clean," he said, looking at the file full of pages crowded with numbers.

Rodriquez and Tremaine swung inside the helicopter and found seats, forcing Shane to slide over, pinning him to the bulkhead next to the door opening.

"Good catch, Salsa," Jody shouted triumphantly. "Way t'dig it outta the dirt."

He reached over, took the gun out of Shane's grip, and popped the clip. "You see the way she flew when your slug hit her? That's 'cause she was flacked, man. Good thing I put one of these in the pipe for you." He pulled a bullet out of his pocket and held it up. The Remington Lights Shane had checked were still in the clip, unfired. "Black Talons. Cop killers! I put one in the breech. Bastards explode on impact." Jody smiled at Shane, who just sat there, unable to get his mind around it. "You never woulda got the job done with that light load."

Shane was reeling.

He had shot and killed a woman whom just two days ago he had decided to marry.

"Hey, lighten up," Jody yelled over the helicopter roar. "You said you wanted her wet. It's done. You made your bones, man. Don't fuck it up. Don't gimme a reason to have second thoughts now."

Shane looked at Jody and forced a smile onto his face, but it felt as wide and ghastly as the grille of an old Buick.

21

THE VIKINGS

They flew straight out over the ocean, staying under the radar, skimming the whitecaps kicked up by a gusty Santa Ana wind. Once they were six miles out to sea, they banked south toward Mexico. Occasionally, Shane could see a large fishing boat off on the horizon, drifting lazily in the chop, packed to the rails with beer-drinking day fishers.

They streaked over a school of dolphins, twenty or more, humping playfully along in the same direction.

Then after an hour, Jody screamed something at the pilot that Shane couldn't make out over the roar of the engine and slipstreaming air that was rocketing in through the missing side doors. It must have been a shouted direction, because a minute later the pilot altered his course and headed northeast, until they passed over the rugged shoreline of Mexico. Then they were flying low over the open sandy beaches of the Baja Peninsula, streaking along above the windblown surf, the seven o'clock morning sun climbing out of the mountains to the east, lighting the frothy tips of waves and throwing long streaks of sunlight across the white windblown beaches. The helicopter's shadow chased beneath them on the sand, catching up to them a foot at a time as the sun began its slow climb.

It was morning on the worst day of Shane's life.

He sat stoically, the racket of the engine and the buffeting wind mercifully killing Jody's normal inclination to talk.

Shane was trying to find a way to deal with his devastation over Alexa. He knew if he didn't get his head working, he would end up just as dead.

He was suddenly struck by the realization that his own death could be a release. Death would take him out of this pain, and transport him to another place. He would be free of himself, away from this soul-destroying guilt.

Or would he?

There was still Chooch to think about. He could see his handsome son in his memory, standing on the other side of the airport metal detector, holding his pads and duffel.

Don't fuck this up with some whack move, Chooch had warned.

Shane had destroyed it beyond their wildest dreams. It was off the scale. But didn't he still owe it to Alexa to see the mission through?

Or should he just dive out the open door—DFO into the sand at eighty miles an hour, snap his neck, cartwheel into the black, leaving it all behind?

In the end, he knew he couldn't give Jody an easy way out. If he was going to die, he'd take Jody with him. He'd have more honor as a kamikaze than as a suicide. He would bring Jody down . . . for himself and for Alexa. He would do it without mercy or regret.

Then, as if he could sense Shane's murderous pledge, Jody shivered and zipped up his windbreaker.

"There!" Jody yelled, and smacked Shane on the shoulder, pointing at a deserted beach at the mouth of a river.

Shane nodded as the pilot again altered his course, shooting across the beach and up a narrow wash, slowing as the hills narrowed on both sides of the low flying chopper. The Bell Jet Ranger continued a few hundred yards up the gully, swapped ends, then hovered over a patch of grass.

A short way off, Shane could see a dusty new blue-and-white, thirty-six-foot, double-axle Vogue motor home parked on a dirt clearing—an expensive rig with all the extras. A satellite dish poked up from the roof. Two men were standing in front, shielding their eyes, shifting and turning away from the swirling rotor sand as the helicopter settled. Even at that distance, Shane could see that one of the men was gargantuan, leaning on crutches, his left leg bandaged from ankle to hip. The last time Shane had seen him, they were faced off over gun barrels behind the noise-abatement house. Shane felt the skids touch ground, and the pilot started flipping switches as the engine wound down.

"Let's go." Jody was out of the helicopter first, followed immediately by Tremaine and Hector Rodriquez. As Shane started to exit, he looked into the expressionless, hazel eyes of the pilot, who wore his weathered complexion like a snake's skin.

"David VanKirk. Jody calls me Lord of the Skies," the man said. "I was in the Police Air Unit until IAD terminated me for flying drugs up on weekends. Now I drive this taxi for the Vikings. Personally, I don't give a shit whether you get a piece of this or not. I'm on a flat deal. But you got trouble here. Watch out for Rod, and Sawdust."

"Sawdust?" Shane asked.

"Yeah. The tall thin guy over there by the motor home. Sergeant Lester Wood—Sawdust. Get it? Jody's got nicknames for everyone."

"Always did."

"See the steroid case on crutches, next to Sawdust? That's Victory Smith. His real name is Peter. You shouldn't a'shot him. . . . Jody thinks he can control them but most a'these guys are doing heavy drugs now. My guess is, you won't last the day."

David VanKirk turned away and finished shutting down the helicopter.

"Thanks for the heads-up." Shane got off the backseat and reluctantly followed Tremaine, Rodriquez, and Jody over to the two men waiting by the Vogue coach. Jody turned to him as he approached.

"This is Hot Sauce," Jody said, laying a protective hand on Shane's shoulder.

All four men glowered at him in silence. Shane found himself trading eye-fucks with the barrel-chested monster on crutches. When they'd exchanged gunfire, Shane had been so jacked on adrenaline that he'd missed Victory's overpowering brutishness. Now, standing in this Mexican wash, he took a better inventory. Viewed piece by piece, he was impressive, but the combined effect was awesome.

Victory Smith was propped up on crutches, the massive slabs of muscle on his shoulders rising and falling slowly with each breath like plates on a weight-lifting machine. His neck triangulated down on overdeveloped trapezius muscles. A MAC-10 was tucked in his belt, and a webbed bandolier full of magnum nines was stretched across a sixty-inch chest; his biceps flexed at least twenty-five inches. Riding atop this angry tower of muscle was a narrow face, pinched and mean, with a complexion as rough as lunar lava, pockmarked and rutted by steroids. Prehistoric, reptilian eyes never moved off Shane, tracking him mercilessly. He was predatory, deadly, and barely in control.

"Our code name is Vikings," Jody was saying. "It was given to us originally by Captain Medwick. I kinda like it, so we've kept it. Hector Rodriquez and Peter Smith are

'Hot Rod' and 'Victory.' They're both ex-SWAT. Tremaine Lane, here, is 'Inky Dink,' and this too-tall, half-mute Texas motherfucker dressed like Clint Eastwood is Sergeant Lester Wood: 'Sawdust.' They were in SIS with me."

Shane had hardly noticed Lester Wood, he'd been so focused on Victory Smith. Now he glanced over and saw a man who radiated silent disapproval. Wood was close to six-four and unnaturally thin, dressed in dusty, worn cowboy clothes. A silver rodeo buckle divided faded jeans from a denim work shirt. He had on a new windbreaker vest, rough-out bull-rider boots, and old-style Ray-Ban aviator sunglasses that were coldly studying Shane from under the brim of a custom-made Charlie Tweddle cowboy hat.

"Shane, I know you two had a little run-in a while back," Jody said, indicating Victory Smith. "But I want you guys to get past it."

Shane didn't say anything; a few more amps of pure hatred spread across the weight lifter's steroid-cratered face.

Jody put his arm around Shane. "This is my old Little League catcher. He's in for an equal share. Nobody fucks with Hot Sauce, or they deal with me, *personally.* Now, olet's break out that beer an' get a fire going. We got plans to make. Bring all that shit down to the beach." Pointing at three coolers sitting on the ground near the motor home, he opened the door and disappeared inside.

Shane found himself looking at four seething ex-cops. Nobody spoke.

"In literature, this is called a pregnant moment," Shane finally said, trying to break the tension.

"Hey, asshole," Victory Smith whispered, "I don't know what you think you got goin' here, but far as I can see, you're just a walking corpse."

"Maybe you should take that up with Jody," Shane answered.

"Fuck Jody," Victory growled. Moments later Jody bounded out of the motor home and set down a cooler of beer. He saw the anger, hesitated, then started pulling cold brews out of the ice chest and flipping them around at the circle of men.

Smith made no move to catch his. It ricocheted off his crutch and landed in the sand.

Jody tried to talk their anger down. "To begin with, let's get a few facts straight. This ain't his fault. He saw me on the freeway. My mistake—not his. He did what any one a'you woulda done if you saw a friend you thought was dead. He looked into it."

Now they were all glaring at Jody.

"He shot an LAPD sergeant for us. Killed the acting head of DSG and took this file." He reached into his back pocket, pulled out the folded manila folder, and waved it at them. "Hot Rod and Inky Dink were there. Right? Tell 'em what you saw."

Reluctantly, Tremaine Lane and Hector Rodriquez nodded, but the nods were so subtle, they were almost imperceptible.

"This file is in code, but it says we're all still alive. Fortunately, it's the original and there are no copies. Right, Hot Sauce?"

"Right," Shane answered.

"It was only hours from being sent to the Questioned Documents Division. We were all about to get made. Without Scully, our whole deal was dust. So, in my opinion, that gets him a piece."

"Then give him your piece," Smith said darkly.

"And what're you gonna do, Victory? You gonna lead cheers and be in charge a'that fuckin' crutch? Who's gonna handle your end of it, now that you're draggin' one leg?"

"I wouldn't be draggin' it if yer buddy here hadn't shot me," Victory said, but his eyes shifted briefly away, then came back.

"You're supposed t'be a SWAT Home Incursion Specialist, so how come you're the one ended up stopping a round?"

Victory didn't answer, but he leaned down, and with a long arm, scooped his beer out of the sand. He ripped the tab off; the can chirped and hissed foam.

"Okay. Let's go have this cookout. Sawdust, get the tattoo kit. Since Hot Sauce is a Viking, we gotta give him his leg piece."

Nobody moved.

"Is somebody gonna have to shed blood over this?" Jody asked softly.

"I ain't down with this shit, and I ain't sharin' my end with this peckerwood," Tremaine growled, but the rest of the Vikings turned, and Tremaine finally followed them toward the beach.

After they left, Jody smiled. "Give 'em a little time, Hot Sauce. They'll get over it."

"Right . . ." Shane said softly. "I'm gonna count on you to make that happen." Then he followed Jody down to the beach, feeling intense emotions directed toward his childhood friend—frustration, disillusion, and murderous rage.

THE VIKING FUNERAL

The small gas generator hummed.

The tiny ink-filled needle whirred.

Tears filled Shane's eyes.

Lester Wood hunched over Shane's left ankle while Jody held it against a driftwood plank to stabilize it. Slowly, Sawdust drew the crude Viking helmet, freehanding the tattoo without a stencil, the horns reaching up the inside of Shane's foot unevenly, curling around his ankle bone.

Sawdust leaned into the needle, painfully blunt-ending the job. Shane could see a dark, sadistic smile twitching at the end of the ex-cop's bloodless, ruler-straight mouth. Shane clenched his teeth, determined not to cry out.

They had been on the beach all day, drinking. Shane had tried to keep away from the alcohol, realizing that his survival depended on a clear head, but the ache inside him continued to grow. Finally, about noon, depression overcame him. He consumed beer after beer until sometime late in the day he realized he'd finished more than two six-packs and now felt bloated, sick, and unruly.

As the morning sun came up, the Vikings had stripped off their shirts, and Shane could see the insanity of Sawdust's body art; most of it done with standard stationery-store black ink. Hot Rod was sporting what street parlors call a Fullback Royal—a badly proportioned hand-drawn eagle emblazoned across his shoulder blades. It was still red and looked as though it was getting infected.

All of the Vikings except Tremaine Lane had the same freehand Viking helmet on the inside of their ankles, with additional designs on their arms and shoulders. It was low-grade prison-quality art, done in black ink with Sawdust's amateurish scrawl. For some reason, the African American ex-sergeant had no tattoos.

"There she be. . . . All done," Lester Wood said in his West Texas drawl. Shane looked down at his ankle: red, raw, and bleeding from dozens of deep new puncture marks.

"That's a tattoo?" he said angrily.

"Right now, it looks like beef day at the Injun Agency, but you wait an hour, then git it in the ocean, wash her off. It'll look fine when she heals." Sawdust snapped his kit closed, got up, grabbed a beer, and wandered off.

Shane's ankle throbbed as he stood. Most, if not all, of the Vikings seemed either wired or wasted. Shane watched as they drifted up the beach, away from him. Throughout the day he caught glimpses of their stash and saw fresh needle marks hiding in tattoo ink. Only Jody seemed to be drug-free, but he had been guzzling beer after beer.

Shane noticed that the unit was divided. Lester Wood sat at the north end of the beach with Tremaine Lane. Smith and Rodriquez stayed at the other end. More than once Shane caught the steroid junkie and the gray-eyed Mexican whispering, making plans and looking in his direction.

The end of the day finally came. At sunset, when Jody

and Shane walked down the beach away from the others, Jody pulled a bottle of tequila out of his pocket. "How 'bout a shot a'Mexican courage?" he said, handing it over.

Shane took the bottle, telling himself he would take only a sip, but once he got it up to his lips, he found himself swallowing hungrily, trying to burn loose the tangled knots inside him. His eyes were closed as he gulped it down, until he felt Jody's hand tugging at the flask.

"Hey, hey, Hot Sauce . . . save some for me." Jody pulled the bottle down to find it half empty.

"Yeah, right," Shane said. "Sorry."

"You hit the number this morning . . . put that round right through the ten ring. Clean shooting, Salsa." Jody was talking about Alexa's murder as if it had been a firing-range event.

Subliminal memories flashed:

Alexa flying backward, arms extended.

Blood spurting.

Eyes lifeless.

Shane winced inwardly and his face contorted. Jody saw the flinch. "Fuck her, man. . . . Give it up. She deserved what she got."

Shane nodded, but Jody's eyes were drilling—reading his thoughts, seeing his devastation.

"Don't do this grief thing, Salsa. Get over it," Jody ordered.

Shane nodded again. "You're right. Fuck it," he finally said. They walked on in silence for a few feet, then: "You got a disaster here, Jody. All these guys are cranked up."

"I know they seem a little fractured, but I'm trying to keep things in balance," Jody said.

"Balance . . . Yeah, right." Shane took a deep breath. "Victory Smith is popping Arnies like they're M&M's. He's got 'roid-rage'; it's the reason he wants to rip the shit outta everybody. The guy's got enough gym juice in him to bench-press a school bus. And Lester Wood . . . I saw his Baggie: cocaine and pills. Tremaine is just an alcoholic, and I think Rodriquez is candy flipping—heroin and Ecstasy. The only straight guy you got is VanKirk, and he just sits in that fuckin' helicopter playing Game Boy. You got a mess here, Jody."

"I gotta cut 'em some slack. I can't ride 'em too hard anymore, or they'll mutiny. The only one I'm seriously worried about is Victory. . . . He used t'be a good hammer, but you're right . . . lately his brains are on tumble dry. He quit functioning even before you shot him. But I'll handle it. Leave him to me. We'll all be straight when the deal goes down." He paused and leaned back against a rock outcropping.

What deal? Shane thought, but didn't ask.

"Back in the beginning, before we started doin' doors for Medwick, I had a tight group," Jody continued. "These guys were the best—handpicked. But once we began committing felonies, the LAPD Rules of Discipline and Engagement didn't cut it anymore. At first Mayweather just had us doin' low-grade stuff, and only against big-time organized criminals. We'd break into some shot caller's house and go through his desk, find out what his action was. Then we'd either dime him out to the appropriate division in the department and let them make a bust they could take to trial, or we'd swing down outta some tree and start capping the assholes, handle it ourselves, y'know? The drug-use thing started slow. At first I didn't know they were using, 'cause they did it in their own cribs at those damn airport houses. But once I thought about it, it made sense."

"Cops using drugs? . . . That's never gonna make sense."

"These guys were warriors, man—the best of the best—and the department had them committing crimes. It was fucking them up. So after some low-grade B&Es, a few started doing a line of coke here and there, maybe a little Mexican grass . . . nothin' too nasty, just a little chemical help after a confusing day. But after we took down Medwick and Shephard, a couple a'guys started seriously freaking. I even had t'lose a guy. He went completely haywire. We buried the poor motherfucker on a beach up in Oxnard. Right now I'm just trying to keep some balance here. I only need to hold it together for a little longer."

"Jody, you've been hanging with 'em too long. You've lost your perspective. These guys don't give a shit about anything. . . . Not money . . . Not life or death. They don't want what you want."

"You got 'em all figured out, huh? You're here six hours and you got the whole thing scoped," Jody said angrily, but handed Shane the bottle. "Give it a rest, Salsa."

They sat on a rock and watched the sun go down. A quarter moon came up and rode low on the horizon, reflecting on the silver-black ocean. Shane looked over and saw Jody staring out to sea; his expression was fixed but strangely wistful.

"I'm not saying it's not my fault. . . . I shoulda seen it coming." Jody was silent for a minute before turning toward Shane. "When you cut to the chase, we all just got sold a buncha shit—end of story."

Shane wasn't sure what he was talking about. Whatever was going through Jody's mind, Shane couldn't fathom it. Somewhere along the way, Jody Dean got lost and this new person he didn't even recognize had taken his place.

The almost-empty tequila bottle slipped from Jody's grasp, then clattered onto the rocks and broke. "Protect and serve . . . Respect for individual dignity, compliance with lawful orders, duty to report misconduct . . . courtesy, gallantry, and morality in the service of the public trust. What a crock, huh?" Jody sounded drunk. "These

Glass House swivel-chair commanders write this shit up. They put it in *The Management Guide to Discipline*. They force-feed it to us at the Academy, and we swallow it whole, like a buncha brain-dead assholes. It's a worthy ideal, but it's ill-conceived because you can't give life-or-death power to a bunch a'eighteen-year-old testosterone cases and not have a recipe for disaster. And the strange part is, the bosses in the Glass House don't give a shit; otherwise, they wouldn't sanction units like SIS or SWAT and fill them up with adrenaline junkies."

Shane remembered the discussions they'd had at the end, just before Jody faked his death and disappeared. Back then, Jody had argued that the department needed these two controversial units. He said it was cutting-edge law enforcement like the Special Investigations Section and Special Weapons and Tactics that held back the tide of criminal pollution.

"I thought you loved SIS."

"I was wrong. They finally let me see what a crock a'shit the whole deal really was." He paused, took a deep breath, then went on: "Right after the Vikings were formed, we were working a big drug laundry out of Southwest. We had forty Mexican bankers bagged and tagged and ready for the bus. Had these guys dirty, on videotape . . . big guys, white-collar crooks, at big banks like Bancomer and Banco ProMex. We had the pricks. The case was solid, so we took it to the bosses, Medwick and Mayweather . . . and guess what?"

"They cratered the investigation."

"Worse. They farmed it out to Justice because they were afraid of the political repercussions. If we arrested all these white-collar crooks in the Mexican banking system, they were afraid of the international pressure that would come down. Then, of course, Justice shut down the investigation to avoid the political turmoil. The same people who keep preaching about how we have to protect our children from drugs limited the scope of the investigation so it wouldn't become an international banking scandal for our NAFTA buddies in Mexico.

"When over a year's work hit the wall, we were already set up on this new sting, the one we're working now. It's even more potent. But instead of working it for the department so they could throw it away when it was time to book the perps, we decided to go ahead and work it ourselves. We had already stumbled onto an independent criminal contractor who was into something too good to turn down. We . . . How do I put this? We moved in on him and took over his action. We eventually had to lose him, too, but now we're runnin' his operation and interfacing with his criminal targets. Only this time, nobody gets busted. This time, we're keeping what we make. We're gonna say good-bye to that pile a'bricks up in L.A., split up and live on the Riviera or some damn place. . . . Anonymous millionaires."

"You had to *lose* him?" Shane asked. "You mean you killed him."

Jody turned and smiled suddenly at him. The smile seemed wide and loose and tinged with madness.

"So what is it?" Shane finally asked, changing the subject to get that scary look off Jody's face. "What's the new play?"

"Not yet, Hot Sauce . . . not yet." He pushed himself away from the rocks and stood. "We're outta here soon as I make a phone call and get the okay. Come on . . . I don't like to leave 'em alone too long to plot against me." He was grinning, but they both knew it was true.

It was after midnight.

Shane was on the beach, trying to sleep, but hadn't been able to shut his mind down. He had his head buried in the crook of his arm, while thoughts of Alexa tormented him. His ankle tattoo was throbbing. Twice earlier that evening, he had asked if he could check the locked motor home for bandages, but the Vikings just looked at him with dead eyes, as if they didn't want to waste precious medical supplies on a walking corpse.

Jody had been up the beach arguing with somebody on a portable satellite phone, so Shane didn't bother him. Finally, he had just torn off the bottom of his shirt, wet it in tequila, and wrapped his lower leg.

Shane was looking up at the stars, the ache of Alexa's loss deep inside him. Then he heard something. . . .

He lay still and heard it again: a rustle, like a puff of wind blowing dry grass.

He felt movement on the packed sand nearby. Although Jody still had his Beretta, Shane had found a palm-size granite rock earlier and had put it next to him for protection. He reached out and slowly curled his fingers around it. The round, smooth surface filled his palm. His heartbeat quickened; neck hair bristled. He knew without looking that the man who was snaking up from behind was about to strike. He waited until he felt the ground quiver.

Shane lunged violently to his right.

A knife thundered down exactly where his chest had been. He scrambled to his knees and tried to spin around, but Hector Rodriquez lunged forward and grabbed him. The Mexican's muscular arms locked around Shane's neck, his gray eyes shining. The knife fell out of his hand onto the sand.

"Motherfucker," Rodriquez grunted, bearing down now, closing Shane's windpipe.

Shane dug his heels into the sand for traction as Rodriquez shifted his grip, going for the police choke hold. Shane had to move fast before his carotid artery was closed, shutting off the blood supply to his brain.

"Die, motherfucker," Rodriquez rasped into his ear, ratcheting down even harder. Shane felt consciousness dimming. He was out of options. He swung the rock in his right hand as hard as he could.

It hit with a mushy thud, and Rodriquez screamed. The Mexican let go of his throat, so Shane struggled up onto his knees, then spun around to face the big Hispanic, whose crushed nose was now spread across his face. Blood, lit by moonlight, appeared almost black and dripped from his chin, splattering in ugly Rorschach patterns on the white sand.

Rodriquez went to his belt with his right hand, pulled out a mini-Uzi, and chambered it. "Cocksucker!" he roared.

Then the muzzle flash of automatic gunfire lit the dark beach.

But it was Rodriquez, not Shane, who flew backward. Most of the Mexican's head was missing when he flopped onto the sand a few feet away.

Shane, startled and exhausted, looked over and saw Jody standing in the dark, holding a short-barrel Heckler & Koch machine pistol.

After a moment of silence, Jody walked over and pried the mini-Uzi out of the dead man's hand. "Dig a hole. . . . Let's get him buried." For the first time since he'd known him, Shane thought his old friend looked shaken.

Shane's eyes found Victory Smith behind Jody. . . . The weight lifter's pockmarked face was stretched into a grimace of hate. Shane knew that Smith had somehow managed to talk Rodriquez into the attempt on his life. Now, with Hot Rod dead, Victory Smith was not going to be held in check, no matter what Jody said.

Shane watched from the doorway of the motor home as Tremaine Lane dug the shallow grave, then Lane and Wood dragged the near-headless body of Hector Rodriquez over and laid him at the edge of the fresh pit. Victory Smith teetered on his crutches in smoldering silence.

Jody came to the motor home, opened a side compartment, and pulled out a five-gallon can of Coleman lantern fluid. "We're gonna give him a Viking funeral. No invitation required. Come on," he said.

They walked to the edge of the hole where the three other Vikings stood, expressionless.

"Okay, let's get something straight," Jody said. "Rodriquez died because he couldn't focus on the problem. I talked to Papa Joe this afternoon, and the plans have changed. He wants us up in the Springs tomorrow night to meet the other players. That means we gotta get movin' now. We've got a week, maybe less, before we cash in. After that, we don't ever have to see each other again. But I can't pull this off if we keep losing people." He looked around at their sullen faces. "Starting tonight, no more drugs. This guy's dead 'cause he couldn't keep the spike outta his arm. I'm friskin' everybody 'fore you get on the coach. If you don't ditch your stash, you don't leave with us. The Lord of the Skies will fly you back, and you lose your cut." Nobody spoke, but they all stood there, glaring. "Okay, let's plant him."

Tremaine Lane and Lester Wood rolled Rodriquez into the hole. He thudded when he hit the bottom, three feet down.

"Anybody wanna say anything?" Jody asked.

"Motherfucker sure used a lot of X," Tremaine finally murmured.

Jody emptied half a can of Coleman lantern fluid onto the body, then dropped in a match. The body exploded in fire. They stood there, around the flaming grave, watching Hot Rod burn until they could no longer make out the shape of him.

As Shane watched, he felt another wave of soul pollution that darkened his world and deadened his senses. The moment stood as a dark premonition of the path his life had taken. The depression brought with it a listless loss of self that made everything seem unimportant—even Alexa's murder.

The body crackled and burned, until finally all that was left was glowing ash.

"That concludes the service," Jody said softly.

LISA

Shane saw the distant lights of Palm Springs shimmering on the horizon like a counterfeit jewel. The motor home was crusted with brown sand from the rutted dirt roads they had taken in Mexico before finally crossing the border at Mexicali, then turning northwest toward the Cochella Valley.

The entire way across Baja and into California, nobody had mentioned the shooting of Rodriquez, but the memory certainly lingered.

Then they were driving through downtown Palm Springs, on North Palm Canyon Drive, past Arby's barbecue joints and faux French restaurants, past golf courses and Bentley dealerships.

They left Palm Springs proper and started to pass through neighboring towns, strung back-to-back along Highway 111 like brightly painted beads. They passed Smoketree Village and Palm Springs Heights, with their estate homes built low on the desert hillsides . . . then drove through Cathedral City, the only tarnished bead on this expensive necklace of resort towns. Used-clothing stores and taco stands stood side by side like passengers at a skid-row bus stop trying desperately to ignore one another.

They drove through Rancho Mirage and Indian Wells, finally arriving at the exclusive development community of La Quinta.

The same three architects must have been making a killing in the Cochella Valley. Everywhere he looked, Shane saw Spanish arches and terra-cotta tile. In La Quinta, every palm tree was bathed in its own 2,000-watt xenon "up-light." All of this costly, brightly lit architecture was draped in colorful purple and red hibiscus and bougainvillea.

La Quinta was upscale housing that stretched along several world-class golf courses.

Jody had driven the last leg of the journey and now turned the big, dusty motor home into a new "behind the gates" development project called La Quinta Esperanza. He pulled up to the guard shack and tapped the horn. An octogenarian in a crisp brown uniform decorated with shiny yellow shoulder patches came out of his flower-draped shack with a clipboard and limped over to the driver-side window.

"Howdy," Jody said, grinning. "I'm Lewis Foster. I think I'm expected. I'm a guest of José Mondragon's."

The man scowled at his clipboard as if it contained the results of his last prostate exam. "Can't see with these glasses," he muttered. "Gotta get me a new prescription."

"Lemme help," Jody said, reaching for the clipboard. He found his alias and pointed to it: "Lew Foster. Right there," he said, handing over his phony driver's license obtained by the ATF Undercover Documents Section.

The old man grabbed the clipboard back and nodded. "Yep . . . Yep, sure 'nuff, there she is," he muttered. "I'll get the keys." He returned Jody's license, then limped painfully back into the shack.

"They musta got this plastic badge from Geezers 'R' Us," Jody growled. "If this dinosaur is our security, we're gonna have t'post our own watch. Inky Dink, you got the first duty."

There was a groan from Tremaine Lane in the back of the motor home, then the old man came back and handed Jody a set of keys. "It's the big Spanish one . . . very end of Desert Flower Drive."

The house was at least five thousand square feet and sat at the end of a cul-de-sac. Jody pulled into the circular drive and parked the Vogue coach in front of a four-car garage. Fairways from the adjoining golf course bordered the hacienda-style home.

The Spanish structure was two stories and, from the landscaping, looked as though it had just been completed. Topiary trees cut into veterinary shapes were lit by pale moonlight and haunted the perimeter of the house, rustling in the desert wind like restless spirits.

They climbed out of the motor home, then passed through the side gate into the courtyard, where a wing of guest suites horseshoed around an Olympic-size pool. A few shanked golf balls were submerged in the deep end.

One by one, Jody opened up the guest suites with his keys, and members of the Vikings picked their accommodations. All of the rooms were big, with kitchenettes, living rooms, and remarkable views of either the fairway or the mountains beyond.

Shane's room had a phone jack but no phone. Not that he would attempt to contact Chief Filosiani under these circumstances. He was supposed to get loose and call in, but so far he'd had no opportunity. Also, he didn't know what to say to the Day-Glo Dago, how to explain the "cop killer" bullet Jody had put in the breech of his gun that resulted in Alexa's death.

He undressed in his bathroom, then put his clothes in the suite's apartment-style vertical washing machine and dryer. He set the wash cycle; then wearing only a terry-cloth robe he found in the closet, Shane went outside to swim a few laps. He hoped some exercise would help get his head clear. He shrugged off the borrowed robe and dove naked into the water. His new, raw tattoo shot pain up his ankle all the way to his knee, but he ignored it and kicked hard to the bottom. Just for the hell of it, he retrieved a Titleist 4 golf ball with a huge smile cut in the side, then he frog-kicked the length of the pool under water. When he came up on the far end, he dropped the ball on the deck, and it rolled slowly to a stop between two patent-leather high-heeled pumps. He glanced up, looking into the jade-green eyes of a blond woman in a black-striped business jacket and matching skirt. A world-class beauty, she was standing at the edge of the pool, holding an ostrich briefcase, smiling down at him with open delight.

"José said this place was well stocked," she mused, studying his nude body, "but this is almost too good to believe."

"Jesus, lady. . . . Where the hell did you come from?" Shane blurted.

"Panama City," she replied, deadpan. "And you would be who? The famous but mysterious La Quinta Water Nymph?"

"Funny. You wanna turn around so I can get my robe?"

"Not on your life."

A man's voice called out: "Lisa, let's go! We're late! You can meet these people later."

Shane looked over the pool deck. Standing in the doorway of the lit living room, about twenty yards away, was a short but powerfully built dark-skinned Hispanic man dressed in a black suit. Despite the Palm Springs heat, he had an overcoat draped on his right arm.

"Coming, José," she called to him, then turned back to Shane, kissed her fingertips, and wiggled them seductively at him. "I guess, as the man says, we're going to have to meet later," she said, smiling. Then she turned and walked away, making a show of it, her calves flexing, her short, tailored skirt flipping playfully against sculpted thighs.

LAUNDRY

"Come on, we need to talk," Jody said, startling Shane. He had just dressed and spun toward the open door, but Jody had already left.

He grabbed his wallet off the bed, stuffed it into his pants, and followed.

Shane found Jody standing behind the house by the golf course, on the edge of the sixth fairway, staring out at the moonlit grounds. As Shane approached, Jody handed something to him in the dark. "Here."

Shane couldn't see what it was, but when he took it, he was surprised to find his Beretta still in its Yaqui slide ankle holster.

"Figured after what happened in Mexico, maybe you shouldn't wander around without that. I reloaded it for ya. Full loads."

The gun that killed Alexa.

Darkness hovered, but Shane pushed it away. He sat on the grass and strapped the holster to his right ankle, which thankfully was not the one with the throbbing tattoo.

Jody squatted down beside him on his haunches, Indian-style. "Okay, Hot Sauce. You won't be much help to me if you don't know what's going on, so here's the deal. I already told you about these Mexican bankers, the ones we lost to the Justice Department. . . ."

"Yeah . . ." Shane waited, and finally Jody continued.

"Well, hiding out at the edge of that bust was this little guy we couldn't identify. Name was Leon J. Fine. Turns out he was an L.A. bail bondsman. He was trying to write some paper on one or two of these Mexican bankers. I got a friendly judge to shut that down fast. All of those guys were big-time flight risks—white-collar crooks with no priors. These Mexican bankers were all sitting in jail having anal-penetration nightmares. The judge agreed that if they ever bonded out, everybody woulda been back in Mexico before the first siesta. Anyway, so here's this little shitball bondsman, L. J. Fine, hanging around the edge of my bank case. Maybe he pissed me off, or something about him didn't add up. Either way, I got interested. After Justice took over our case, I had some time on my hands, so I put one or two days in on the guy just to see what his story was . . . and guess what this schmuck was doing?"

"Beats me."

"He was going out to airports, getting on private jets that belonged to Fortune 500 companies, and flying all over the place like he was Prince Abu Dabi or somethin'. So I'm saying to myself, What does my little low-rent L.A. bondsman have on these big corporations, and why are they flying him around in their twenty-million-dollar corporate jets?" Jody smiled at him. "Wanna guess?"

"Why don't you just tell me."

"You ever hear of something called the parallel market?" Jody asked.

"No, I haven't."

"Don't feel bad, neither had I. It's a little confusing till you get the hang of it, but basically, a lot of big Fortune 500 corporations are using their product to launder Colombian drug money. And it's bigger by a bunch than the Mexican bank bust, 'cause hundreds of these U.S. companies are doin' it . . . and have been for over twenty years. Any company with a product that's worth a lot, but doesn't weigh much—like cigarettes or booze or electronics—is prime for the hustle."

"You're shittin' me," Shane said, thinking he must have heard wrong.

"That's what I thought at first, but it's true. The deal we're working right now is with All-American Tobacco. I guess it's not enough these guys are killing us with their cancer sticks, now they're also laundering Cali cartel drug money."

Shane asked, "How do cigarettes or liquor products wash drug cash?"

"It took me a couple a'months to figure it out, but here's the headline on how it works. Let's say my little schmendrik—my bail bondsman, Leon Fine—wants some money to buy a new house, or a speedboat, or some other damn thing. He calls around to drug dealers he knows—guys he's written paper on, and he asks, 'Hey, Pedro, how much money have you got stored up?' Let's say, for easy math, Pedro has ten million in an L.A. collection house, and it's Cali cartel money, and he needs to get it laundered for his *patron* in Colombia. So he says to Leon: 'I got ten cartwheels, but I gotta do the deal with a black marketeer in Colombia, 'cause my *jefe* wants the cash to end up in Colombia. Then Pedro, the drug dealer, puts Leon in touch with some Colombian black marketeers. Actually there are six families in Medellín who specialize in parallel-market goods. After Leon sets up his deal with Pedro and the black marketeers he calls the Blackstone Corporation—"

"Who?"

"Blackstone. It's a big Swiss free-market trading corporation. There are a bunch of foreign trade companies who do this shit. Blackstone is one of 'em. They're the guys who run the duty-free shops in airports—they also run duty-free zones all over the place. And, Shane, you won't believe this, but these foreign duty-free corporations are running the biggest drug laundries in the world, and have been for two decades."

"How could that be? I been a cop for twenty years and I never even heard a'them."

"Me neither," Jody said. "Anyway, my bondsman, Leon, says to his contact at Blackstone: 'I got ten million in drug cash from Pedro in L.A. to buy cigarettes, and I have a deal set with Colombian black marketeers, so I need the smokes delivered to Aruba.' Aruba is inside the Caribbean duty-free zone and it's legal for All-American Tobacco to ship as much product there as they want." He paused. "Got it so far?"

Shane nodded.

"Okay, good . . . The Aruba duty-free zone stretches from Aruba across to South America, specifically to Caracas, Venezuela, which is, lo and behold . . . right on the Colombian border. Leon's black marketeer has his smuggling business in a little border town out in the desert, called Maicao." Shane remembered that Maicao was one of the towns circled on the map he found in the noise abatement house on East Lannark Drive. Now everything's set up and ready to go." Jody continued, "Blackstone calls All-American Tobacco and says: 'Ship ten million dollars' worth of Virginia Fives to Aruba for the parallel market.' "

"Virginia Fives?"

"Yeah . . . top-quality Virginia tobacco. See, a lot of the product sold in South America is shit: Turkish leaves or stuff grown in the South American jungle. The top quality V-Five is what everybody wants. So now the guy at All-American says, 'Okay, we'll take a meeting.' Then Blackstone puts a sales distribution executive from All-American in touch with my L.A. bail bondsman, Leon, and they cut a deal. Still with me?"

"Yeah. The bondsman is making a deal with a major drug dealer in L.A. for cash. Then he makes a deal with All-American Tobacco to buy the cigarettes with the drug money, using this Swiss duty-free company, Blackstone, as the middle man."

"Exactly. You got a real knack for this, Hot Sauce. Okay, next, Papa Joe Mondragon, who is Blackstone's head of Latin American Ops, gets in touch with the Cali cartel leader in Colombia. Let's say it's the Bacca family. Papa Joe confirms the deal. The cash is then handed over to Leon, who picks it up in L.A. using a step van, because that much cash is bulky as hell. Leon takes it to a compliant bank, where he deposits it and wires it to one or two other U.S. banks, to wipe out the paper trail. Then he wires it to a numbered account in a bank in Aruba, where it's held and earmarked to go to All-American Tobacco to pay for the cigarettes when they finally arrive in Aruba. That gets both the cigarettes and the drug money to pay for them out of the U.S. and safely into the Aruba duty-free zone. You with me still?"

"Yeah. . . . Two bank transfers to throw off any suspicious bank examiner, and now the drug cash is in Aruba along with the smokes."

"Exactly. What makes this deal really sweet for the tobacco company is, normally AAT sells a case of cigarettes, which contains fifty cartons, for a base price of a hundred dollars in the legitimate market. But remember, they have to pay U.S. federal cigarette taxes, so that pushes their sales price per case up to three hundred dollars."

"The federal duty on a case of cigarettes is two hundred dollars?" Shane asked, surprised by the amount.

"Cigarette taxes are a bitch. Except on this deal, these cigarettes are gonna be smuggled out of the duty-free zone, into Colombia, and All-American is never going to have to pay the taxes. But AAT sells them to Leon for three hundred dollars a case anyway, just as if the taxes were attached. So instead of making a hundred dollars a case on these smokes, they're actually making three hundred. A much, much better deal for All-American."

"So the parallel market in Colombia is way more profitable for them than the legitimate market."

Jody nodded. "Then the cigarettes are shipped by All-American to Aruba and smuggled into Colombia, where they're sold. Then my little schmendrik, Leon, collects the drug cash, which is in the Aruba bank, and wires All-American Tobacco their money. He also pays Blackstone, which takes a three percent cut. Leon gets his percentage. Then the cigarettes are sold in the Bacca cartel black-market malls in Colombia. That completes the circle, because once Bacca sells them, he gets his L.A. street cash back. The Cali cartel loses about forty percent from the original ten million for this laundry service, but he can now say he's a legitimate cigarette broker and claim his income without fear of prosecution. Everybody goes away rich and happy."

"You're shittin' me."

"That's what this little bald geek, Leon, was doing. And get this: Leon's end of the deal is thirty percent of the gross amount. Off that original ten million bucks, he would be making three million. This little piece a'shit was doing better than the president of All-American."

"So what happened?"

"We picked him up, beat the snot outta him, and got him to introduce us to all his contacts . . . especially José Mondragon, who is head of Latin American Product Placement at Blackstone—the godfather, as far as all this is concerned. Papa Joe has to bless every deal, or AAT and the Colombian drug lords won't play."

"Why are you running the laundry? Why not just rip the drug dealers and take all the money?"

"That was my first plan, too, but if you rip these greaseballs, they'll never stop lookin' for you, and there's enough in this deal so our thirty percent is plenty."

He paused to let that sink in, then went on. "After we got Leon to duke us in with Papa Joe, we also got a list of Leon's contacts at all the other Fortune 500 companies he'd been dealing with. Once he told us all that, Leon didn't seem like such a critical element anymore, so we just took the business away from him and set him up with a six-foot hole and a bag of lye on Dead Man's Beach in Oxnard." Jody smiled. "If the tide changes, that beach is gonna spit up more bones than a Halloween horror flick. In the meantime, we're cutting our deal on those cigarettes tonight with José Mondragon and All-American Tobacco."

"Who's Lisa?"

"Lisa St. Marie. She's AAT's account exec on this deal. Bitch is a tough negotiator. She'll try and cut our percentage to improve All-American's take."

"But you can handle her, right?"

"Yep. Good-lookin' piece of trim, but she's cold as a polar bear's nuts. She's also something of a sport fucker and I'm told by those who've tried her out that she's a world-class lay. Just do me a favor: if you decide to haul her ashes, don't tell Victory. He's got a crush on her, and so far she won't give him any play."

Shane nodded his head. It was hard to believe that Fortune 500 companies would be engaged in this kind of criminal behavior, but he believed what Jody was telling him was true.

"So that's what we're doin', Hot Sauce. Only the deal

we're cutting tonight's not for ten million dollars . . . it's for fifty."

"What's the split?" Shane asked.

"Thirty-three point five of the fifty million buys the cigarettes and goes to AAT, the other sixteen point five mil is commission. Three percent, or one point five mil, goes to Blackstone; thirty percent to us. Our end of this fifty million dollar deal comes to a cool fifteen mil. No taxes, no record of the deal . . . it's cash in a bag. After this is done, each of us is gonna get a little less than three million dollars apiece. David VanKirk gets a half a mil to fly the chopper."

Shane let out a low, long whistle.

"Now you can see why we crossed over; why Medwick, Shephard, and Hamilton had to disappear."

Shane said nothing.

"If I hadn't watched my little bail-writing shitball do this, I wouldn't've believed it myself. But it's for real, the payday of a lifetime, and as of now, you get Rod's share." Jody let out a long breath and smiled. "Welcome to the Vikings, Hot Sauce. And don't ever say I never gave ya nothin'."

PAPA JOE

Everybody called José Mondragon "Papa Joe." Aside from the house at La Quinta, he also kept a villa at the Ritz-Carlton in Rancho Mirage, where he transacted his business. Tremaine Lane had security duty, but the rest of the Vikings left for the eight o'clock meeting at a little past six. They stopped on the way to pick up some food and new clothes, parking the motor home in a pay lot in Palm Desert. Then Jody doled out some money that Papa Joe had given him to buy the scruffy unit a more terrain-friendly wardrobe.

Shane wandered the shopping malls with Jody, but eventually they split up and he found himself at Don Vincent's Store for Men, on North Palm Canyon Drive. He selected a lightweight blue blazer, gray slacks, and a pale-blue shirt with a white collar, along with new underwear, socks, and shoes; then he rolled up his old clothes and put them in the store bag. Shane was just coming out of the dressing room when he was stopped in his tracks by a rayon nightmare. Lounging in a nearby chair, dressed in a new shimmering mint-green shirt, which stretched ominously across his overdeveloped chest, was Victory Smith.

"Hey, Scully," the huge weight lifter said. "Two hours I been wandering in these stores buyin' stuff, but I ain't happy, man."

"It ain't easy bein' green."

"Rod was my home slice. He and I rolled up scumbags together for two years in SWAT. I loved that guy. Because of you, he got dusted, an' it's pissing me off."

"Whatta you want from me?" Shane asked, setting down his bag so that both hands were free while feeling the comforting weight of the automatic on his right ankle.

Smith saw him freeing up and smiled: "Hey, dickwad, I'm not gonna try for you in a Palm Desert men's store. Gimme a little credit here."

"I don't want any trouble. Why don't we put this behind us?"

Victory Smith pulled himself to his feet. He had dropped one of the crutches somewhere and was now using only one. He propped it under his left armpit and leaned on it casually. "You know where the abductor canal is?" he said lazily.

"North Michigan, up by Lake Erie."

"Keep the jokes comin', asshole." They glared at each other. "The abductor canal is in the mid-thigh. That's where your slug hit me. You'd be surprised how much really necessary stuff goes through the abductor canal: you got your deep femoral perforation artery—carries blood to your feet; your femoral nerves—fuck with them and they hurt like a bitch. Then y'got all the other abductor muscles—your abductor minimus and magnus; plus a lotta tendons and shit, too numerous to mention. After you shot me, this leg looked like a plate a'spilt spaghetti—a fuckin' mess. Beyond that, my Beaner doctor musta got his license at the Tijuana School of Terminal

Agony. How much of this is ever gonna work right again is anybody's guess."

"You trying to tell me something?"

"Just fillin' you in on what happened, Scully; what you did to me." He turned and hopped toward the door, then stopped and swung back. "I got one real bad habit. Even back on the job it kept getting me in trouble. Wanta guess what that was?"

"You fart in squad cars."

Smith ignored the remark. "I'd go outta my way to make things right. Didn't leave no negative balance on the books. Fuck with me an' you got some payback comin'. No exceptions, no reprieves."

"I'll consider myself warned."

"It's not a warning, Hot . . . Sauce," stretching it out, making the nickname sound ridiculous. "No, sir, not a warning."

"Then what?"

"A promise, a fact of life. Course, I gotta wait till I'm feeling a little stronger. . . . Couple a'days and I figure these stitches oughta hold. Then, after I see what's left a'my leg, I plan on givin' you my own Viking funeral . . . very small event . . . just you, me, Rod's ghost, some gasoline, and a match." He turned again and, using his one crutch, hobbled out of the store.

They all met back at the motor home at seven-thirty as agreed, but Smith was late. All of the Vikings except Shane were now dressed like breath mints. Jody had on a plain, light blue, spring-weight sport coat, aqua blue shirt and linen slacks, with a pair of two-tone brown-and-white shoes. He looked like a cartoon gangster. Even Lester Wood had shucked his Western garb in favor of tan slacks and a light-purple shirt. He had a new off-white linen jacket. The rough-out cowboy boots and aviator glasses were all that remained.

Jody studied Shane's conservative attire: "This is the Springs, Hot Sauce."

"I didn't realize we were supposed to dress like Disney characters."

"Where's Smith?" Jody grinned.

They heard the crutch poke-poking along on the sidewalk around the corner from them. Then the massive ex-cop limped into view, and stopped.

"Where you been?" Jody asked.

"Me an' Hot Sauce went shoppin' together."

Jody nodded, not registering the implausibility of that idea. "We gotta get up to Papa Joe's before eight. While I cut the deal with Lisa, you guys hang out by the pool and back me up. Papa Joe says there're only gonna be one or two other people from All-American Tobacco there, so this should only take half an hour. Then we'll find a bar and celebrate."

The Ritz-Carlton Hotel sat on twenty-four landscaped acres in the foothills of the Santa Rosa Mountains, overlooking the Cochella Valley. Jody drove the motor home to the front gate, gave José Mondragon's name, and was directed to the Palo Verde villa at the end of a road that skirted the hotel grounds. The view looked across Frank Sinatra Drive into the twinkling lights of Rancho Mirage. The Palo Verde villa, like everything else in Palm Springs, had sweeping arches and Spanish tile, all of it wrapped in flowering bougainvillea.

As they pulled up to the villa, they could hear a band playing swing music somewhere inside. The melody leaked out across the grounds. Valets in red Ritz-Carlton jackets were grabbing the car keys of arriving guests, jumping into the vehicles and running them backward up the drive at breakneck speed to park them in the overflow lot above. The motor home was jamming up traffic, causing a difficult parking problem.

"Half the fuckin' world's here," Victory complained. "I thought this was a private little deal with just one or two tobacco executives."

"So did I," Jody said, getting out of the motor home and handing the keys to the attendant. "Sorry, nobody up at the gate told me this was so tight down here," he said to the valet. "Who are all these people?"

"AAT executives and their wives," the valet answered. "They're having their Western Regional Sales retreat."

"How do we do a deal with all this goin' on?" Victory said as they headed into the villa.

The band called themselves the Majestics—a string quartet, plus piano, drums, and bass. They seemed stuck on forties music, which the mostly gray-haired men and women in dark suits and cocktail dresses danced to energetically. The Spanish-style living room had been emptied of furniture to accommodate the makeshift dance floor.

Jody was gazing down at his pastel outfit with concern. "Shit," he growled, "we look like a buncha ushers at a Mexican wedding."

After a minute the man who had called out to Lisa when Shane was in the pool walked up, and Jody introduced him as José Mondragon. As Shane shook hands, he could see that the short, powerfully built man was dripping with pricey accessories; a twenty-thousand-dollar gold Cartier watch peeked out from under diamond-studded French cuffs.

As they released the handshake, Jody patted Shane's shoulder, "José, this is my friend Shane I told you about. Of course you remember Victory and Lester."

"Mucho gusto." José shook hands all around, then smiled at Jody. *"Con su permiso, por favor."* He smiled, dismissing them curtly as he took Jody's arm and led him off, leaving Shane and the other two Vikings standing there.

"*Bésame la pinga,* asshole," Smith growled. "Since we all know this fucker went to Harvard, why don't he speak English?"

Without inviting him to join them, Smith and Wood moved off, leaving Shane alone.

He pushed into the bar and ordered scotch on the rocks, then wandered slowly through the party, feeling out of place and suddenly very lonely. He desperately missed Alexa and Chooch. Finally, he wandered onto the veranda and leaned against the concrete rail, looking out across the twinkling lights of the valley.

"I liked your swimming outfit better." A rich contralto voice interrupted his thoughts.

Shane turned and once again found himself looking into the remarkable jade-green eyes of Lisa St. Marie. He wondered if she got that color by wearing contacts. She had changed out of her business suit and was now dressed for maximum effect. It was a high-fashion balancing act, teetering precariously between sexy and slutty. Her neckline plunged, her short dress was slit way up one side, all the way to her abductor canal. She had on just enough jewelry to accent her alabaster complexion, but not too much to detract from her eyes. A single pearl rested between her swelling breasts, diamond earrings twinkled from behind shoulder-length wings of honey-blond hair.

"Is it too soon in our relationship to make a personal observation?" she smiled. Her teeth and personality glittered.

Shane didn't feel compelled to answer; she was working hard enough for both of them.

"You have a magnificent tush."

Shane gave her a slow smile. "I'm trying not to get into any trouble with you, Ms. St. Marie."

"I must have made a good first impression. You bothered to find out my name," she enthused, then moved closer to him and slid her right hand through his arm.

He pulled out of her grasp and put out his hand. "I'm Shane." She shook it formally.

"Nice to know you, Shane. Lisa."

"Aren't you supposed to be having a business meeting with Jody right now?"

"I might get around to Jody, but right now I'm more interested in you." She brushed up against him, pressing a breast against his arm.

"You always leave this many skid marks?" Shane asked. "We could both get whiplash. Why don't we start by trying to be friends?"

She studied him for almost half a minute while the Majestics switched to "Stardust." Then she kissed the tips of her fingers; this time, instead of wiggling them at him, she gently touched his cheek. "Nobody can resist me for long, Shane." She smiled at him seductively. "Let me get you another drink; then we can get started on our new friendship. Or better still, why don't you keep me company? Come to my meeting with Jody."

Shane finished his drink to buy time. He didn't want to piss off Jody . . . at least not yet. But this was a heaven-sent opportunity to stand up close and watch the players in this deal. The ice cubes clinked against his teeth. As he set down his glass, he had a strange flashback.

Alexa was standing in his backyard, at the canal house, looking up at Chooch and talking earnestly. Shane's heart froze with the memory, followed by deep pain and intense longing. Then Alexa and Chooch were gone, and Lisa St. Marie remained, frowning at him. She had seen the painful look pass through his eyes.

"Whatever that was, I don't want any," she said.

"I was just remembering something," he muttered.

"Follow me, I'm betting we'll have some fun."

So he followed her . . . across the dance floor full of swirling executives and into the bedroom where José Mondragon, Jody, and three other men were waiting.

TRIPPING

The bedroom was large, dominated by a king-size Spanish-style poster bed. Four men turned simultaneously as Lisa opened the door. A frozen tableau.

Jody, dressed in powder blue, with two-tone shoes, his drink halfway to his mouth, glaring; José Mondragon, by the desk, looking up from a sheaf of papers, startled, like a kid caught cheating on a test. And then there were three gray-haired AAT tobacco executives who were standing together by the plate-glass window. As the door opened, these three West Coast cancer distributors stared as Shane and Lisa entered the room.

"I don't think we need any more people here than is absolutely necessary," José said, now speaking in perfect, unaccented, English. He had completely dropped his bullshit *"cómo está"* act.

"I can vouch for Mr. Scully," Lisa said. "He's working with us on distribution. He's also an extremely qualified deep-end retrieval expert." She twinkled this nonsense at them, and the room tension dissolved in her smile like an Alka-Seltzer tablet in a sea of sexuality.

Only Jody seemed unmoved. In fact, there was a crazy tightness to his mouth and around his eyes, as if he had just been insulted and didn't know where to park the anger. Finally he nodded—a jerky, almost spastic movement not at all like him.

Lisa motioned toward one of the lung-cancer salesmen. "This is Chip Gordon, head of our overseas subsidiary, American Global Tobacco," she said, smiling at a tall, narrow-shouldered man whose face in profile had the shape of a quarter moon. "And this is Arnold Zook," she said, motioning to a nondescript, pudgy man with a laurel wreath of gray hair circling a shiny pate of open scalp. "He supervises some of our other Latin American duty-free transactions." She turned toward the third man, dressed in black: "And our host this evening, Louis Petrovitch." She didn't mention his corporate title, but it was obvious that Petrovitch was the power player. He had a Prussian general's military bearing—tin-colored short hair, a mile of jaw, and eyes the approximate color and texture of poured concrete. He didn't acknowledge the introduction.

"Shall we go out onto the patio, where it's safe?" José suggested, fearful of listening devices. He swung open a pair of double doors, and the group walked out onto a large deck, almost twice the size of the bedroom. Shane followed, finding a spot near the door where he could observe but would hopefully be forgotten. The rest of them walked to a glass-topped table ten or twelve feet away. The lit golf course stretched out, fragrant and verdant below them. Shane watched as Jody sat; he seemed stiff, uncoordinated.

Where was that old fluid grace . . . Jody's athletic elegance . . . where was the casual economy of motion?

Lisa was the last to join them. She slithered into a chair and wrapped her legs to the side, showing a lot of well-shaped thigh. Chip Gordon, Arnold Zook, and the formidable Lou Petrovitch stood nearby, holding glasses of melting ice. When Lisa crossed her legs, Shane heard Petrovitch inhale sharply.

He's sleeping with her, Shane suddenly realized.

Lisa smiled at Jody with jade-green confidence, while Papa Joe started the meeting.

"Lisa will conduct this transaction for AAT," José said. "As the representative for Blackstone Duty-Free Imports, I will act as a court of last resort in any dispute. My company will also control the drafting of the transaction, and the contract will be held at the Blackstone office in Geneva for obvious reasons. Acceptable?" The question was aimed at Jody, who simply nodded. Strangely, Jody's hands were trembling on the tabletop.

What the hell's wrong with him? Shane wondered.

"Okay, Ms. St. Marie, you're on," José began.

"Señor Mondragon tells us you want to buy some duty-free, V-Five product and market it in Aruba," Lisa said. "Aside from distributing product, we can also handle all the shipping, warehousing, and insurance. I'd like to pitch a package deal."

"Skip that. Let's start with the cost per case." Jody's voice was shaky. "Since we're dealing in bulk, I think five percent to Blackstone and three hundred dollars a case to All-American is fuckin' nuts. You're not even paying federal taxes. It's way too high. We're gonna need a break on those numbers." Unexpectedly, Jody started rubbing his eyes. The people on the deck watched him with growing concern until he finished and squinted up at them. *"What?"* he said angrily, catching them staring.

"It's always bad form to look into someone else's pocket, Mr. Dean. I think if you want to do a deal, we need to transact it along traditional lines. Whether or not we have a federal tax burden just isn't any of your business," pudgy, dark-suited Mr. Zook said.

"Traditional lines? How many guys you do business

with want to buy fifty million in V-Fives in one shipment? I'm looking for a discount and a lowered percentage for volume."

"Let's get back to who handles the product-shipment insurance and warehousing," Lisa said, smiling across the glass tabletop at Jody, trying to calm him down.

Jody didn't answer; instead, he rubbed his eyes again. It was almost as if he couldn't see properly.

"We'll ship for fifty cents a carton," Lisa said. "We'll insure for another dollar fifty. We'll warehouse in our building in Aruba for two hundred dollars a pallet on an amortized weekly rate."

Jody dug into his pocket and pulled out a folded paper with some math scribbled on it. He squinted as if he could barely read his own writing.

"Either that," Lisa said, "or you can get your break from José out of Blackstone's five percent. That's up to them, but All-American is not cutting our three hundred dollar per case base price."

Petrovitch nodded. He seemed proud of her.

"Leon Fine said there was room to negotiate on volume," Jody protested.

"Ahhh, yes, Leon. . . . Whatever happened to poor Leon? He sorta up and disappeared," Lisa said softly. "And since Leon isn't here to confront that issue directly, maybe we ought to leave him out of it."

"Who do you fucking people think you're dealing with?" Jody asked, his voice too loud and badly out of sync with the setting.

Shane took another hard look at his old friend: Jody was smarter than this, yet Shane saw something in his eyes that he had never seen before. Jody's eyes were on fire. Gone was the cold appraising confidence. Shane wondered if he was on something. He couldn't believe Jody would be stupid enough to get high and then come to this meeting, yet he seemed clearly out of it.

"There's no need for rude behavior," Lisa said.

"Fuck you, honey!" Jody responded hotly, exploding to his feet. "Just 'cause there's no history here, don't think you can fuck me over! You people act like this is a business transaction. It's not! It's a criminal conspiracy. Let's not forget that you're all money launderers. I make one call and this whole deal goes into federal court and back to the taxpayers."

The Prussian general cleared his throat: "Get this . . . this person out of my party." Petrovitch turned and left the deck, taking his two flunkies and most of the available oxygen with him.

Jody was left standing, glaring awkwardly. José Mondragon turned and followed Petrovitch.

Lisa finally rose from her chair while Shane put a hand on Jody's shoulder. "Come on, man. Cool down."

"Get your fucking hands off me!" Jody screamed and backhanded Shane's arm off with his fist.

"What'd you take?" Shane asked, looking at Jody closely. "You're on something. . . . This isn't you."

"No . . . no . . . I'm . . . I wouldn't . . . I didn't . . ." And then he fell backward.

Shane had to scramble to catch him before he cracked his head on the tile. "Somebody slipped him something," Shane said, looking at Lisa.

"Get him out of here," she replied. "Go back to José's."

"What's going on? Jody wouldn't use drugs. He's trying to get everybody *off* drugs."

"I think I know what happened. I need to do some damage control. Just do what I say. I'll be there as soon as I can." She turned and left the deck.

Shane got his hands under Jody and half dragged, half carried him off the patio. He laid him down on the damp grass at the side of the villa. Jody was groaning. Inside the party, the Majestics ended "Begin the Beguine," finishing up with a corny drum riff. Jody rolled over and vomited on the grass.

"Always a music critic," Shane mumbled.

"Get me outta here, Salsa," Jody moaned. "I feel like shit."

A few minutes later Shane found Sawdust and Victory on the far side of the room, pounding down scotches like construction workers at a neighborhood bar.

"Let's go. Jody's outside," Shane said, and left without waiting for them to reply.

They found Jody on the grass where Shane had left him, but now he was unconscious, snoring loudly.

"What'd you do to him?" Lester growled.

"I didn't do anything to him. Somebody spiked his drink. It was weird . . . some kinda mood-altering substance, maybe GHB. He went nuts . . . blew the whole deal."

"What?" Sawdust said, then looked at Shane suspiciously. "Who would drug him? Everybody's in this for the money. These people need us to move their product. You did this to him!"

"It wasn't me," Shane said. "You want a guess? I think we got some competitors inside All-American who don't want this deal to happen."

Victory stood leaning on his crutch while Sawdust ran to the parking lot above and retrieved the motor home. When he pulled up, Shane and Victory dragged Jody inside. They drove back to José Mondragon's villa to wait for Lisa St. Marie.

But she was already there, standing with Tremaine Lane out by the pool.

THE REBOUND

While the rest of the Vikings put Jody into bed, Shane talked it over with Lisa.

"I think I can still save this," she told him. "I know what happened. At least I'm pretty sure I know. I think I can convince Lou . . . but we need to . . ." She stopped because Victory Smith had just come out of the house and was hopping around the deep end of the pool, over to where they were standing. He leaned in on his crutch, glaring.

One by one, the rest of the Vikings came out and formed a circle around them.

"You ain't supposed to talk to her. Jody does the deals," Victory growled.

"Somebody, and I won't mention who, dropped hydroxyl methylphenidate into Jody's drink," Lisa said.

"I'm not a fucking druggist. Talk English, lady," Smith said.

"MDMA-two, a form of juiced up Ecstasy. It's a big-time depressant, causes irrational behavior," Shane replied, and Lisa nodded. Apparently, Victory had been so busy at SWAT, kicking doors and doing kneecaps, he missed out on his drug tour in Vice.

"We don't have any time," she continued. "If you guys still want this deal, I have a chance to save it. Mr. Petrovitch is leaving on his private jet in two hours. I either put this back together by then, or it's dead." She was cool and in control. Her jade-green eyes seemed to twinkle with excitement. Or was it amusement? Shane couldn't shake the feeling that she was thoroughly enjoying herself.

"I need to cut a deal *now*," she pressed.

"If Jody's X-ing, he won't be up to anything for hours, maybe a day," Tremaine said.

"I need to take Lou a deal tonight, in the next hour. I know I can square things with Papa Joe. It's Petrovitch we need to capture. Jody threatened him, and frankly, Lou doesn't like being threatened. I may have a way to straighten that out, but I want one of you to cut the deal with me now. I need to bring him an offer."

"One of us?" Sawdust asked.

"Him," Lisa said, pointing at Shane.

"Fuck him. He not even scheduled t'live till Friday," Victory growled.

"It's him or nobody . . . and, whatever he and I work out, you've gotta make Jody stick to it."

"Maybe it was you, spiked Jody's drink so you could front up and kick Scully's ass on this deal," Tremaine Lane said lazily from a chair a few feet away, his feet propped up on a glass-topped table.

"Okay . . . have it your way. See ya around," Lisa said, then started to walk to the far end of the pool. They all watched, mesmerized by the hip action. Shane guessed she was probably not doing it intentionally. She'd learned that walk in high school when she first realized it turned every guy's brain to mush.

"Hang on a minute," Lester drawled. "We'll do it your way."

Lisa stopped and turned theatrically to look at them.

"What if Jody don't like the deal once he comes to?" Victory asked.

"Hey, boys," she said softly. "The big money is in the smuggle. You guys are gonna make your percentage off that. You wanna blow this over whether it ends up being two seventy-five a case or three hundred?"

They stood glaring at her, trying to decide what to do.

"What's it gonna be? Once Mr. Petrovitch's plane takes off, this is over. He won't revisit it. We're out of time."

Victory Smith leaned forward on his crutch and whispered softly to Shane, so nobody else could hear: "Okay, Party Boy, go ahead. But if you get shorted by this bitch, the balance comes out of your end."

"Y'mean I'm gonna be around for the payoff? I thought I wasn't gonna make it till Friday."

"Keep yer hands off her. I'm the one's gonna be doing her. You fuck her, you're dead."

"Is this on or off?" Lisa asked from the far side of the pool, where she waited impatiently, hands on her hips.

"Go on, gaffle with the bitch," Tremaine said softly, his deep ghetto voice rumbling.

Lisa crossed back, took Shane by the hand, and led him around the side of the house to the front drive, where her car was parked. It was a white Mercedes convertible with the top down. She slid behind the wheel and got it started.

"Where're we going?" Shane asked, still standing by the passenger door.

"I'm not gonna try and cut a deal here, with all these testosterone cases leaning on me. We'll find a nice quiet spot. Get in."

Just before sliding in beside her, Shane looked up and

caught Victory glaring out of the living-room window. Shane shot him a wide grin, then grabbed his crotch. Smith was still there as they pulled away from the house.

"It's Arnold Zook," she said. "I can't prove it, of course, but I'm pretty sure he's the one who spiked Jody's drink."

"Who? You mean the little round short one who looks like he should be stacking cans at Ralph's?"

They were parked halfway between La Quinta and Rancho Mirage, off Bob Hope Drive, in a small, sculpted park. Up-lit date palms stood over them, swaying in the breeze like giant eunuchs waving fans.

"He was the product executive who was working with Leon Fine. When Leon disappeared, Jody preferred working with me. Arnold lost the account, and he didn't take it too well."

"What's the difference? Don't both of you work for All-American Tobacco?"

"Our individual financial arrangements are complex, but they're tied to product placement. If Jody made an ass of himself and pissed off Mr. Petrovitch, Arnold Zook wouldn't lose any sleep over it."

"Okay, so how do you get Petrovitch to come around?"

"Leave that part to me," she allowed. "I just need to know what we're talking about."

"And, like Tremaine said, you picked me because I looked like the biggest moron."

"I picked you because you're the only one who isn't fucked up on drugs. You can still think. I swear . . . Jody's let these guys get completely out of control. This is my first and last arrangement with him."

"Okay, let's hear your offer."

"I can't cut a deal on product price. Mr. Petrovitch won't go for it. Our parallel market is in place and has been operating along set guidelines for a very long time."

"Over twenty-five years, I hear."

"Yeah, maybe. And if word gets out that I cut you a discount price on product, it's gonna haunt me on every other deal I make in the world."

"So, you smuggle tobacco and launder drug cash in places other than just Colombia?"

"I don't like to use words like 'smuggle' and 'launder.' I'm a tobacco-company account executive, negotiating a deal with you to supply the Blackstone duty-free zone in Aruba with cigarettes to be sold there. Period. End of discussion."

"Lisa . . . you're laundering Colombian drug money for the Cali cartel."

"I'm not laundering anything."

"The Vikings set this deal up with a Cali cartel drug dealer in L.A., then Jody cut a deal with Papa Joe at Blackstone. They brought All-American in to supply the cigarettes, which get shipped to Aruba, paid for with drug cash, and smuggled back into Colombia, where they're sold by the Cali cartel, who then gets its money back. If that's not a laundry, then I'm Pippi Longstocking."

"Where Jody or anybody else gets the money to buy our product is their business, not mine. Listen, Shane, I'm cutting you a lot of slack here. Don't make this impossible."

"Okay, so you won't negotiate on the cigarettes. How 'bout the shipping and insurance and warehousing—all that other stuff you were talking about?"

"I'll give you ten cents per case off the shipping, and forty cents on the insurance—"

Shane put up a hand and interrupted her, "Slow down. I don't even know what we're talking about."

"We're talking about all the ancillary expenses."

"Hell, I don't even know what's good or bad . . . or what competitive bids on those services might be. I'm negotiating blind here."

"So, then, how are we gonna make a deal?"

"You have rate cards on all this shit? For your legitimate deals? The shipping and insurance and warehousing?"

"Yeah."

"Okay . . . fifty percent off on the entire package, per your rate card."

"What?"

"I want those services at cost."

"I heard you, but that's ridiculous. I'd be cutting my price by over . . ." She reached into her purse and pulled out a calculator and began poking at the keys, her lacquered nails clicking as she punched in numbers. Shane watched her while she worked, her features shimmering in the moving lights from the swaying date palms. After a minute, she looked over at him. "Thirty percent. Best I can do."

"Fifty percent, Lisa. Don't fuck with me on this. If I cut too bad a deal, Jody's just gonna tank it. You can sell this to Mr. Puffenguts, I know you can."

"Petrovitch," she said, smiling.

"You guys will be running your shipping, insurance, and warehousing at no profit, but you're still getting a full three hundred dollars a case on the smokes; like Jody said, it *is* a huge shipment."

She looked down at the computer in her hand. "Fifty percent off." She punched in a few more figures. "That comes to a little more than seventeen dollars a case."

"Okay, that's the deal then. Yes or no?"

She tapped her thumb on the Texas Instruments computer, which had a twelve-digit LD screen instead of the normal ten.

"Okay. But if I can't sell this to Lou, I'll need you nearby. I want you to wait for me in a place where I can get back to you without having the rest of Jody's animals contributing their opinions."

"Where?"

"AAT rented me a separate villa at the Ritz-Carlton, down by the tennis courts. How 'bout there? Lou should still be at the hotel, packing. That way, if we need to adjust anything, you'll be handy."

"Okay."

She put the car in gear. They pulled out from under the date palms, shot down Bob Hope Drive, and turned right again on Highway 111. Lisa St. Marie was holding her head erect, her shoulders straight. She seemed lost in thought while she drove: intense, hard and beautiful, no flirtatious nonsense now. She had turned back into a very busy executive on an important lung-destroying mission.

Shane wondered if she was planning to blow the Prussian general to get the deal done.

CANDY KISS

Her room was full of shiny masonry, Italian terra-cotta, and Spanish tile. Expensively framed but marginal abstract art hung on the walls. Like everything else in the desert, this junior-executive suite had a pastel-peach color scheme. Except Lisa's suite was without the magnificent views of the valley or the golf course. Shane could see a lit tennis court out the main window and hear the steady *thunk-thonk* of a singles match, mixed with energetic grunts and squeaking shoes. The match was obscured behind a green screen that hung on the chain-link fence a few yards from the window. The shadows danced and lunged on the colorful canvas like ghostly memories.

Lisa was still with Petrovitch. Shane looked at her telephone and again considered making a call to Filosiani. But he didn't want the LAPD number to show up on her bill, so he decided to wait. Instead, he took the opportunity to get to know her a little better.

He started his search where most cops do—in the bathroom, where you often learned personal secrets. Lisa's bathroom was no exception. She had the standard beauty aids: eye shadow, makeup brushes, and Vaseline; two round metal hairbrushes, each tangled with honey-ash strands. He pulled several loose. There were no dark roots—a natural blonde. Lipsticks by Lancôme: Iced Amethyst and Bronze Fire. No eyewash or contact-lens case, so it seemed the jade-green color came direct from the factory. Then he found two small, brown plastic compacts stuck way down in the webbing of her cosmetic travel case. The powder inside was not from Revlon, but Colombia. Fine and white, it dusted the mirror. Shane ran a wet index finger across the stuff and tasted it. . . .

Bingo. *El diablo!*

Lisa St. Marie kept that high-strung motor of hers redlined with toots of Inca whizbang.

Shane closed the compact and put it back where he found it.

Well, he mused darkly, *there are worse things than snorting coke . . . you could always punch a round through your girlfriend's heart.*

He moved through the rest of the place.

The closet contained mostly expensive designer stuff. She either did very well at All-American Tobacco or General Puffenguts bought her a lot of high-priced collectibles. The shoes were strictly from the Imelda Marcos shelf: Prada, Charles David, Manolo Blahnik.

Her jewel case was locked inside the flimsy key-locked room safe, which Shane opened easily with his picks. The case was just a small leather box, but with impressive contents. Shane wasn't much at appraising jewelry and wished he had Murray Steinberg there to scan them with his loupe, but they looked authentic—expensive settings glittering with designer elegance.

He closed the safe and kept snooping.

The refrigerator was where he found Lisa's moonwalking kit. The heavy artillery was tucked in the freezer compartment behind the ice trays: amphetamines, methamphetamines, and, oh yeah ... some MDMA$_2$. So maybe Tremaine had called that one right. Maybe Lisa had sabotaged the deal with Jody so she could knock down the price with Shane.

There were also some tabs of something that Shane thought looked like LSD, making them the only ingestibles. This was gyro-hydro, but there was no needle. Lisa didn't do her cooking in a spoon. She didn't violate that perfect alabaster skin with track marks. Everything in here but the acid and the Ecstasy went up her nose.

He closed the refrigerator and wandered back into the living room. The tennis game had finished, so Shane slumped into the big, overstuffed club chair by the window. He was bone-tired, and without planning to drift off, he was suddenly somewhere else ... asleep, but maybe not; dreaming, but it felt terribly real ... like he had passed into some other dimension intact, summoned there for an audience and a scolding.

She was dressed in her sergeant's uniform, the one she had worn at the Medal of Valor ceremonies, and she was still holding the medal in its beautiful leather case.

"Shane, we can never make this work. . . . You know that, of course." She was scowling at him, but there was also disappointment.

"Why, Alexa . . . why can't we?"

"Because there's darkness in you. Whether it's because you were abandoned by your mother . . . left at that hospital as an infant, or because police work made you cynical isn't important anymore. Darkness is darkness, no matter where it comes from. And it's been there as long as I've known you. Even when we laughed, it was there, hiding behind your smile, frightening me."

"Alexa . . . no . . . please . . . I can change."

"It never would've worked. Never. We were kidding ourselves."

"No . . . no, it could have, because I loved you. I still love you."

"God decides these things," she said sharply, standing in the beautiful pulpit now, preaching down at him. He remembered that pulpit. As a child, he had gone to the Episcopal church each Sunday with the Deans, looked up in wonder at its carved perfection, studied it while sermons droned. It was ornate and encrusted with symbols. Angels with their wings outstretched held the corners of the desk aloft. On its polished surface rested the powerful book of words. A scroll was carved on the front face of the pulpit. He'd wondered what important truths were on that document, what overpowering wisdom. He went up and tried to read the scroll, but the letters were only tiny scratches in the polished wood; like so much of his early life, only there for effect. *"God makes these choices for us,"* Alexa continued. *"You went your way, I went mine."*

"No . . ."

"It's done. The deal is closed."

"No, Alexa, not yet."

Suddenly, somebody touched his shoulder.

He opened his eyes. It was Lisa. She was standing over him, dressed in a black linen coat.

"I said, The deal is done, and who the fuck is Alexa?"

"Hi," he said, still troubled by the nature and content of the dream. "Nobody . . . old friend. She's dead."

"Mr. Puffenguts will do the deal as negotiated." Lisa smiled. "Papa Joe is writing the contract over in Lou's suite. If you sign it before you leave, the ball is back in play."

"Oh . . ."

"And now for the celebration." She held out a bottle of champagne she'd been hiding behind her back.

"I don't like champagne much." His head was clogged; the heavy sleep and troubling dream lingered.

"How 'bout this, then?" she said, and let the coat fall

off her shoulders. She was standing naked in front of him, wearing only her high-heeled pumps.

"Jesus," he said, and struggled to sit up in the heavily upholstered chair.

"You showed me yours. . . . How do you like mine?"

She turned and showed him her gym-trained glutes. Sexy and very beautiful . . . no denying that.

"My . . . I . . ."

"Your what?" she said, smiling. And then, before he could say another word, she dropped into his lap and put her arms around his neck. "You can touch. Go on . . . feel me here," she said, then took his hand and placed it between her legs. He started to pull away but she held it there. "I need to feel you. I need for us to know each other this way."

"Why . . . why is . . . ?"

"Now for the candy kiss." Then her mouth was on his, open and hungry. She pushed her tongue between his lips; he suddenly felt something on his tongue . . . bitter and stinging, it was dissolving, being quickly absorbed.

A candy kiss? . . . Cocaine? . . . LSD? He started to pull away, to spit it out.

"No," she said, never taking her mouth off of his. "Go with it, baby. Go with it—you'll fly." He felt the substance running off his tongue, around his tonsils, down his throat. She had her hands on his belt and was undoing it, stripping it off.

"I need to feel you. I need to touch you, to taste you," she whispered as her hand reached into his pants, stroking him.

"Goddamn," Shane thought, or maybe he actually said it. He wasn't sure. He tried to pull away—at least he thought he tried . . . *wanted* to have tried.

"Alexa . . . Alexa!" his mind screamed, but all he heard were her dream-remembered words.

"Shane, we can never make this work. . . ."

"Why, Alexa . . . Why can't we?"

"Ahhh . . ." Lisa purred. "That's better. You're so hard. Let me help you . . ." and his pants were coming down, sliding around his thighs. She took her mouth off his and found him down there . . . found his traitorous erection.

"It never would have worked. We were kidding ourselves," Alexa scolded.

"Isn't that better? Doesn't that feel nice?" Lisa whispered.

"It could have worked because I loved you. I still love you."

He felt her lips on him, her tongue on his hardened shaft.

"There's darkness in you. Even when we laughed, it was there, hiding behind your smile."

Lisa rose, adjusting herself on his lap to face him, her hips rising up slightly, then she slid his erection deep inside her. "There," she panted. "There . . . there . . . harder . . . harder . . . harder . . . Fuck me, you bastard!" Her voice guttural and craven.

Shane felt the drug inside him, spreading fire and ice.

"You went your way, I went mine."

He wanted to scream—*No!*—but his mind blurred with carnal darkness.

"Now, now . . . Do it now!" Lisa commanded.

So he did. He released, spasming inside her. She threw her head back and rode him, moaning out loud with unabashed pleasure.

It was a chilling moment for Shane, as if the depravity that had been hovering, beating its dark wings, had finally settled on him, devouring his morality and self-respect all in one lustful encounter.

Unfortunately, it was the best sex he'd ever had.

THE LOOK

Shane's fragile psyche fell in on him. He remembered Lisa's kneeling over him, feeding him something . . . maybe more pills, or tabs; he wasn't sure. He vaguely recalled signing the agreement, the paper swimming in blurred vision, and Lisa's voice, musical but furry. He wasn't sure how he got back to Papa Joe's house. He had a momentary recollection of Lisa's dashboard clock, wondering if it could really be four A.M. He guessed she'd driven him. His mind buzzed and snapped like a broken speaker.

A few memories stood out.

The front door, with Tremaine standing in the threshold holding a .38 snubby, muttering, "You're fucked up, too?"

Jody, sprawled in a lawn chair in the bright midday sunlight, moaning and crying, then suddenly leaning over and vomiting into the pool.

Victory Smith standing over him, whispering softly: "It would be so easy now, motherfucker . . . so easy."

The fog he was swimming in didn't clear until almost

six that evening. When it did, it was all at once, as if somebody had yanked up a shade. He was suddenly back behind the wheel, driving a swerving, disabled brain.

He was with Jody in mid-sentence when he snapped back, and Shane had no idea what they'd been discussing. His own words lingered in his head like a remembered dream: "... I could do ..." was what he had just said. One moment he was nowhere, and the next he was stretched out on the sofa in Papa Joe's borrowed room, feeling like shit while Jody, sitting on the bed, scanned a two-page document.

"The best you could do?" he said, throwing the papers back onto the bedspread. Shane could see his signature scrawled on the bottom. "She jacked you up, man. I hate this deal ... it was signed under duress. You're still babbling like an idiot."

"I'm okay. . . . I'm better now." Shane's head was pounding, but the real pain, the one deep inside him, was an unbearable feeling of loss—this time not for Alexa or Chooch, but for himself.

"This bitch got the full three hundred dollars. Leon Fine said he bargained her down to two seventy-five. Leon woulda got an extra twenty-five bucks a case on his deal."

"Yeah, Leon's doing great. Let's hear it for Leon."

Shane sat up, then stood and went into the bathroom, washed his face, and glanced at himself in the mirror. He looked as bad as he felt; three days of stubble under furtive eyes that belonged to a frightened loser stared back at him. Shane couldn't bear to look at the wreck he had become, so he left the bathroom and returned to the living room. Jody was still holding the papers, scowling down at them.

"I ain't gonna do this deal. Call her back."

"Jody, she says Petrovitch won't renegotiate."

"*She* says? Like I give a shit what she says. Fuck her . . . but of course, you've probably done that, too."

"Jody, remember what Captain Clark always told us?"

"Y'mean that prick from the Fiscal Support Bureau who kept running audits on our expense sheets in Southwest?"

"He said dollars are fungible. And they are." Shane's head was at least functioning now.

"What does that mean?"

"It means, it doesn't matter where they come from as long as you get to the same number in the end. We got a seventeen-dollar-a-case discount on ancillary services. Leon says he woulda got twenty-five dollars off on the sale price, which, since he never closed the deal, is questionable. But he probably woulda paid full boat on all this other shit—the warehousing, insurance, and shipping. That means, if he wasn't lying to you, he mighta done eight dollars a case better than us. Who fucking cares?"

"I care," Jody said as he stood up. "These people are crooks. They're laundering money for scumbags, putting it back in the hands of greaseball cartel bosses who're using it to sell more drugs to kids."

"So are we. Let's just take the deal and get on with it."

Jody walked to the east window and looked out at mountains that were slowly turning purple in the evening light. "Yeah . . ." he said, softly, "so are we." Then Jody turned and faced Shane, changing the subject abruptly. "You're still fucked up over shooting Sergeant Hamilton, aren't you?" Shane's muscles froze; somewhere deep in his psyche, survival instincts took over.

Jody didn't wait for an answer. "At first that pissed me off. I wanted you not to give a shit, but I've been thinking about it, and now I know if you weren't fucked up over it, you'd a'been faking. Since you're unwinding, taking drugs and balling a skank like Lisa St. Marie, I know you're on the level. Otherwise I'd be suspecting a setup.

I can see inside you, man. You're eating yourself up, just like you always did when things weren't John Wayne perfect."

Shane didn't answer.

" 'Member all that night music . . . back when we were kids . . . planning what we were gonna be?" Jody went on.

"Yeah . . ."

"You always knew. 'Cept at first. At first it was a fireman, remember? Then you switched to a cop, and you never changed. I never knew what I wanted. I became a cop because you did. Dumb fucking reason, huh?"

Shane's head was killing him. He could barely think.

"It's funny . . . when you grow up with everything, you don't know what to wish for." Jody was studying Shane while he spoke. "I mean, pitchin' for the Dodgers . . . what kinda bullshit dream was that?"

"Maybe you could've done it if you'd tried."

" 'Cept I never wanted anything bad enough to put out for it. Things just sorta always happened for me. You worked selling ice cream at Huntington Beach t'get that old piece-a-shit Ford you loved so much; hand-washed that pile a'rust three times a week. I got a new Mustang convertible for my sixteenth birthday. I never washed it once, 'cause I never really cared about it."

"Right." Shane didn't want to hear any of this. Worse still, he suspected Jody was working up to some kind of soul-cleansing confession.

"You always had a code. When you fought for shit, it was for honor or something corny like that. You never just beat on some kid for his lunch money. Underneath all my jokes, I guess I admired that."

"Can we give it a rest?" Shane muttered.

"I never told you this, Salsa, but I always envied you. I wanted things to matter for me like they did for you. I wanted them to be more important. But they never were, and the funny thing was, the less I cared, the more people seemed to do what I wanted. You were the only one who didn't completely buy into my bullshit. I had to really work to capture you, 'cause you had all those lofty ideas. Used to piss me off, too, 'cause I never could understand what the big deal was . . . and then one day, I found out why I could never care." He turned slightly and was now looking out the window at the mountains. It was almost half a minute before he continued: " 'Member that course at the Academy on criminal psychology?"

"Yeah."

"That was a real wake-up call for me 'cause I fit one of the criminal classifications dead on. You know which one?" He turned suddenly to look back at Shane.

"No."

"Sociopath. That was me. No feelings, no emotions, all the time pretending; acting emotions I couldn't feel, but knew I was supposed to . . . pretending sorrow when my dog died, pretending love on Mother's Day . . . never feeling anything. Not one damn thing. We were from opposite ends of the spectrum. What a team—the bleeding heart and the sociopath, the ultimate high-low block. No wonder we always kicked ass."

"But here we are in the same room, both doing this same shit, so let it go. Please . . . I don't need to hear this." Shane desperately wanted to end the conversation; he was afraid of it.

But why?

A few years ago, when they had the arguments over SIS, Shane suspected that Jody had lost his conscience, but it had never occurred to him that Jody never had a conscience to begin with.

So, does it really matter now if Jody felt anything back in sixth grade?

But it did. It was critically important, because Jody's boyhood friendship had been one of the only pillars of strength in Shane's youth. It had formed a significant part of his value system.

More night music: "Y'know one of the other reasons I fucked up?" Jody said softly. "It was my dad . . . good old easygoing Fred Dean. What a world-class jerk." Jody shook his head in wonder. "What a train wreck that guy turned out to be."

"I loved your dad. Your parents treated me like I was their own."

Jody shrugged and turned again to look out the window. "When he went broke, he left me hanging out there with no fuckin' values . . . nothin'. You didn't have money or parents, but you had everything. You had beliefs. You had your code, corny as I thought it was. I cared about nothing. Worse still, I couldn't settle for less than we'd always had, and couldn't find any legal way to get that standard of living back."

"So you make this score and then all your problems go away?" Shane's headache was pounding, but Jody's confession was even worse.

"You always loved being a cop," Jody continued.

"Yeah," Shane answered softly. "Yeah . . . It seemed like a great profession. I thought it was noble . . . blue knights standing up for the innocent. I thought the battle was about right and wrong. But it wasn't about right and wrong; it turned out to be about legal and illegal, rules of evidence . . . the Police Discretionary Clause . . . the Miranda. Make some tiny technical mistake, and a confessed child molester goes free. I loved it until it turned me into a cynic."

"I never loved being a cop," Jody said quietly, turning back to study Shane's reaction. "I loved what it let me do. Turning on my gumball, and running a red light to get to a ballgame on time. I loved being able to get some asshole down on his back in an alley with nobody watching, then shove my piece in his mouth and listen to him beg. I loved seeing that look in his eyes. The look, man . . . better than sex or drugs. It validated me, y'know? The look said, 'I know you can do it. You can light me up and walk away, and nobody will even ask why.' The look said: 'I know you're all that's between me and eternity. I'm alive for only as long as you allow it.' Shit, nobody had to say anything. It was there, pure and clean . . . no misunderstandings, no technicalities, just a beautiful fact." His eyes were almost glowing as he spoke. Then he paused and studied Shane. "You never felt that on the job, when you pulled down on some asshole? Never felt the pure joy of that?"

"No," Shane said. "I was in it for something else."

"Yeah." He snorted. " 'Service in the public trust.' "

"Maybe we could've stood for something, Jody. Maybe we still can. Chief Filosiani's different. He wants to try and put it back the way it should be."

"Chief Bada-bing? You're dreaming, Salsa. You trust Filosiani and he'll fuck you over just like the rest a'them swivel-chair heroes on the sixth floor of the Glass House. And that's not cynicism; it's *truth*. But, hey . . . go ahead and fantasize. That's what I always liked most about you. You knew how to have dumb-ass dreams." He turned and, without another word, walked out of the bedroom, snatching Papa Joe's contract up off the bed as he passed.

Shane turned on the TV news.

He never should have, because Alexa's funeral was the headline story. Shane sat, mesmerized, as Chief Filosiani spoke about her courage under fire:

"It is with tremendous regret that I am here this afternoon," the chief said to almost two thousand of L.A.'s finest, who were standing in their dress blues on the Police Academy training field. Even Chooch was there. Shane caught a glimpse of him standing with his head bowed as the TV shot panned over to Buddy. Chooch looked as though he was crying. Shane put out his hand and touched the TV screen.

The blond female news anchor came on camera, continuing the story with a slide show over her right shoulder: "Sergeant Hamilton, a recent Medal of Valor recipient, was gunned down by her ex-boyfriend, Detective Sergeant Scully."

No! What is this? Shane was on his feet.

He leaned forward and stared. Shane's picture appeared over the shot of the Police Academy memorial service. It was his Academy graduation picture. He looked youthful and proud. "Sergeant Scully had been undergoing a psychiatric review and was deemed by his LAPD commander to be emotionally unstable when apparently he was driven to murder."

No . . . It was an accident. Why are you saying this?

The shot switched to the police brass band playing "Taps." There were shots of a Helicopter Air Unit fly-by: five black-and-white Bell Jet Rangers and a Hughes 500 passed low over the field. Then more shots of Buddy dressed in a black suit, somber and grief-stricken . . . shots of the ceremony later, at Forest Lawn, as the casket was lowered with a twenty-one-gun salute. Buddy was handed the flag off the coffin, folded into a tight, career-ending package.

Shane stared in disbelief at the screen until the newscast switched stories.

His mind kaleidoscoped. His thoughts tumbled. Images flashed before him:

Lisa on top of him, her head thrown back—guttural and feline: "Fuck me, you bastard!"

Chooch standing in the airport, carrying his helmet and shoulder pads: "Give her the ring, Shane."

Jody, just a minute ago . . . his words soft, but horribly prophetic: "You trust Filosiani and he'll fuck you just like the rest a'them swivel-chair heroes."

And finally, Alexa . . . in her dress-blue uniform, stand-
ing before him, disapproving and remote: "There's dark-
ness in you, Shane. It would never have worked. You went
your way, I went mine."

WHO AM I?

The speedometer on the Vogue motor home hovered near seventy while its tires sang in the rain cuts on the concrete highway. The ornate grille reflected the dotted white lane markers on the chrome bumper, hoovering up lines like a Main Street junkie.

Shane was trying to sleep in the big blue crushed-velvet club chair, forward of the galley. Jody was stretched out on the bed in the rear compartment. Tremaine and Lester Wood were up front, engaged in whispered conversation, while Victory Smith was in the booth nursing a beer and brooding.

But Shane was restless. His mind kept touching the edges of new, soul-defining realities: Alexa's death, Chooch left in the wake of this catastrophe, the powerful memory of sex with Lisa—a woman he knew was corrupt and dangerous but whose darkness he was inexplicably drawn to.

When he thought about everything that had happened, he knew Jody was right.

If Tony was on the level, why would the LAPD be

calling him a murderer on TV and making him a shoot-on-sight fugitive for every law-enforcement agency in America? The Day-Glo Dago had picked a scenario that eliminated Shane from the equation. It was now pretty obvious to Shane that Filosiani didn't want to face the consequences of his own mangled plan. A plan that had resulted in the death of a police officer under his direct supervision. With this news story, he had cut off Shane and forced him to run. Shane was completely alone.

The weird thing was, it didn't seem to matter much. His perspective had changed. He felt like someone else. His world had lost the vivid colors that had always characterized his thoughts and feelings. In their place, a gray mist had descended, taking the volume way down. Shane suspected he no longer had very many things he really cared about. Maybe he had become like Jody. Although the treasured memory of Alexa and Chooch lingered, even these once powerful performers in his life failed to fully penetrate this new fog of listless disinterest.

He began to realize that the ache inside him was really more of a craving. He needed something . . . something to brighten this reality.

How had Jody put it?

A little chemical help after a confusing day.

He was looking at Lester Wood's travel case sitting on the blue carpet, not five feet away. He wondered if Wood had found a way to smuggle one of his little Baggies past Jody's inspection. Or maybe he had found a connection in Palm Springs and hooked himself up, scored some *polvo blanco*. So Shane stretched his foot out around the case and began to nudge it closer.

"You banged the bitch, didn't ya?" Victory interrupted his thoughts, dropping into the chair in front of Shane. "I told ya t'leave her be."

"Get away from me," Shane said softly.

"I told ya not t'fuck 'er."

"I don't take my orders from you, Vic. 'Sides, with all those anabols and oxys you pop, you couldn't lay a carpet."

"Gonna teach you a lesson, then blow yer worthless head off." Smith was sitting with his huge legs spread out in front of him, leaning back in the chair, acting as if all of this was his choice and on his terms.

Shane shifted his right foot and let it fly . . . kicking the steroid junkie right between the legs.

The weight lifter screamed in agony, doubled over in the chair, then dropped to his knees on the carpet, moaning. His left hand cradled his balls, but his right was snaking toward the Uzi tucked into his belt.

Shane yanked the Mini-Cougar out of his ankle holster, pushed it toward Smith, thumbing off the safety as he slammed the muzzle hard into the man's simian forehead. Shane beat Smith's draw by a full second. Victory was caught with one hand on his nuts and the other on his half-drawn Uzi.

"Go on. Bust a move. Let's see what ya got," Shane whispered. He could actually feel the weight lifter's heartbeat pulsing through the muzzle of the Beretta.

Jody exploded out of the bedroom and in an instant was standing over them, his own Mini-Light pulled and chambered. Shane could feel the motor home gearing down as Tremaine Lane slowed, turning around to see the drama that was playing out behind him.

"Put it down, Shane," Jody ordered.

"Him first."

"Unhook, or I'll lose the both a'ya right now," Jody commanded.

"This ape's been threatening me for two days. I want this over with," Shane demanded.

"Fuck you," Smith said.

Jody fired his Mini-Light. It was on auto-fire, and half a dozen bullets ripped holes in the carpet between them.

The rounds blew chunks out of the floor of the motor home and ricocheted off the pavement below, then whined away across the desert. Somehow, miraculously, nothing hit the gas tank or driveshaft. The insanity of the event carried the moment.

Victory Smith let go of his weapon and put both hands out to his side.

Shane still didn't take the Mini-Cougar off the giant's pockmarked forehead. He found himself actually contemplating pulling the trigger, his fingers twitching inadvertently on the cold steel. Then he finally saw fear in Smith's eyes.

In that second, Shane knew he owned the man. He'd have to risk death to pull the trigger because Jody really might take him out, but Shane was seriously tempted to end it—kill Victory and let Jody shoot him for it. It was Shane's call in that split second, and everybody knew it.

And then Shane felt it.

Jody was right. There was a spark of pure joy in this simple equation. It emanated from Victory across the two feet of bullet-torn carpet into Shane. He saw the fear of imminent death register in Smith's pig-mean stare. Shane desperately wanted to seal his own fate. He couldn't remain caught between what he used to be and what he was becoming. He needed to be one thing or the other.

Jody reached out and slowly pushed Shane's wrist aside, shoving the gun away from Victory's sweat-slick forehead. "This ain't it, Hot Sauce."

And then it was over.

"This pile a'shit gets near me again, I'm gonna put him down." Shane's voice, as well as his whole body, was shaking.

Victory was still on his knees, rocking slightly back and forth on the bullet-ravaged blue shag carpet, cupping his balls in both hands. "Lose this motherfucker, Jody," the weight lifter whispered. "There's a five-state manhunt for him. He's poison. Get rid of him."

Jody didn't respond. Instead, he reached down and yanked Smith's Uzi up off the floor. "Let's have yours, too," he said sharply to Shane.

Shane shook his head and put the gun back into his ankle holster. Then he walked to the back of the motor home, into the bedroom, and kicked the door shut. He sat on the queen-size bed with his head in his hands. He could hear the others talking low, as the vehicle once again picked up speed. Jody's voice was louder than the others. Shane couldn't make out the words, but he could feel the vibe right through the paneled bulkhead. Jody was scared. They had started pulling guns on each other, and he was losing control. The mix had turned dangerous, with a strong suicidal flavor.

The gray mist settled lower, engulfing Shane inch by inch. He had been half an ounce of a trigger pull away from murder. Half an ounce from putting a round through Peter Smith's head.

It was exactly what Jody had talked about: getting a guy down, seeing that look—the look making you feel pure and alive, but also driving you . . . pushing you. In Victory's weakness, he felt rage; in his total surrender came a surge of unreasoning violence.

He remembered a saying from somewhere but couldn't recall where it came from . . . perhaps a Sunday school lecture, or maybe just some barroom psychologist: *When a man is severely tested, only then does he discover who he really is.*

So who the fuck am I? Shane wondered.

31

HOUSE IN THE VALLEY

It was almost eight P.M.

Jody told them they wouldn't be needing the blue-and-white motor home, so they spent twenty minutes wiping their prints off every surface, then left it in a pay lot off Ventura Boulevard and walked four blocks to the Sherman Oaks Inn, on Valley Vista. As they climbed the stairs to the second-floor room, Shane could see the orange-and-black Charger in the adjoining lot, parked next to an unmarked blue step van.

The room Jody led them into was several notches up from the one in Sunland. The two-room studio apartment was colorless, decorated in beige and brown. The furniture was new and nobody had left cigarette burns on the wood or vomit stains on the carpet.

They had said very little since the incident in the motor home. Victory Smith had remained silent, his eyes furtive and brooding. But the one time that Shane had locked stares with him, he saw hatred so intense that it froze him momentarily. Jody must have sensed trouble, because he'd kept Victory's Uzi locked in the motor home.

Lester Wood, whom Shane had learned was born in southern Texas and was fluent in Spanish, moved to the phone, took out a slip of paper with a telephone number scribbled on it, and dialed. He spoke quietly in Spanish, then a few moments later hung up. "That was one a'her Spic bodyguards. Juanita's on the way."

"Wait'll you see this bitch, Hot Sauce. Real *guapita,* but hard as asphalt. The spill on her is, she's already dropped six guys. She's Raphael Bacca's niece."

Jody turned to the other Vikings. "Because Rodriquez is gone, we gotta change the lineup. Inky Dink, you're driving backup. Stay at least two blocks back; use the GPS. Hot Sauce, you're with Tremaine. Victory, you're in the gray van with Sawdust."

"I don't wanna stay with the fucking monitors," Smith growled.

"I don't give a shit what you want, that's the way it's going down."

"What monitors?" Shane asked.

"The white step van parked in the lot down there is the one we're using to pick up the cash. It has three pin-cams mounted on it. Tiny little bastards're about the size of a shirt button. One is on the back of the rearview mirror, shooting out the front window. Gives us a wide shot. One's in the grille, pointing down; one is mounted under the bumper, looking back."

"Why?"

"I wanna know where they keep the cash. Since I'm gonna be a hostage and blindfolded, the cameras will tape the whole deal. Send the pictures to the monitors we got in the gray van."

"Once they give the money to us, what's it matter where they keep it?" Shane asked.

"A guy I know in SIS is gonna get the videotape mailed anonymously. We'll be long gone, but Juanita and her band a'scumball *ladrones* are gonna face an SIS hard takedown. Most greaseballs don't survive those." He smiled at Shane. "I don't want any *cholos* left behind to point a finger at us, pick us outta some picture lineup."

Tremaine Lane suddenly walked out of the room, and Shane wondered where he was going.

They waited.

The Colombians arrived at a little past eight-thirty. There was a knock on the door, and Victory got up to open it.

"Hola," one of the men outside said softly.

"Yeah, right," Smith growled. "How's yer asshole?" He stepped aside, letting them into the room.

There were two men and a woman, and as Jody had promised, Juanita Bacca was quite a package: shoulder-length, shiny black hair framed a dusky complexion and deep almond eyes. She was wearing a long black skirt wrapped tightly around her slender waist, slit in the middle almost to her crotch.

Jody nodded to her. "Juanita. *Cómo estás?"*

She didn't acknowledge him; instead, she rattled some Spanish at the two men standing behind her, who immediately separated and flanked her protectively.

It was then that Shane got his first good look at both bodyguards. The one on the right was going to be big trouble. He was six-foot-two, unusually tall for a Colombian, and had flat, uninteresting features. The tattoos on his neck ran down into his open shirt collar. His name was Octavio Juarez, and Shane had busted him three or four times when he'd been working with the Valley Vice team. As soon as Octavio spotted Shane, he nudged Juanita.

"Ay, cabrón! Es cuico," he whispered.

In a second, everyone had a gun out, including Juanita Bacca, who squatted slightly and grabbed between her legs through the folds of her split skirt. A spring-release holster chimed loudly, a chrome-plated .45 caliber Hard-baller suddenly appeared in her hand.

They all held position, glaring over gun sights. No one seemed jittery, either ... just another day at the office. Then Tremaine Lane appeared from the corridor behind them and tromboned the slide on his auto-mag. The sound brought the first flicker of fear into the faces of the two black-eyed bodyguards, but they didn't turn or flinch. Only Juanita's and Jody's eyes hadn't changed; both were prepared to go down.

Victory Smith, unarmed, was standing in a crouch, his huge mitts helplessly out in front of him.

Juanita rattled something in Spanish to Octavio.

"Sí," he replied. *"Este cerote me puso en el bote."*

"Hey, in English!" Jody demanded.

Shane spoke enough street Spanish to know Octavio had said, "This piece of shit put me in jail." And it was true. Octavio was a good bodyguard but a less-than-gifted street dealer who kept selling drugs to Valley Vice cops throughout the mid-nineties. Shane had roughed him up three times in one eleven-month period. A Valley Division record.

"Tu compañero es policía," Juanita said suspiciously to Jody.

"He says what? A cop? You're nuts!" Jody was stalling.

"Jody, go buy this bitch a newspaper 'cause I'm all over the front page," Shane said.

"That's right," Jody brightened. "Tremaine, we got these greaseballs covered. Go down to the lobby, get the *L.A. Times*." He motioned at Shane. "He's wanted by the cops for the murder of a police officer. Tell her, Sawdust." Lester Wood rattled the translation at Juanita.

"No ... Miguel, vete!" Juanita said, motioning to a bodyguard who was holding a Tech 9 on Shane and Jody.

She barked something else in Spanish, then Miguel backed out of the room past Tremaine.

"Inky Dink. Go with him!" Tremaine followed. They were all left standing in the room, gripping their iron, hoping nobody would get nervous and squeeze off a round by mistake.

A minute or two later, Miguel reentered the room with a copy of the *Los Angeles Times* and handed it to Juanita. Tremaine appeared in the threshold behind him.

On the front page, above the fold, was a picture of Shane, along with the story of the murder of Alexa Hamilton. Juanita scanned the paper quickly, looked at the picture, glanced up at Shane, then over at Jody, her beautiful face composed in a silent question.

"He's not a cop anymore," Jody explained. *"Ya no es policía.* He's wanted for murder . . . he's with us now." He looked at Sawdust helplessly. "Is she getting any of this?"

Lester Wood rattled off a long sentence. Then all of them seemed to be talking at once. Finally Juanita lowered her Hardballer, and the others followed suit.

"¿Tienes los numeros? ¿Te los dió mi tío?" she asked.

Shane knew about "los numeros" from other drug stings he'd worked. She was asking Jody for a secret number given by the cartel boss to both parties involved in a street transaction. Bacca was the cartel boss, and this was his money. The ID number was proof of his consent that the cash could be turned over to the Vikings. Since there were no contracts protecting the transfer, it was Jody's knowledge of this code that enabled Juanita to hand over millions of narco-dollars with no questions.

"The number? Yeah . . . It's 457, from Raphael," Jody said.

"Cuatro cinco siete de Raphael," Lester said.

"Okay. *Vamos. Usted solamente,"* Juanita ordered, pointing at Jody.

204204204 STEPHEN J. CANNELL

"Absolutely." Jody smiled. "Me only." The tension in the room had eased slightly.

"*Vamos en su coche,*" she said to Jody. Adding in horrible English: "We load. For is done. You go back. *¿Es suficiente?*"

"Works for me." Jody smiled at her again. "You guys wait here."

"*Dame las llaves.*" She turned to Miguel. "*¿Cómo se dice?*"

"She wants the keys to our car," Shane said.

"*Sí,*" Juanita answered. "Keys."

"It's the blue step van in the lot downstairs," Jody said to Miguel as he handed him the keys. The bodyguard immediately left the room.

Through all of this, the still-suspicious Octavio Juarez never took his eyes off Shane, not for a moment believing that a cop who had hooked him up three times in one year was now a fugitive.

"Let's do it," Jody said.

Juanita and Octavio flanked Jody, and with no further discussion, they walked out of the room and closed the door, leaving the rest of the Vikings behind.

"Why're we waiting? Let's get outta here," Shane said after they were gone. He moved to the door, but Lester and Tremaine were still at the windows, watching as the step van, followed by a new black Cadillac, pulled out of the lot.

"Be cool," Tremaine said to Shane. "With this satellite rig, we can tail them from miles back . . . it shoots a tracking signal back to us from outer space."

They waited for almost three minutes before Tremaine nodded and Shane opened the door. They walked out of the apartment, down the stairs, and into the parking lot. Shane and Tremaine climbed into the black GMC truck with the pool-cleaning logo on the side. Victory Smith and Lester Wood got into the windowless gray van with the monitors. Tremaine had already switched on the dash-mounted GPS: a map of the entire West Valley down-loaded onto the LCD screen. Then they saw a small blip moving near the center of the readout, indicating the route the step van was taking. It was heading east, down the Ventura Freeway toward Studio City.

"Let's go. That's them," Tremaine said. Then he pulled out. The gray van, with Victory driving, followed right behind them.

"Where'd you get all this high-tech stuff?" Shane asked.

"Rod stole it from SWAT. They got the best shit," Tremaine answered, his deep voice resonating in the sound-deadened cab.

They were on the freeway now, following the flashing dot on the GPS, heading east. The white step van was at least a mile ahead of them.

Shane looked over at Tremaine, his shaved head glis-tening, reflecting the passing freeway lights.

Of all the Vikings, Shane thought Tremaine was the most puzzling. The ex-SWAT sergeant had a cool intel-ligence and natural leadership that he masked with pro-found silences, mixed with spurts of ghetto-speak. But every time he spoke, Victory, Lester, and sometimes even Jody stopped talking and were suddenly alert, like street punks listening to a distant siren.

Tremaine glanced over and caught Shane looking at him. "Whattcha think you starin' at?" he demanded an-grily.

"Nothin'." Shane shifted his gaze to the LCD screen. They rode in silence for a minute.

"Why don't you get it the fuck off your mind," Tre-maine suddenly said.

"You know this is coming unglued," Shane said. "Two guys already dead and buried. Victory's a mess. Sawdust doesn't give a shit, and Jody's on autopilot. You saw him

back there, ready to swap lead with a buncha street dealers."

Tremaine continued driving, and a slight smile passed
across his face, then disappeared, barely visible, like a
shadow on a dark wall. He shook his head slowly. "You
got it all worked out, huh?"

"So when it all comes apart, then what?"

"You best slow yer roll, Chuck. You don't know me.
. . . You 'bout t'make a bad mistake here."

"I'll tell you something else I'm wondering."

They drove in silence, the target vehicle flashing on
the LCD screen between them, heading down the curving
freeway map, being measured from deep space by a satellite while Tremaine drove and said nothing.

"All these other guys've got Sawdust's shitty pictures
drawn all over 'em," Shane said. "You . . . you've got no
ink . . . no nothin'. Not even the little Viking helmet. I'm
thinking, Why is that? It raises questions."

Tremaine didn't look over at Shane, but he had lost
the slight smile. His knuckles gripped the wheel hard as
he drove.

"Tell you something else," Shane continued. "You hate
being called 'Inky Dink.' Every time Jody calls you that,
it's like you got kicked in the ass. So I'm wondering how
come you put up with it; why you lettin' Jody 'Tom' you
like that."

Tremaine looked over. His eyes had become cold black
warnings.

"Here's my guess . . ." Shane continued recklessly.
"You ain't completely down with the program, and if the
rest of these guys weren't so zooted, they'd spot it."

The speedometer was ticking up in the seventies while
the truck radials hummed.

"I ain't no Sega radio," Tremaine finally said. "Go play
those tunes somewhere else, white boy."

Then, the beeping light on the LCD screen turned off

the freeway. A few minutes later Tremaine made the same turn. The windowless van containing Victory and Sawdust followed like a gray shadow, sharking along behind them.

Ten minutes later they watched the map screen as the step van turned left on Shadow Drive, then right onto a street called Glen Haven. It stopped at the last house, at the end of a cul-de-sac.

A few minutes later Tremaine drove into the same high-income neighborhood with his headlights off and parked up the block out of sight of the house. The gray van parked behind them.

Tremaine switched off the GPS and got out of the truck.

They went over to the van. Tremaine knocked on the side door, then as soon as it opened, they jumped inside.

Victory Smith was already tuning in the three TV monitors, revealing that the white step van was parked in a hedge-lined driveway.

"Always the same deal," Sawdust said. "Expensive house at the end of the cul-de-sac with a view of the whole street. The Beaners living inside are just window dressing sent up here from Colombia. It's all on page one of the playbook."

They watched on the wide-angle lens coming from the camera stuck behind the rearview mirror as Jody, wearing a blindfold, was led into the house.

Once he was inside, Miguel opened the garage and Octavio pulled the step van inside. They could see the garage door come down behind it from the rearview camera. The grille-mounted camera now showed an expensive Spanish tile floor in the large, empty, four-car garage.

Octavio took off his jacket, grabbed a pickax out of the storage cabinet, then walked to a spot in front of the van and swung the ax high over his head, bringing it down hard, smashing the decorative tiles.

"Must have their money room under all that expensive tile," Sawdust drawled.

They watched on the monitors as Octavio, then Miguel, took turns breaking up the three square feet of flooring. Next they shoveled out four inches of subsoil, revealing a trap door. Octavio pulled the door up and turned on a light, exposing an underground room. Then, one at a time, the Colombians went down a short flight of stairs, disappearing off the monitor for a moment, only to reappear, carrying large rectangular canvas bags that looked to Shane to be about three feet long by two feet high and wide.

"Show me the money, boys," Tremaine rumbled softly in his rich baritone as the two drug dealers put the canvas bags into the back of the step van, then returned for more.

The whole treasure hunt took less than an hour. The step van was almost completely filled with bags of cash. Then Jody was led blindfolded out of the house and helped back into the front seat of the step van.

They watched on the rearview-mirror cam as the truck backed away from the house. In the process, the front-end cameras neatly panned the mailbox and the house number on the curb. Then the step van took off, up the street, again followed by the black Cadillac, its front license clearly photographed by the rear-bumper camera.

The two vehicles swept past the van, rocking it with slipstreaming air. "We'll let 'em get a block or two ahead," Tremaine instructed, then after a minute, added, "Okay, now."

Shane and Tremaine got out of the gray van and returned to the truck. They switched on the GPS and again followed the step van from several miles back, watching on the LCD screen until it stopped moving.

Both tail vehicles pulled over and waited. The beeping light on the GPS continued blinking but remained stationary. Five minutes later the cell phone in the truck rang and Tremaine pushed the speaker button. Jody's voice filled the truck cab.

"Okay, they're gone. I'll drive the van and meet you back at the Sherman Oaks apartment. We'll see what we got here."

What they got were thirty large canvas bags containing fifty million dollars in banded bricks of used cash.

RUSTY

Jody had a deal with a crooked armored-transport company driver to move the thirty bags of cash to the Union Bank in San Diego. They unloaded the step van and put the cash in the back of an armored truck that had been borrowed without permission from the transport company's service department. At a little past eleven P.M., it pulled out with Tremaine riding shotgun and headed toward San Diego.

"You ever heard of a guy named Giovanni DeScotto?" Jody said to Shane as they rested in the back of the empty step van.

"Yeah, he's a banker or something, suspected of doing bank wire transfers for the Cali cartel. I read a department one-sheet on him. He was never busted."

Jody grinned. "Wrong! I busted the fuck. Got him dead-bang during the Mexican drug case. Caught him on videotape, offering to launder twenty mil."

"You flipped him?" Shane asked.

"Amen, brother. Burned him and turned him. He's our guy now. He's working at a bank in San Diego as vice president of Latin American deposits." Jody was grinning. "He's gonna take delivery of this armored-truck shipment and pass it through his bank." Shane knew that once the money was deposited in a bank, Jody was home free. Bank-to-bank wire transfers were exempt from Treasury Department supervision. There was no federal record kept on these transactions. It was a major loophole in the Justice Department's anti-drug policy. This one fact alone was responsible for the existence of the drug laundries operating in both Mexico and Colombia.

"Tremaine rides in that armored truck down to San Diego and gets our money logged in to the bank there as a cash transfer from Bancomer in Mexico," Jody continued. "Giovanni writes up the phony paper to record the deposit, then he does the cybertransfer to a little bank I found here in the Valley where I got some serious leverage with the VP of regional operations. From there, it gets wired to Aruba." Jody smiled. "Two bank transfers, and the money is off-shore."

"Slick," Shane said, and watched Jody smile.

The West Valley Bank of Commerce was located just off Ventura Boulevard on Beverly Glen, nestled into a landscaped commercial park five blocks from some of the most expensive real estate in the Valley.

They left Victory in the car outside, with instructions to cover their backs.

Tremaine had called an hour before, to say that the transfer of funds to the San Diego bank was complete. He was headed back to L.A.

It was nine A.M. when Jody, Shane, and Lester walked through the swinging glass doors. The West Valley Bank had a minimalist decor and looked as though it had been designed by Frigidaire. A few black-and-white Impressionist paintings dotted the shiny white walls.

Jody asked a passing bank employee if Bob Miller, the

vice president of regional operations, was around.

"You mean Rusty." She smiled. "I'll get him."

After five minutes Bob "Rusty" Miller walked up. Shane thought he was fifteen years and at least one hair transplant past his nickname.

Rusty led them to a private, windowless office in the back of the bank and closed the door.

"Both of these gentlemen are police officers as well?" he began without preamble. He seemed agitated and definitely in a hurry to get Jody out of there.

"That's right." Jody smiled. "This deal is going to work just like the Mexican bank sting. Same MO, only this time we're gonna wire slightly more cash . . . fifty million. It goes to a personal account in Aruba."

"*Slightly* more?" the pudgy banker exclaimed. "You can't be serious. That's five times more. . . . and isn't Aruba in the Caribbean?"

"The Lesser Antilles. Twenty-five kilometers from the Venezuelan coastline."

"That's outside of the continental United States."

"Yep. Last time I checked."

"Sergeant, this branch is currently undergoing a federal bank examiner's review. It's going to be very difficult to handle that large a sub rosa transfer at this particular—"

Jody held up a hand and interrupted him. "You're going to do it because this is police department business, and a failure to comply will bring all kinds a'nasty shit down on you, Bobby."

"Jeezus, when is this gonna end?"

"Never," Jody snarled.

"I can't just keep doing this," he whined.

"Then you shouldn't a'been banging that teenage boy in the Valley, Bob. Shit like that has consequences. You know what happens to pedophiles in prison?"

"Look . . . I . . ."

"You're gonna be home plate at pole-vaulting class."

"Stop it, please."

"I'm just trying to reset the table for you. Let's not get stupid and lose our perspective here."

Rusty was perspiring dark half-moons under the armpits of his designer blue shirt.

"Another bank-to-bank transfer?"

"Right. The cash is in this numbered bank account in San Diego." Jody handed him a slip of paper with the number on it.

"Okay," Rusty wheezed. "Who's this go to?"

"Wire it to the First Mantoor Bank of Aruba, marked to Lewis Foster's account there," Jody said, using the same alias he had given the geriatric gate guard in Palm Springs.

Rusty's face had gone pale.

But Shane had no sympathy for him. Worse still, he was appalled that Jody had rolled this creep instead of booking him. In Shane's mind, there was no worse crime than pedophilia. Yet Jody had apparently caught this guy and had let him slide in return for performing a banking favor on his Mexican bank sting.

In the wake of his disgust over doing business with Rusty Miller, Shane felt the old cop anger return, the sense of right and wrong that had propelled him toward police work in the first place. In that second, standing there in the back room of the bank, he felt for a moment like the old Shane Scully who cared about justice. He desperately wanted to be that man again. So he stood glowering angrily at the fat pedophile with a teenager's nickname, trying to turn back the clock ... trying to be what he had once been, to reclaim feelings he had lost.

Then Rusty left the room with the account number to arrange the transfers.

"You rolled a child molester?" Shane asked as soon as the banker was out of the room and the door was closed.

"We caught this bozo by sheer accident." Jody grinned.

"We were staking out the Mexican bankers, had a video trap set up to shoot through some glory holes in the motel rooms they had rented on Canyon Boulevard, not half a mile from here. We were waiting for them to get back from dinner, and unknown to us, the guy on the lobby desk was 'hot cotting' rooms, letting a buncha chocolate cowboys use already-rented suites for an hour or so, for cash. Rusty stumbles into our video trap with a fifteen-year-old male prostitute named Bunny. No shit, that's this kid's street name. When it turned out Rusty was in the banking business and we desperately needed a U.S. bank to wire our department-issued sting cash from . . . it was too good to let slide. So Rusty became our CI on that op."

"This guy victimizes children. How can you make him a confidential informant?"

"All the John Wayne bullshit's really starting to get old, Hot Sauce," Jody snapped.

A few minutes later Rusty Miller came through the door. The trip to the wire-transfer room had done him some good. His color had returned. He handed Jody a slip of paper. "Here's your wire confirmation," he said.

Jody looked at the slip, then pulled out his wallet, managing to flash his sergeant's badge for good measure as he put the receipt inside.

"You stay out of trouble, Mr. Miller. I don't wanna hear from any of my Vice contacts that you're out boning kids on the Strip. If I do"—he nodded toward Shane—"my man, here, is gonna chop-block your ass."

"Please, leave me alone," Rusty squeaked.

"Right . . . Lemme take that under advisement," Jody said, and led the frightened pedophile out of the room.

Lester looked at Shane after they had gone. "This guy turns my stomach," he drawled. "Was up to me, he'd be doing a telephone number in the joint." A telephone number was con lingo for a long sentence.

Then Lester exited the room, and Shane found himself

alone for a moment. He wanted to speak to Chooch, even if it was just for half a minute. Without worrying about the consequences if he got caught, Shane reached out, picked up the phone, and quickly dialed his home number. One ring . . . then two . . .

Come on, Chooch . . . Pick up, please.

Then his answering machine clicked on.

"What the hell are you doing!" Jody interrupted, glaring at Shane from the doorway.

"Calling my machine."

Jody exploded into the room, grabbed the receiver and put it to his ear. Shane could hear his own voice recording leaking into the small room.

"Whatta you, nuts? They could trace this call through the phone-company records, come here, and roll Bob Miller. You don't talk to anybody. I thought we had that straight." He slammed the phone back in the cradle.

"I was just gonna leave a message for my son," Shane said.

"No messages. Nothing. You don't exist for that kid. You're history. Now let's get moving. They're waiting."

Shane didn't ask who was waiting. His heart was slamming in his chest.

In that moment, he had a premonition that he would never see Chooch again.

FLIGHT

"Victory's back on steroids," Shane said, just loud enough to be heard over the whine of the starboard engine. He was seated in a plush Gulfstream 5 that was owned by All-American Tobacco. The jet was parked at the Peterson Aviation private jet terminal in Van Nuys.

"You're dreamin', Salsa."

"Hey, Jody, I blew this guy's thigh to shit just under two weeks ago. Look at him . . . he's already walking without crutches. Only way he could be healing this fast is if he's slamming steroids."

"Get off this, will ya?"

"The guy is fixing. Once his leg is solid, he's gonna try for me. I can't do what you want and be watching my back at the same time."

"We got less than three days and this thing is done. You'll never see him again. Don't make a problem now."

"Why don't you just go ahead and admit you can't handle him, that you're afraid to confront the guy?"

Jody spun and glared across the narrow aisle at Shane. "Get off my jock, for Christ's sake. I told ya I'd take care of him, and I'll take care of him, but I don't need you all the time in my ear about it."

"You planning on doing that before or after he makes another play for me?"

Just then, a pretty young blond woman dressed in a blue uniform with shoulder boards came up the stairs into the plush jet. "Hi, I'm Lily," she announced happily to the Vikings, who were spread out in the comfortable club seats. "I'll be your stewardess. If any of you want to order a special meal, I can take care of that now, but it will delay departure. I suggest the selected menu on the embossed cards in the back of each seat."

"We're fine," Jody said, his voice still tinged with anger.

They heard footsteps on the jet staircase, and Lisa St. Marie came aboard, followed by José Mondragon.

"Okay, Lily," Lisa said. "Tell Matt and Carl we're all here." She was the only AAT employee on the plane and seemed to relish being in charge. She had chosen tropical colors for the flight, an off-the-shoulder Hawaiian print dress and matching sweater that she tied around her waist like a sash. José, in his trademark black Armani and glittering links, poured himself a drink from the chrome-and-crystal bar, then settled into an empty seat as the stewardess disappeared into the cockpit. Momentarily, a hydraulic mechanism hummed and the staircase came up, air-locking tightly into place.

The port-side engine wound up as Lisa walked down the aisle, pausing at Shane's seat. "I thought I'd sit back there," she said, pointing to the sofa in the aft compartment. "It's more private, and I'd love the company."

"Sure," he said, shooting a look at Victory as he unbuckled his seat belt and followed her to the rear of the plane, where they both sat on the champagne leather sofa.

She took his hand and smiled. "It's a long flight. We

generally cruise at around forty-five thousand feet, and you know what that means. . . ."

"No, Lisa, what does that mean?"

"You're about to become a satisfied member of the Mile-High club."

"I am?"

"We can be brave and do it here after everyone's dozing, or we can go to the lav, but once they're asleep, I'm planning to screw your brains out."

"Do I have any choice? Or is it always your call?" He could already feel the effect of her . . . her scent, her vibe, her wanton sexuality.

She reached down and felt his erection. "Look who's ready to go," she purred.

When she smiled at him again, he turned his face away. He promised himself he would not make love to Lisa again. But even as he made this pledge, he could feel lust beginning as a warm, sick feeling in the pit of his stomach, growing inside him, spreading to his loins like deadly poison. They took off and climbed quickly to their cruising altitude.

It was going to be a long flight, and Shane's resistance to her brand of spiritual darkness was low. After the stewardess served dinner and collected their trays, Lisa started in on him . . . teasing at first . . . reaching out to him, feeling him, pulling her dress off her shoulders, exposing herself, pulling his face down, her nipples already hard with passion. Shane glanced nervously at the others sprawled out in the forward cabin, sleeping in their reclining chairs.

What was it about this woman, whom he didn't even like or care about but couldn't seem to resist? Why did she have this carnal hold on him? Like an addict, he was no longer in charge of his impulses.

Suddenly, she was unzipping him, leaning down and placing her mouth on him.

"No . . . no . . . please, no," he mumbled feebly. She

was dangerously close to his core, close to destroying the last valuable remnants of him, and yet he desperately wanted her.

She glanced up, delight twinkling in her jade-green eyes. "What do you mean, no? This is my gift. Everything else I do just fills up the spaces in between."

"No," he said weakly, pushing her away and zipping up.

And then, filling in for his faltering resolve, brutish Victory Smith was towering over them, stooping slightly in the six-foot cabin. "He giving you a problem, Lisa?" the steroid jockey asked softly. " 'Cause if he is, just say the word and I'll take care of it."

"Excuse me." She got up off the sofa with no further comment and, swinging her hips, walked all the way to the front of the jet, passing through the small door into the pilot's cabin.

A strange sense of gratitude for the weight lifter swept over him.

"Check it out," Victory said as he did a slow, deep-knee bend. Pain registered on his face, but Shane was shocked to see that he could squat all the way down and then rise up again. "Pretty good, huh?"

"Looks like the old abductor canal is back in business."

"Jody ain't gonna be here to protect you forever. I'm gonna pick a time when it's just you and me, no witnesses. This is your last day on planet Earth, pretty boy. Try and enjoy it." He turned and lumbered back to his seat in the front, and never looked back at Shane again.

Seven hours and three time zones later, they landed on the small Caribbean island of Aruba.

ONE HAPPY LITTLE ISLAND

Queen Beatrix Airport was on the eastern side of Aruba. They taxied up to a Customs shed located between the Mantoor executive-jet terminal and the regular commercial-jet boarding areas.

Out of the window of the private jet, Shane could see a handsome, forty-five-year-old dark-skinned man in white linen trousers and a flowered shirt leaning against the fender of a black, seven-passenger Mercedes SUV. His sandaled feet were crossed at the ankles, his arms laced comfortably across his chest.

Jody had promised that there would be no Customs or Immigration check, so Shane left his Beretta strapped to his ankle. Except for Victory, the rest of the Vikings were also packing. Shane wasn't sure what had happened to the weight lifter's Uzi. He just hoped Jody hadn't returned it to him and that it wasn't hidden in his gym bag.

Shane followed Lisa, José, and Jody off the plane into the humid tropical morning. The rest of the Vikings trailed behind with their small satchels and stopped near the waiting man.

José gave the man a bear hug. Then Lisa took her turn, administering a couple of pecks on his swarthy cheeks. José turned toward the Vikings, who had arranged themselves in a semicircle, squinting in the nine A.M. tropical sun.

"This is Sandro Mantoor," José said. "Sandy is going to take us to the hotel." All of this was spoken in perfect Ivy League English. "Sandro and I attended Harvard Business School together." He added proudly, "We were in the same Eating Club."

They all exchanged names and handshakes, Sandro exposing two rows of porcelain-white, orthodontically perfect teeth. "I've arranged for our best villas at the La Cabana Beach Hotel. I think you will be quite comfortable there."

"Sandy owns the hotel." José smiled proudly. "But you'll come to see the Mantoors own almost everything on this island." Then, to prove his point, José grinned up at the Mantoor Aviation sign hanging on the front of the private-jet terminal.

"Isle de Mantoor," Lisa said happily.

"I've arranged for a second vehicle to take us to our accommodations. Customs and Immigration have already been dealt with, so we can leave without delay," Sandro informed them. "José, perhaps you and Ms. St. Marie could travel with me. I have a few things to discuss before the meeting this afternoon."

"Of course."

José, Sandro, and Lisa got into his Mercedes and pulled out just as an identical SUV arrived. Shane noticed that both vehicles were brand-new, with dealer plates in chrome holders that read: MANTOOR IMPORTS. The island's motto was inscribed on the yellow and red license plate: ONE HAPPY LITTLE ISLAND.

They all got into the second SUV, Jody choosing the

passenger seat next to the driver—a large, Germanic man who said his name was Eric.

Shane was jammed in next to Lester and Victory in the second row. Tremaine had slightly more room in the back.

The capital city of Oranjestad was only five miles away, and they arrived minutes later. The outskirts of the port town were surrounded by tin-roofed shacks, happily dressed in bright Caribbean colors—red with green trim, or yellow with blue. Boxed palms lined the streets and swayed in a brisk trade wind. As they neared the center of town, the red, tin-roofed houses gave way to traditional Dutch and Queen Anne architecture. The port was picturesque, with quaint, brightly painted, stern-tillered fishing boats anchored in the magnificent horseshoe harbor, waiting for dusk. A medieval fort and a lighthouse were on opposite ends of a pair of stone jetties.

Then they were in the center of town; they passed the First Mantoor Bank and Commerce Company, located in a two-story Dutch turn-of-the-century manor house. It dominated most of one block in downtown Oranjestad. Mantoor Travel, a Donatella Mantoor Corporation, sat on Main Street, along with the Fredrico Mantoor Shipping and Freight Forwarding Company. Farther down the street was the King Venezuelan Shipping Line—a Daveed Mantoor Corporation, and so on.

Eric kept up a running dialogue in a thick Dutch accent, pointing out sights: "The Mantoor family is, how you say . . . tradition of Aruba. She is a business dynasty formed by late grandfather, Elias Mantoor, yah. Elias, he come here, was Lebanese Christian . . . migrated to Latin America over hundred years ago. He do . . . how you say . . . trading all along da Caribbean coast. Dere on corner is Mantoor Corporation headquarters." Eric pointed to a plantation-style house on two acres taking up an entire city block in the center of town. "Used to be colonial governor's mansion until Elias, he buy in 1896, for corporate headquarters. Da Mantoor family all become citizens of Netherlands, like me, with Dutch passports. Sandro Mantoor . . . one day soon, he make the control for all this. The great-uncle, Milos . . . he very ill." The spiel continued like that until Eric turned into a floral-landscaped, tree-lined drive.

The La Cabana Beach Hotel and Casino was a beautiful Dutch Colonial structure: rococo white wood railings, fronted slanting wooden porches like delicate lacework. Huge paddle fans turned in the open lobby, swirling hot tropical air lazily around inside the exposed-beam entry.

Shane was given the Orchid Suite. He went inside, closed the door, and set down his gym bag. The room was large, beautifully appointed, and done restfully in light blue and white. He looked through the sliding glass doors to the Caribbean waters just a few yards beyond. A twenty-five-knot wind was snapping the palm fronds just outside his window. The crescent white-sand beach was teeming with sunbathers. Bodysurfers competed for wave space with half a dozen streaking sailboarders who shot diagonally back and forth across the turquoise lagoon. Paddle balls and Frisbees flew recklessly. Sailing above it all were a few hang gliders, crisscrossing over this frantic activity like colorful winged creatures circling for a spot to land.

"Pretty cool, isn't it?" Lisa interrupted. He spun around and found her standing in his bathroom door. She had changed into white shorts, sandals, and a pastel orange blouse tied in a knot at the middle.

"Are we roommates?" he asked.

"Actually, my room is next door . . . but I scammed a key to yours, so I guess we get to be whatever we want." She crossed the room and kissed him lightly on the lips, then pulled away, spinning slightly to her right, showing herself to him. Certainly seductive and inviting, but Shane thought it was also a little too choreographed.

He was being manipulated. This suddenly seemed like the too-planned dance of a professional . . . and in that moment, the spell she had cast over him was broken. She suddenly seemed sad, comic, and slightly desperate.

"We'll have to save our party for later. I've got a meeting with the Harvard Marching and Chowder Society in ten minutes. When we do this again, I don't want us to have to rush." She smiled. "What did you think of Sandy?"

"The Mantoor family is something," Shane said. "What don't they own around here?"

"You don't know the half of it. Aside from their legitimate businesses, the Mantoors control the trans-shipping of all drugs and parallel-market product in this duty-free zone. They're the new pirates of the Caribbean. The Mantoors and Paco Brazos control most of the negotiations for black-market product down here."

"And who is Paco Brazos?" Shane asked.

"He's a Colombian nightmare—a 'San Andresito.' "

"A what?"

"The San Andresitos are the five families that control all the smuggling into Colombia. They get that name from black-market malls called San Andresitos that are located all over Colombia. The malls are owned by the Medellín cartels. Paco's malls are owned by the Bacca family, the same people that Jody's L.A. drug cash came from. Our smokes will be sold in their malls, and that's how the cartel gets its money back. The five smuggling families— the San Andresitos—operate out of a desert town called Maicao. Since we're running such a huge load of cigarettes, and no one or two families can place that much product, Paco Brazos has subcontracted the deal to include his competitors. But he's charging the other families a big commission, and this could cause a problem. The other San Andresitos don't want to pay him. That's why

I'm off to meet Sandy, José, and Paco. We're trying to hose these guys down. Then at four, José and Paco are meeting with the rest of the San Andresitos to do the deal." She walked toward the door. "These smugglers make me a little nervous. I can hardly wait to finish this and get back to L.A."

"Do we all go to the four o'clock meeting?"

"No. Just Sandy and José. I won't be there, either, because—"

"Because as an All-American Tobacco executive, you don't really have a clue what's going on, right? You're just selling duty-free cigarettes."

"Don't be a shit, darling."

She smiled, planted another kiss on her fingertips, and wiggled them at him from the door, then turned and walked out of his room, a sexy package designed for trouble.

After she left, Shane sat on the bed and thought about what she had told him.

The problem was, he didn't seem to care anymore. He felt a heavy layer of depression just off the edge of his psyche . . . a rolling fog of guilt and darkness. It was threatening to overcome what was left of him . . . to make him completely disappear.

35

THE DUTY-FREE ZONE

"You look like Ricky Ricardo," Shane said to Jody, who was standing in the hall outside Shane's door, wearing a wild flowered island shirt. It was ten minutes to four in the afternoon.

"Just bought this in the gift shop. We're comped." Jody grinned. "Everything's on Sandy. Despite his greasy look, I'm beginning to really acquire a taste for that guy. This place a'his ain't bad, either. You should see all the A-caliber trim hanging by the pool." He smiled broadly, then added: "Let's go. Eric's waiting downstairs. We're supposed to be at the duty-free dock for a meeting with the Colombians in ten minutes."

"I thought we weren't invited."

"An hour ago we weren't; something musta changed."

They met the rest of the Vikings in the lobby and again found themselves packed into the black Mercedes SUV, Shane wedged in behind the driver's seat, staring at Eric's Teutonic wrinkles. Lisa wasn't with them, and Papa Joe had taken the seat up front.

"We got a little problem," he said to Jody as soon as

the vehicle was in motion. "Unfortunately, it's not something I can fix."

"Unfixable problems are a Viking specialty," Jody said, smiling.

"Paco Brazos decided to cut one of the San Andresito families out of this deal. The man he left out is Santander Cortez. Santa is not a man you get rid of easily. He's something of an enigma out in the desert . . . a black marketeer with a political agenda. He will undoubtedly make trouble."

"Don't worry," Jody said. "We'll take care of it."

José shook his head. "Don't be so sure. There are frequent kidnappings and murders surrounding parallel-market transactions in Maicao. It's out in the desert. There is no law, no police or civil government. Worse still, there is only one road in and out. Once you go in, you are in a trap. Making things more complicated, the leftist guerrillas and the right-wing death squads hide in that desert preying on each other and the San Andresitos' shipments. As white Americans, you will be easily spotted. Everyone in Maicao will know you are there from the first minute you arrive. There are no Anglos in Maicao. You will have only Paco Brazos standing between you and all this, and Paco cannot easily be trusted."

When they arrived at the port, Eric drove the Mercedes to a fenced-off wharf with a guarded gate. Signs identified it as the MANTOOR SHIPPING COMPANY FREE-TRADE ZONE. NO TRESPASSING warnings were printed on the gate in four languages. A uniformed guard with an out-of-date carbine swung the bar arm up and allowed Eric to drive the German-made SUV down the bustling pier. There were several old three-hundred-foot freighters tied to the wharf. All the ships were registered to different countries. English, Japanese, Dutch, and Venezuelan flags tugged at their halyards, snapping energetically in the stiff breeze.

Crane engines roared as loaded containers swung from cables over the dock and above rusting freighters, creating a deafening racket. Green John Deere forklifts, piled high with boxed merchandise, were zipping around, scooting loads of duty-free in and out of ten huge warehouses located on the pier.

The wharf was immense, almost fifty yards wide, and swarming with people and product.

"How come they don't warehouse onshore?" Shane asked. "Why store all this stuff out on the dock?"

"Because none of it is going to stay here more than a day or two," José answered. "It's all contraband. Parallel-market goods heading into Colombia."

"All of this is going to Maicao?" Shane asked as he watched a forklift with three crated washing machines whiz by in front of their vehicle.

"Maicao and Culcata, Panama," José said. "It is no wonder the Mantoors control so many businesses, no? They have much money to invest."

Shane nodded as he again remembered the maps he had found in Jody's airport house. Culcata was the other city that was circled.

Eric drove the Mercedes into the last warehouse on the pier and parked. "This building contains only cigarettes and liquor," José told them.

Shane was looking at billions of cigarettes from every U.S. manufacturer: Phillip Morris, Reynolds Tobacco, Liggett & Meyers, and Lorillard. On the other side of the warehouse were the liquor products: huge wooden pallets were stacked forty feet high with cases of Seagram's, J&B, Early Times, and Beefeater.

"Our cigarettes came from Norfolk, Virginia, yesterday, on that Dutch freighter tied up across the pier. They are now on those pallets over there." He pointed to more than three hundred large shipping containers stacked near the door, with the AAT logo stamped on every box. Each carton also sported a big red duty-free sticker. "They will soon be loaded on a Venezuelan ship to cross the channel."

"How many cigarettes is that?" Shane asked.

"There are twenty cigarettes in a pack," José began. "Ten packs to a carton, fifty cartons in each case, and nine hundred sixty cases in each of these containers. We have shipped three hundred fifty containers." He paused for effect. "That comes to ninety-six million cigarettes."

As soon as they got out of the SUV, Sandro Mantoor came out of a door a few yards away and headed toward them, his leather soles clacking on the shiny concrete. "This way, my friends," he said, and led them through another door and up a flight of stairs, into a plush suite of offices. They walked down an air-conditioned corridor, then entered a small conference room. A plate-glass window dominated the far wall, overlooking the bustling warehouse operation below.

There were four men standing in different parts of the room, and despite their expensive tropical clothing, they all looked like extras from the movie *Rio Lobo* . . . round, sweating men with crooked teeth turned brown by tobacco. Greasy smiles lurked menacingly under hungry eyes. If one of them had started cleaning his teeth with a knife, it wouldn't have surprised Shane. Tucked in their pants, under loose shirttails, he could see handguns bulging.

"Paco, mi amigo," Sandro said expansively as he embraced Paco Brazos, who was only five foot four and bald on top but wore his fringe hair long and pulled back in a ponytail.

He had on tan slacks and a Mexican guayabera with two Snickers bars stuffed into the breast pocket.

"Buenos días, mis compañeros," Paco said to all of them with something approaching two-faced warmth.

Then Papa Joe introduced Jody, who introduced the rest of the Vikings.

"These are my dear friends and trusted business associates," Papa Joe said first in Spanish, then turned to Jody and translated it all into English.

"Bueno, bueno," Paco Brazos said, nodding and bowing all in the same motion, then introduced the three other men in rapid Spanish.

Spartacos Sococo was the tallest at around five-seven. He had the worst haircut Shane had ever seen. It looked as if he had attempted to cut it himself using garden shears. Emilio Hernandez was five-five, fat, and had a recent-looking red-welted scar that cut through his left cheek, running down his neck into his collar. Octavio Randhanie, the only skinny San Andresito, just smiled at them, never removing his straw hat or dark glasses.

The San Andresitos kept stretching their humorless grins over hard eyes that were expressionless as licked stones. Shane had done enough undercover gun and drug deals in Los Angeles to spot the deadly crosscurrents.

The six men began speaking rapid Spanish. Shane was struggling to keep up, but their Colombian accents sounded different from the Mexican Spanish he'd encountered on the streets of L.A. It appeared that the San Andresitos were arguing over how many containers of cigarettes each family would handle. At one point, Spartacos Sococo slammed his fat brown hand on the table. *"¡Ay que huacho!"* he said angrily as he got up and made an elaborate false exit.

"No tengas miedo, vete," Paco replied sharply, calling Spartacos's bluff, challenging him to go ahead and leave.

Spartacos finally turned and went back to his chair. More shouted conversation was followed by more curses and posturing. Then, ten minutes later, the men stood quickly and glowered at one another. Nobody shook hands as Paco showed them out of the room.

"The deal's done." José sighed. "Paco got an additional ten percent of each of their profits, which they are all very unhappy about. He also got the most product—fifteen million dollars in cigarettes. Each of them got only five. They wanted an even split, but this is more than they would normally handle, so hopefully they will get over it."

They left the warehouse and drove to Sandro's bank to disburse the fifty million dollars.

The First Mantoor Bank of Aruba was magnificent. Brass and leaded-glass doors fronted the executive offices, which were done luxuriously. English antiques squatted on white plush pile.

Jody presented his wire-transfer confirmation slip from the West Valley Bank of Commerce, then accessed the fifty million in L.A. drug cash that Rusty Miller had wired to the bank to be held under the name of Lewis Foster. Jody showed the bank president his phony ID, took possession of the account, then wrote out the instructions to wire thirty million dollars to American Global, which was All-American's European company in Geneva. It was payment in full for the cigarettes. Five million was wired to Blackstone in Geneva, which covered their commission for brokering the deal. Fifteen million was put in escrow to be jointly held by Papa Joe until the Vikings had delivered the cigarettes to Maicao, Colombia. Once the product was safely there and the four families had taken delivery, the money would be released to the Vikings. The Bacca drug cartel would be repaid its original L.A. drug cash once the cigarettes were sold in their cartel-owned black-market malls, completing the laundry.

36

BETTING THE HOUSE

"Look't that rusting bastard," Jody said to Shane. They were standing on the duty-free pier, studying the old Venezuelan freighter being loaded with containers of cigarettes. It was seven P.M. that same evening. The only paint on the vessel's brown steel hull was some fresh white lettering on the stern that read *Subu Maru,* which Papa Joe had explained meant "bright star." Shane thought the rusting bucket looked more like a falling star. They had been told the ship was leased by the King Trading Company: a Mantoor-controlled Venezuelan shipping line.

"This rusting piece a'shit only handles contraband for the drug trade," Jody said.

The *Subu Maru* was at the end of her days, stuck in the service of the devil, making the short, twenty-five-kilometer run from Aruba to the port of Maracaibo, which sat just inside the Gulf of Venezuela.

As they stood on the dock, watching their containers of cigarettes being lowered into the black hold, something strange happened to Shane—a darkening of Shane's spirit, worse by far than any of his other episodes. It kept building throughout the afternoon, until his chest was tight with anxiety and he was short of breath. Suddenly, he felt he couldn't stand to go on for even another hour.

Although the rest of the Vikings had left the pier, Shane and Jody watched until the last containers were loaded on board. The sun had begun to set, treating them to a luscious, multicolored sunset, before slipping below the surface of the Caribbean Sea, bringing down the curtain of night.

"I'm gonna see if I can find a woman," Jody said with a grin. "How 'bout it? Wanna come? No pun intended."

"No . . . No . . . I think I'll get something to eat at the hotel, walk around a little," Shane said as a frightening notion began to haunt him.

"If you change your mind, call me."

"Gimme your cell-phone number," Shane said as he picked up a Spanish newspaper off the dock and handed it to Jody, who wrote down his number and handed it back. Shane folded it carefully, then put the newspaper in his back pocket.

He caught a cab to the hotel but didn't want to go to the room for fear that Lisa would be there, stripped down to her high heels, waiting to destroy what was left of him. Shane got out of the cab, and as he walked through the lobby, he knew that he was at the end . . . knew he couldn't go on. Spiritual darkness overwhelmed him. All of his thoughts, no matter the content, just served to drive him lower.

He wandered toward the pool, looking for something, anything, to free him from this suicidal grip. It was a few minutes past eight. Nobody was out there. The lights in most of the cabana suites were on. He could see guests moving back and forth in front of the curtains, getting ready to go out, their lives full of adventure and romance, while his was now only about loneliness and despair. He sat in a pool chair and rubbed his eyes.

There was nothing that mattered to him anymore—not even his pledge to destroy Jody. There were Jodys everywhere, men who lived violent lives without remorse. What was one Jody, more or less?

He felt himself sink deeper.

In desperation, he tried to lock onto something positive.

Chooch.

He focused on the feelings of love for his son. He loved Chooch desperately but now began to realize that his son would be better off without him. He sat on the corded pool chair, wondering how he had become so completely lost.

He got up suddenly and walked into the lobby. "Could I have a piece of paper and an envelope, please?" he asked the pretty island girl at the concierge desk.

"Of course, sir," she said, handing it to him.

He walked across the lobby, then sat at the small writing desk and began a short letter.

He couldn't address it to anyone in particular, because he had no one left at the LAPD whom he trusted, so he began:

> *TO WHOM IT MAY CONCERN:*
> *The following facts have been obtained regarding a massive money-laundering scheme involving the illegal sales of parallel-market V-5 All-American Tobacco products into Colombia . . .*

Then Shane laid out the entire scheme, with every detail he could remember. The letter went on for three pages. He named all of the Vikings and included Jody's admission that he had killed the two heads of the Detective Services Group. Shane wrote about Leon Fine, dead and buried on the beach up in Oxnard; he named the All-

American Tobacco executives: the Prussian general, Lou Petrovitch, and his two helpers, Chip Gordon and Arnold Zook. He described the Mantoors, how they used their power and influence in Aruba to subvert their own duty-free zone for illegal profit. He named the five San Andresito families, spelling their names as carefully as he could, hoping he had them right. Then he confessed to pulling the trigger on Alexa Hamilton in the Tony Filosiani–supervised plot, intended to set his cover for the Vikings, explaining how he fired, not knowing Jody had reloaded his gun with a Black Talon. Finally, he wrote about Lisa St. Marie, who probably, more than even Jody, had presided over his ultimate corruption. He asked the LAPD Scientific Investigations Division to scan the enclosed newspaper for Jody's fingerprints, proving that he was still alive at the date of publication.

He ended the letter with a message to his son:

Forgive me, Chooch. You will be better off without me. I did the best I could, but it was not enough.

He signed it:

LAPD Sergeant Shane Scully

He put the letter into an envelope along with the dated Spanish newspaper containing Jody's cell number and fingerprints. Shane sealed the envelope, then walked back to the concierge, bought two stamps, affixed them, and addressed the envelope:

COMMANDING OFFICER
LAPD INTERNAL AFFAIRS DIVISION
304 SOUTH BROADWAY
LOS ANGELES, CALIFORNIA 90007
U.S.A.

"Would you please mail this for me?" he asked the concierge.

"Of course, sir," she said as she took the letter. "I'm afraid it won't go out till the morning. . . ."

"That's fine," he said.

She dropped it into a mail slot and smiled at him. "Have a nice evening."

"Yes," he said. "Of course." He turned and headed back out to the pool, but he didn't stop there. He continued toward the lagoon, walking on numb legs.

When he reached the beach, he turned right. It was deserted, no longer the colorful playground of a few hours ago.

He felt the weight of the Beretta on his ankle, heavier with each step. He walked almost a quarter mile from the lit seaside cabanas before he sat down and began untying his shoes.

I'm taking off my fucking shoes just like eighty percent of the dumb-ass suicides I worked, he thought.

He finished removing his shoes and placed them neatly beside him. Then he peeled off his socks, the weight of the Beretta heavier with each passing second.

His mind was lasering back and forth across this final decision, searching for one last handhold—one positive emotion that would save him.

But when he really examined it, there wasn't anything left for him. Chooch was going to be in college in eighteen months. With no one to vouch for him, Shane would be vilified by the LAPD and eventually caught and convicted of Alexa's murder. He couldn't face Chooch's reaction to that.

He had no friends left on the department. Alexa had been the last, and he had killed her.

He had once felt brotherhood and love for Jody, but now he knew that Jody was a sociopath and had just been using him all these years, pretending love and friendship but feeling nothing. Worse than that was the realization that Shane was becoming more like Jody every day.

All he wanted to do now was to get off the ride.

Slowly, he pulled the 9-millimeter automatic out of its slide holster.

He chambered it.

The unusually loud click rang in the empty night.

One last important decision: Where to place the muzzle?

Under the chin at the mandible? Aiming up through the horizontal palatine bone into the anterial cranial fossa—coroner's terms echoing back at him from hundreds of autopsies.

Perhaps he should stick the muzzle in his mouth, go for the medial soft palate uvula . . . drive that two-ounce pill right up into his cerebral peduncle. Usually a sure thing, but on one or two occasions, he'd seen that path produce total brain vegetation but not death.

Maybe he should just stick with the reliable old temple shot. Put the muzzle on his inferior temporal line, just above the ear . . . pull the trigger and hope for the best. Hope that the slug wouldn't ricochet around inside his cranium but leave him breathing through a tube for ten years, until he finally rotted from the inside out.

As a cop, he'd seen all of these muzzle positions fail to get the job done. His last meaningful decision.

What a dumb fucking problem, he thought ruefully.

The old homicide dicks called this dilemma "betting the house." Slowly, Shane brought the gun up and stuck it into his mouth. His hand was shaking. He could taste the Hoppe's gun oil on his tongue, pressed flat by the weapon. His teeth began chattering on the barrel.

"God help me," he said quietly, his words slurring on the cold metal.

He tried to pull the trigger, but something stopped him . . . some last-second doubt. And in that moment, everything changed.

Somebody came out of the dark and hit him hard from behind, knocking him forward.

The gun flew out of his hand, splashing into the water while Shane was thrown, face-first, onto the wet sand.

He felt a huge weight land on his back. A massive arm locked around Shane's throat. In that instant, he changed from a potential suicide to a potential homicide. With this change in category came a desperate will to survive.

He fought and clawed to get the man's arm off his windpipe, struggling to keep from being strangled on that deserted stretch of beach.

"This is for shooting me, and for killin' Rod, and for screwing Lisa," Victory Smith whispered, the gasps of hot air filling Shane's ear.

Shane managed to tuck his chin down and get his hands around the grizzled arm, which was slowly choking him.

Suddenly, Victory's grip slipped.

Shane got his mouth on the weight lifter's huge forearm and bit down hard.

"Fuck!" the steroid jockey screamed, letting go.

Shane rolled out from under Smith and came up on his knees, just in time to field a left hook that caught him on top of his head, ringing his ears, starring his vision, and knocking him back into the light rippling waves at the edge of the lagoon. Shane landed on his ass in two feet of warm tropical water. Pain shot up his spine. He had come down on something hard. Instinctively, he reached down and grabbed it—

His Beretta.

As Victory Smith ran toward him, splashing water, Shane brought the gun out from under him and pulled the trigger.

The Black Talon shell casing had resisted the seawater, and the gun fired, bucking loudly in his hand. The exploding slug took Victory in the center of his simian forehead, blowing it wide, but the weight lifter kept coming . . . cerebral fluid and brain tissue spilling down his pockmarked face as he ran. The muscled giant took two more faltering steps and fell toward Shane, his arms out in front of him, grabbing Shane in a lifeless hug as he landed. Shane felt Victory's heart beat twice before it stopped.

It was suddenly quiet.

All Shane could hear was the gently rippling surf and the distant sound of rustling palm fronds. He let go and pushed the huge man off, watching as Victory rolled onto his back into the churning surf. Seawater washed the sickening hole in his head, turning the swirling surf dark with blood and brain matter.

Shane staggered to his feet, then looked down at his fallen adversary. Why hadn't he just let Smith finish the job he'd already started? What had made him fight so desperately to survive?

Shane stood over the corpse, watching it roll and turn in the light surf. A lifeless ballet. The swirling black patterns of Victory's strange personality washing out of his skull into the seawater. He knew this memory would be locked in his subconscious forever.

Finally, he reclaimed himself and pulled Victory up onto the beach, dragging the two-hundred-fifty-pound man . . . tugging, struggling to pull him up to the berm, where the white sand met with a ridge of low, tropical vegetation.

Shane got down on his knees and started to dig a hole, using his hands to paw up the granules until he got down where the sand was damp. Buried shells stabbed at his fingers as he dug, breaking his nails and making his hands bleed.

He could hear someone crying softly and looked around, afraid he was being observed. Then he realized he was the one crying.

He locked his mouth shut and forced himself to stop. Finally, Shane had dug a trench that was two feet deep and seven feet long; hardly big enough to hide this hulking giant for long. The first strong wind would uncover him, but Shane could dig no longer. He was completely spent. He took Victory's wallet and rolled the steroid junkie into the shallow grave, then covered him up until nothing was left but a foot-high mound of packed sand.

He picked up the murder weapon, wiped the Beretta clean on his shirt, then threw it as far as he could into the lagoon. He heard a faint splash somewhere way out there as it hit.

When Shane got back to his room, it was empty. Thankfully, Lisa wasn't there, but he saw that there was something on his pillow, glittering and colorful. He walked to it, wondering what it was, and whether Lisa had left it there.

He picked it up and stared at it in confusion. It was a two-inch round medal, with a red ribbon attached.

The LAPD Medal of Valor.

"You were the one who really earned it, so it's only fair that you should keep it."

He turned, and she was standing just outside on the balcony.

She walked toward him, took him in her arms, and held him. Then he could feel her pressed against him. Suddenly he was kissing her, holding her head in both his hands.

But he had shot her, watched her fly backward . . . watched as the huge pool of blood spread around her. Yet somehow she'd come back. Somehow she'd survived.

Alexa Hamilton was alive.

RESURRECTION

"I'm so sorry, so sorry," she said, holding him. Shivers ran through both of them.

"I thought I killed you . . ." he stammered.

"I wasn't hurt," she said softly.

He finally let go of her and stepped back, the joy of holding her overtaken by heart-wrenching fear that Lisa or Jody would suddenly return and that he would lose her all over again. "We can't stay here," he blurted.

"I've got a room up the beach. Come on . . ." She pulled a high-frequency radio out of her bag and triggered it. "This is Three. Are we clear out there?"

"Roger, Three. This is One. Come on," a man's voice said.

"Who's that?" Shane asked.

"I'm down here with federal backup. Tony set it up . . . DEA guys . . ."

"Shit, Tony's got half the free world out looking for me."

"We had no choice. I'll explain everything, but we've gotta get outta here first."

She led the way to the door, but Shane stopped her before she could exit. He kissed her one more time, her mouth soft on his, feeling such sweet warmth radiating inside that it brought tears to his eyes. He released her, then cautiously opened the door and peeked out. The corridor was empty.

"What's your backup look like?" he asked.

"Jo-Jo Knight—tall, black, linebacker type—fashion disaster . . . Dacron shirt and plaid Bermudas. The other one is a little round Cuban, Luis Rosario. They never stop rippin' each other, but they're pretty good guys. They're tasked outta Treasury."

They left the room and ran down the corridor into the stairwell, where a tall, wide-bodied African American was waiting with a radio.

"Howdy-do," he said. "I'm Agent Knight. Hang on a sec while I check in with Beaner Central." He triggered his walkie-talkie. "Two, this is One. How we lookin' out there?"

"Smooth as Cuban cookin'. Bring 'em on. Got ya covered," a soft voice with a Cuban accent replied.

"Where's Miss Shake an' Bake?" Jo-Jo asked.

"In the bar. Got the gringos in there all pitching tents in their pantalones. We'll go out the back, through the service entrance."

"Roger that," Jo-Jo said, looking up at Shane. "Your friend Lisa."

"Business associate," Shane corrected, wondering if Alexa knew about his relationship with the sexy tobacco executive.

They took the stairs two at a time, finally exiting into a service area, where they found a short, round Cuban with a dark complexion, infectious smile, and porkpie hat.

He glowered at Jo-Jo Knight. "Your people maybe got rhythm, but you got no timing? I'm gettin' flat arches out here, waitin'." Rosario turned and led the way through the

service area and down a narrow corridor that was filled
with laundry hampers.

They ran out the back door to where a car was parked.
Jo-Jo got behind the wheel; the Cuban opened the back
door and they piled in, then the car pulled out and headed
across town.

Shane held Alexa's hand, squeezing it hard, afraid to
let go. He couldn't believe he was sitting next to her
again, couldn't believe she was alive and back in his life.

Her room was on the beach at the Divi-Divi Resort
Hotel, on the outskirts of Oranjestad. Luis Rosario and
Jo-Jo Knight took cover positions where they could watch
the front and back of the hotel. Alexa opened her suite,
then she and Shane entered.

Once the door was closed, she turned and they kissed
again. Finally she pulled away, reluctantly.

"Fun as this is, we don't have much time," she said,
still holding his hand. "I'm sorry for what we did to you,
Shane. It wasn't fair. I didn't want to do it, but the DEA-
SAC in L.A. insisted. Tony finally had to go along."

"Good old Tony."

"Don't blame him. He didn't want to. Sit down, I'll
fill you in." She led him to the bed where they sat side
by side.

She looked into his eyes and began her story. "After
you didn't report in, we went to your house. We saw
blood on the kitchen floor, the broken screen and window
in the bedroom. We knew you'd been kidnapped. Tony
picked me up and we had a meeting in his office. Right
about then, the Questioned Documents Division broke the
number code on the logbook we found in Mark's safe. It
was Medwick's account of how the Vikings were formed,
how all five of them were removed from the city payroll
records. You were right. The whole experiment was set
up under Deputy Chief Mayweather."

"There were six of them," Shane said. "Jody, Tremaine

Lane, Victory Smith, Lester Wood, Hector Rodriquez, and some Hispanic cop they killed and buried up in Oxnard."

"The records say only five. There's no mention of anybody named Tremaine Lane . . ."

Shane thought about that for a minute, and a new idea started to form, but for the moment he filed it. "Okay . . . Go on."

"The whole parallel-market thing was in Mark Shephard's logbook, including the Fortune Five Hundred companies, Aruba—everything. It was undoubtedly written before Jody decided to go bad and take over Leon Fine's business. Once Jody made that decision, like you suspected, he had no choice but to kill Medwick and Shephard because they knew what the Vikings were working on. Chief Filosiani notified Washington and brought in a Treasury SAC from the L.A. office. Once those guys were aboard, everything started to play like a James Bond movie."

"Those two feds outside play more like a Cheech and Chong movie."

"They were Chief Filosiani's picks. He worked some joint-ops cases with them when he was in New York. They're best friends, and good guys once you get past the constant ethnic ribbing."

"I shot you with a Black Talon," Shane said. "How could you have survived that?"

"Remember those paintings in Chief Brewer's office?"

Shane nodded.

"He sold them to get new equipment. Flack vests."

"Yeah."

"Well, they weren't just ordinary vests. It was brand-new body armor designed at the Pentagon. They're level-three tech vests, called Ultimas, capable of stopping anything, including Cop Killers, Teflon loads, armor-piercing stuff—the works. Tony was afraid that Jody would switch guns on you, so he had me fitted for one as a precaution. And then, to make it look real, he got a friend of his, a Hollywood special-effects man, to rig a blood squib and give me a bladder full of cow blood. I had a pump I could squeeze down on under my arm."

"Why? Why would you do that? I was so fucked up, I almost—"

"I know . . . I know . . . I guess that was sorta my fault. I told them you thought Jody could read your thoughts. Then the Treasury SAC began to wonder if you could pull it off. He felt if you believed you really killed me, your reaction to my death would be more authentic. Your life was at stake, so Tony and I finally agreed. But when we lost you after the shooting, our plan got totally scrambled. We didn't count on a helicopter being in that hangar. We didn't think we'd completely lose contact with you. When we didn't know where you were, the DEA decided we had to put on a full media funeral . . . because that's what would have happened if I'd really died two days after winning the MOV. They were afraid that if Jody was in L.A. and it wasn't a big media deal, he would know it was all bullshit, and he might kill you. We didn't know where you were, so I sat home and watched my own funeral on TV."

"And Chooch?"

"I told him. I forced them all to let him in on it. I couldn't let him think you'd killed me and gone bad. It wasn't fair. Buddy knows, too."

"For whatever it's worth, they were right," Shane said. "Jody told me he probably would have suspected something if I hadn't been as screwed-up as I was."

She nodded, then went on. "We knew that the Mantoors were part of this because it was all in the logbook. We hoped you would eventually show up in Aruba, so I came down here with Luis and Jo-Jo and we waited. This morning, when that jet pulled up at Mantoor Aviation and you got off, my heart broke, baby." She put her hand over his. "I could see how far down you'd gone. Sometimes I can see inside your head, too. Maybe I can do it even better than Jody. I knew you were close to the edge, so I begged them to let me contact you, and Tony agreed. He finally just overruled that tight-ass Treasury SAC in L.A. and did it without their approval."

"You were almost too late."

"I was waiting in your room, with Rosario watching Lisa, hoping she wouldn't come back before you did."

"I'm sorry about Lisa, I—"

"Shhh," she said softly. "You thought I was dead. You don't talk about Lisa St. Marie, I won't talk about Mark Shephard. We'll mark it down as history and move on. Fair enough?"

"Fair enough."

"I love you, sweetheart," she said softly. "I can't tell you how bad I feel about the way this went down."

"It's okay . . . it's okay. It's over now. I have you back."

"But you've got to go. You can't be missing for too long."

"I need a gun," Shane said. "I had to lose mine."

"Here . . ." She opened her purse and handed him a Spanish automatic. It was a 9-millimeter Astra with a short barrel and an eight-shot clip. Shane chambered it and stuck it into his ankle holster. "I've only got one spare clip," she said, handing it over to him. Shane stuck it in his back pocket.

They stood up. "Hold it," she said. "I almost forgot something." She reached into her purse and handed him a bottle of pills.

He looked at the label: "Blood pressure pills?" he said as he unscrewed the bottle top and rolled one little white tablet into his palm. "What's this for?"

"It's not a pill. It's a satellite-tracking device; a satellite transmitter with microcircuitry. You take it as soon as you leave port. It lives inside you and broadcasts your position. I don't want to lose track of you again. It'll pass through you in twenty-four hours, but hopefully this whole thing should be over by then. That thing will tell us where you are within a yard."

"You're kidding me."

"Your tax dollars at work." She smiled. "The Frisbees have great toys. Now, get going. I don't want Jody looking for you, asking questions. We're less than twelve hours from the takedown. We'll save our reunion till then." She got him up off the bed and led him to the door.

He turned to face her. "Alexa, wait . . . There's something I need to ask you first."

"No time."

"No, I need to ask you now."

He pulled her closer.

"When I thought you were gone, it seemed like my life was over. Now I can't let you go without asking." He took a deep breath. "I love you. Will you marry me?"

She stood before him for a long moment, tears welling in her eyes. "Of course I'll marry you, you idiot. What took you so damned long to ask?" She kissed him. The kiss lasted almost a minute, and when it was finally over, she pulled him back into the room and led him over to the bed where she pulled him down.

"I thought there was no time." Shane teased.

"Changed my mind . . . female prerogative."

She made slow love to him, and in that moment came Shane's redemption and resurrection.

In that coupling, he was reborn.

38

MARACAIBO

"So, where the fuck is he if he's not in his room?" Jody asked angrily, looking at Tremaine Lane, Lester Wood, and Shane. But mostly he was glaring at Shane.

It was ten past eight in the morning; the black Mercedes SUV was a few feet away in the porte cochere with the trunk lid up and their canvas bags already inside. Eric was standing nearby, watching.

"You're asking me?" Shane said. "Since when am I in charge a'that steroid case? Like you advised, I'm giving that asshole all the room I can."

"Victory knew the *Subu Maru* was set to leave at eight. We're already late."

"We could split up and go lookin'," Sawdust drawled, not putting much energy into the statement.

"Okay, scout around; we'll meet back here in ten minutes," Jody said.

While Tremaine, Lester, and Jody took off, looking for Victory, Shane went to the reception desk.

"I gave the concierge a letter to mail for me last night,"

Shane said. "I changed my mind about sending it. Has it gone out yet?"

"Yes, sir. The mail left an hour ago."

Shane nodded and saw a Caribbean guidebook for sale. He picked it up, peeling off five U.S. dollars.

"How come I get the feeling you're not telling me everything, Hot Sauce?"

Shane spun around and found Jody standing right behind him.

"I really love this . . ." Shane said as his mind suddenly filled with the vivid image of Victory lying dead in the surf, his dark brain contents washing around in the light surf.

"You're thinking about some shit swirling around in the water," Jody said. "What's that all about?"

It was frightening how he did it. Shane forced his thoughts away, forced them on nothing . . . a trick he had perfected when they were kids.

Jody straightened up, and his expression changed. "It's gone," he said softly.

"Victory Smith is your problem. You wanna know how I feel about him going missing? I feel great. The guy was an unguided missile. Somebody probably did us all a favor and pulled his drapes."

"Papa Joe wasn't fooling about this Santa guy. He's an Argentine fugitive, a political terrorist, and he could be big trouble for us. We need Victory. He might be nuts, but he gives us a comfort zone."

"We should forget him and get moving."

Eventually, that's what they were forced to do.

Jody talked to them on the dock just before they boarded the ship. "I don't know what kinda bullshit we could be facing, so I got Sandy to score us some better firepower." He handed each of them a brand-new Polish MP-63

9-millimeter machine pistol. The weapon was compact, with a flip-down grip and retracting stock. Then he handed each of them two forty-round clips. The machine pistols fit easily into their gym bags. "If we get jumped by the whole town, we're pretty much fucked, but at least we'll take some greasers with us."

The *Subu Maru* pulled away from the Mantoor Duty-Free dock an hour past schedule. Its mostly Venezuelan crew gathered in heavy, oil-stained mooring lines as the gap widened between the freighter and the dock.

The old Caterpillar engines clanged into reverse, and the ship creaked in protest as the stern made a slow journey back and to starboard, pulling the ship away from the wharf.

Jody was on deck, somewhere aft as the bow of the *Subu Maru* swung slowly around and was now pointing toward the mouth of the harbor.

The breeze was ten knots on the stern and the slow-moving ship just managed to make up the difference, leaving them engulfed in a tropical stench, fouled by its own diesel smoke.

Then they cleared the jetty and were out of the harbor in a light following sea, the slow-turning propellers churning up a white wake, pushing them toward the southwestern horizon and Maracaibo, thirty miles away.

Shane stood at the rail feeling so content that even the clogging heat and stink of the ship didn't bother him. He was grateful to whatever divine force had prevented him from pulling the trigger, until Victory saved him for Alexa, Chooch, and their future together. Only yesterday at this same time he had felt empty and used up; now Shane was overcome with excitement and expectation. All he had to do was stay alive for one or two more days.

And that reminded him . . .

Shane reached into his pocket and took out the bottle containing the white transmitter pill. He unscrewed the top, then looked at his watch: 10:15 A.M. He shook the pill into his hand and was about to pop it into his mouth when Lester Wood materialized at his side.

"Got a cold, pard?"

"High blood pressure," Shane said as he popped the pill into his mouth and dry-swallowed it. He showed Sawdust the prescription bottle.

Woods looked at the label, then handed it back. Shane threw the bottle into the sea.

"Guess what?" Sawdust said.

Shane didn't answer but kept his eyes on the horizon.

"While I was out lookin' for Victory, I heard that some soft-drink vendor found a body up on the beach real early this morning. The corpse was buried in the sand."

"Why tell me?"

"I hung out down there and listened to them bean-eaters shootin' the shit. Kinda got the gist of it. The way they were talkin', the stiff was a big, ugly guy, lotsa muscle, flowered shirt, tattoos, American. Sound like anybody we know?"

"To these islanders all Americans look big and ugly."

"Appears this guy got on the wrong end of a corpse-and-cartridge party. Course, I didn't see the body, but they say he was built like Schwarzenegger. Tell me this don't sound like our own anabol-slammin', iron-pumpin' steroid case."

"Lotta big guys with muscles down here."

"I ain't making no accusations, Hot Sauce, but all them anabolics was makin' Vic buck real close t'the ground. I think maybe he finally came after ya, forced ya to burn some powder. But like I say, I'm not losin' no sleep over it." He paused, reached into his pocket, and pulled out a tin of chewing tobacco. "Course, Jody might see it differently."

"Is this a threat?" Shane said softly.

"A negotiation." Sawdust took a pinch of Skoal and

put it into his mouth. "With Victory dead . . . that means we only got us a four-way split now. I'm thinking this information might could stay between just the two of us."

"How much?"

"With Victory outta the mix, that means the fifteen mil now only gets divided by four. That makes each share worth three point seven-five mil, give or take a pony. I'm thinking, you kick back a mil to me. With Victory's cut thrown back in the pot, you still walk away with almost three million."

"You've got no proof," Shane said. "Your word against mine."

"Yer right . . . but we ain't in court here, pard. This ain't about proof, it's about anger and paranoia. Jody's stressed. Takes one phone call to the Mantoors back in Aruba. Dandy Sandy checks the body, finds a Black Talon parked in Vic's head, and you're in a heap a'grease, pard."

"Okay," Shane said softly.

"Good goin'." Sawdust was smiling, swaying with the rolling deck, his Ray-Bans kicking moving spots of tropical sunlight up and down Shane's face. "Nice tradin' time with ya." Then he spit a line of tobacco juice over the rail into the ocean before ambling off.

An hour later Shane could see the faint outline of the Peninsula de Guajira, which made up the western end of the Golfo de Venezuela.

Ninety minutes later they were steaming into the Straits of Zapara, which narrowed until they were in the spacious Bay of Tablazo, passing anchored freighters flying hundreds of different flags, each one waiting for its turn to offload cargo at the main dock.

Amazingly, the rusting *Subu Maru* steamed right past all of them, heading straight to the front of the line. Shane mused that drugs certainly had their place in the Latin American scheme of things.

The huge Venezuelan shipping port of Maracaibo loomed on all sides as the *Subu Maru* groaned and moaned, then jockeyed her ugly bow toward the dock, first in slow forward, then slow reverse, backing down on the port engine, straining to pull her canoe stern up to the concrete wharf. Commands were shouted angrily in Spanish over the loudspeaker from the bridge. Monkey-fist knots that gave weight to thin strands of nylon line were heaved overboard by sweating deckhands and hit the dock, where other men in blue overalls grabbed them and pulled hard, dragging the heavy oil-stained mooring lines they were attached to ashore. The heavy lines were then hooked to dock cleats, winched tight, and spring lines were set.

The growling engines on the *Subu Maru* were finally shut down, but loud dock sounds immediately replaced them. Cranes hummed and men shouted in Spanish.

They were in the Venezuelan portion of the Aruba duty-free zone.

The Vikings were about to embark on an insane journey that none of them had bargained for.

39

TRUCKIN'

Tremaine Lane and Lester Wood stayed with the cigarettes while Shane and Jody found Paco Brazos in the shipping office on D Dock, where he was getting their cargo manifests logged in at the duty-free desk. A uniformed Venezuelan Customs inspector was banging his rubber stamp on countless egress forms without bothering to read them. Next to him was a uniformed Colombian colonel with shoulder patches that read EFECTIVOS DE COLOMBIA. Despite his nonresident status, the colonel seemed to be in charge of the trans-shipping of their cigarettes.

"Están seguros," he said sharply, indicating a stack of import invoices.

The Venezuelan Customs official nodded and kept stamping the forms furiously.

Paco finally glanced up at Jody and Shane. "You have nice the travel?" he said in his broken English.

"If you don't mind choking on diesel fumes," Jody answered.

"We go soon. Customs, she all fix, no?"

"What about the other San Andresitos?" Jody asked.

"Hernandez, Sococo, and Randhanie. Aren't they supposed to be here to take delivery?"

"Ahh, is very good . . . yes . . ." Paco smiled. He didn't seem to have a clue what Jody had just asked him.

They moved out into the hot afternoon sunlight. A line of five trucks were just pulling through the guard gate on the duty-free dock—old Mexican Fords with chipped paint, broken headlights, and fenders redesigned by traffic. Wooden stakes held up stained covers that arched over the truck beds like dirty brown rainbows.

"Los camiones," Paco announced.

The trucks came to a stop, then ten or twelve private armed guards, known in Colombia as *celadores,* jumped out of the back of each vehicle. They wore threadbare, faded khakis tucked into shiny new paramilitary jump boots, and each guard carried an identical olive green machine gun—old Mexican Mendozas. The out-of-date thirty-ought sixes had wooden stocks and twenty-round box mags that loaded from the top. For a while the Mexican gangs in L.A. had been using these weapons, but as the drug business quickly became prosperous, they all switched to Russian auto-mags. Shane remembered that the old-style Mendozas were prone to jamming.

Paco rattled off a few sentences in Spanish. Jody looked over at Shane for a translation.

"I didn't quite get it. Sounded like he said you and he should ride in his bubble, whatever that means," Shane said. "He wants the rest of us in the back of the trucks."

"Your bubble?" Jody asked Paco.

"Sí, sí. Mi bubble es mi carro. Tengo nuevo—Land Cruiser." Paco pointed proudly at a new black Toyota that was parked nearby.

"A bubble." Jody grinned. "Yeah, looks kinda like one, don't it?"

Ten minutes later the other San Andresitos arrived, also in new Land Cruisers. The SUVs were all loaded with extras: chrome rims, whip antennas, and roll bars with deer lights. The custom interiors were tuck-and-roll. They all had TMX sound systems that could blow the fur off a rabbit.

An hour later the cigarettes were safely loaded and the caravan was turned around, ready to leave.

"Hokay," Paco said, pushing his ugly brown teeth out from between puffy lips. "We go. *Vamos a la ciudad de Maicao.*"

The Vikings retrieved their gym bags containing the comforting weight of their machine pistols and boarded the trucks, which were now full to the top with All-American's cigarettes: one truckload for each of the three San Andresitos families, two for Paco Brazos. Paco got into his Toyota Land Cruiser, with Jody in the passenger seat beside him, and pulled to the head of the line. Shane was assigned to the back of the second truck with two of Emilio Hernandez's teenage guards.

Shane's vehicle was so filled with cases of cigarettes that there was almost no room to stand. He looked at the guards and guessed them to be about seventeen or eighteen. Their smooth faces and round cheeks had not yet been hardened by adulthood, but their eyes were those of predators. These teenagers had seen death or had caused it—Third World eyes, burning with anger and determination, in faces only slightly older than Chooch's.

The trucks moved slowly off the dock and through the duty-free gates, into the old town of Maracaibo.

They rocked dangerously in and out of deep potholes, rolling down the narrow streets like a parade of lumbering elephants, past a seven-block-long green island that sat in the center of town like a huge grass runway.

"*¿Qué es esto?*" Shane asked one of the guards, pointing at the rectangular grass strip.

"*El Paseo de los Siglos,*" the teenage *celador* said sharply, and turned his back on Shane. The rough translation was "Passage of the Centuries." It meant nothing to Shane.

Finally, they reached Avenida 15 and hung a left. One after the other, the trucks and Toyotas rounded the corner, then proceeded north through the new part of Maracaibo.

Tall skyscrapers and flat-roofed, one-story shacks stood within yards of one another, giving the place a feel of unstructured growth.

Soon they were in the countryside, passing arid fields and slanting wooden fences, blowing road dust out from behind each truck as they headed into the desert.

La Guajara was described in Shane's Caribbean guide-book as a semi-desert, but to him it looked bleaker and hotter than Death Valley. Brown cactuslike vegetation clung to the few sandy washes, hoarding precious drops of moisture like thirsty castaways.

They passed straggling tribes of nomadic Indians herd-ing half-dead burros along the dirt road. The nomads ran to get out of the way of the caravan, as the smugglers blasted the air horns in their shiny new Land Cruisers. The Indian men shouted at their frightened children, grabbed the halters of their braying donkeys, and glared with impotent hostility at the trucks that sped past, leaving them engulfed in a curtain of brown dust.

Shane tried to ask one of the guards about the Indians, but the boy just shrugged. "Wayu," was all he would say. Shane wondered if that was the name of the tribe or a curse, or both.

Soon they crossed out of Venezuela into Colombia. The border was marked by an old yellow sign shot full of bullet holes, outside the small town of Paraguación.

Paraguación seemed right out of a Sam Peckinpah western. The trucks slowed only slightly as they jounced down the dirty main street, past dusty cinder-block stores with broken glass windows. Rough-hewn corner posts supported tin roofs on buildings that leaned precariously.

A dry fountain dominated the center of town, across from a general store.

The trucks and SUVs swept through Paraguación like a Panzer division. A few Indian children stood on the boardwalks, holding on to their mothers' cotton dresses. They watched with black-eyed wonder while a few of the trucks carelessly clipped the circular base of the fountain as they rushed past.

The convoy had just passed out of Venezuela, into Colombia. There were no Customs stops, no government officials, nothing.

Nobody in the town of Paraguación, or the two nations it separated, seemed to care that ninety-six million cigarettes had just been converted from duty-free product into illegal contraband. It had happened in the blink of an eye as they shot through that little village under the uninterested gaze of a few desert Indians.

They picked up speed again, heading across the "semi-desert," scattering jackrabbits and rattlesnakes in their path, heading west toward a lawless hell town known as Maicao.

40

MAICAO

Shane could actually smell the town before it came into view, a malodorous combination of sewage and rotting garbage drifting east on the desert wind.

They soon reached what Shane assumed was the airport, according to the Colombian guidebook he'd picked up at the hotel. But it was unlike any airport he'd ever seen.

What had first been a meandering dirt road, rutted and treacherous, suddenly became a two-way, poured-concrete highway that ran for a mile and then miraculously widened into six perfectly straight lanes complete with runway arrows, footage markers, and landing lights. The caravan of trucks rolled over old rubber landing marks left there by the four-ply jet tires that had touched down in both directions. After five miles, the six lanes narrowed again, becoming a two-lane highway and then, as if it had never been there at all, they were back on dirt bouncing along again. The field had no tower, no hangars, no gas pumps or support buildings. The Maicao International Airport was just six lanes of concrete, some telltale skid marks, arrows, and a few landing lights. Shane guessed that night flights put down unannounced to offload cargo and left just as quickly.

"*¿Aeropuerto?*" Shane asked a teenaged *celador,* whose scraggly new chin whiskers stubbornly announced the coming of manhood.

"*Sí, aeropuerto,*" the angry youth answered. Two words this time. They were having a verbal festival.

Shane's guidebook said that Maicao was a town that should not be visited. Shane could never remember seeing that kind of statement in a guidebook before. Under this startling warning, it said the town had a population of fifty-five thousand, all of it apparently living on the outskirts of town in slum housing with no plumbing or electricity. Shacks now dotted the sandy desert on both sides of the road, without the slightest hint of organization or city planning. The terrain was littered with shanty tilt-ups and lean-tos made out of wooden packing cases and discarded sheets of corrugated metal. Worse still was the smell that became more intense as they pulled into town. Every block or two they passed six-foot-high mounds of reeking garbage. Big greenback flies strafed the piles of refuse, prospecting ferociously.

Very few people could be seen standing outside, as the oppressive midday heat pushed into triple digits.

They bounced around a curve and saw a Colombian military garrison located on the east end of town, protected by a nine-foot-high razor-wire fence. Two white-helmeted gate guards stood in the sweltering heat but paid no attention as the five truckloads of contraband rattled into town.

They entered the business district, which Shane thought was even more depressing than the slum housing they had just encountered. The first and most remarkable thing about this section of Maicao was the prodigious amount of discarded packing material. It was everywhere.

It seemed that the boxes full of contraband, once opened, had simply been shucked out onto the street. Bubble wrap, as well as old wood and cardboard from broken-down containers, covered everything. A layer of white Styrofoam popcorn was blowing over it all. It scattered in the trucks' wake, finally piling up against the curbs. In a curious example of urban eco-balance, human waste ran in the gutters, rotting the packing material from the bottom, slowly making room for next week's load. Concrete lane dividers, once intended to be planters to enhance city beauty, were now just catch basins for old cardboard boxes and rusting metal banding tape.

The trucks slowed to ten miles an hour as they drove down Calle 16.

The few men walking on the heat-shimmering sidewalks turned to watch as the five-truck caravan with its Toyota SUV escorts rumbled into town.

Shane noticed that there were no women, and the men he saw were all packing dangerous-looking weapons. Pistols were stuck into webbed canvas belts. Machine guns of every make hung by faded leather straps.

They drove past the Heda Hotel, where there was supposedly a cantina called the Corraleja. The guidebook said it was named after a particularly dangerous bullfight where the spectators could come down from the stands, enter the arena, and take their chances with the bull.

The center of town was more of the same, except as they got closer to the warehouse district, the refuse and garbage grew in height, overflowing the curbs. The Styrofoam popcorn now dominated the landscape, swirling over everything, drifting like Rocky Mountain snowbanks.

They finally turned off Calle 16 into the warehouse district, and it looked like no place Shane had ever seen. Most unusual and out of place were the half a dozen or so untended and underfed cows that wandered aimlessly in the street, grazing on God knows what, blowing the popcorn aside with angry snorts to get at the rotting garbage below.

Each of the five San Andresitos families had magnificent warehouses there. The first one they drove past was located at the mouth of the street: a large, paranoid building that seemed designed to repel an invasion force. The windows resembled gun ports. Castle-type exterior doors were banded with heavy metal. CORTEZ LTD was written in silver letters across the side of the building.

Farther down, Shane could see four more mammoth buildings, two on each side of the street—one to each square block. In front of every warehouse was a modern, architecturally designed showroom that displayed the San Andresitos families' black-market products.

Santander Cortez's showroom followed his castle motif: steel and granite walls with narrow slit windows, each containing spotlit radios and watches. The glass looked thick enough to be bulletproof.

Emilio Hernandez had gone for a massive French Provincial showroom. For Octavio Ramandi, it was Colonial. Greek Orthodox for Spartico Sococo. Paco Brazos had really gone fishing. His showroom was a black and red Japanese pagoda-style building, with Macy's-size front windows filled with merchandise. The glass was protected by silver alarm tape.

The canvas-backed trucks began to peel off, each one heading to its respective family headquarters.

The truck Shane was in stopped halfway down the street, and the engine shut off. He waited while the tailgate was dropped and his two teenage *celadores* jumped out, then Shane picked his way through the shifted cases of cigarettes and dropped down onto the street. He landed on two feet of compressed packing wrap in front of Emilio Hernandez's French Provincial showroom.

From where Shane stood, he could see the other four

trucks parked in front of their respective warehouses. Paco Brazos was standing a block away in front of his large pagoda monstrosity, grinning broadly.

Jody was just getting out of Paco's black Toyota as Tremaine jumped down from Sococo's truck farther up the street. Two blocks ahead, Shane could see Lester Wood was already making his way carefully down the street toward Jody, his boot heels sinking in the muck.

"*¿Qué está allá'?*" Shane asked one of the teenage guards, who just turned and walked away without answering. "Eat me," Shane muttered softly.

Suddenly a door opened on the side of the warehouse, and a dozen more armed teenagers jogged out to stand in a semicircle around the truck. They weren't packing the old Mendozas. These guys were strapped with shiny blue-steel auto-mags, which they held at port arms. A pair of elephant doors on the warehouse clattered up behind them, and two battery-powered yellow forklifts hummed out and parked nearby.

"*No es necesario que usted se quede,*" Emilio said, dismissing Shane. His sweating round face showed disdain.

Shane could see Jody waving for him to come over. "Okay . . . *bien. Adiós,*" Shane said, then turned his back on the hate-filled eyes of fifteen heavily armed teenage boys and made a slow, treacherous journey across the garbage-filled street to join Jody and Paco and the other two Vikings in front of Brazos International.

He walked carefully past a dozen more *celadores* who were protecting Paco's two truckloads of cigarettes. They watched him like prison guards until Shane finally pushed open the two-inch etched glass door and joined Jody, who was standing just inside. Entering the showroom was like stepping back into air-conditioned sanity.

The room was cooled to sixty-eight degrees, and Shane's sweat-soaked shirt immediately began drying ice-cold against his skin. The stench of Maicao was left behind, and a sweet lilac scent of an expensive room deodorant took its place.

"Some little township they got here," Jody said softly.

"Jesus, I didn't know there was this much bubble wrap on the planet," Shane answered.

"You see Santander Cortez's place?" Jody asked. "From those gun-port windows on the second floor, he could control the whole street with less than ten guys. What's that about?"

"They got a whole new take on commerce out here," Shane answered.

"I don't like the way this feels. We need to complete our business and get the hell outta town before Santander gets back."

"Back from where?" Shane asked. "I thought he was up here, layin' in the cut, waiting to slit our throats."

"According to Paco, he had to go to Medellín on business."

"*¿Quieren ver a mi tienda?*" Paco interrupted them as he entered the showroom.

Jody cocked a questioning eyebrow at Shane.

"He wants to show us his store."

"Yeah, *bueno,*" Jody said. "But let's not take all day."

Paco led them through his magnificent showroom with its glass cases full of radios from Motorola and TVs from GE. Electronic conveniences glittered under recessed lighting, each one on its own Japanese-style jade marble stand. Tremaine Lane and Lester Wood trailed behind, their eyes flickering across the incredible display of goods.

Paco walked them through the appliance room with its ultra-size Sanyo, Panasonic, and Sony TVs. Dishwashers from Westinghouse, microwaves from Revel, refrigerators and washer-dryers from Maytag and Kitchen Aid. Almost every make and brand imaginable was represented. The cigarette and liquor display was in a hallway about forty feet long that stretched between two appliance rooms. The corridor was walled with glass cases full of every U.S. cigarette brand. Bottles of Russian Stoli sat next to carved decanters of Chivas Regal—all of this twinkling merrily under recessed product lights.

From there, they walked out into the warehouse.

Shane didn't know how long they were in the cavernous concrete-block building, but the tour was a definite mind bender. The three-story, open-spanned structure was so full of goods that they had to often walk sideways to get down the aisles. Men in straw hats driving forklifts whizzed past on the center aisles, moving things around in the massive air-conditioned building.

It was hard to determine how much product was stored there, but if Shane guessed several hundred million dollars, he couldn't have been too far off.

Paco kept talking as he led them through his black-market kingdom, keeping up a fractured-English spiel worthy of a Disneyland riverboat guide: "General of Electric, *aquí*. Packard Bell, *allí*." But he saved the best for last. *"Y la plata está en el fondo adentro."*

Jody shot Shane a look off the last sentence.

"I think he's saying the money is inside." Shane smiled.

"I like that. Let's go see the money." Jody grinned back.

They climbed a flight of stairs. Paco opened a door, and they entered a plush suite of offices. For the first time since arriving in Maicao, Shane saw women—all young and pretty. Each sat in front of a computer, furiously clicking their mouses and scrolling inventory screens. Paco Brazos was thoroughly enjoying the effect his tour was having on them, and he had obviously saved the best for last.

He punched a code into a very sophisticated computer

lock, swung open a three-foot-wide metal door, and turned on the lights; then all of them entered.

The room was about sixty feet square. There were several upholstered chairs, and in the center a computer monitor sat on an antique wooden table. The screen showed the peso exchange rates all over the world. Banded bricks of every kind of currency imaginable were stacked on the shelves that lined the walls, overpowering the room with the sweet, musty smell of paper money.

Each section had a label indicating the currency stored below: U.S. dollars, Swiss francs, Greek drachmas ... Colombian, Venezuelan, or Mexican pesos. Floor-to-ceiling displays of cash dominated every inch of wall space.

"Es mi cambio," the short, fat black marketeer beamed proudly. "My ... How you say? Exchange for *todo el* business, no?"

"Yeah, yeah," Jody said, his eyes locked on the fortune in the room, his breath suddenly short with envy.

"Time to go. We must to meet others," Paco said, looking at a diamond-encrusted Rolex Presidente. "For to get delivery receipt. Then maybe *señorita,* some fucky-fucky, no? *Entonces vámonos a la Maracaibo antes de que Santander vuelva."*

"This jerk-off thinks if we hurry, we might have time to get laid before Santander gets back," Sawdust drawled.

"Tell him we'll take a rain check on the pussy," Jody said.

"Sí, sí," Paco chirped, getting the gist of that. *"No señoritas. Lo siento."* He led them out of the room, carefully shielding the lock with his body while he reset it.

"You believe this, Salsa?" Jody whispered.

All Shane could do was shake his head in wonder.

"Tengo sed," Paco said. *"Bebemos fuerte con los otros San Andresitos."*

"He's thirsty," Shane said. "He wants—"

"I got it," Jody interrupted, looking at his watch. "Only one beer while we get the delivery receipts, and then, adios."

"Sí, sí, está bien, mis amigos." Paco grinned, showing teeth the approximate color and texture of an old wooden fence.

Paco led them to his Toyota, then they got in and drove up the street.

Five minutes later they were parked next to the three other Toyota Land Cruisers in front of the Corraleja Cantina—the very bar Shane had read about in the guidebook.

It was just past two in the afternoon and the businesses in town had closed for siesta, but nobody seemed to be sleeping. Inside they could hear laughter and Mexican music playing on what sounded like an old scratchy forty-five. Then a glass broke, followed by hoots of laughter.

"Ándale," Paco said, grinning, as he led them into the cantina. The Vikings took their gym bags with them as they got out of the Toyota and cautiously walked through the door.

Even though it was named after a Colombian bullfight, Shane thought the place looked more like the bar from *Star Wars*. Adrenaline and beer were being mixed in dangerous quantities. Sweating men were talking loudly.

Forty pairs of angry eyes swung toward them.

Suddenly the room went deadly silent.

41

BAR FIGHT

"This joint don't feel too friendly," Jody said, one hand on his gym bag, the other fingering the hard place under his jacket where he kept his chambered Heckler & Koch.

"Hola, mis amigos," Paco shouted expansively to the other San Andresitos, who were in a booth at the back of the cantina. Paco led the way through the bar full of Colombian misfits, to where Spartacos Sococo, Emilio Hernandez, and Octavio Randhanie were perched on hard, butt-polished vinyl, grinning like three hungry vultures on a split-rail fence.

Shane and Jody wedged in next to Emilio Hernandez and Spartacos Sococo, while Paco Brazos, Tremaine, and Lester found seats next to Octavio Randhanie. The San Andresitos forced smiles onto their faces while the background noise in the bar began to build again slowly.

The cantina was quite large, dominated on one side by a scarred wooden bar and mismatched furniture. The men in the place all seemed to be made of gristle and knotted twine. Their brown muscles glistened with sweat. There was no air conditioning; a big paddle fan with wicker blades turned ineffectively from the ceiling while an old Wurlitzer jukebox screeched American rock and roll through blown-out speakers.

"Qué bueno, ¿no?" Paco said. "Good pussy, *abajo. Pero no tienes tiempo para la fucky-fucky, no?"* He grinned, spreading his lips happily. His bullshit brown–toothed grin was really beginning to wear thin.

"Look, boys . . . *amigos,*" Jody said. "We don't need to get laid, we need our paperwork—our receipts proving that the merchandise got delivered up here safely, so we can collect our money from Sandro Mantoor in Aruba. You got that for us?"

Five sets of stone-hard eyes met Jody's question, glaring volumes of guarded thought, but no hint of what was to come.

"Sawdust, tell 'em what we want."

Lester Wood rattled it off in Spanish, and the San Andresitos all nodded, sipping whiskey from shot glasses, but nobody made a move to hand over anything.

"I'm thinking we got us a little problem," Sawdust said. "These boys don't seem t'wanna ride in the wagon."

"Tell 'em we don't get our receipts, we're gonna take that info back to Sandy. And if they got some dick-brained idea about us not getting outta this town in one piece, then Sandy Mantoor isn't gonna send any more product up here. He's guaranteeing our safety."

Lester Wood translated this, but after he finished, all four of the San Andresitos just stared. Nobody was smiling any longer.

"Kinda like barkin' at a knot," Lester Wood drawled.

"Okay, what's going on? Where's our bottom line here?" Jody asked.

Paco rattled off some Spanish, and the other San Andresitos nodded.

Sawdust translated: "Seems we're being kidnapped. They won't let us go unless *we* pay *them.*"

"You want us to give you money to let us out of here?" Jody growled.

"*Sí . . . sí, dinero*. Money for to go. *Es correcto,*" Paco said.

"You fuckin' people . . ." Jody snapped. "I'll die here before I pay one fucking cent."

"Jody . . . let's think this through," Shane said softly. "Let's get a number from 'em. Why should anybody die if we're only talkin' about one or two grand?"

"No," Paco said, understanding instantly when the subject was money. "*No es suficiente.*"

"How much?" Jody was smiling now, but Shane knew that smile. He'd been dealing with it since the sixth grade. It was a deadly warning.

"*Te va a costar veinte por ciento.*"

"He wants twenty percent," Sawdust drawled. "We need us a laugh track t'go with this."

"That's about three million dollars!" Jody said. "You sure that's gonna be enough, you fucking *ladrón*?"

The four San Andresitos froze. Shane realized most of them had taken their hands off the table where they were now dangerously out of sight.

"Jody . . ." Shane said. "Take a look around in here . . ."

Jody swung his gaze across the bar. Most of the men had silently risen off their stools and were now forming a loose circle around their booth. Shane continued: "I think I saw some of these people driving forklifts in Paco's warehouse. They lured us in here. We've been set up."

The bar had gone graveyard quiet, except for a bad version of "Blue Suede Shoes" screeching over the blown speakers, sounding more like a catfight than music.

Suddenly, Jody yanked his H&K P-7 out of his waistband and shoved it in Paco's face. Simultaneously, all eight men in the booth had guns in their hands.

Half the men in the bar had also found weapons in that split second.

Twenty pistols were cocked and aimed at the Vikings sitting in the booth. It had happened fast, but Jody had beaten Paco's draw. Paco Brazos was in no-man's-land, frozen, with Jody's gun an inch from his face, his own weapon not quite out.

"I'm ready! Go for it, asshole! Let's do the dance." Craziness lit Jody's face like the changing colors of a raging fire. It was all there—excitement, adrenaline, and a willingness to die, all of this registering in one crazy heartbeat. "Come on. Start blasting. But no matter what, you're on the bus. You're goin' first, greaseball."

They were all stretched out in deadly postures, each one shoving a gun across the table at the enemy opposite him. None of the Vikings had time to get to their Polish MP-63s but instead had gone for their handguns. Shane had snatched the Spanish Astra out of his ankle holster and was trading aims with Spartacos Sococo's huge Desert Eagle. They posed there for several dangerous moments before a slow, impish smile broke across Paco's dirt-brown face.

"*No quiero disparar . . .* no shoot. *Tomamos y comemos y luego tus papeles.*" He turned to the other San Andresitos. "*Mis amigos . . . no más . . . no más.*"

"He's changed his mind. . . . He doesn't want to shoot us. He's gonna give us our papers," Sawdust said, holding his Colt Commander on Emilio Hernandez, who had a blue-steel Beretta 9 aimed right back at him.

"Tell 'em to put their guns away," Jody ordered, and Sawdust did.

All of the San Andresitos slowly reholstered their guns. The Vikings didn't.

"Get the rest a'these shit burners outta here," Jody ordered, indicating the men standing in a deadly circle around them.

"Vete, vete afuera," Paco said to the sweating contingent of armed men.

Slowly, the men in the bar shouldered their weapons or repacked them in faded canvas holsters. They sauntered toward the door, trying to look tough in the middle of a retreat, dragging their pride like heavy sacks behind them.

Only then did Jody nod for the Vikings to put their guns away.

"Muy bien, muy bien," Paco said, heaving out a tortured sigh.

Spartacos Sococo, Emilio Hernandez, and Octavio Randhanie stood angrily, then pushed their way out of the booth.

"Where are the fucking receipts?" Jody asked. With no need of translation, the San Andresitos reached into their pockets and pulled out the delivery vouchers, handing them to Jody, who in turn handed them to Lester Wood. He read them and nodded.

"Yep," he said, returning them to Jody, who put them in his back pocket.

Just then a phone started ringing. Nobody answered it. Paco shouted at the bartender.

"Teléfono!"

The old man behind the bar crossed and picked up the phone. *"¿Cómo?"* he said, and listened for a long moment. *"Sí . . . sí. Gracias."* He hung up and looked over at Paco.

"¿Qué es?" Paco demanded.

"Cortez viene al pueblo."

"Santa's coming," Sawdust translated. "This might be a good time t'blow town."

42

SANTA'S COMING TO TOWN

Tremaine said, "They're plannin' something. We need t'break hard on these assholes before it gets outta hand."

They were standing on the curb outside the cantina. The San Andresitos were clustered over by their cars.

"How d'ya figure to do that, Inky Dink?" Jody said. "There's four of us in a town of fifty-five thousand gun-toting *pendejos*."

Paco broke away from the others, approached, and slapped Jody on the back as he rattled some Spanish. Jody frowned and glanced over at Lester Wood.

"He says we gotta get going before Cortez returns."

"So, let's do it," Jody said.

All five of them jammed into Paco's Toyota. He turned his bubble around and headed back toward his warehouse on Calle 16, leaving the three other San Andresitos standing in front of the cantina, staring down at designer-name watches as if their futures were ticking away on each dial.

"Where's he going?" Shane asked. "We should be heading west. That's the only way out of town."

Paco answered in Spanish, and Sawdust turned to Jody.

"He says we need to pick up some *celadores* at his business, for our safety. He says Santander won't attack us if we have enough protection."

"Now he's worried about our safety?" Shane asked. "Five minutes ago this prick was trying to hold us for ransom."

"Good point," Jody said, then pulled the P-7 out of his side pocket and put it against Paco's rib cage.

"*¿Qué es?*" Paco said, glancing at Jody, then down at the gun.

"So you don't go stupid on us, *amigo.*"

They made a right onto Calle 16 but had to stop as soon as they turned because they were stuck behind a strange column of armed men and vehicles. A sole man pushing a wheelbarrow was leading the parade. Walking on each side of him, guarding the wheelbarrow, were four *celadores,* their machine guns aimed in all directions. An empty flatbed truck rumbled along behind.

"What is this?" Jody snapped.

"*Para comercio* . . . How you say? *Dinero por* trade, *Hernandez no tiene* dishwashers, *de modo que va a comprarlos en mi tienda.*"

Sawdust said, "If one of them doesn't have what he needs for his market in Colombia, he buys it from one of the others."

"*Sí,*" Paco said.

"They going to your place?" Jody asked.

"*Sí, a mi tienda* . . ."

"What's in the wheelbarrow?"

"*Dinero Colombiano.*"

Paco managed to pull around the column, and as they drove past, Shane looked out the window. Sure enough, the wheelbarrow was half full of stacks of Colombian pesos.

Paco stopped the Toyota in front of his warehouse. A moment later the wheelbarrow full of cash and the empty truck arrived. Two yellow forklifts zipped out of Paco's warehouse with pallet-loaded boxes of Maytag washing machines stacked three high. A dozen *celadores* stood out front, facing Hernandez's *celadores* over glistening new auto-mags. The man with the wheelbarrow upended it unceremoniously onto the Spanish-tile sidewalk in front of Paco's showroom.

"Cha-ching," Jody said softly.

Three of the women whom Shane had seen in the office upstairs now rushed out of the building and bent over the bundles of cash, rifling through them, their nimble fingers counting. Calculators hummed and LCD screens printed out figures. Once again, Shane noticed that the calculators were the big twelve-digit Texas Instrument computers. He finally realized that when tabulating these huge sums in pesos, the regular ten-digit calculators ran out of decimal points.

Suddenly, from the end of the street, they heard the sound of big truck engines growling loudly. Shane looked over and saw two old army trucks with at least twenty men in them, rolling over the garbage-strewn street.

"Adentro! Adentro! Ándáles!" Paco said as he began to move toward the warehouse.

"Not so fast, asshole," Jody said, grabbing Paco by the collar, now putting the P-7 to his head. "You're not quite through here yet."

All of the *celadores* swung and pointed their weapons at the Vikings, but Jody ignored them and pointed up the street at the approaching trucks. "Whose guys are those? Is that Santa?"

"Sí, Santander viene," Paco said. Unreasoning fear was in his eyes and spreading over his face.

"Let's go," Jody said, jamming his gun barrel hard against Paco's temple, freezing the army of *celadores* on the sidewalk.

Paco shouted at them, *"No disparar! No disparar!"*

The women on their knees kept gathering and tabulating. They never looked up.

"Somebody get a piece on this guy," Jody commanded, and Sawdust put his pistol to the back of Paco's head.

Jody jumped out of the Toyota SUV. Then he ran around and got behind the wheel, pushing the fat San Andresito over into the passenger seat beside him. Tremaine broke out the glass of the two fixed windows in the rear of the Toyota, using the barrel of his pistol. Gymbag zippers ripped open in the car, followed by a chorus of forty-round mags slamming home and sliders being tromboned.

"Only one way out and that's past those guys up there," Jody said. "It's gonna be reckless, so hold on." He backed up, turned, then headed up the street directly toward the approaching vehicles and twenty armed men.

"No! No, está loco . . . somos muertos!" Paco said, sweat pouring down his round face, drenching his shirt collar.

A happy madness distorted Jody's features: "We may die, but we're gonna take a few motherfuckers with us."

In seconds, the first bullets rocked the Toyota. Fired from a half a block away, they thudded into the grille and shattered a side mirror.

"Get busy!" Jody shouted.

Shane leaned out one of the broken side windows and aimed his Polish MP-63 up the street at the column of army vehicles. The badly rocking SUV distorted his aim as its tires spun, looking for purchase on a street covered with decaying garbage. He started blasting, aiming blindly with one hand, the bolt clattering maniacally as the machine pistol fired, spewing hot brass out into the street.

It was hard to assess what happened next because it was a blur of spinning tires, rotating landscapes, and chattering gunfire. Jody was heading right at the lead truck, then yanked the wheel to the left at the last second. The radial tires spun garbage out behind them, slushing badly in the rotting muck as the SUV hit a curb and bounced up, then, somehow, they were on the sidewalk in front of Sococo's showroom.

Ten automatic weapons broke out simultaneously, shattering the remaining windows in the Toyota. Jody kept his head low while the entire front windshield starred and then rained chunks of glass in on them.

Shane dropped the first clip and jammed his last one home. Tremaine was firing out the window on the far side of the SUV. With the windshield gone, Sawdust was aiming straight out the front, his MP-63 barking loudly inside the car, throwing a stream of spent casings at Paco in the front passenger seat. The sweaty San Andresito screamed in panic as Sawdust's hot brass hit him, the bullets whizzing past his ear. They were now opposite Cortez's two army trucks.

Santander's men had taken cover behind the vehicles and let loose as the Toyota roared past on the sidewalk. The Vikings fired until the weapons were empty and the slides locked open. Heavy 9-millimeter bullet hits rocked the SUV but, miraculously, it didn't stall.

Shane grabbed his Astra and emptied his last clip until he was pulling the trigger maniacally, dry-firing, unaware that he was empty because of the booming retort of the Colt Commander that Sawdust was using right next to his ear. The chattering racket of ten incoming machine guns set up a deadly cacophony only twelve feet away.

"I'm dry!" Shane yelled. They were now past the column of men and trucks. Almost immediately, Jody's P-7 flew over the seat and hit him on the shoulder. Shane scooped it up, turned, and kept firing out the back window.

Somehow they got through the violent maelstrom and bounced back onto the street.

"Anybody hit?" Jody yelled.

"Yeah, I'm leakin' some," Lester Wood drawled.

"How bad?"

"Well, it's . . . it's . . . I think I'm okay . . ."

Jody was making a right turn, back onto Calle 16, heading out of town. The Toyota engine sounded as if it had been hit—running rough and getting worse by the minute.

Sawdust's face was drained of color, but his denim shirt was drenched in red. "This ain't good back here," Shane said. "Sawdust looks bad."

The SUV was losing speed, coughing and bucking.

"We gotta get to that garrison at the end of town," Jody said. "We'll deal with it then."

"No!" Paco said. "No militia."

"I'm through listening to you!" Jody shouted, spinning the wheel to avoid another wandering Hereford grazing on garbage in the middle of the street.

They headed back through town. The Toyota was barely moving when the garrison finally came into view.

Shane could see out the back window that Santander's jeeps had gotten turned around and were now behind them, closing fast. "They're four blocks back," he announced.

The SUV was lurching badly as it bucked and coughed down the street. Shane pried the Colt out of Lester Wood's hand and emptied it out of the broken back window.

"No! No militia!" Paco shouted again. Jody ignored him and lurched the Toyota onto the paved road leading into the military base. The two gate guards swung their weapons down on polished shoulder straps, aiming them at the Toyota as it pulled to a stop at the main gate.

"Police," Jody said, yanking out his LAPD badge and holding it out the window. "American *policía.*"

"*Necesitamos socorro,*" Lester Wood rasped.

Santander's trucks pulled into the driveway behind

them but slowed down fifty yards away and inched forward like jackals at the edge of firelight.

"Fuck this," Jody said, watching them in the one remaining side mirror. Then he hit the gas. The Toyota bucked forward, smashing the wooden bar arm across the base road, shattering it.

"No!" Paco screamed.

An alarm started ringing, and almost immediately fifteen soldiers ran out of a wooden building slamming banana clips into a variety of automatic weapons, clicking off safeties as they approached. In seconds, they had the Toyota surrounded.

Jody got out of the vehicle with his hands up and his LAPD badge held high. "American *policía*," he repeated to the soldiers, who were staring in disbelief at the bullet-riddled vehicle. Shane looked back at Santander's trucks parked just a few feet outside the garrison. At first it seemed they were afraid to come closer. Then Shane began to wonder if perhaps they were parked there to block a possible retreat.

"Sawdust, tell this guy we demand political asylum," Jody said. "Tell 'em. Tell these guys we're American cops on a U.S. government mission. Go on, do it!"

Shane was studying the dusty look in Lester Wood's vacant eyes. "We're gonna have to find a way to tell 'em ourselves. Sawdust didn't make it."

43

THE WHITE ANGEL

It was an empty structure: no windows, a tin roof, wooden shelves, and a poured-concrete floor. It looked like a supply locker. Once the door was locked, Tremaine sat glumly on the floor while Jody and Shane began pacing.

"What now?" Tremaine challenged, his low voice turned flat and cold as slate.

"Okay, look, this is a Colombian military unit," Jody said slowly. "America has diplomatic relations with Colombia, so we try and get a message out to the U.S. embassy, get them to cut through all this, get the embassy t release us into U.S. custody." He looked up into Tremaine's angry, disbelieving stare.

"You're kiddin' me, right?" Tremaine glared at Jody. "Didja forget, we're supposed t'be dead."

"We're also laundering fifty million in Colombian drug cash," Shane said. "If we call the U.S. embassy, we're not gonna get released; we're gonna get extradited."

"Okay, Hot Sauce, then you tell me. . . . Whatta you wanna do?"

"I'll tell you one thing," Shane said. "There's something very wrong about this military base. Did you see the weapons those troops were carrying?"

"Yeah, what of it?" Jody growled.

"Some of it was prototype stuff, brand-new Beretta 92s. But I also saw some twenty-year-old Chinese assault rifles. I think one of those guys even had an antique Lee Enfield. He'd be better off using that thing as a club."

"So what?"

"Doesn't the army of a sovereign nation generally issue standardized equipment?" Shane continued. "Doesn't the Colombian government supply its soldiers with unitized ordnance? These guys are packing everything from auto-mags to slingshots."

"He's right," Tremaine said, looking up with concern.

"So what am I supposed to do about it?"

"Nothing. I'm just wondering why. And what happened to Paco Brazos? They pulled him outta the car with us, but they didn't put him in here. How come?"

"Maybe he drinks beer with these assholes. Who the fuck knows?" Suddenly Jody didn't have very good answers.

"This afternoon we rolled in here with almost a billion contraband cigarettes, right past those guards," Shane said. "Nobody gave a damn. You saw that building of Paco's. . . . How much contraband had to go past this base, unobstructed, to fill up that warehouse, not to mention all the other San Andresitos?"

"Okay, so somebody's getting paid off," Jody said, frustrated. "Stop asking all these dumb questions."

"Let the man talk," Tremaine said, turning toward Shane. "Whatta you thinkin'?"

"You were saying that José told you about the political situation in Colombia. I've read some department one sheets about it—it's supposed to be treacherous," Shane said, still pacing slowly in the locked room. He stopped and looked over at Jody, who was a few feet away, a strange expression on his face. "What is it? Do you know something?" Shane prodded.

"Yeah, that's what Papa Joe told me, too," Jody said.

"What'd he say?" Tremaine demanded.

"To tell you the truth, when he told me, I wasn't paying a whole lot of attention. He said something about—"

"What? Come on, man," Tremaine rose off the floor, moved across the room, then grabbed Jody's shirt and yanked him up close. "What did José tell you, man?"

"Get your hands off me, Inky Dink. Who the fuck you think you're pawing?"

"I wanna know who those green jackets out there belong to."

"Then get your fuckin' hands off me!"

There was a long, electric moment before Tremaine finally let go of Jody's shirt and took a step back.

"What did José Mondragon tell you?" Shane asked again.

"I don't remember, exactly. I'd been drinking. Something about two Marxist armies fighting with the government, or some shit. He said there's a lot of kidnapping out here. These Marxist guerrillas snatch people, mostly U.S. oil-company executives working on desert drilling rigs, or any Anglo they can get their hands on. They ransom you back to your family or your company—whoever will pay the most money to keep you alive. He was telling me about this insurance you can buy, kidnapping insurance. He said nobody from Blackstone or All-American will set foot inside Colombia without it."

"You tellin' me we coulda got kidnapping insurance?" Tremaine said. Now he was right in Jody's face.

"Inky Dink, you put your hands on me again, I'll knock your lights out. How we gonna buy insurance? We're all supposed to be dead."

"We got aliases. We coulda worked somethin' out through José," Tremaine shot back.

"We're not a bunch a' fucking oil-company pussies. Nobody's got the stones to kidnap us."

"Am I just imagining this, or are we all locked in a goddamned windowless room here?" Tremaine glowered.

"Fuck you," Jody growled.

Shane stepped between them. "What else did José tell you?"

"Just that there are these two leftist armies that prey on the San Andresitos and on each other. All the San Andresitos pay a percentage of their black-market profits to the guerrillas so they'll let the contraband go on into Colombia—a political contribution made at gunpoint."

"Who are the two armies?" Shane asked.

"They've both got acronyms . . . one is like RAFC. Stands for something like the Revolutionary Armed Forces of Colombia. And the other is NLA, the National Liberation Army."

"Sounds t'me like you paid more than a little attention. You got all this down pretty good," Tremaine challenged.

"What're you tryin' to say?" Jody threatened softly. "You got something on your mind, lay it down, asswipe."

"How 'bout we focus on the damn problem," Shane said. "If these guys aren't regular army, then is that good for us, or bad?"

"One other thing José told me . . . There's another guy up here. It's probably not important, but José said he's the joker in the deck, an ex–Argentine army colonel who leads a death squad—a right-wing fanatic with white-blond hair. He supposedly trained in the U.S. at the School of the Americas, in Fort Benning, Georgia."

"Never heard of it." Tremaine glowered.

"It's some kinda counterterrorist school, run by our Pentagon. Latin American army officers from OAS get nominated by their governments to go there. Instructors from the Pentagon teach greaseball commandos how to

get info out of captured commies, how to pull out fingernails with pliers—shit like that."

"I love it," Tremaine said.

"Papa Joe told me this Argentine colonel gets off by
torturing and killing."

"What's his name?" Shane asked.

"Don't know his name, but they call him the 'White
Angel.' Papa Joe said The Hague finally charged him with
war crimes committed while he was in Argentine Intelligence. He was sentenced to death in Argentina, but he
escaped and fled to Colombia. He settled up here, in the
desert."

"So I guess we got two choices," Shane said. "If these
guys are regular Colombian army, we play the American
embassy card. If they're Marxist guerrillas, we get down
on our knees, start begging, give them a cut of what we
got in the bank in Aruba."

"And if we been captured by this other dude, the White
Angel?" Tremaine asked.

"It's not him," Jody said. "He's a right-wing extremist
. . . an outlaw hiding from the government in the desert."

"But isn't the Colombian government a right-wing democracy?" Shane asked. "Wouldn't the White Angel be
closer politically to them than to a buncha Marxist guerrillas?"

Nobody answered Shane's question. Finally Tremaine
changed the subject.

"You're an asshole, ya know that, Jody?" he said. "We
coulda had insurance. We had us some insurance, then we
coulda got the fuck out of here."

Jody took a swing at him, knocking Tremaine back
hard against the brick wall. In an instant, the two were at
each other, snarling like animals.

"This is great," Shane muttered.

They came hurtling back toward him. Shane tried to
get out of the way, but the room was small, so he was

pinned as the two crashed hard against him. He caught an elbow in the head and went down under a pile of flying fists and sweating bodies. He finally managed to roll free and get up. He grabbed Jody, who had gained control and was now on top of Tremaine, pummeling him with both fists.

Shane yanked Jody off and threw him against the far wall. "We got enough trouble without this!" Shane shouted.

Tremaine wiped some blood off his mouth with the back of his hand, while Jody slid down the wall and sat on the floor.

"You fucking jerk-offs," Jody mumbled. "How'd I get stuck with such pussies?"

"You picked us!" Tremaine shot back.

They sat on opposite walls of the room, all staring at their feet.

An hour later the door opened and a tall, handsome Hispanic man they had never seen before entered the room. He was wearing a perfectly cut tan suit and a red silk ascot. He kept his jacket buttoned despite the oppressive heat inside the windowless, metal-roofed room. There were two armed guards beside him, but they weren't adolescent teenagers with bristling chin whiskers—these men had expressionless eyes like dark holes cut into cardboard.

"Good evening," the man said. His English was perfect, and he spoke with an American accent. "My name is Santander Cortez and I'm sorry you have been forcibly detained. I know you probably think that because of our business difficulties, I mean you harm, but let me assure you this is not the case. I hold Paco Brazos responsible for leaving me out of your cigarette transaction."

"You got that right," Jody said, standing.

"And you, I wager, are Mr. Dean?"

"Yes."

"I would like to discuss options with you, if that is convenient." He was smiling warmly.

"Sounds good."

"You other two gentlemen, if you'll please bear with me, I think everything can be amicably arranged. I'm sorry if this has been stressful. I'll be back to you two shortly." He motioned to Jody. "Mr. Dean?"

Jody moved across the room and exited with the tall, handsome man. The door was locked behind them.

"Maybe we finally caught us a break," Tremaine said.

"Yeah," Shane answered. But one thing troubled him about Santander Cortez.

The man had a full head of snow-white hair.

44

CHAT

Four hours passed, but Jody never returned.

The more Shane thought about it, the more he was sure that Santander Cortez was the White Angel. He sat in the dark, running their predicament over in his mind, studying it from every possible angle. The first thing he needed to do was pick up some coordination with the man silently brooding a few feet away.

"Tremaine . . . ," he said.

Tremaine raised his head and glowered at Shane.

"You and I need to work together if we plan on staying alive. We've gotta stop fighting and do some thinking."

"We're fucked," Tremaine said softly. "What we gonna do to change that?"

"For starters, how about the answers to a few questions?"

Tremaine stared at Shane but didn't respond.

"I still wanna know how come you're not inked . . . why you didn't get that Viking tattoo like the rest of us."

"I don't buy into that. That's white-boy shit."

"That's one reason, but you wanna hear another?"

Tremaine didn't answer.

"I think you're a department mole. Internal Affairs, or something."

Tremaine's lip curled into a snarl . . . or was it a grin? It was hard to tell in the dark room.

"I know you came aboard late, after Jody had already set up the Vikings," Shane continued. "Wanna hear my theory?"

Tremaine still didn't answer, so he went on.

"Somehow, you or somebody in IAD found out about the Vikings, so you got yourself assigned to SWAT. Then through your friendship with Rodriquez, you put a move on Jody and got picked to be the last Viking. But since you were workin' undercover, you weren't listed in Medwick's log. Cops hate tattoos. You didn't want a tattoo, 'cause you weren't really a Viking. You were only there to find out what they were doing and bust 'em. You were the only one in the unit who wasn't on drugs—same reason. How'm I doing so far?"

"You got a big imagination."

"Jody isn't coming back. He's gone. You and I are next. We're all gonna die. There's no police to protect us up here, and there's no government to save us, just criminals, flies, and garbage."

"You doin' fake jacks on me now. Tryin' t'fuck with my mind."

"I'll tell you something else that doesn't quite stack up. Your jive ghetto bullshit reads like street cover to me. Every now and then when you get surprised, it slips. I think it's just camouflage for Jody, but Jody's gone, so you're wasting this hot-shit performance on me."

"Zat right?"

"Yep. And laugh this one off if you can. . . ." Shane paused. "I'm workin' undercover, too. I think we're both department plants running games on each other. Problem is, there're no Vikings left to bullshit. So maybe we oughta come clean with each other—start from there."

"I saw you cap Sergeant Hamilton . . . saw her bleed out. No fuckin' way you're workin' undercover."

"It was rigged. She was wearing a vest."

"Ain't no vest gonna stop a Black Talon."

"You're wrong. It's called a level-three tactical vest . . . developed by the Pentagon. I'm working a special undercover assignment for Chief Filosiani."

"Bullshit."

"Listen, Tremaine, whether you're Internal Affairs or not, we still need to work together. There used to be six of us. Now it's just you and me."

"Okay, smart guy . . . so let's hear your plan."

Shane glanced around the room. "You suppose those shelves will come down? We could pry loose those heavy two-by-four supports underneath."

Tremaine looked up at heavy wooden shelves and the two-by-four frames holding them. "Yeah," he said. "So?"

Then he gave Tremaine the rest of his plan.

45

CAT AND MOUSE

The door opened an hour later, and two of the hardened mercenaries entered the room. Shane and Tremaine were pressed flat against the wall. Each swung a three-foot-long two-by-four at his man. The two Colombians doubled over and went down. Shane and Tremaine sprung out and searched them for weapons but found none. Suddenly a volley of machine-gun fire exploded through the door from four backups positioned outside. The bullets whined and ricocheted around inside the small enclosure, sparking off walls like manic fireflies.

Shane felt hot pain sear in his thigh, then another slug hit him in the side of his neck. A moment later he was pounced on by three men and went down in a pile. Their blows rained down on him; he was clubbed with a gun butt until his vision blurred. Consciousness hovered against a black mist that finally descended and swallowed him.

When he awoke, everything ached. He was alone in the room; Tremaine was gone. He pulled himself into a sitting position and took a quick, fuzzy-headed inventory of his bruised, bleeding body. He had a nasty-looking through-and-through on his upper thigh that was still leaking blood and had completely numbed his left leg. The slug was close to his abductor canal. *Karmic payback.*

The second bullet had grazed his neck, and he had a furrow an eighth of an inch deep running across the right side of his throat. The blood had crusted, but that wound had stopped bleeding. His lip was split and two front teeth were loose; his head ached, and everything else felt horrible.

He slumped onto the floor, and for the next hour felt the temperature slowly drop as the desert night cooled the tiny tin-roofed room until he was freezing. Then he sat with his arms wrapped around him, his teeth chattering. He didn't know how long he waited. He dozed off once but awoke with a start when the door flew open.

Four men rushed in, grabbed him, stood him up, and laced his hands behind his back with wire. Using pliers, they twisted the wire tight until it cut painfully through his skin. Then they pushed him brutally through the door.

He was stumbling ahead of them, one leg almost numb, lurching across the lit compound. Every time he slowed, somebody would give him a hard push, knocking him forward. They herded him past the parade ground toward a small wood-frame building.

The house was painted white with green shutters; it had a peaked roof and slanting porch. A bright redbrick chimney completed an out-of-place Iowa farmhouse look.

He was dragged and pushed up the steps, then shoved through the front door.

The living room was American Gothic with a turn-of-the-century rocker and quilted chairs. Framed fox-hunting paintings of jumping hounds and horses dressed the walls. The mercenaries shoved him through an oak and glass door into a small, cozy den and pushed him down onto the floor.

"Abajo solamente, no te muevas," the guard ordered.

Shane nodded and waited for what would come next.

A few minutes later the tall Hispanic man walked into the room. He had removed the tan suit jacket; in its place was a blue three-quarter-length silk smoking jacket, belted at the waist. He wore sharply pleated tan pants and a white shirt. His bullshit red silk ascot was still peeking out from underneath. "This is not what I wanted. Please, will somebody remove those restraints?" he said in perfect American English, but now Shane could also hear something else in his speech. Flat Boston vowels tinged his accent.

The guards either knew what he was saying or had been through this so many times before that they knew what was required of them, because they rushed to Shane, pulled him up, and began clipping the wires.

"Gently, gently," Santander said. "We're civilized men; let's try to behave that way." He smiled at Shane as wire cutters snipped the restraints on his wrists.

"Perhaps the armchair," the white-haired man instructed.

The guards led Shane to the chair and motioned for him to sit, then backed off a short distance, their eyes like those of starving men staring at a steaming meal.

"What happened to Jody and Tremaine?" Shane said. The Hispanic man's smile widened, but he didn't answer. A grandfather clock tick-tocked from the corner of the room, its brass pendulum rhythmically slicing up the minutes.

"They are doing just fine," the white-haired man finally responded. "As will you. But first we must get to know one another . . . chat for a spell. I look forward to my all-too-infrequent civilized visitors."

"I'd like to believe that, Colonel."

"You should." He smiled. "You see, living out here in the desert, I don't have much opportunity to talk to men who have opinions formed by Western culture or world literature. These men are uneducated." He motioned to the four armed *celadores*. "They can endlessly discuss sex or the Old Testament, but as a steady diet, even those worthwhile subjects can become pretty stale."

"So you are a colonel, then." Shane's words seemed to surprise him.

"I beg your pardon?"

"I called you Colonel, you didn't correct me."

He smiled slowly. "And what do you think that proves?"

"You're the White Angel?"

He began slowly turning a diamond ring on his index finger. "Since I'm a man who has, on occasion, targeted my enemies with extreme forms of death, I have been given many names: the 'White Angel,' the 'Crow,' and earlier, before my promotion to colonel, 'Captain Death.' Childishly colorful, but quite useful nonetheless, because these names strike fear into my enemies. Fear is a useful currency." He seemed to choose each word with great care, delighting in each syllable, like a man tasting a perfectly seasoned dish.

"You take yourself pretty seriously."

"Yes, as a matter of fact, I do—and for good reason. What I do affects the politics of nations. If you are a wise man worthy of my interest, you will take what I say seriously as well."

"So what is this little talk really about?"

"Weakness," Santa Cortez said softly, his voice now almost a whisper.

"Yours or mine?" Shane asked.

"It will be a shared experience." An evil shine came into his eyes, a penetrating madness that Shane didn't like at all.

"How so?"

"This is hard for a man such as myself to admit . . . but my weakness has defined me since adolescence. At first it frightened me, even sickened me, because I couldn't control or understand it. Later, I saw it for what it really was and began to take a measure of strength from it."

Shane was beginning to dread what he was about to hear.

"It started when I was a child. I would, on occasion, catch and set fire to a neighborhood pet—a cat or a small dog. I had an uncontrollable urge to administer pain . . . to watch an animal die painfully . . . to put my hands on it as it passed over the threshold, to feel it convulse . . . take its final breath. It was as close to a feeling of love as I have ever been able to experience.

"My father eventually caught me. He was an admiral in the Argentine navy, a man of strict discipline and rules. He took me to a doctor, who said I had a disassociative, psychotic disorder. So I was sent to Boston, to a clinic, where I lived until college. In America I learned about democratic principles. I learned to love freedom and a constitutional government. After I returned to Argentina, I chose to fight for democracy in my own country—to drive the Marxist dictators out of power. As an American, I'm sure you share my hatred of left-wing governments. I fought Marxist thieves in my country, but since my conviction for political murder, I have had to fight them from my neighbor state, Colombia. So you see, I am a freedom fighter much like your own Founding Fathers. I have deep-seated political beliefs, but underneath, I still have my deadly cravings. Pain and death seem to nourish me, so I have made this childhood weakness a political strength."

"You kill people—torture them."

"My violence is labeled madness. Fear is my Trojan horse. My enemies ingest it, absorbing it inside them, where it then spreads and weakens them."

"Why are we sitting in Aunt Bea's den, discussing

this? I can't absolve you, and you can't change."

"I find my excitement is magnified when I take the time to interact with my targets."

"So, we're talking about my torture?"

"We are."

"Maybe you and I can make a deal," Shane said as fear suddenly swept through him.

The White Angel smiled, gently touching the longish hair at his temples, brushing it carefully behind his ear with his fingers. "You were saying?"

"I have a million dollars in a bank in Aruba. I'd be willing to arrange a wire transfer. You need funds to fight your war. I can help you."

"Ahh, I see. So you have money to negotiate for your safety?"

"A million U.S. dollars, in cash, to turn me and Tremaine loose."

"And how would this transaction be accomplished?"

"Because of the escrow instructions, it has to be done in person. You, and one or two of your *celadores,* come back to Aruba with me. We contact Sandy Mantoor, his bank releases the funds, then I turn them over to you. Once you take delivery, you can wire the money to any bank in the world."

"I see." He put a hand up to his delicate mouth. "I'm disappointed you didn't start with your best offer," he said softly. "I know you have much more than that. But you see, Sergeant, it really doesn't matter, because I have already made an acceptable arrangement with Mr. Dean."

"With Jody!"

"You thought he was dead, and he would have been—just like you and the Negro. But Mr. Dean had ten million in kidnap insurance. We concluded a transaction with his insurance company an hour ago. The funds were transferred when I turned him loose. You'll have to admit, it's much cleaner than trying to go to Aruba and deal with that criminal Mantoor family, take a chance on being captured on foreign soil, sold to my Marxist enemies for cash. I put nothing past the Mantoors. So . . . thank you, but I must decline your offer."

"Jody paid you?"

"Worse. He also contracted me to kill you and Mr. Lane." He smiled at Shane. "So, like the cat who has cornered his mouse, I can play with both of you for hours, bat you around, watch you try and get away, maybe put a paw on your tail, chew your head and ears, listen to you squeak. Then slowly you will become tired; shock will numb your nervous system. You will have no fight left, and like the cat, I will become angry with you for not playing. In retaliation, I will make your end . . . well . . . interesting." He smiled again, and Shane couldn't help noticing that this time the smile was warm, almost as if the White Angel had developed true affection for him.

Then Santander Cortez moved to the window and looked out at the lit compound. "The Negro didn't hold up as well as I would have thought. Sometimes men surprise me . . . strength of will is a unique and rare quality."

"Where is he?"

"I'll show you. . . ." He turned to the *celadores.* "*Afuera al Negro, ándále.*"

The guards quickly moved to Shane, yanked him to his feet, and led him out the back door of the house and across the compound.

They went through a locked gate and were soon off the base, moving across the desert. The cold night air lessened the stench of the surrounding town, but it was still there, lingering stubbornly.

Shane didn't know where they were heading or what horrors were in store for him.

Then he saw Tremaine, lit by the light of a portable generator.

He was tied to a chain-link fence, bleeding from a hundred cuts, his head down on his chest, vomit puddling at his feet. Enormous strips of his skin had been removed.

"You son of a bitch," Shane said softly, the spectacle taking his breath away.

"Not a pretty sight, I admit, but fun while it lasted." Santander paused to let the moment sink in. "And there are hidden benefits: these guards will tell the story—how I skinned the *pobre* Negro, cutting him in slices while he screamed, finding ecstasy in his agony. The story will grow with each telling. The Trojan horse of my legend of terror will be dragged into the depths of my Marxist enemies and fester in their imaginations: win-win."

Shane moved on rubbery legs toward Tremaine. He could barely believe the human wreckage in front of him. Then the destroyed man coughed, and blood ran out of Tremaine's mouth.

"Shit! He's still alive," Shane murmured.

"Go ahead. Get a good look," Cortez whispered. "Ask him how he liked it."

As Shane moved closer to Tremaine, he heard a gasp or a rattle, or maybe it was a whisper. He was close enough to see that Tremaine's right eye was wide open, staring at him, disembodied. Then he heard the rattling sound again, followed by a cough and a sigh. He thought Tremaine was trying to tell him something.

"What?" Shane asked, his own voice a croak. "What is it?"

Shane's left thigh throbbed, so he used his right knee to kneel. He got as close as he could until his ear was next to Tremaine's shattered mouth.

Then he heard the noise again . . . a weak stirring of sounds against a rush of exhaled air. "Werrrr . . . riigghh . . ." Tremaine breathed softly into his ear.

Shane watched as Tremaine's lips trembled.

"Sheee . . ." the black man said, and coughed up more blood.

"What?" Shane whispered. "She?"

"Ifffff . . ."

"If?" Shane asked.

Tremaine Lane let out what air was left inside him like a long pensive sigh of exasperation. Then his head dropped, and Shane knew he was gone.

Suddenly Shane knew what he had been trying to say.

She . . . if . . . Sheriff.

Tremaine Lane was working undercover.

46

THE SOLEMN PROMISE

Shane was yanked to his feet and pushed toward the floodlit fence, which had been securely anchored in concrete. He was held firmly by two *celadores* as Tremaine's dead body was unwired, then slumped to the ground at Shane's feet.

"Next," Santander said, smiling slightly.

Shane was turned and pushed up against the fence. One of the *celadores* began to wire his right wrist to the top rail as the other one grabbed his left and did the same. The White Angel unsnapped a leather box he had been carrying. When Cortez opened it, Shane could see surgical scalpels mounted on blue velvet. They glittered ominously in the generator's harsh light.

"I think, to start, perhaps the number-three handle with a four-four size-ten blade. It makes a nice, shallow three-millimeter cut." Santander picked a long, bent, chrome-handled instrument out of the case, reached in with his fingers, and selected a small curved blade, then snapped it onto the end, tightening it with the set screw. "I am sorry that I am forgoing normal surgical sterilization techniques. I used to scrub for the fun of it, but it was really just foreplay, because you'll be long gone before any infection could set in."

"Knock yourself out," Shane murmured as the White Angel moved forward, holding the scalpel delicately between his thumb and forefinger. "We'll need to get that shirt off." Santa turned and barked the order. "¡La camisa!" One of the *celadores* ripped Shane's shirt. Then the White Angel stepped forward and placed the tip of the scalpel under Shane's nipple. He pressed lightly, and Shane felt the blade pierce his skin.

"Is this not a feeling close to ecstasy?" Cortez said, his voice turning husky with sexual passion.

Shane spit in his face.

Out of nowhere, gunfire erupted on all sides of them. Shane spun his head in time to see half a dozen separate muzzle flashes in the desert. All four *celadores* standing near him went down quickly, riddled with bullets. Immediately, Santander Cortez fell, blood spurting out of a huge hole in his neck.

Shane heard orders shouted in Spanish and saw movement at the edge of his vision. Then twenty men dressed in faded khaki ran toward him while reloading and firing their auto-mags.

He heard Alexa scream, "Not him! Don't shoot! Not him!"

He thought he saw Luis Rosario, in his porkpie hat, also yelling in Spanish.

Seconds later, hands were pulling at his wrists, untwisting the wire. He fell, with his wounded leg buckling under him. Then Shane was on his back, looking up into Alexa's blue eyes, her hand cradling his head as he lay in the sand. Jo-Jo Knight appeared over her shoulder, a smoking Uzi clutched in his fist.

"Ahh, damn . . . lookit you," Alexa said sadly, studying his beaten face. "I can't leave you alone for a minute."

He forced a weak smile just as more automatic weapons cut loose. Soldiers standing near him were now being cut down by a vicious barrage of machine-gun fire coming from the direction of the garrison. The troops around him dove into a shallow wash, proned out, then began returning fire. Jo-Jo Knight and Luis Rosario grabbed Shane.

"Let's get this gringo outta here," Rosario said. They lifted him quickly and began carrying him as best they could away from the firefight.

Alexa spun and emptied a 9-millimeter clip in the direction of the fort, trying to set up some cover fire but at the same time exposing herself dangerously. Miraculously, she wasn't hit. They began moving across the uneven desert terrain, stumbling in the dark, Rosario and Knight half-carrying, half-yanking Shane along, dragging him like a sack of vegetables.

"Will you guys put me down? I can walk!" he yelled as Rosario and Knight, each supporting a side, kept running until they were a safe distance away, then stopped to help Shane get his feet under him. Alexa pushed the eject button on her Astra, dropped the empty clip onto the sand at her feet, then slammed in a new one. They kept moving, but more slowly now, Shane struggling to keep his leg working under him until they finally came to an old English lorry with primered fenders parked by the road with several other army surplus trucks.

"Let's take this one," Rosario said. They helped Shane onto the back of the truck while Jo-Jo Knight got behind the wheel. He turned a switch on the dash, which substituted for an ignition key on most military vehicles. The engine started.

Alexa and Luis jumped up on the back of the flatbed next to Shane.

"Roll it!" she yelled.

The lorry rumbled across the desert, past three or four other deserted military vehicles. They could hear the sounds of the firefight receding behind them.

"Who were those guys?" Shane asked.

"Marxist rebels," Alexa said. When Shane looked surprised, she added: "We take help wherever we find it."

Soon they were back on the dirt road, heading out of Maicao. The old English lorry creaked and groaned and bounced through potholes. A few miles farther they hit pavement. The heavy sand tires vibrated on the two-lane concrete road that announced the beginning of Maicao's unconventional airport.

Shane saw a small blue and white Citation jet with U.S. tail markings taxiing on the ground near them, already turning around, and readying itself for takeoff. The lorry swung under the starboard wing and stopped.

Somehow, they got Shane out of the back, carrying and dragging him to the waiting plane.

"Will you guys let go of me?" he demanded. They ignored his request and pushed him roughly up the ladder into the jet.

"Okay, 'Darker Than Me,' let's do this dust off," Rosario said to Jo-Jo Knight, who was pulling the Citation's cabin door closed behind them.

Almost before the door was latched, the jet was rolling. They hurtled down the poorly lit runway, engines screaming to rotation speed, and then the small executive jet lifted off the tarmac. The strange, six-lane runway fell away beneath them as the government pilot banked right, heading north toward the Caribbean Sea fifteen miles away.

"Thank God you found me," Shane said.

Alexa grinned. "I told you that pill would locate you within a meter." Shane smiled and took her hand.

"We found out from a CIA internal briefing in Washington that this garrison was being used to billet a right-wing Colombian death squad, commanded by an ex–

Argentine colonel named Raphael Aziz," Alexa continued.

"Aziz?" he said. "Is he the White Angel?"

She nodded. "We knew from the satellite tracking that you were on that base. Rosario has some very interesting contacts. He got us hooked up with that band of Marxist guerrillas through a drug source he has in Medellín. So we made a deal with Aziz's guerrilla enemies, who were already near here. They agreed to give us some backup in return for finding out where Colonel Aziz was. We surrounded the place, but before we could move, out you came."

"He skinned Tremaine Lane alive," Shane said softly.

She didn't answer but squeezed his hand. "You need a hospital."

"I'll settle for a kiss."

So that's what they did until Luis Rosario and Jo-Jo Knight dropped into the two seats facing them.

"Is this what white people do after a gunfight?" Rosario asked. "Cubans just drink and sing."

"I thought Cubans drank and made love to sheep." Knight grinned.

"Okay, okay." Alexa grinned. "Knock it off, you guys."

Jo-Jo said, "Unless you want this bird to circle over the water, we need to figure out where we want to go. Here's what me and this little freeway dancer figured out: your buddy Jody tried to cash in the escrow account in Aruba, but Sandro and Papa Joe beat him to it. By the time he showed up, they already cleaned it out. I think Papa Joe also set up the Vikings to be killed by the San Andresitos in Maicao after you delivered the product up there. You guys were just donkeys; he was never gonna share that money with you."

"After Jody went to Aruba and discovered the money was gone, he disappeared on a charter flight to Florida,"

Rosario said. "We lost the trail in Miami. Can't figure why he'd be going to Florida, anyway."

"Jody's not going there," Shane said. "He might have filed his flight plan for Miami, but trust me, he's going wherever Papa Joe and Sandy Mantoor are. Jody's gonna kill those two for setting him up and taking his money." Shane ran it over in his mind for a minute. "Papa Joe's got a house in Palm Springs. Maybe there."

Alexa shook her head. "After we broke the code book and found José Mondragon's name, we hit that desert house looking for clues to where you might be. I'm afraid that site got burned. José won't be going back to the Springs."

Shane gave it some more thought. "L.A.," he finally said.

"Why L.A.?" Alexa frowned. "That's the hardest place for him to hide. Three thousand cops there know he's alive and what he looks like."

"Because that's where Lisa told me she was going, and Lisa's his only contact to Papa Joe. I know this guy. It's personal. . . . Jody is gonna get his money back, or die trying."

Alexa went forward to tell the pilot while Shane put his head back on the seat and closed his eyes. He was bone-tired. Sleep came in seconds.

They were at Ryder Field . . . back in the sixth grade. Jody in his Pirates uniform, smiling at Shane . . . slamming a ball into his pitcher's mitt, pulling it out, throwing it back again. "Good game, Hot Sauce . . . Way t'call the hitters."

"You threw the Ks," Shane answered, his own voice bright and happy.

"We're a team. Nothing can ever change that." Jody grinned.

Shane suddenly felt the need to tell Jody how he really

felt: how much his friendship meant . . . what it was like to have been left at a hospital . . . to have never known his own parents . . . to be raised by strangers. How he never knew his mother. How he would lie in bed wondering why she had left him. Who was she? Why didn't she care enough to keep him? "You're all I have," Shane finally said. "You're the only one who ever cared about me."

Little Jody grinned and dropped the ball, throwing his arm around his ten-year-old buddy. "Don't you forget it, Hot Sauce."

"I'll never forget," Shane said, with all his heart. "You have my solemn promise."

47

CITY OF ANGELS

They made a fuel stop at Love Field in Dallas. Alexa had radioed ahead and arranged for a medical team to take a look at Shane's leg. The bullet had passed through the lastus laterus muscle, barely missing the abductor canal.

So much for karma.

The slug had threaded its way through a complex maze of potential disasters while doing very little damage. They stitched and bandaged him up, gave him a shot of antibiotics, then told him to check with a doctor in L.A.

They took off from Love Field an hour later.

Los Angeles was in the middle of a horrible inversion layer that trapped the city's smoggy pollutants like smoke under a blanket.

The Citation landed at Van Nuys airport at three-thirty in the afternoon, taxied up to the small Customs shack at the end of Runway 2-6, and shut down.

Tony Filosiani was waiting for them beside the grandfather of the Crown Vics. The old beige and brown Ford fit the funky L.A. day.

"I'm sorry about the way this went down, Sergeant,"

the chief said as they deplaned. "I know we mind-fucked ya, but I didn't know what else t'do."

"It saved my life," Shane admitted as he limped over to the car and stood leaning against it. "It fooled me, so I fooled Jody."

"We been trying t'get a fix on this Lisa St. Marie person you radioed me about," Filosiani said, getting right to business. "We finally got an address from the whadda-ya-callit . . . from the taxes."

"The State Real Estate Tax Board?" Alexa corrected.

"Yeah. She bought a condo in Century City two years ago. The address just came in. I got a five-man jump-out squad stationed over there. They say, according to the doorman, she's upstairs. They got the place covered till we get there."

"Let's go. I'll fill you in on the way," Shane said through punched and swollen lips. Then he turned to Jo-Jo and Luis. "Thanks for the backup, guys." He shook hands with Knight.

When the fed pulled his hand back, he found that he had the STD transmitter in his palm.

"I found that floating in the airplane toilet," Shane said. "Guess it's yours."

"Damn . . . I hope ya washed it off," Knight said, glowering at the little white pill.

Shane shook hands with Rosario. "Stay in touch, *amigo*," he said, then turned and opened the rear door of the plainwrap. As he slid into the chief's musty car, Shane could see that true to form, the Day-Glo Dago had cut himself no slack when it came to the perks of office. The backseat was torn, and the car smelled of stale tobacco.

Alexa paused to say good-bye to Jo-Jo and Luis, kissing both of them lightly on the cheek. "You guys are the best," she told them.

"Hear that, you little Cuban faggot?" Jo-Jo said, grinning. "I'm the best."

"Ain't what she told me," Luis said, winking at Alexa. "She told me she thinks you're the biggest, slowest sack a'shit this side a'the post office."

"At least I don't roast no live chickens in motel bathtubs, you greasy Santeria."

Chief Filosiani shook his head in mock distress, but he was grinning as he settled behind the wheel. Alexa followed, and Chief Filosiani pulled away from the Customs building.

"Them two . . . Jesus," he said, shaking his head. "They never stop with that shit."

Filosiani turned onto the 101 Freeway, took it to the 405, then over the hill into West L.A.

In less than twenty minutes they were in Century City, pulling up to a twenty-story high-rise with a huge marble monument sign out front that announced the building: CENTURY PARK WEST.

The tall steel-and-glass tower poked up through the afternoon sky, its top-floor mirrored windows disappearing into the brown L.A. muck.

They were met by Lieutenant Lincoln Heart, who was leading the team of jump-outs. Heart was ebony black, and his short-sleeved Class C uniform barely concealed a physique of rippling muscles.

There were two blue-uniformed officers waiting in the lobby. They learned that two more were already up on Lisa's floor, watching her apartment.

"You got a floor plan?" Filosiani asked.

"Yep, got it from the building manager. Ms. St. Marie's got an east view, two-bedroom," Lieutenant Heart said as he opened a folded Xerox of the plan. They studied it while Heart continued: "According to the doorman, she came home last night 'bout midnight. Her car's still in the underground garage. Far as he knows, she hasn't left and nobody's been up to see her." Lieutenant Heart reached into his pocket and produced a key. "Here's the master to that floor."

"How you wanna do this, Lieutenant Hamilton?" Filosiani quizzed Alexa. It was his management style to be a coach to his officers but let them run the operations.

Shane smiled when he called her "Lieutenant," realizing that in his absence, her promotion had come through.

"We need to get Ms. St. Marie to cooperate, and I think Shane has the best chance of turning her. We may need to use her as bait to lure Jody. If she knows where Papa Joe is, we'll need to get that, too." Alexa looked over at Shane. "For all those reasons, Shane should be on point," Alexa said.

"Good analysis," Filosiani noted. "I agree."

"How's the leg feel?" Alexa asked.

"Okay," Shane said, and surprisingly, aside from some occasional throbbing and muscle weakness, he had very little pain. "Lemme give it a try. But I have to do it alone. If we do a SWAT-type entry, she'll clam up."

Filosiani nodded.

"Anybody got a piece I could borrow?" Shane asked.

"Here," Alexa said, "I have a backup." She handed him another Astra 9.

"What is it with you and these little Spanish Astras?" He grinned.

She smiled. "Great little purse gun, eight-shot clip, no hammer, doesn't snag coming out. Stop complaining . . . you still owe me four hundred for the last one."

He chambered the Astra and stuck it into his belt, zippering his light windbreaker over it. Then the four of them stepped onto the elevator.

They rode in silence, listening to the innocuous elevator music and light chimes that announced each passing floor. As the elevator stopped, Lieutenant Heart gave Shane the master key.

They exited on sixteen—Lisa's floor. As they got out

of the elevator, they saw two more of Lieutenant Heart's blue shirts watching Lisa's door from the stairwell up the hall.

"You're up," Filosiani said. "Number sixteen-twelve."

Shane limped on his bad leg across the plush carpet to Lisa's apartment while Filosiani motioned to the men in the stairwell to stay back.

He rang the bell next to a pair of massive oak double doors. He could hear the chimes inside, waited, then tried again.

Nothing.

He knocked on the door and, when nobody answered, took out the master key and silently fitted it into the lock. He pulled Alexa's Astra, jacked a round into the pipe, then quietly pushed the door open.

The hallway was mirrored on both sides to give the narrow corridor a wider feel.

An old fear hit him.

Shane hated going through mirrored entries when he was shaking a house; too easy to get spotted. He took a deep breath before quickly slipping into the white-on-white condo. He stopped just before entering the living room, keeping his back flat to the mirrored wall on the right, using the mirrors opposite him to search the living room. His ears were straining for any sound of movement. Nothing.

Out of the corner of his vision, he saw Alexa appear in the front doorway with yet another Astra in her right hand. She had more of those little automatics than the Spanish Mafia. He put a finger to his lips and motioned for her to stay outside.

She nodded and held her position as Shane moved carefully into the empty living room. He slid past the wall-to-ceiling plate-glass window and checked the kitchen.

Nothing.

He worked his way down the apartment's center hall, pausing at the guest bedroom door, pushing it slowly open, checking inside.

Empty.

He continued on to the master suite. He had a premonition of death, almost as if he could see around the corner into the future. A cold fear was beginning to ice the edges of his stomach. He cracked the bedroom door and looked in. The bed was mussed, but empty. He entered cautiously, checking the perimeter of the room first. The suite was spacious, dominated by a king-size bed and a plate-glass window that took in the smog-drenched Hillcrest Country Club sixteen stories below.

The bedroom was deserted. The bathroom wasn't.

He found her there, naked.

It wasn't pretty.

What human beings were capable of doing to one another sometimes horrified him.

She was lying in her tub brutally shot in five places. Both kneecaps were shattered, as well as both elbows. The kill shot had opened a gaping hole in the center of her chest. Lisa had been blond and pale in life, but lying in her tub, naked and bloodless, she looked like a broken doll in its white porcelain container. Papery skin wrapped her lifeless body like thin, transparent tissue. Her blond hair was tipped in dried blood, turning the feathered ends red.

Sex goddess in repose.

"Shit!" Shane heard himself say, then called out in a loud voice, "I've got her! It's clear, master bath!"

In seconds, Alexa and Filosiani entered with Lieutenant Heart and the two jump-outs from the stairwell.

"Okay," Filosiani said as soon as he saw the body. "Everybody out. This here's a crime scene. Let's not foul it for Forensics with our own prints and fibers."

They all backed out of the bathroom and stood in the hall.

"Jody's our doer," Shane said softly.

"Then he's turning into a monster," Alexa said softly.

"No," Shane answered, "he's just decided not to hide it anymore."

Filosiani said, "I'll get Homicide out here. My guess is, if she knew where Sandro Mantoor and José Mondragon are, then Jody musta found out before he killed her."

"She was pretty tough," Alexa said, with a tinge of admiration as she looked toward the bedroom door. "She must have taken all four joint shots before she talked. After he got what he wanted, he put the fifth round through her heart."

"Sure is the way it looks." Shane shuddered.

"So how do we find Papa Joe?" Alexa said. "If Jody gets to him first, he'll get the money, kill Sandy and José, and run. Once he gets out of the country, we'll lose jurisdiction and probably never find him."

"There's a guy, an ex-Air Unit pilot named David VanKirk," Shane said. "IAD terminated him for making night flights, smuggling dope in from Mexico with his police helicopter. If you've still got an address, I'd send somebody out to his place to sit on him. Jody may try and use that chopper to get outta California."

"Good idea," Filosiani said. Because his cell phone wasn't working in this steel-and-glass building, he ran toward the elevator on his way outside to call Homicide and gather up a surveillance detail on David VanKirk.

"This is a dead end, of course," Alexa said softly. "Without Lisa, we've got nothing . . . nobody . . . no place to start. My guess is Jody won't take a chance on VanKirk."

Shane nodded.

However, there was one other possibility that began tickling Shane's thoughts. It was a huge long shot, but he had been on such a cold streak, he figured he was due. He hoped it was time for him to finally cash a winner.

48

MESSENGER

"Tremaine Lane was an L.A. County Sheriff." Shane was standing outside of Century Park East with Alexa and Filosiani. The Homicide team had just arrived, and the Forensics techs were unpacking their blue windowless van.

"Tremaine wasn't in Shephard's file. We don't have any background on him," Alexa answered.

"He was working undercover. The whole Viking thing started at the Sheriff's Department. I always wondered if maybe the culture had somehow migrated to us, through one of these joint-ops task forces we're always running. Tremaine and Hector Rodriquez were tight. Is there any way to pull Sergeant Rodriquez's assignment jacket to see if he ever worked a joint-op with Tremaine Lane?"

"Easy enough," Filosiani said, then picked up the radio on the nearest squad car and got a patch through to the Records Division. He identified himself, told them what he wanted, and asked for a rush.

"Roger that, sir," the female Records Division clerk said. In less than a minute, she was back on the air. "In

July of '99, Sergeant Hector Rodriquez of SWAT was assigned to the Cobra Unit in the Valley. Cobra was working with L.A. Impact, which included half a dozen county sheriffs. They worked a big arms deal in the Sunland. Ten Class A felony arrests came down."

"Do you have the names of the other sheriffs who were in on that bust?" Filosiani asked.

"No, sir. You have to get that from Sheriff Messenger's office."

"Call over there and tell Bill Messenger I need a meeting. Tell him it can't wait. I'll be there in ten minutes."

At five-foot-seven and 135 pounds, Bill Messenger barely made the Sheriff's Department height and weight regs. He was a dark-complexioned, second-generation Egyptian American with close-cropped, silver-gray hair and a penchant for perfectly tailored, double-breasted suits. The jacket he was wearing had brass buttons on it, giving him a distinct Napoleonic tilt. Titanium-framed glasses, as spartan as his waistline, rested atop a Roman nose.

"What's the emergency, Tony?" Messenger said, negotiating his way across his cream and tan office, threading past two form-over-function Danish modern chairs that squatted on delicate tapered legs like futuristic spiders. He shook hands with Tony, Shane, and Alexa. The two L.A. law-enforcement heads were exactly the same height, but that's where the similarities ended. Standing nose to nose, they were the yin and yang of law enforcement. The Day-Glo Dago radiated warmth of personality, while William "Bill" Messenger had the emotional temperature of a garden snake.

"We got a problem," Tony said, looking at the door. "Mind if I close that?"

"My secretary doesn't leak," Messenger said testily.

"Yeah, but her husband might." Tony kicked the door

shut, and by mistake it closed too hard, slamming loudly.

Bill Messenger winced.

"Who are these people?" the sheriff asked, looking at Shane and Alexa.

"This is Lieutenant Alexa Hamilton," Tony began.

"The Medal of Valor winner who died a week ago?" Messenger said, and cocked a bushy eyebrow.

"I'll get to that. And this is Sergeant Shane Scully," Tony added.

"The man who killed her. You run a strange shop, Tony." Messenger was glaring at both of them.

"The staged killing of Lieutenant Hamilton was part of an undercover op," Filosiani said. "This pertains to the problem you had a few years back with that rogue group of sheriffs who called themselves Vikings."

"Not to quibble, but that didn't happen on my watch. Sheriff Bloch hosted that disaster. However, I ended up with the mop and pail after he died."

"The culture has spread to us," Tony said bluntly.

"Too bad. The Vikings were racists . . . minority-hating sheriffs who took their suspects down into county aqueducts and beat them. I had my hands full, and was never sure I rooted them all out. I fielded three civil-liberties lawsuits when I tried to arrange a lineup to check my men for that silly tattoo they all had on their ankles. 'Illegal body search,' the courts called it. 'Unconstitutional' . . . 'Lack of probable cause.' " He shook his head sadly. "They want a perfect department, but they won't let me do what it takes to weed out the bad apples."

"The LAPD Vikings aren't racists," Shane said. "But they are killers."

"What makes you say they're not racists?" Messenger challenged. " 'Cause my Vikings did everything but burn crosses and hang people from trees."

"I know they aren't, because I've been undercover with them for the past week."

"That's why you staged the phony shooting?" Messenger said, looking at Tony. "To set his cover?"

"Yeah, but it's a long story, and I don't really have time for it now," Filosiani said. "The reason we're here is that we found out one of your deputies, Sergeant Tremaine Lane, was working inside that LAPD deep-cover unit without my knowledge. We now believe he was a Sheriff's Department plant reporting back to you, Bill."

"I think not," Messenger said, but his bearing had suddenly turned rigid.

"Your undercover is dead," Shane said. "Cut to pieces. Skinned alive by a death-squad maniac, then left to die hanging on a fence in Colombia. I was there when it happened."

"I see." Messenger didn't move.

"I understand you have a responsibility to protect the identity of your UCs," Tony said. " 'Specially since you've been infiltrating a sister law-enforcement agency without notifying its chief in advance," he added sharply. "But the fact is, we're running short on time and I'd really appreciate it if I could cut through the fuckin' cow shit and get a straight answer here before more people die."

Sheriff Messenger finally moved. He crossed the room and actually threw the lock on the door, which moments before he had insisted they leave open. Then he turned and walked back to the center of the room, using the little journey around his spacious office to compose his thoughts.

"Okay," he finally said. "Let's say, for the sake of argument, that Sergeant Lane *was* working a special assignment for me . . . and now you say he's dead?"

"Yes, sir," Shane said. "He had joined an off-the-books LAPD squad who also called themselves Vikings, complete with the same ankle tattoos as your sheriffs. I think Tremaine got duked into the unit by one of our SWAT sergeants, Hector Rodriquez, who worked a joint-ops with him in the Valley two years ago."

"How do I know my guy's really dead?" Messenger said.

" 'Cause I'm telling you. I was there! I saw him die!"

"Excuse me for doubting your word, Sergeant, but I watch the news. I understand your own department ran a psychological profile on you just last year. You could be delusional, a disenfranchised troublemaker. Owing to the sensitivity of all this, you're going to have to tell me something more to convince me."

"Tremaine and I got captured in Colombia, in a town just across the Venezuelan border, called Maicao. His skin was peeled off in strips. Jesus . . . what the hell else you want from me?" Shane was starting to get hot, glowering at the emotionless little man.

"Calm down, Sergeant," Tony said softly. "Bill's gonna help out . . .'cause if he don't, I'm gonna run a stick through his nuts and roast 'em over a slow fire in the governor's office."

"Yeah, and just how you think you're gonna do that, Tony?"

"You put a guy in my department without clearing it with me first. I'll get the district attorney to subpoena your Command Directive, then I'll roll it up and jam it so far up your ass, you'll be able to start breathing through it."

The county sheriff took off his titanium glasses, pulled a silk handkerchief out of his pocket, and went to work giving the lenses a thorough cleaning . . . then he slipped them carefully back onto his nose.

"Okay, let's also say, just for the hell of it, that I might acknowledge that Sergeant Lane was working in an undercover capacity inside your department." Messenger was speaking slower now, as if his words had solemn weight. "And let's say he stumbled into your rogue Viking unit. Since your man here says he's dead and can't report in, that would seem to end it. How am I supposed to help you?"

"He'd been undercover for two months. . . . I don't know how you guys supervise UCs, Bill, but over in my 'strange' shop, we set up phone drops, get interim reports. So unless you're running this place like a Carnival Cruise, you got his re-back file. We need those reports. We need to know everything Sergeant Lane found out, 'cause this thing is coming unglued. Most of that unit is already dead, and the ones who ain't are running for the airport. Like I said, we don't have a lotta time."

Bill Messenger pushed his titanium rims higher up on his nose. He went to his desk, opened a bottom drawer, then took out a metal lockbox. He opened it, pulled out a file, and threw it on the desk between them.

"You keep the ops reports in your desk drawer?" Tony said, smiling.

"For obvious reasons, I was supervising the Viking mop-up myself," Messenger said in a hard, clipped voice. "What do you need to know?"

"We're trying to get a line on an Argentine national named José Mondragon," Tony said. "We need to know where he lives when he's in L.A. We think one of our Viking cops is about to kill him. We need José alive, to make a money-laundering case we're settin' up."

"I can already tell you his L.A. residence's not in there. He stayed in hotels," Messenger said, motioning toward the manila folder. "But help yourself."

Shane picked up the file, opened it, and found the section on José Mondragon. "House in Palm Springs," he read. "We already know about that."

"No kidding," Messenger complained. "You hit that place harder than a Mexican piñata. That was the one good contact point we had."

"Maybe if we'd known you guys were in on our case, we coulda worked something else out," Tony fired back.

Shane scanned Tremaine's report quickly: "José is married to a diplomat's daughter. Didn't know that. Lives half the year in Argentina." He looked up. "Anything in here about an Argentine colonel named Raphael Aziz?" Shane asked.

Messenger shook his head sharply, so Shane kept scanning Tremaine's UC report. "Polo . . . Says here José's a member of the L.A. Polo Club. Plays polo at Will Rogers Park in Santa Monica." Shane looked up at Messenger.

"We checked that out. José stopped playing there two years ago, then shipped his polo pony back to Argentina. It's a dead end."

Shane kept reading. "His license plate number for his Jag is in here. Did you run it?"

"Yep," Messenger said stiffly. "Car is registered to one of Blackstone's companies in Switzerland, no local address."

"Dead end," Alexa said.

The sheriff nodded.

"Known associates, Lisa St. Marie," Shane read.

"She'd be a good place to start," Messenger said quickly. "Go find her. José Mondragon used her as a sexual spy, so if you roll her, she probably has some good stuff on him."

"Lisa ain't gonna be much help," Tony said.

"Why not?"

"She just ain't."

"I thought we were cooperating," Messenger snapped.

"She was tortured and shot five times in her condo a few hours ago. She's at the morgue."

The diminutive sheriff didn't react.

Shane kept reading: "He once kept a single-engine plane at the Santa Monica Airport, but sold it two years ago." Shane looked up. "If he played polo in Santa Monica and flew his plane out there, I wonder if he had a house out there, too."

"Don't know. Sounds like a good place to start." Messenger glanced at his watch, anxious to be rid of them. "Why don't you check it out?"

Shane closed the file and looked up at the sheriff. "Can we get a copy of this?" he asked. "I'd like to look it over more carefully."

"If my man is dead, then you can have it. But you'll have to take a poly first. I want to know you're telling the truth about all this."

"Good going, Bill. Good cooperation," Filosiani snapped.

"Tony, Tony, Tony," Messenger sighed. "You never cooperated with anybody. Not once in your whole career. I can't take any more bad press on this Viking thing. This all started here at the Sheriff's Department, so if you kick it up again, I'm gonna have to suffer through a bunch of newspaper and TV recaps. We looked like a buncha Klansmen when the *Los Angeles Times* broke that piece three years ago. I'm finally getting past it. If it's spread to your department, I'm sorry, but my responsibility is to see it's not back here. That's what Sergeant Lane was trying to determine."

"I'll take the polygraph," Shane said suddenly.

"All you gotta do is convince my poly operator that Sergeant Lane is really dead. If that's the case, then I can't protect him anymore, and you can have his files."

Shane took the polygraph and passed.

Half an hour later they left the sheriff's office with a copy of the classified folder.

When they reached the parking lot, they looked up and saw Bill Messenger staring down at them from his office window on the fourth floor of the big, boxy Sheriff's Building. He looked even tinier standing behind the huge expanse of glass.

"First time I actually liked that prick," Tony said as they got into the Crown Vic and pulled away.

49

RULES

They read the file in Chief Filosiani's sparsely furnished office. There was nothing in the Sheriff's Department folder that gave them any clue to José Mondragon's whereabouts. After going over it several times, they began to lose hope.

Shane used the phone in the chief's office to call Chooch at Filosiani's house.

"Thank God, you're safe, man," his son said, relief in his voice.

"Get your stuff ready; Alexa and I will be over to get you in an hour."

They checked the Santa Monica Polo Club and talked to the club manager, who confirmed that José Mondragon had not been a member for years. The club had no address on file for him, or anybody else for that matter; they didn't even have a membership list because all you needed to play was a horse and enough friends to make up a team. The team captains rounded up their players and scheduled the matches. The manager did remember José's horse, though, because he said it was a world-class polo pony, a coal-black Arabian named Sir Anthony of Aquitaine. He confirmed what Bill Messenger had told them. The horse had been shipped to Argentina two years ago.

The polo club was a dead end.

So was the airport where José had kept the plane. The Cessna he flew didn't even belong to him. It was leased from an FBO and, true to José's practice, the Blackstone Corporation was the only name on the lease. Nobody at the airfield even remembered him.

"I'm out of ideas," Shane said as he limped out of the chief's office with Tony and Alexa. They walked across the seafoam-green carpet, past the blond-wood paneling, and finally got into the large elevator. "Jody's so far ahead of us that if he knows where José is, he's already working on him like he did on Lisa," Shane continued. "José will be dead. Jody will have the money and be gone."

"But nobody knows where José is," Alexa countered. "Maybe Jody can't find him, either."

"Maybe," Shane said, but he didn't have much hope.

They climbed back into the chief's Crown Vic, Tony behind the wheel, Alexa in the front, Shane in the back. His leg was now throbbing horribly, but he clenched his jaw and tried to ignore the pain.

Twenty minutes later they pulled up in front of a very modest two-story Tudor with a small lawn and, judging from the depth of the lot, almost no backyard.

Chooch was waiting out front with his overnight bag at his feet. If the chief looked like a butcher, then Mary Filosiani was equally well cast as the butcher's wife. A pleasant, dark-haired woman in a print dress, she was standing beside Chooch. She kissed him good-bye, and Chooch walked up to the car.

Shane got out and gave his son a hug. "Boy, am I glad to see you," he said in Chooch's ear.

Chooch just hung on, his arms unabashedly around Shane. When he finally pulled back, he had tears in his eyes. "Man, I was so worried about you," Chooch said, looking at the damage to Shane's face.

"How was quarterback camp?"

"Get the fuck outta here," Chooch smiled. "I was only up there for ten hours before you got your big dumb ass kidnapped. So I came right back."

"Oh, yeah," Shane grinned. "I forgot. And watch your mouth."

The chief let them borrow the Crown Vic to drive back to Venice. "I been thinkin' I'd trade it in for a fresher model anyway," he smiled. "It's one thing tryin' to set a good example for the troops; it's another to ride around in a garbage can with wheels."

Shane threw Chooch's luggage into the back and got behind the wheel.

They were silent for most of the drive back to Venice. Several times Shane looked over and saw Chooch or Alexa smiling at him.

"What?" he said, and suddenly they all started laughing.

They pulled into the garage at the canal house and parked next to Shane's dusty Acura, then walked into the small kitchen, where Shane opened the freezer and pulled out a package of four frozen New York steaks. He set them on the counter to defrost.

"Let's get the barbecue going, Bud," he said to Chooch, who grinned and pulled a bag of charcoal briquettes from the cupboard. The boy took it outside and filled the orange Weber barbecue that was sitting on a small patch of poured concrete in the backyard.

It was just about dusk. Shane put his arm around Alexa as they looked out the sliding glass door at his son, starting the fire in the backyard. It was wonderful to be home, but bubbling under that relief was a strange, unsettled feeling.

"I know what you're thinking," Alexa said softly.

"Now you and Jody both can do it, huh? Walk right inside my head, without knocking."

"You feel like it's not over, but it is. Sometimes things just don't wrap up perfectly."

"Yeah, I know . . . it's just . . ."

"We're alive and we're together, babe," she said. "You and me and Chooch. What more can we ask for?"

"You're right, as usual." He snapped his fingers. "Just a minute. I forgot something." He turned and limped down the hall into the bedroom, where he opened the top dresser drawer and pulled out the engagement ring in Murray Steinberg's slightly crushed black-leather box.

Shane walked back outside, where he found Alexa and Chooch poking at the briquettes with long-handled tongs, spreading them out.

Shane turned and faced Alexa, took her hand, then slipped the two-carat engagement ring onto her finger. "There," he said, "now it's official."

"It's about time, is what it is," Chooch said, smiling. "But aren't you supposed to ask her first?"

"She said yes two days ago," Shane told him, taking her in his arms as Chooch smiled his approval.

As the setting sun lit the edges of the rippling canal, Shane cooked the steaks, Alexa made a salad, and Chooch set the table.

They sat in the backyard and ate quietly, counting their blessings, grinning like children.

Later that night, Shane and Alexa made love in his bed while Chooch watched TV in the living room.

Shane felt as if he had completed an impossible journey. He had been looking for something that didn't exist, but in its place he had found something even more valuable.

If only he hadn't lost Jody. If only Jody hadn't confessed that he'd never cared . . . that he hadn't loved

Shane the way Shane had once loved him. That realization caused a sadness that he suspected was produced by betrayal as much as by loss. It touched on old issues of abandonment that he had lugged around his entire life. Shane's parents had dumped him at a hospital's back door like human trash. He had been infant number 732. City Services finally named him Shane. He had picked the name Scully, after his favorite baseball announcer, Vince Scully. But that first betrayal by his parents had caused an ache inside of him that had never left.

Why did my mother leave me like that? Didn't she care?

He had asked himself these same two questions over and over again, day after day, year after year, until they had almost lost their meaning.

The Deans had filled in some of the emptiness, until Jody had snatched it away again, coming back into his life two weeks ago.

Alexa had fallen asleep beside him, but he lay awake, thinking and listening to the TV in the other room.

He fell asleep some time during Leno.

Jody had his back to a field where beautiful horses ran, galloping around the edges of the wooden perimeter fence. The horses came to an abrupt halt each time they reached the rail, sticking their magnificent heads over, snorting angry air from flared nostrils, looking across the fence line at the distant city, before turning and galloping back across the field to the other side. But Jody didn't turn to watch them. His eyes were only on Shane.

"You don't get to play unless you sign up," Jody said. "You have to register first."

"I know," Shane answered. "But it sure would be fun to play."

"They have rules about that," Jody said seriously.

"I know," Shane said. "Rules."

"It's not like Little League, where everybody can play," Jody continued. "Here, you have to register. They have to know who you are."

"I know," Shane said. "Rules—you have to register."

Riders were now magically up on the horses, galloping across the open field in their team shirts, swinging their polo mallets at the little white ball that flew energetically with each whack. As it came close to where they were standing, Shane was surprised to see that it was a baseball they were hitting.

"I have to go," Jody said. "You can stay and watch, but don't get too close. They have rules about that, too."

"I know . . ." Shane said.

Then Jody turned and walked out of the dream.

The horses were now galloping near the fence. The baseball flew by the spot where Shane was standing, and the horses raced to catch it. He could feel the slipstreaming air against his face as they thundered past.

"Rules," Shane said softly in the darkened bedroom, the word still on his lips as he opened his eyes.

When he spoke, he woke Alexa, and she turned over and looked at him. "What?" she asked.

Shane wasn't sure. He just knew that he was terribly troubled by the innocuous dream, as if something were lying there on the bottom of his subconscious, something important that he'd forgotten to pursue, but he didn't know what it was. "Rules in polo," he said. "Everybody has to register, or they can't play."

"What?" Alexa looked at the digital clock. "God, it's twelve-thirty," she said, turning on the bedside lamp.

"Maybe we should make sure Chooch got to bed and isn't sleeping on the couch out there." She got up, put on her robe, and left the bedroom.

"Rules," Shane repeated, trying to figure out what his subconscious was trying to tell him. "Everybody has rules." He sat up in bed, his heart pounding because he knew this was important but didn't, for the life of him, know why.

He had spoken for ten minutes on the phone to the polo club guy. They *didn't* have rules; that was the point. The man had stated that all you needed was a horse and a team to play on. "Rules," he said again, as Alexa returned to the room.

"What?"

"Everybody has rules. You can't play without registering first."

She turned off the light. "Chooch is in his bedroom, conked."

"Good."

"What on earth are you talking about?"

"A dream," he said. "I was with Jody, watching a bunch of men playing polo, only they were hitting a baseball, and in my dream he said, 'You don't get to play unless you register,' that you can't play because there are rules. . . ."

She looked at him. "Okay, there are rules. How does that apply?"

"I don't know. . . ." He looked at her and shook his head ruefully. "Polo . . . rules in polo. Of course, there're rules in polo. Shit."

She smiled and kissed him, then got back into bed. Shane hugged her, feeling her breath on his neck, the slow beating of her heart, and then, wrapped in her safe cocoon, he was quickly asleep.

He was back on the polo field. Only now he was petting a huge Arabian horse that poked his nose over the fence where Shane was standing. He knew, without asking, that the horse was Sir Anthony of Aquitaine. He was coal-black and eating a cube of sugar out of Shane's hand.

"I've never seen a horse as beautiful as you," he said in the dream.

The stallion snorted. His black coat was shining. "I'd

sure love to have a horse like you," Shane said in wonder. "If you ever have a colt . . ."

Shane suddenly woke up again, this time with a start. His heart was pounding, slamming in his chest. *Shit,* he thought as he lay in bed. *What is this?*

He got out of bed and quietly limped out of the room. Wearing only his Jockey shorts, he went down the hall, then out into the backyard, where he sat in one of the metal chairs and watched the quarter-moon ripple on the still water. His thigh had been bandaged with white medical wrap, but some of the stitches must have broken loose, because a dried bloodstain the size of a grapefruit had leaked through the gauze. He was going to have to get his wounded thigh re-dressed.

"Rules," he said again softly, returning to his dream. "Horses . . . polo . . ." *You can't ride. . . . Why can't you ride? You can't own an Arabian horse without . . . without what? Shit.* He sat there turning it over in his mind. *You have to register to ride . . . to play? Why do I want a damn horse, a colt? Why? I'd have to register. I'd . . .*

He lunged out of the chair, headed into the house, turned on the lights in the bedroom, and put a hand on Alexa's shoulder.

She rolled over and glared at him. "What are you doing?" she asked. "Are you ever going to sleep?"

"Listen, if you owned an Arabian horse, wouldn't you have to list him with some kind of Thoroughbred registry?"

"I guess . . ."

"You do, you have to. There're rules about it. I think I read somewhere with all Thoroughbreds, you have to register them to protect the bloodlines and stud fees. Thoroughbred horses are registered at birth . . . when they're colts. There's some kinda Arabian horse registry."

"So?"

"It'll have the address of the owner."

"Unless his horse is registered to Blackstone Corporation in Switzerland, like everything else this guy owns."

"Sir Anthony of Aquitaine?" Shane smiled. "No fucking way. That horse is his status symbol. He might register his car or a house to the company, but this animal's a champion. . . . It's in Papa Joe's name. Count on it. José is in the fucking horse registry, I'll bet you anything. It'll be somewhere on the Internet."

She rolled out of bed and put on her robe. "Let's get Chooch out of the sack. He's our best computer jock."

It was so easy, it was almost ridiculous. The registry was called exactly what Shane had guessed: the Arabian Horse Registry. Sir Anthony of Aquitaine was in the stallion listings. Below that was a lot of stuff about his bloodline: out of this sire and that mare, going back six generations, but at the bottom was the owner's name and address, right there on the screen:

José Luis Mondragon
2457 Malibu Canyon Road
Malibu, California

50

COWBOYS AND INDIANS

They called Tony Filosiani from the Pacific Coast Highway, waking him up.

"Malibu?" he said after Alexa filled him in over her cell phone. "You guys go in the county without Sheriff's Department jurisdiction and Messenger will throw one a'his Egyptian conniptions."

"Then call him and get us some backup," Alexa said.

"I'll try."

Shane slowed down the Acura to make the turnoff from PCH onto Malibu Canyon Road. That two-lane highway climbed up into the coastal mountains, becoming a dark, treacherous, winding two-lane that widened periodically to include a center passing lane. The road snaked along a ridge above a deep river gorge, and they flashed by a sign that said they were leaving Ventura and passing back into L.A. County. Shane was slowing, looking for the address. There were very few intersecting roads on the two-lane highway and even fewer driveways. Shane had to be careful not to overdrive his headlights and shoot past 2457 Malibu Canyon Road.

Then he saw it.

The address was painted on a mailbox on the left-hand canyon side of the road. Shane braked hard, snapping his headlights off as he made the turn, heading slowly down the dirt drive into the canyon below. The driveway was rutted from a recent rain. It headed down, switching back and forth, into the narrow valley.

"Wait a minute," Alexa said. "Stop."

Shane put on the brakes. "What?"

"We can't go down there without Sheriff's backup," she said.

"If Jody's down there, I want him."

"You aren't thinking straight."

"Is that any way to talk to your future husband?" he scowled theatrically. "Gimme my ring back."

"You're not man enough to take it, buster." She hit him playfully on the shoulder with the back of her hand. "If we wait, we get two things—we get backup, and we get jurisdiction."

"I haven't had a shred of jurisdiction since I choppered outta that fuckin' hangar two weeks ago. And as far as backup goes, guess what?" She stared at him apprehensively. "You're it."

"Okay, but at least don't drive all the way down there. Let's find a hole in the bushes and park it."

"Good suggestion. I've got enough Bondo in this sled already."

They rolled slowly down the road, keeping the headlights off and the engine on, with Shane riding the brake.

Finally, they could see the roofs of some ranch buildings below, so Shane started looking for a place to stash the Acura. He found a good spot about a quarter mile from the end of the dirt driveway: a trash area with two large Dumpsters. Shane rolled the car in between the two metal bins and shut off the engine, then reached up and pulled the bulb out of the dome light on the headliner. He had long before removed the plastic cover for easy access. He stuck the bulb in the ashtray, then both of them quietly opened the doors and slipped out of the car.

"Okay," he whispered, "I'm taking point."

"Will you cut it out with the John Wayne bullshit? Let's just move on this together."

"No," he said sharply. "I want you back twenty yards at least."

"Why? Because you're afraid I might stop one?"

"Yeah," Shane said.

"Or is it because, if you find Jody, you're gonna take him out and you don't want a witness?"

Shane gave her such a withering scowl that she shrugged. "Just asking."

They headed down the drive with Shane out front, limping badly but keeping about twenty yards of separation. When he came to the end of the road, he kneeled down to check the surroundings. Pain shot up his leg.

There were two horse barns, some stables, and three houses in a cluster next to a training corral that contained a center turnstile. Long metal bridle poles used for breaking horses carouseled out from the turnstile. There were lights on in the main house and a couple of spots on light poles over by the corral that threw a dim glow over the entire front yard. Two empty cars were parked by the main house.

Then Shane saw the big blue and white motor home. It was under some shade trees, about thirty yards to his left.

"Jody's here," Shane whispered to Alexa, who had moved up and was just kneeling down beside him.

"How do you know?"

He pointed at the thirty-seven-foot, double-axle rig. "That's his. We used it to go to Palm Springs, dropped it in the Valley before we left for Aruba."

"How did he get that monster down this narrow, winding road?" she asked.

"You're right. There must be another way in and out of here."

"What're you gonna do?"

"There used to be an auto-mag in that rig before we left town. It was Victory Smith's. Maybe it's still there. I'd like to get my hands on it. Not that I don't love these little Spanish Astras," he said, smiling.

"Shane," she said softly. "I think . . ."

"I know, wait for the sheriff. Tell you what, why don't you go back up the road and flag him down when he gets here?"

"Right. Great idea, dick-brain."

Shane didn't respond but moved off, heading toward the motor home.

He was thankful for the quarter moon that gave a little light but didn't flood the yard. He crept along the perimeter, out of range of the corral lights, hugging the moon shadows until he was at the back of the motor home. He paused to listen, heard nothing and snuck up the side, pulled Alexa's Astra, thumbed off the safety, and tried the door handle.

Unlocked.

Shane pulled open the metal door and looked back. Alexa had moved up behind him to take a cover position at the rear of the vehicle. She had her gun in both hands, held slightly up in a range-ready firing stance. From there, she was in a good position to protect his back. He nodded at her, then carefully climbed up the three steps into the motor home.

Sandro Mantoor was inside . . .

He had been hacked to death, then dismembered. His head was sitting in the sink, staring with lifeless eyes at a spot about a foot over Shane's head.

"Fuck," he whispered, afraid to inhale, swallowing

hard to keep his stomach bile down. The carnage was almost impossible to absorb. Blood squished in the carpeting under his feet. He found Sandy's arms on the double bed; his torso in the stall shower. Then he heard movement behind him. He spun and aimed the Astra at the door.

Alexa's face poked through the opening, looking in at him. Shane hurried to keep her from coming inside. He met her at the threshold, blocking her view of the mutilation, quickly pushing her outside and closing the door behind him.

She saw his pale expression. "What is it?" she asked. "What's in there?"

"He . . . he . . ." Shane stopped, took a deep breath. "It's a mess in there. You don't wanna see it. He butchered a guy—Sandro Mantoor. He's in pieces all over the place. Head's in the fucking sink."

"God, no . . ."

Shane was shaking now; his wounded leg felt weak and was beginning to go numb.

"When you're on backup you're supposed to cover the exit line, not come inside," he said, anger replacing shock.

"I think I saw somebody coming out of the house a minute ago. He went into the barn carrying a valise."

"Was it Jody?"

"I don't know. I couldn't tell. Too far away."

"I'm gonna get closer. This time, back me up, okay? Don't move in unless something goes down."

He took off toward the house, his heart pounding. It took him almost five minutes to reach the west wall because he was favoring his left leg and because he had to stay wide to keep out of the light coming from the two poles by the corral. He hugged the perimeter of the yard before finally reaching the side of the house. He stood and peeked through the living-room window.

Papa Joe Mondragon was sitting in a chair, facing a

wall. His head was slumped over, and he looked as though he was sleeping. Other than José, the room appeared empty. Shane made a slow circuit around the house to get to the east-side window, which would allow him a better view.

When he got there, he wished he hadn't. José's face had been beaten to a red pulp. He looked as if he was still breathing, but blood was running down his chin, dripping and staining his collar and crotch.

Shane wondered how Jody could have gone so far out of control.

Suddenly, cars were coming down the road. He turned around in time to see two Sheriff's Department black-and-whites barreling into the yard. They weren't using sirens, but drove in with their gumballs flashing, throwing colored light all over the place.

Before Shane could plan his next move, two shots rang out—flat, barking sounds that came from the direction of the barn. One of the sheriffs who had just gotten out of his car went down immediately and started screaming in pain.

The sheriff's cars' bar lights strobed red and blue patterns across the front of the barn. Then Shane saw Alexa moving toward them, holding up her badge.

"Stop, throw down your weapon!" the second sheriff's deputy yelled at her, leveling a riot gun at her over his door.

"LAPD," she shouted, but kept coming.

"Throw down your gun. Get facedown on the ground!" the sheriff yelled back.

Now Shane heard a horse galloping. He turned and faced the sound but couldn't see anything, so he made his way around the side of the barn just in time to see a fleeing dark shape. The rider's head was low on the horse's neck, behind the mane. He spurred the animal on, galloping fast down the narrow trail, into a riverbed that was framed by narrow canyon walls.

Shane made a limping run across the open space toward the barn door.

Two more shots rang out. Then he heard Alexa scream, "No! He's a police officer." But the sheriff opened up on Shane anyway. Bullets whizzed all around, pinging and ricocheting off nearby farm equipment and thunking into the soft wood of the barn walls.

Shane dove inside the barn and slammed the door shut. The building was huge, with stalls on both sides. Shane had never been much of a horseback rider, limiting his saddle time to a couple of weekends at a dude ranch in Arizona, where he'd been more interested in his date than in any of the swayback nags stabled there. He grabbed a halter off a nearby hook, then opened the nearest stall containing a horse. It was a large chestnut bay with a black mane and tail. He wrapped the halter around the horse's neck and tied it to a corner post, found a bridle hanging in the stall, grabbed it, and tried to push it into the horse's mouth. The animal reared up and spit the bit back at him.

"Nice horsey," Shane said, sounding like a seven-year-old.

He finally wrestled the bridle on but decided he'd have to forgo the saddle. He'd wasted too much time already.

Shane pulled the stubborn bay out of the stall and led it out the back of the barn, where he tried to mount it. With his blown left leg, he was having no luck, so he pulled the horse over to a nearby stable rail and managed to get on by climbing up, then swinging aboard. He suddenly heard more sirens as additional sheriff's cars arrived.

He kicked the horse in the withers and it bolted out of the open corral with Shane barely aboard.

He was flying down the road behind the barn, desperately holding handfuls of the horse's coarse mane, almost dropping the reins and the Astra 9—all of them tangled in his white-knuckled grip.

The horse was galloping down the trail full tilt when Shane saw dark shapes coming at him fast. At the last second, he ducked and avoided being knocked senseless by a low branch. Soon he was away from the farm, galloping along the wet, sandy wash, the horse's metal shoes splashing water and ringing on stones. Shane's eyes were straining for any shape that resembled a man on horseback up ahead.

He was bouncing painfully on the horse's bony back, his nuts slamming mercilessly up between his legs.

Fuck this, he thought, reining in the horse and slowing him. The horse's footing was unsure in the rocky wash. He didn't want the animal to stumble and go down.

The wash narrowed, and Shane was forced to ride slowly down the center of the rocky stream. He was leaning down close to the horse's neck to avoid another low limb when a shot rang out and clipped a branch not three feet from him.

Shane lost his grip, fell off the horse, and splashed loudly into the stream. He lay still, the icy water flowing over him. The eight-shot Astra 9-millimeter was still in his hand. He'd managed to hold it high, keeping it dry.

He wasn't sure how long he waited there, but it seemed an eternity. He was freezing now; his whole body feeling as numb as his left leg.

"Who you think you're kidding, Hot Sauce? How long you gonna try and play dead?" his old friend called out to him from somewhere in the dark. Shane didn't answer. He tried to pinpoint the direction the sound was coming from.

"You were always a better catcher than an Indian." Jody's voice came down to him from about forty or fifty yards away, up high and on the right. Shane didn't think

Jody could see him, or he would have fired again. He was trying to lure Shane into a conversation so he could find him and end it.

When another shot rang out, Shane's suspicions were confirmed. The bullet thunked into a rock forty or fifty feet to his right.

"So, Hot Sauce, who woulda ever figured it would come to this, huh?" Jody called out. "You an' me crawlin' around in the dirt. Cowboys and Indians."

Shane began to move slowly away from the voice, being careful to not splash any water. He thought he might have a slight advantage because he now had a rough fix on where Jody was, while Jody was obviously still trying to locate him. Jody had always won these games of hide-and-seek when they were kids. It was uncanny the way he could tell what Shane was thinking, where he would try to hide next.

Then, true to that memory, Jody echoed that very thought. "I could always find ya, Hot Sauce . . . and this won't be any different. Course, it doesn't have to end that way. We could make a deal."

Shane slipped out of the water, up onto the bank on the east side of the wash. He managed to squirm up the slight incline in front of him, finally reaching a spot behind some scrub brush. Once he was there, he used the foliage for a screen and sat up slowly.

"So, Shane . . . think it over. It doesn't have to end with you dead. Maybe we can still find some flex in the deal."

Shane thought he could see Jody about twenty yards off to the left behind some rocks, lit by the faint quarter moon. His old friend was looking down and to his right, searching the stream. Shane started to travel in a counter-clockwise circle, staying out of Jody's vision, being careful not to crack a twig or kick a pebble.

"Throw out your gun and stand up," Jody called out.

"We'll work something out. There's plenty here for both of us."

Shane kept inching slowly up the hill and around to his right. He finally worked his way to the flat ground behind Jody. He could now see the back of Jody's head and a piece of his right shoulder as his childhood friend huddled down behind a rocky outcropping. Shane edged closer, not sure if he could muster the courage to actually do what he now knew he had to.

And then, without any warning, Jody sensed him and spun around.

Something, God knows what, kept Shane from pulling the trigger and killing him in that instant when he had the chance. Immediately his advantage was lost, and now they were about ten feet apart, both holding handguns aimed at each other, the barrels glinting in the moonlight.

Shane could see the madness in Jody's eyes.

"Put the gun down, Jody." Shane's voice was shaking.

"You can't win, Hot Sauce. I'll know a split second before you do, and I'll beat ya."

"Put it down . . ."

"I'm sorry about what I told ya in Joe's desert house. That was a mistake. I never shoulda told ya I didn't care. I could see it in your eyes. . . . I broke it between us when I told ya that." He smiled weirdly. "But when I said I never felt love, well . . . that's not exactly right, Salsa. There were a few times I felt it, but I was always inside your head. I felt it through you."

"Put the gun down." Shane's voice was weak.

"I'll give ya a piece a'my end." Jody kicked the bag at his feet. "José transferred the cash. Hundred-thousand-dollar bearer bonds. The whole fifty mil is in this gym bag. I'm not talking a fifty-fifty split or anything screwy like that, 'cause I been through too much . . . been too far. But how 'bout ten percent? That's a good payday. Five mil. Then you and I go our separate ways. Least we don't end it this way . . . with you dead."

"Why did you butcher Sandro Mantoor like that?" Shane asked, his voice still shaking.

"Felt like it," Jody said without emotion. "Matter of fact, there's something kinda sweet about it when ya do it slow like that."

Shane knew he had to end this. He had to pull the trigger. He couldn't trust Jody to the courts. He was smart and handsome. He might find a way to O.J. his way out, just like he always had before.

"Don't do it, Hot Sauce," Jody warned sharply. "Don't even think about it."

In that moment, Shane lost his resolve. Even though he knew Jody was a sociopath, a monster, he couldn't pull the trigger. Jody must have sensed that, too, because he went on talking.

"I may not have loved you, man," he said softly. "But that was only because I couldn't. That piece wasn't in me . . . just wasn't there. But, Shane, I respected you more than anybody I ever knew. That's why I'll cut this deal. I want us both alive. What's love anyway? It's just a buncha horseshit and a four-letter word."

And then, as if a long-hidden door had opened, Shane was suddenly inside Jody's head, just as Jody must have always been inside his.

What Shane saw was indescribable and horrible— black, poisonous, and beyond all reason.

They fired simultaneously.

51

HUNTINGTON HOUSE

"All the children have their own beds and foot lockers," she said. *"We have set morning bathroom times, and of course, we all eat together in Spring Hall. He'll be one of the youngest, but I think he'll be fine."*

Shane was looking up at her. She was pleasant-looking with a round face, but she had acne. She smiled at him, so he smiled back.

"Will he go to school here, at Huntington House?" a woman he couldn't see asked.

He was holding her hand, but she was out of sight above him. Shane felt very tiny, forced to crane his neck up to see the pleasant woman with the acne.

"Yes, school will be here at Huntington House until the sixth grade and then, depending on how Shane does, we'll arrange for him to attend either St. Augustus Elementary School, which is just a few blocks away, or he can go across town to Havenhurst."

"Well, then, it's all settled," the invisible woman said.

"Fifty over ninety and falling," a man's voice said,

piercing Shane's consciousness. A siren was somewhere
behind him.

"Hit him with another A-shot, fifty cc's," a voice commanded.

*"Come on, Shane," the pleasant woman with acne
said. "We'll show you around." He held her hand, but he
had never felt so alone. He was becoming agitated, even
frightened. He could feel his heart begin to beat hard in
his chest. What would happen to him? Who were these
people?*

"Heart rate and BP up again, but he's leaking inside.
We're gonna need to get him typed, stat."

*"Here's the playroom," the pleasant woman said.
"Look at all the nice toys."*

*Shane tried to move toward the toys, but a hand pulled
him back. "No, not now. It's not a play period yet."*

*He looked up at her but could no longer see her, either.
He could now only hear her voice: "Play period's at three
in the afternoon."*

"Stand by with a crash unit. We've got a Code Blue
coming in. ETA four minutes."

*They were walking along a corridor where the walls
were getting narrower and higher, until Shane felt overwhelmed and dwarfed by the place. It was getting dark,
too. The lights suddenly dimmed.*

*"We'll show you where you're going to sleep," the
pleasant woman said, but she now seemed far away. . . .
Suddenly Shane was wandering alone in the dark and
narrowing hallway. He was getting smaller and smaller
with each step. But a bright light, beautiful and pure, was
coming from a crack under a doorway down the hall.
Then he heard Jody.*

*"A fireman? Really? You wanna climb through a win-
dow with a hose? What kind of bullshit job is that?"*

"But Jody, wouldn't it be neat to save somebody's life?"

"A fireman? Shit, I don't wanna be a fireman."

"What do you wanna be?"

"I don't know. I never know."

"This guy's in de-fib! Hit the paddles! Clear!"

He felt a sharp pain in his chest.

They were at Ryder Field in their Little League uniforms. Shane was rubbing the sore place on his chest.

"Jody, when I give you the curve sign, don't throw the fastball. You hit me in the chest. I wasn't ready," Shane said. It was almost dark, and the park ranger hadn't turned on the field lights yet.

"Just the heater." Jody grinned. "I'm gonna stick with the heater."

"Outta the way; hit him again! Clear!"

Something buzzed. A jolt hit his chest.

They were in Jody's bedroom with the lights out. Night music.

"A cop?" Jody sneered. "I thought you were gonna be a damn fireman."

"If you're a cop, you stand between right and wrong. You'd really get a chance to count."

"You believe that?"

"Hit it again!"

Sharp pain. A buckling explosion in his chest that for a moment brought the lights back on in Jody's bedroom.

He was looking at Jody in the other bed, propped up on an elbow, staring at him speculatively.

"We'll be friends forever," Shane told him, glad the lights were back on.

"No, we won't, Hot Sauce. It's not in the plan!"

"But that can't be, Jody. I'm like your brother," Shane pleaded.

"I'll give you something 'fore you go—something so you won't forget me."

"What is it?" Shane asked. "When do I get it?"

"When it's time. It's a secret," Jody grinned. "A special gift."

"I'm losing him," the man's voice said.

The towering walls disappeared, and Shane was bathed in a light so white and pure that he marveled at it. Then, almost as if he were being lifted by an invisible hand, he was flying fast and low, but rising quickly. Up . . . up . . . he went.

"My God, what fun," he laughed, banking into the light, streaking toward it until he almost reached its center. But then, without warning, he pulled up and hovered there, bathed in its radiant beauty. He glanced over and saw the Dean family floating somewhere beyond the light. Fred and Marge waved at him. . . . "Shane, we're so glad you're here," they told him.

He looked down and saw Alexa and Chooch below him.

Jody was there, too, standing on the pitcher's mound, frowning down at the rosin bag in his hand.

Suddenly, a woman he didn't know was floating toward him, smiling. She was beautiful, with rich, chestnut hair and his same blue eyes. She reached out to him.

"Come with me, son. We're together now." Her voice was soft, like music. "I never meant to leave you, but I couldn't help it. It was an accident."

"Are you my mother?" he said, thinking this was perfect. He wouldn't have to stay at Huntington House with strangers. Now he could finally have a real home with a real family.

"Yes, I'm your mother," she said. "You have to believe I always loved you. I wanted to keep you, darling. I had to leave, but I was always here waiting, and now you've finally come to me. Now you're finally—"

Without warning, everything ended.

52

JODY'S GIFT

When Shane came to, he was in ICU and it was two weeks later. They told him he'd been in a coma produced by a gunshot wound to the head. Jody's bullet had entered his scalp just above the hairline at the parietal bone and had traveled a scary, improbable path, hugging the subcutaneous connective tissue between his scalp and skull. It cracked the bone over the cerebellum in three places, then exited the back of his head at the base of his neck at something called the lamdoidal suture, without ever entering his brain cavity. Shane had suffered multiple concussions, and his head had to be opened to release the pressure of built-up cerebrospinal fluid inside his skull.

They had kept him sedated for two weeks so he wouldn't thrash around and possibly cause more discharge inside his cranium.

When he finally regained consciousness, nurses and doctors swarmed over him. Shots were given, blood pressure taken, and strict orders posted: NO VISITORS.

The wall opposite his bed in ICU was all glass; he looked up and saw Alexa and Chooch with their noses pressed against the window, like children watching a glassed-off exhibit. He stuck his tongue out at them weakly, and they both waved and laughed.

Later that day, when he woke up again, Alexa was holding his hand.

"Alexa," he whispered. "I . . . I . . ."

"Shhh," she said. "I had to raise hell to get in here. If you set off that heart monitor you're hooked to, I'll never get back in again."

"What happened?" Shane asked. The last thing he remembered was sitting in the backyard, telling Chooch he was going to ask Alexa to marry him.

"Jody's dead," Alexa said. "You hit him right between the eyes. Pretty nice shooting for a cop who can barely get weapons-qualified each June."

"No . . ." Shane said. "Jody . . . Jody committed suicide two years ago, in the Rampart Division parking lot."

"Jeez, you lost a big piece," she said, looking worried.

"I what?"

She leaned down and kissed him, brushing her lips gently across his. "Maybe it's for the best," she told him.

Eventually, it all returned. Little bits floated back like ugly puzzle pieces drifting in on a brown memory tide.

There were still a few holes in his calendar, but they gradually began to fill, creeping back like ghastly visitors, wandering in the ballroom of his memory until they finally found their correct chairs.

He left the hospital two weeks later, rolled out into the parking lot by a nurse pushing a folding wheelchair. When he stood, he felt twenty feet tall and two inches wide. He teetered precariously before lowering himself into Alexa's car. His scalp had been stitched and bandaged. His neck was already healing. There was an ugly puckered welt there from the gunfight in Maicao. The hole

in his thigh was now a pink divot the size of a quarter.
All in all, he was damn lucky to be alive.

Chooch was in the backseat and never took his hand
off Shane's shoulder, as if letting go, even for a second,
might cause some kind of permanent separation.

"We need to set the wedding date." Alexa smiled.
"You keep saying you remember asking me, but I think
I'd better close the deal while you're still lucid."

"How 'bout this weekend?" Shane said. "By this weekend, I'll be kickin' ass." But despite this bravado, he felt
light-headed and was forced to lean back against the head-
rest.

Actually, the date they set was two months later. It was
a late September wedding that took place at the Police
Academy Chapel.

The service was small, but importantly attended. There
were a dozen cops from his old homicide table, along with
their wives, as well as some old partners from Patrol. Of
course, Buddy made the trip. No way to freeze him out.
Buddy slapped backs and talked retailing.

Chooch was the best man, and Buddy gave the bride
away. Because he didn't have anyone else, and because
something told him it would mean a lot, Shane asked
Tony Filosiani to stand up for him, to be his one and only
usher.

They were married at four in the afternoon. The ceremony was short and simple, but the emotions were not.
Alexa cried when they exchanged rings. The reception
was behind the chapel. After it was over and the guests
had left, they lingered outside, smiling as Tony and his
wife, Mary, traded guarded looks with Buddy. Shane,
Chooch, and Alexa stood on the steps looking out at the
San Gabriel Mountains, majestic, almost purple in the
bright, smog-free California afternoon.

"Some weddin'. Glad t'be part of it," Tony enthused.

"You guys should know, when I'm in a wedding, I make marriages that last. You two got an obligation not to screw up my perfect record, not countin' my sister."

Shane smiled and nodded. "Yes, sir. That order is accepted."

"Good. And now, I got another little weddin' gift, Shane. I put you in for the MOV and the Police Board approved it. Gonna get the medal at this December's ceremony."

"His-and-her medals." Alexa smiled.

"Once Papa Joe gets outta the hospital, he'll testify." Tony went on: "We're gonna kill this billion-dollar parallel-market scam for good. The Justice Department has already opened their investigation. Without laundries, these drug cartels can't function. We hit 'em where they live—in the pocketbook. The CEOs of the companies laundering this shit are gonna be toast. We brought it to 'em, Shane. You made the difference."

Finally Buddy went back to the hotel to pack. Shane, Alexa, and Chooch slipped away to Venice.

They were glad to be safe at home. They changed out of their wedding costumes and met in the backyard ten minutes later. Shane was in shorts, a T-shirt, and flip-flops. Chooch was in his baggies and saggies, Alexa in a sweatshirt and leggings.

Shane poured them all flutes of cold champagne. They toasted the wedding and stood on their patch of grass, watching the sunset over the blue Pacific a block away.

"Where's the honeymoon?" Chooch asked, grinning.

"How about Aruba?" Alexa said, smiling. "I still have my room key." She dug in her purse and threw it on the glass-top table.

"How about anyplace on earth but there?" Shane said.

"I'll miss you guys while you're gone," Chooch said.

"No, you won't," Shane grinned.

"How come?"

" 'Cause we're gonna wait till Christmas and you're going with us," Alexa finished.

"Really? Is that allowed, taking your kid on the honeymoon?"

"From now on, this family stays together," Shane said.

That night Shane lay awake in bed, listening to Alexa sleep beside him . . . the slow breathing, the warmth of her next to him. They hadn't made love. It was strange not to consummate their marriage on the wedding night, but Alexa had been told by the doctors not to do it for a month, because they wanted to keep his heart rate and blood pressure down until they were sure everything had stopped leaking inside his head. There was one week left on that ridiculous sentence. Shane had argued, but Alexa stood firm. He probably wasn't going to win many arguments with her, or as the Day-Glo Dago would say, "Fugedaboutit."

So instead of sex, he lay on his back, looking at the ceiling, turning his new wedding band around on his finger, reflecting, trying to make sense of all that had happened.

He'd been very close to death. The docs told him that his heart had stopped twice. He'd flown down that heavenly corridor, chasing a column of pure white light. He'd seen all of the people in his life that had mattered: the Deans, Jody, Chooch, and Alexa.

Then he thought of the beautiful chestnut-haired woman whom he had known on sight was his mother.

"I'm sorry," she had said. "It was an accident. I didn't want to leave you."

What kind of accident would take you away from your child, make you leave him at the back door of a hospital? Then suddenly he realized that she had *not* put him there; she'd died and somebody else had. She'd come to him in a near-death experience and told him that she always loved him . . . always wanted him. Shane didn't think that when you had a near-death vision, it included lies.

Whatever caused her disappearance, he now knew it hadn't been her fault. His mother *had* loved him, and with that realization, a piece of the darkness that had always haunted him finally slipped away.

He closed his eyes and tried to see her again. He could almost create the vision, but not quite. Yet in its place there was a memory of her love . . . gentle and pure and full of warmth.

"So what is love, anyway?" Jody had scoffed. *"Just a lotta horseshit and a four-letter word."*

Boy, Shane thought, *poor Jody. Jody had missed out on everything.* Suddenly, Shane felt sorry for him—sorry he couldn't have found a way to fix that.

Jody might not have been able to love Shane, but Shane had loved Jody, and in his memory he still did.

He closed his eyes and wondered if the gift Jody promised to him had been the bullet that took him to the edge but gave him a chance to meet his mother, to feel her warmth, to finally experience her love, if only for a few precious seconds. Seconds that had changed him and taken away his painful darkness.

Before he fell asleep, he decided that was it. That was Jody's gift.

From the very beginning, that must have been God's plan.

POSTSCRIPT

All-American Tobacco is a fictitious company, but some of the underlying events of this story were inspired by national headlines. There is currently a billion-dollar civil case pending against Phillip Morris, filed by the Colombian government, over alleged lost cigarette taxes. In 1998 a Reynolds Tobacco subsidiary settled a case involving taxes on cigarettes transported from Canada and paid fifteen million dollars in fines and penalties. A former executive of that company went to jail. Hundreds of other Fortune 500 companies were investigated by the U.S. government. Finally, Bonnie Tishler, Assistant Commissioner of the U.S. Customs Service, in a statement before the Congress of the United States, on June 19, 1999, stated that the Treasury Department had elected not to pursue prosecution. "It is very difficult, with a large Corporate structure, to get your hands around exactly who may or may not be facilitating the business of money laundering. . . . By punishing the U.S. Corporations, we may in turn be punishing . . . their ability to sell their products to countries such as Colombia. It could hurt our ability to export and cost us jobs, while at the same time not really making any progress against the drug cartels. . . . The object of our investigation is not to put U.S. companies in jail."

Instead of prosecuting corporate officers, the federal government elected to mail out warnings to hundreds of U.S. companies that helped launder billions in Colombian drug dollars.

To date, no further action has been taken.

ACKNOWLEDGMENTS

Again, there are many people who have helped me get this book into print. Grace Curcio, my loyal co-worker (she makes me call her that), has been a friend and adviser for twenty-five years and typed the rough drafts on all seven of my novels. Since I work seven-day weeks, she gets very little rest. She is my secret weapon and my treasure.

Kathy Ezso inputs everything into the computer, does countless rewrites, offering helpful notes and suggestions. Without her, I would be lost.

Christine Trepczyk has read this draft, checked it for logic, and pitched in when we needed an extra hand doing cleanup.

Thanks to Jo Swerling, who read and encouraged me through the writing, and to Roy Huggins, who has been a wonderful "last eye" on all of my manuscripts.

Wayne Williams, my friend and editor, has done his usual great job of criticizing, nitpicking, and reorganizing sentences, always making the book stronger and tighter.

I want to thank Charles Spicer, my editor at St. Martin's Press, for his friendship and editorial help. He has worked tirelessly to push me further and higher, always with a gentle style that bespeaks his nature.

A huge note of gratitude to Sally Richardson, my publisher, who has been a believer from the beginning and helped keep me on the road with excellent advice.

Thanks to Dorsey Mills for her assistance and to John Murphy for great publicity.

To my wife, Marcia, and my three children, Tawnia, Chelsea, and Cody. Your love makes me strong, and at the end of the day, I'm really only showing off on paper, trying to look worthy in your eyes.

Read on for an excerpt from
Stephen J. Cannell's next book

HOLLYWOOD TOUGH

AVAILABLE IN HARDCOVER FROM ST. MARTIN'S PRESS!

THE BAD JOKE

Nicky Marcella was waiting to get into the bathroom
when Shane opened the door and the two of them looked
at each other like two art thieves at a Sotheby's auction.

"Shane, my God, Shane Scully," Nicky said. He was
wearing a beautifully tailored, if somewhat gaudy,
orangish-brown suit . . . or was it brownish-orange . . . ?
Hard to tell because the colors strobed when he moved.
Either way, it took some doing to pull it off. Maybe it
was helped by the fact that there wasn't all that much of
it—Nicky being only five-foot-five, top to bottom including his stacked Cuban heels. Nicky Marcella was rail-
thin—Sammy Davis thin. He had black hair, close-cut on
the side, and slightly longer on the top. He was wearing
a silk shirt with a few too many gold chains. His smile
was warm, but strangely ferret-like.

"Nicky, how you been?"

"Staying outta jail, I'll tell you that much."

"Glad to hear it," Shane said, and he was. He hadn't
seen Marcella in four years. Nicky was a Hollywood character. When Shane first met him he was doing street cor-

ner cons—green-goods hustles, and pigeon drops. Shane had first busted him when he was still a rookie working vice in Hollywood. He'd rolled him up twice more in the Valley when he was riding around in a plain Jane doing a straight eight in uniform. Sometime in the mid-nineties, Nicky had switched from short cons to running bets for bookmakers and had taken a short fall for that. He'd ended up doing a bullet in county jail. When he got out, he moved on to straight-up bookmaking, writing betting slips out of a porn shop on Little Melrose. Nicky Marcella had dabbled in the criminal arts for almost the whole fifteen years Shane had known him, and now here he was, in Farrell Champion's house, rubbing shoulders with Hollywood's elite.

"Whatta you up to? Or should I just count the silver?" Shane smiled.

"Can't blame you for that, Shane. But I'm clean as the Board of Health these days. Just a minute, don't go away, gotta tap a kidney."

Nicky pushed past him into the bathroom while Shane stood outside wondering what on earth Nicky Marcella, a low end street hustler, was doing at this party full of heavy lifters. Even so, Shane had to admit that, over the years, he'd come to enjoy the guy. Nicky had an infectious personality and never took himself too seriously. Of course he was shamefully easy to arrest . . . No toe-to-toe scuffling and bruised ribs with Nicky. At five-feet-five, he was not the kind of criminal who fried your nerve synapses with adrenal overload, so that probably had something to do with it. Nicky was also a fountain of gossip. Shane would sometimes put the word out on the street, with his CIs and snitches, that he needed some particular piece of intelligence, and more times than he could remember, Nicky Marcella would be the one to call in and drop the science on him.

Another strange thing was, Nicky never wanted anything in return. It was almost as if he was trying to buy Shane's friendship, not his conscience. And slowly, over the years, Nicky had managed to do it. Shane had really come to like the little grifter in that strange way that cops can like criminals and still not respect them.

The door opened and Nicky walked out smiling. "Man, you look great. You got a trainer?" Nicky asked.

"Yeah, the PT instructor at the Academy."

Nicky nodded and shifted his weight. "Don't tell that to any of those silks out there," he said, pointing toward the room full of celebrities. "In this crowd, you gotta have a personal trainer and he's gotta have a schtick like the Tybo guy. Trainers around here interview the celebs, not the other way around."

There was a pause while both of them were pondering the same question: *What the hell are you doing here?*

"Okay, you first," Shane finally said.

"I'm in show-biz now," Nicky smiled. "I guess I always was in the business of show. Hey, what is a street corner pigeon drop on an old lady, if it's not a good performance? I'm not selling bets on the nags any more either . . . I'm selling bets on movies . . . which we bullshitters in the cinematic arts always refer to as 'film.'"

"You're in the film business?" Shane said, finding that hard to believe.

"Yep, Producer. Got my own company, Cine-Roma Productions. We're in pre-production on a film right now. I've also got a big development deal with Farrell over at Paramount on a novel I bought called *Savages in the Midst*."

"The sequel to *Gorillas in the Mist*?"

"Midst . . . midst, with a 'd,' Shane. Like in our midst . . . like that. It's about the meat-eaters in show-biz, and a girl from Illinois who's looking to be a star, and about savages in suits who destroy her dreams, and eventually, her body. We could cast the fucking thing off this party's guest list. Farrell is talking Gwyneth, but I'm not so sure. I'm thinking more like Liz Shue. Do it a little harder edged. Make the statement seem integral . . . amp up the verisimilitude."

"The what?"

"Verisimilitude . . . means the appearance of truth. You have to learn these words if you wanna be a player." He put his hands in the pockets of his ridiculous, multicolored suit, rocked back on his Cuban heels, and regarded Shane. "Now you."

"Huh? Oh . . . Just Alexa and Farrell's fiancée, Nora Bishop, are old friends. Nora used to be Alexa's babysitter when she was a kid."

"I like mine better," Nicky said.

"Me too," Shane admitted.

"Listen, bubbie, seeing you here might be fortuitous."

"Yeah?" Shane looked puzzled. "How's that?"

"I was thinking of calling you last week. Isn't that a mitzvah? Haven't seen you in four years, thinking about calling you . . . Kaboom, here you are. That's what we in the biz call . . ."

"Verisimilitude?"

"Yeah, with a heavy dose of righteous karma," he smiled. "Shane, I'm looking for a girl who's dropped out of sight. This is silly really but I bet you could pull this off for me. Her name is Carol White. She's perfect for a part in this movie I'm casting.

"*Savages in the Midst.*"

"No, the other one, the one I'm doing at my shop . . . at Cine-Roma. Farrell and I are only in development on *Midst*. Development is a term we use meaning creative hell. This film I'm talking about already has its green light—it's what we call a firm go. The girl, Carol White, is perfect for the part of Cherri, which is a showy little role . . . the lead character's best friend. Carol has this ethereal quality, which is a word we use in film, meaning translucent–delicate–refined . . . very hard to find these qualities in a young actress. Okay, so here's my problem. She used to do some low budget stuff around town and some TV, shit like that, and then she kinda disappeared. I checked with SAG, and they got no current address on her. I think she may have even dropped out of the business altogether. I don't know who her current agent is."

"I can promise you, I'm not representing her," Shane said.

"I was thinking you could maybe go into the police computer. Carol White . . . ten little keys that spell Big Break. If she's had a traffic ticket or owns a car, you could get the girl's address and I give her the part that kickstarts and totally redefines her career. When they do the 'E!' Celebrity Profile on her five years from now, she's gonna be up there saying I owe it all to an L.A. cop and a helluva guy, Shane Scully."

"Listen, Nicky. You probably haven't heard, but I've been on a medical leave of absence for almost a year. I don't go back on the job until next week. So, I don't really have any way into the police computer. They change the access codes all the time. Mine's not even current anymore. So as much as I'd like to help and all that . . ."

"Right," Nicky smiled but stopped tipping back on his stacked heels. "Hey, listen, I was probably way outta line there anyway. I mean, the police computer isn't exactly dial-a-job."

"Right."

"Hey, well, it was just a thought. You're looking good, man. Stay healthy and God bless. You're on my prayer list."

"Your what?"

"Found Jesus. Lot happens in four years, go figure. Spent twenty years living a bullshit life before I discover Jesus is my savior . . . Now I got Jesus and Louie."

"And just who the hell is Louie?" Shane was grinning.

"Louie is the god of all movie-making. If Louie smiles on you, you get big stars, big grosses and it never rains on your beach shoot. In the film business we learn these things. Take care, Shane."

Nicky turned to walk down the corridor, and Shane felt instantly bad about brushing off the favor. How hard would it be to help little Nicky? Nicky, who had helped Shane with dozens of useful tips and never asked for anything in return . . .

"Hey, hold on," Shane called out and Nicky turned to look back. "I changed my mind. Gimme your card. I'll punch up this girl for you. I gotta go down to my old homicide table tomorrow to get my duty jacket anyway. I'll get somebody to run her."

"You always were my favorite copper, even when you had the cuffs on too tight." Nicky grinned and pulled out an alligator wallet, removed some expensive-looking cards, then handed one to Shane. There was a logo of a phoenix in embossed gold. Under that it said:

Cine-Roma—Nicholas Marcella, C.E.O.

"Carol White," Nicky said, "spelled just like it sounds."

"Okay. I'll call you tomorrow if I get anything."

They separated and Shane prowled around. He was really having a good time now. He had a second scotch on the rocks, spent some time talking to Angelina Jolie and then later, Alexa was back at his side.

"Hi. Where'd you go off to?" Shane asked.

"Just meeting the other bridesmaids and looking at pictures of our dresses that Nora ordered. I can't believe they're getting married in ten days. Talk about whirlwind."

"Right, right . . . I was just saying the same thing to Angelina Jolie," Shane said, a smile twitching the corner of his mouth.

"Get outta town . . . Where?"

Shane pointed to the beautiful actress who was wearing capri pants and a crop-top. She caught Shane's eye as he pointed her out to Alexa and waved back.

"Down, boy," Alexa warned, then she fixed another look on her face. It was her no-nonsense look, the one she wore downtown at Parker Center.

"I've gotta go. We got a 187 out in Sunland that the CRASH Unit is worried about. They want me to roll on it." She held up her cell phone. "Just got the call."

"Really? Who died?"

"They think it's Kevin Cordell, but the DB took so much lead that they're gonna have to do it with dentistry."

"Another one bites the dust . . ." Shane said, thinking it was about time that somebody put Stone on the ark. He'd been a murdering gangster for over twenty-five years, and except for a nickel jolt at Soledad for accessory to second-degree murder, he'd pretty much escaped justice.

"If it's really Stone, it could create a power vacuum and we could end up with Crips and Bloods shooting each other and anybody else who gets in the way," Alexa said.

"You need the car . . . I can drive you . . ."

"No. Nora will be really upset if we both leave early. The sheriff's department is doing us a favor and is sending a unit over from the substation here. They'll taxi me over the hill."

"You really think they need the head of the whole Detective Services Group standing at a crime scene, looking down while a bunch a' the lab techs roll the vic?"

"Hey, they're my detectives. I go whenever I'm asked. Besides, I'm only the *acting* head of DSG so I try harder. I'm just holding that post till the chief appoints a captain to the job."

"Honey, Filosian isn't going to replace you. You're acting head only because you're still a lieutenant, and technically, they can't have a Looie in that position. But he's not going to put somebody over you. I can read that guy . . . you got the job. You is de man."

"Right . . . right. Well, de man gotta take her ass to work."

"I'll stick around here for another hour until they do the steak fry, then I'll drive over the hill and pick you up. You got an address?"

She handed him a slip of paper, then kissed him on the lips. "Only one more thing before I leave . . ."

"Say goodbye to Nora?"

"No, that's done. I gotta run this bitch in the pedal-pushers off my guy."

"Come on . . . she's married."

"In Hollywood, marriage is an eight-letter word with the half-life of a Mrs. Fields cookie."

Alexa moved off, stopped next to Angelina Jolie and said something to her. The two stood there for another moment before Angelina threw back her head and roared with laughter.

Alexa turned and smiled at Shane, then went out the front door to the entry hall to wait for the sheriff's car.

That would have been all that was noteworthy, except for one last thing that happened just before he left the party. Shane had finished his barbecue, and it was fabulous. He'd had another Dewar's, which was one past his limit. He'd spent half an hour talking to James Garner and his lovely wife, Lois. Garner was one of his all-time favorite actors, and as it turned out, a really genuine guy.

He said goodbye to Nora and was heading up from the beach. He decided to cut through the pool house and save the longer walk around the side of the estate to get to the front. He went in the beach entrance and was immediately greeted by a heavy cloud of cigar smoke and male laughter coming from the front room. Shane walked down the hallway toward the sound, listening to Farrell's voice. He was telling some kind of story. Then Shane reached the back of the main room.

The pool house was large, about the size of his entire house in Venice. It had windows on the north that overlooked the ocean. The windows on the other side fronted Farrell's Olympic-sized pool. Nora had decorated the pool house in a quasi-African theme: lots of bamboo, grass rugs, and native art. There were ten or twelve men in the room with Farrell, all of them smoking big Cuban Cohiba cigars. Nobody was paying any attention to Shane when one of Farrell's friends changed the subject with a question.

"So, Farrell, you get Kenny to draw you up a pre-nup like I advised?"

Farrell took a swig of his drink and smiled; his white teeth gleamed, his blue eyes twinkled.

"Listen, that kinda shit's good for you guys who can't take care of business, but I don't need no fucking pre-nup." Doing that last part like the Mexican bandit in *Treasure of the Sierra Madre*.

"Everybody needs a pre-nup. It's the law west of the Pecos," the man persisted.

"Not me." Farrell seemed a little loaded. "Didn't need one with my last two wives . . . when I got tired of those ladies, they both had the good sense to go out and eat some bad shellfish and die of food poisoning." There was some laughter—not much—but some. Farrell swung his eyes around the room until his gaze ended up on Shane.

It's hard to explain to a civilian how a cop's hunches work, because they live in some intellectual and emotional no-man's land between feelings and guesses. In the end, they're not really hunches at all. They're based on keen instinct mixed with physical and emotional observations. In this case, the physical part was in Farrell Champion's pale-blue eyes when they found Shane in the back of the room. They hardened momentarily. Even from twenty feet away Shane could see it; a tightening of the skin around the sockets and a shadow on the cornea that came and went so quickly it would have been easy to miss if you weren't trained to spot it. Then the look was gone and the smiling Farrell was back.

"Hey, Shane . . . That was just a joke, buddy. Don't get your handcuffs out."

"No sweat," Shane said. "Nice party."

"Just a bad joke . . ." Farrell said. "How do you suppose I keep my rakish image?"

"Right." Now Shane was feeling awkward . . . sort of on the spot, as everyone in the room had turned to stare at him. "So, listen, Farrell. Thanks for the great time. Thanks for having us."

"You bet. You bet . . . Good you could come."

Then Shane left. He could feel Farrell's eyes on him as he exited the pool house and headed across the broad expanse of stone pool decking.

Another valet delivered the Acura. It had picked up more dust from the beach. He pulled out of the Colony wondering what, if anything, he should do with this unexpected piece of intel—this bad joke. *Hey, Shane, don't go over the falls in a barrel*, he lectured himself. The man was half drunk and Shane didn't really know him, didn't know what kind of sense of humor Farrell Champion had. But he had seen the look in Farrell's eyes, the game of eye-tag, and the shadow—the microscopic glimpse into Farrell Champion's soul.

It could have been embarrassment . . . could have been regret at making a stupid joke in such bad taste . . . could have been, but something told Shane that there really were two dead women in Farrell's past who had died of food poisoning.

"Shit," he muttered to himself as he drove over Malibu Canyon heading toward Sunland.